Praise for *Notes on Your Sudden Disappearance*

An Indie Next pick for Jun...
Named a Best Book of 2022 by NPR
A *USA Today* Must-Read
Named a Most Anticipated Book of May by *The Millions*

"Riveting."   —*People*

"Fans of Alison Espach's first novel, the wonderful *The Adults*, have had to wait eleven years for her follow-up. Good news: it's more than worth it. . . . Espach's book is often quite funny, and the structure—it's told in the second person—is fascinating. Espach once again proves that she's a brilliantly talented author."

—**Michael Schaub, NPR**

"Terrific."   —*Chicago Tribune*

"Incongruously funny . . . Ms. Espach uses irony well."
—**Sam Sacks,** *The Wall Street Journal*

"Inventive and powerful . . . Espach captures the minutiae of love and loss with unflinching clarity and profound compassion, and pulls off the second-person point of view unusually well. Readers will be deeply moved."   —*Publishers Weekly* (**starred review**)

"This tragicomic bildungsroman in the shadow of loss will invade your heart and hold on tight."   —*Kirkus Reviews*

"A marvelous exercise in voice . . . Never contrived, the novel is beautifully written, making even the quotidian details of Sally's life fascinating, in part because the story invites such a deep emotional involvement with the fully realized characters and, indeed, with the entirety of this splendid and memorable book."

—*Booklist* (**starred review**)

"*Notes on Your Sudden Disappearance* is heartbreaking and funny, often in the same sentence—a deeply felt, finely wrought, and highly satisfying novel. Alison Espach has created a family whose every sorrow, joy, and idiosyncrasy is utterly, vibrantly real."

—**Claire Lombardo, *New York Times* bestselling author of *The Most Fun We Ever Had***

"Tender, eloquent, and wise, this is an intensely beautiful book by a supremely gifted writer." —**Karen Thompson Walker, author of *The Dreamers***

"Unputdownable, insightful, funny, and emotionally profound. A book that swirls and glitters with strangeness and delight, as much a portrait of grief as a love story, both love and grief hinging on the ways we negotiate with things we cannot control, how we sit in the cockpit of the self, what we dare to share with others and what remains ineffable. Gorgeous." —**Rufi Thorpe, author of *The Knockout Queen***

"Oh how I loved this novel! Alison Espach masterfully examines the effects of devastating loss with enormous wit, charm, and intelligence. This is truly a novel like no other."

—**Joanna Rakoff, author of *My Salinger Year***

"In Alison Espach's hands, a teenage girl on the cusp of understanding, a dazzling older sister, and a small Connecticut town become a beautifully described world filled with characters I wanted to meet, characters I still think about. Their trials and tribulations and adolescent longing and awkwardness, their love for each other—it all felt amazingly real. *Notes on Your Sudden Disappearance* is the rare kind of book that made me both laugh and cry. It is hilarious and moving and deeply felt, and I was sad when it ended."

—**Anton DiSclafani, author of *The Yonahlossee Riding Camp for Girls***

"Espach is an immensely talented writer, and her prose unfolds with a devastating lightness of touch. This novel is deeply moving, always excellent, and often unexpectedly funny."

—**Emily St. John Mandel**, *New York Times*
bestselling author of *The Glass Hotel*

"Writing from a black hole, 'soundless and windless and without gravity,' Alison Espach has alchemized unimaginable tragedy into a story that's deceptively funny, tender, and ultimately life-affirming. Novels like this are what the art form is for."

—**Teddy Wayne, author of *Apartment***

ALSO BY ALISON ESPACH

The Adults

NOTES ON YOUR SUDDEN DISAPPEARANCE

NOTES ON YOUR SUDDEN DISAPPEARANCE

A Novel

ALISON ESPACH

A HOLT PAPERBACK

HENRY HOLT AND COMPANY

NEW YORK

Holt Paperbacks
Henry Holt and Company
Publishers since 1866
120 Broadway
New York, New York 10271
www.henryholt.com

A Holt Paperback® and ⓗ® are registered trademarks of Macmillan Publishing Group, LLC.

Distributed in Canada by Raincoast Book Distribution Limited

The Library of Congress has cataloged the hardcover edition as follows:

Names: Espach, Alison, 1984– author.
Title: Notes on your sudden disappearance : a novel / Alison Espach.
Description: First edition. | New York : Henry Holt and Company, 2022.
Identifiers: LCCN 2021047370 (print) | LCCN 2021047371 (ebook) |
    ISBN 9781250823144 (hardcover) | ISBN 9781250823151 (ebook)
Subjects: LCGFT: Bildungsromans. | Novels.
Classification: LCC PS3605.S59 N68 2022 (print) | LCC PS3605.S59 (ebook) |
    DDC 813/.6—dc23
LC record available at https://lccn.loc.gov/2021047370
LC ebook record available at https://lccn.loc.gov/2021047371

ISBN: 9781250871442 (trade paperback)

Our books may be purchased in bulk for promotional, educational, or business use. Please contact your local bookseller or the Macmillan Corporate and Premium Sales Department at (800) 221-7945, extension 5442, or by email at MacmillanSpecialMarkets@macmillan.com.

Originally published in hardcover in 2022 by Henry Holt and Company

First Holt Paperbacks Edition 2023

Designed by Gabriel Guma

Printed in the United States of America

1   3   5   7   9   10   8   6   4   2

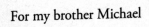
For my brother Michael

THE STATE
OF THE UNION,
1998

You disappeared on a school night. Nobody was more surprised by this than me. If I believed in anything when I was thirteen, I believed in the promise of school nights. I believed in the sacred ritual of homework, then dinner, and then the laying out of our clothes for the next morning—something Mom insisted on from the very beginning.

Mom said it was important to wake up having made the decision about what to wear. So, each night, we made the decision. We brushed our teeth. We stared at each other in the mirror as the foam built and built in our mouths, and eventually one of us would speak. "Hello," you'd say, and this would be so funny for some reason that I can't understand now. You would start laughing, a loud burst of confetti out your mouth—and so I would start laughing, an ugly inward sucking sound that always made Mom run into a room and say, "Sally, are you okay?" which made us laugh even harder.

"She's just laughing, Mom," you said.

We got into our beds. We stared up at the glow-in-the-dark stars that were arranged on the ceiling to spell our names—an idea I hadn't liked at first, since I wanted the ceiling to be an accurate reflection of the sky. But you said that was impossible. You said, the ceiling will never be the sky, Sally, and I didn't argue, because no matter how old I became, you were always three years older than me. You always knew things I didn't know, like there are eighty-eight constellations in the sky and only twenty-two stars in the pack. Just enough to spell our names. So we stuck the stars to the ceiling, and I spent the rest of my childhood looking up, listening to KATHY tell SALLY about all the other things she knew: The sky isn't actually blue. The rain evaporates and goes back up to the sky.

"And did you know that trees can feel pain?" you asked.

"No," I said.

But I wasn't surprised. I had suspected as much ever since Dad told us that the maple tree outside our bedroom window was nearly dead. It was so old, Dad said, it might have been planted by an actual Puritan, a fact that did not impress me as much as it scared me. The tree sat on our lawn, hunched and tangled, and I didn't like looking at it the way I didn't like seeing the bone spurs on Dad's feet when he took his socks off at the beach. Or the bottom row of yellow teeth that were only visible when Mom laughed really hard. It was death, I knew, waiting in the most unexpected places—inside Mom's laughter, at the end of Dad's toes, in the bright green leaves outside our bedroom window that couldn't have looked more alive. So I pulled down the window shade each night before I crawled into your bed. You never pushed me away then. You liked feeling the soft tips of my fingers braiding a strand of your hair.

"Well, they can. That's what Billy Barnes told me," you said. "He knows things like that. His dad's a florist."

Then, I was a very *good listener, very attentive*, the teachers often wrote on my report card. I always had a follow-up question.

"Who's Billy Barnes?" I asked.

"Who is *Billy Barnes*?" you said, like I was supposed to know. But I didn't know anyone except the people in my first-grade class. We were kept hidden away from the older kids, safe in our own private wing of the school. "I'm only dancing the Football Tango with him tomorrow."

"What's the Football Tango?" I asked.

"Just some dance the teachers made up to celebrate Thanksgiving," you said. "I don't really get it. But who cares? That's not the point."

The point was, you were in fourth grade and he was in fifth, and you shouldn't have been partners, but you were paired up anyway. You were the same exact height. It's fate, you said. And it was—the next morning, it happened. You dressed up as a cheerleader and he dressed up as a football player and you tangoed across the gym and he whispered something nice about your hair and that was that. You were in love.

"What did he say about your hair?" I asked.

I was starting to learn that I did not have the right kind of hair. It was nothing like yours, which dried straight out of the shower. Mine was curly, hard to control, like one of those evil cartoon trees that pull people in with their branches when they get too close. That's what Rick Stevenson said on the bus, anyway, just before he told me all about his chinchilla at home, the one that had recently started to eat its own babies.

"I don't know," you said. "Billy didn't specify."

After the dance, you started talking to me about Billy all of the time at night. But you never spoke to him at school.

"What would I even say?" you wondered.

I was surprised you'd ask me—what did I know about speaking to boys then? I could hardly even speak to my own grandmother and grandfather when they sat on our couch during Christmas. I would quietly pick at the hem of my dress, while you asked them questions about their old coal stove and all the milk that used to arrive at their doorstep in bottles. You accepted their gifts with an enthusiasm I couldn't fake. "Thank you so much for the Make-Your-Own-Bubble-Gum kit," you said to Grandma like you meant it, and I was in disbelief. Were we actually excited about making our own bubble gum? I couldn't tell. You were so good—a natural, Dad said once, after we watched you be Peter Pan in *Peter Pan*.

But talking to Billy was not as easy for you.

"Billy's in fifth grade," you said. "And he's going to be a famous basketball player one day. That's what all the teachers say."

So you just watched him from afar, paid close attention to him at recess. Collected information to bring back to me each night. Listed off all the things Billy liked: Pepperoni pizza. The Chicago Bulls. Praying mantises. And his dad, who had recently broken his neck.

"It's really tragic," you said. Then you told the story as if you had been at Bill's Tree and Garden when Billy's dad fell off the ladder. "He must have fallen twenty feet through the air, Sally! It was crazy! He cracked his spine in two places."

"Is he going to die?" I asked.

I couldn't imagine someone breaking their neck and not dying. I imagined Billy's father's neck, bent at a right angle.

"No," you said. "He'll be fine. But still. It's really scary. I mean, who knew being a florist was so dangerous?"

I remember you sounded proud for some reason, like you had broken your own neck.

You told me so much about Billy that by the time I actually saw him, it felt surreal. We stepped out of Dad's car and onto the parking lot of Bill's Tree and Garden, and you clutched my arm like you did whenever we saw a fox in the woods.

"It's Billy Barnes," you whispered.

We knew foxes lived here, but we were always surprised to see one in our yard. It was Connecticut. It was the suburbs. We lived one street away from a Dunkin' Donuts. We never expected to be so lucky, to be in the right place at the right time. In the same parking lot where Billy was moving small white trees out of a van.

Dad went inside to get marigolds for the mailbox, but we stood quietly by the entrance. We plucked petals off a nearby rosebush, pretended like we weren't watching him, but we were, of course. We were studying him very closely, though now it's hard to remember much about the moment. All I can picture is his hair, so thick and brown, like it was made of plastic. Like he was one of my Fisher-Price toys.

"What are you still doing out here, girls?" Dad said when he returned with two pots of gold flowers. The moment was over.

"Nothing," you said, but we both knew we were guilty of something. We stuffed the red petals into our pockets before Dad could see, and you promised me it wasn't stealing because the petals would grow back bigger and brighter, like the worms we sometimes cut in the woods. When Dad started driving, you pulled a petal out of your pocket and started running it along your bottom lip.

"It's so soft," you said, handing it to me. "Feel."

I pressed the rose petal to my lip and felt its softness and that was that.

Talking about Billy became part of the nightly ritual. Like a prayer before bed. Every night that year, we turned off the lights and I pulled down the window shade and you told me about how he gave you a pencil for no reason in the hallway. Ate a bumblebee at recess, also for no reason. Brought in carnations for the entire school. For Valentine's Day.

"Isn't that nice?" you asked.

"Isn't his dad a florist?" I asked.

Some nights, we wondered about the things we didn't know, things we could never know about Billy. What would it feel like to kiss him, and do you think he'd be a good husband?

Of course, we decided.

"I bet he'll take his daughters to the Grand Canyon," you said.

"He'll give them whole dollars when they lose their teeth," I said. "Not like Dad."

In the morning, we woke up and we were always disappointed by the clothes we had laid out the night before. We changed our minds about what to wear, which you said we were allowed to do, and yet I felt bad for the rejected clothes all during breakfast, sometimes apologized to them before we ran to the bus. When you heard me doing this, you laughed. "Sally, they're just shoes!" you said. "It's just a shirt!" But I couldn't stop feeling that they were more than that, that everything was secretly alive, which was why I also said goodbye to the radiators before we left.

After his dad broke his neck, Billy became famous for doing stupid things, too, like putting a carrot in the pencil sharpener before lunch and jumping off the roof after school.

"Who dares me to jump off this roof?" Billy shouted down to us all on the blacktop.

Nobody did. Not even Rick Stevenson, who had spent all of lunchtime crushing his SweeTARTS into a fine powder and then snorting them up his nose. Rick just looked concerned.

"It's too high!" Rick shouted. Then he turned to us. "Billy's going to die."

We looked up at Billy, high on the roof like the American flag. For the first time in his life, Rick seemed right. Billy was going to die. You and I exchanged a secret glance.

"Billy is so dumb," you said to me, but you smiled as you said it, as if it were the best thing a boy could be.

The fall was quick and hard. We ran to Billy, but we were all too afraid to touch him. On the pavement, unconscious, Billy didn't look like Billy at all. He was too still, and it made no sense, because whenever you talked about Billy, he was always moving, like a car that never shut off. But the longer I stood above him, the more unfamiliar he became. Gave me the same feeling I got when I saw Grandpa at his wake. He looked like a total stranger in his casket, stiff and covered in someone else's makeup.

"Somebody help him!" you shouted.

I ran for help. But the whole time down the hallway, I was confused. *If we don't know Billy by this point*, I thought, *who could we ever know?* And then I got the nurse, who was, you said, not really a nurse.

"What is she then?" I asked you.

We watched her wipe the blood off Billy's arms and legs.

"She's just Priscilla Mountain's mom," you said.

We stood on the pavement for a long time after that, like two beads strung on the chain of Billy's life.

B illy broke his leg in two places, which made him a celebrity at school. When he returned from the hospital, everybody lined up to sign his cast, even the teachers. Some girls drew pink hearts next to their name, and some girls, like Priscilla, wrote their phone numbers on his kneecap.

"Why did you *do* that?" you said to Priscilla, not like you were mad, but like maybe you should have done something like that.

"I like him," Priscilla said, and shrugged as if it were no big deal, and yet it annoyed me for the same reason it annoyed me that she was sleeping over. Put her sleeping bag between our beds and a framed picture of her parents on our nightstand and talked about Billy as if he belonged to her.

"We liked Billy way before he broke his leg," I said.

"Sally!" you said.

It felt important—to have loved Billy before he jumped off the roof. To have danced the Football Tango with him way back when. But Priscilla seemed skeptical.

"You like Billy?" Priscilla asked. "You never talk about him."

Now it was your turn to shrug. "He's okay," you said.

You were actually quite shy when you were in fourth grade, something I did not realize at the time, since you were never shy around me. In our room, at night, you were always most yourself.

"I feel like I can say anything to you," you confessed to me after Priscilla left.

But Billy was too popular to talk to, you said. And once his leg healed, Billy was always surrounded by boys, always playing games in the side yard at recess. Football. Soccer. Then basketball. Billy didn't care about talking to girls. Billy didn't care about anything but the Chicago Bulls and how many pull-ups people did during gym class. And dogs. Billy loved dogs. Brought his father's service dog in once for show-and-tell and we followed him through the halls all day. Billy never looked back at us, only bent down to ruffle his dog's head. A yellow Lab.

You tried to get his attention in other ways. At the end of the year, you auditioned for the Disney Spectacular. You dressed up as Annie Oakley for our school's Famous Women Throughout History convention at the end of the year. When all the girls in our school came as famous princesses or queens, you put on your cowboy hat and put a plastic gun in your pocket, because we could do things like that back then. We went to the cafeteria, where our teachers passed out buttons that said "Push Me," and you came alive when people pushed your button. You twirled your gun and delivered your best western twang. Everybody clapped, except Billy. Billy reached out for your plastic gun, turned it over and over, as if he were an antique dealer, appraising it.

Meanwhile, I was dressed in black, all the way on the other side of the cafeteria. People looked at my button, which for some reason said, "Plush me" instead of "Push Me." Boys from my class circled around and Rick Stevenson said, "Ha, Ha. Plush Me. Sally wants to get plushed." I stood straight and thin lipped with one hand on one hip. I felt severe in my bonnet. I didn't know what getting *plushed* was, but I knew I didn't ever want it to happen to me. I knew it would never have happened to Annie Oakley. *She*, I thought, *got a gun*.

"So, what are you?" Billy asked.

During all of our nightly conversations, it had never occurred to me that I might actually speak to Billy one day. I had loved Billy the way I loved Hawaii or Paris, two places we talked about visiting at night, but knew we'd never see because Dad claimed he was too tall to fit in an airplane for that long. So we put up posters of Paris in our room and talked about the kind of croissants we would eat at the base of the Eiffel Tower and that felt like enough.

But here was Billy, standing before me, waiting for a response.

"I'm Florence Nightingale," I finally said.

Mom's idea, which sounded like a good one when she suggested it, but stupid as soon as Billy said, "Is that some kind of a flower?"

"No. She was a famous nurse," I said. "In the Crimean War."

I had a long speech prepared, about how heroic she had been, how her great skill was careful observation. I was even going to mime stitching someone's wound. But Billy said, "Sorry, never heard of it," and then walked off with his friends to the water fountain. He dipped his head low enough to get his hair wet, which must have felt nice. It was mid-July. Too hot to still be in school, in the gym, sweating underneath this nurse's robe, which was really just your old choir uniform. It was a relief when Billy pushed open the double doors on his way out and let in the cool breeze.

I wouldn't see Billy again for years. He went to middle school, and then, a year after, you left to be with him. That's what it felt like. Like I had been left behind in elementary school. Each day, I looked forward to getting home and hearing your updates on Billy.

But some nights, you wouldn't talk much. Some nights, you would put on your headphones and hunch over your homework, and say, "Shhh" whenever I tried to speak. But you always answered me if I asked about Billy. You couldn't resist telling me about your chance encounters with him in the lunch line or how he let you dissect his owl pellet at the science fair or how he held the door for you on the last day of seventh grade.

"He didn't even have to," you said. "I was all the way on the other side of the hallway."

But Billy stood at the door, waiting for you in a suit and tie, which was what the boys had to wear on game days in middle school. It made Billy look older, you said. Taller. It made you think that what Mom had said was right: you girls will be treated with more respect when you dress like you deserve it. Because Billy wore white shirts and ties on game days and then walked down the hallways and the teachers high-fived him. "Hey, great job at the game last night," they said. "Way to take down Dalton." He walked down the hallways as if he owned them, and maybe he did. Maybe that's why he was always holding doors for people.

"He just watched me walk down the empty hallway," you said. "It felt like it took forever to get there."

"That's so awkward," I said. "What did you say?"

"I said, Hey thanks. And he said, No sweat."

And then you walked under his arm and in that moment, you felt something pass through you. You felt truly seen by Billy for maybe the first time in your life.

"Do you guys have a game today?" you asked. A stupid question, you knew. Clearly, he had a game.

"Yeah," he said, and, in your reports, that was all he ever seemed to say. Yeah. No. Maybe. I don't know. He didn't seem to need to speak. Billy's body spoke for him. Even I could hear it, from afar, from our bedroom.

"Does this mean he likes you?" I asked.

"No," you said. "Billy doesn't like anybody."

The only thing Billy cared about in middle school was basketball. He even slept with his basketball some nights, you told me once. At a certain point, I stopped wondering how you knew things about Billy and just processed what you were telling me as fact.

"Why?" I asked.

"Because he's got to learn to love it," you said. "That's what his dad said."

I never had much to report to you at night, except my own academic achievements. The boys of fifth grade did not hold doors for me. They didn't even hold doors for themselves. Rick Stevenson liked to kick doors open with one foot, so hard it always slammed back in his face and made him laugh. The boys I knew did most things with a kind of violence then, even the nice ones like Peter Heart, who tried to flirt with me on the way back from Mystic Seaport by pretending I had been mutilated in a terrible car accident.

"Sally, you're in terrible pain," Peter said, leaning over me. "Now let me put this healing Band-Aid on you."

He put it directly on my lips. Pressed it down firmly. And I thought for a moment that he might kiss me—I had hoped he might kiss me—but then he ripped the Band-Aid right off.

"You have another wound," you said. "A terrible gaping wound on your leg. I think we're going to have to cut it off."

It was all very weird, I told you.

"Oh, it's not that weird," you said. "It just means he likes you."

You were right. A few weeks later, Peter sent me a note in English, asking me to be his girlfriend.

"And what did you say?" you asked.

I said yes, of course. But then we didn't speak for months. Not until I won the fifth-grade spelling bee. I spelled E-L-E-C-T-R-O-N, which upset Peter, because he always won. "Do you even know what an electron is?" Peter asked, and I didn't. I looked it up in the encyclopedia later that night, after everyone fell asleep. I read the entry twice, but still, I didn't understand. What was a subatomic particle of negative electricity?

"Huh?" you said, when I woke you up. "What are you talking about?"

I flopped onto my bed.

"I don't even know what an electron is!" I confessed. "I'm a fraud."

"Oh my God, Sally," you said. "Nobody knows what an electron is."

And besides, you said, that wasn't the point of the spelling bee— the point was to spell the word and that's what you did and that's why they gave you an ice-cream cone and that's why they took a picture of you for the newspaper and everybody who sees it will be like, Sally Holt! Wow. She's so smart.

And you were right. That was what people said after the spelling bee. But it never sounded the way it sounded when you said it. When Rick Stevenson said it at the bus stop, he made it sound like the worst thing about me. When Mom said it, she sounded concerned, like maybe this was the reason I was often alone, in some corner, with a book. And when Grandma said it, it was always just after she called you beautiful.

"You're so beautiful, Kathy," Grandma said. "You could be an anchorwoman one day!"

And then she turned to me. How desperate I must have looked, standing next to you, waiting for my compliment.

"And you, little Sally," she said. "You're so smart and quiet and well-behaved. I bet you'd make a great nun someday."

I froze. Why would Grandma say this to me? Why would I want to be a nun? Couldn't she tell that all I wanted, then, was to be you? I wanted to be older and pierce my ears and grow my hair down to my waist. But Mom wouldn't allow it. Mom dragged me every six weeks to get a trim, long after she stopped dragging you.

"Get in the car," Mom said.

On the way, Mom assured me that hair grew longer the more we cut it, and though this did not seem possible to me, I sat in the chair and trusted in Mom's magic and was disappointed when I looked in the mirror after to find my hair shorter, sitting just above my shoulders like some large brown triangle. It made me feel like a nun.

"But what if I don't want to be a nun?" I asked you later that night.

"Why would you have to be a nun?" you asked.

Nuns didn't get a choice; that's what Valerie Mitt said at CCD class. Her aunt didn't have a choice. Her aunt was just sitting on some park bench, reading her book, minding her business, when God spoke to her. Called her to worship the Lord. And so she became a nun.

For years after Grandma's comment, I worried about God finding me like that, too. Whenever we were out in public, walking to the car or through the mall, I made sure to stay three steps behind you, so God would choose you first.

And when you got to high school, you were chosen. Chosen to be Annie in *Annie*. To be Cinderella in *Cinderella*. To be lead soprano in the women's choir. To sing the National Anthem before the boy's high school basketball game, and you were only a sophomore. I couldn't believe it.

"You're going to have to sing in front of Billy?" I asked.

You refused to act like it was a big deal. "Calm down," you said. "Everyone in the choir gets asked eventually."

Then, in the back seat of the car, you practiced your breathing.

"But why do you have to practice breathing?" I asked. "You already know how."

"There are right ways and wrong ways to breathe," you said. Mr. Fiske, your choir teacher, had taught you how to sing from your belly, how to breathe and keep your voice steady, how to think of yourself as deserving of opportunity. "Especially while you sing."

Walking into the gym felt like walking into an alternate universe, one I had only read about in the newspapers while Mom made breakfast before school. Billy was going to be a star, you read aloud over our pancakes. What made Billy stupid also made him great on the court—Billy had no fear. "That kid could make a three pointer with a bull running right at him," the coach said.

But I was always afraid then. I was nervous for you as you walked to the microphone in the middle of the gym, and Billy and the boys all stood up alongside their bench. Even though there was no need to be—you took the mic and sang the National Anthem the way you had so many times before in the shower, except in the gym, it sounded extra beautiful. Maybe it was the microphone or maybe it was the big expanse of the room or maybe it was knowing that Billy was watching you sing, admiring you the way I was admiring you.

Or maybe it was just the National Anthem. It was the perfect song, you always said. Has almost every note. And, I admit, it gave me chills as you sang the final word and the team stood up, clapped, whistled for you. You smiled so hard, you stopped looking like yourself for just a second. But then you returned to us at the bleachers.

"I'm going to sit with Priscilla and Margaret, okay?" you asked.

"Of course," Dad said.

The game began, and Dad started shouting things out at the players like he knew them.

"Get the ball, Barnes!" Dad yelled. Then he turned to me. "Sally, do you see the way that kid just dives headfirst to get the ball? That's how your father used to be. A maniac."

This is what I saw: Billy missed most of his shots that night. Billy had a bad game, and the team ended up losing. Later, Billy would tell me it was because he knew you were watching. He would tell me that he had fallen in love with you as you sang, and it distracted him to know you were somewhere in the bleachers.

But at the time, he didn't even seem aware of your existence. As we walked to the exit, he didn't look over at us. He gathered his team at the baseline to do sit-ups, push-ups, laps, because that's what the coach made them do after they lost a game they were supposed to win.

Billy seemed oblivious to us as we watched them move up and down, up and down, so in uniform, it looked like breathing. It surprised me, to see the secret discipline that lived inside Billy. Billy was a terrible student, you said. Billy was always sleeping in class. But there was Billy, doing fifty push-ups in a row because someone told him to. He looked like a machine. Like he was not a boy anymore, just a body with a function.

The other boys, too. Fred Jenkins, you said, who farted the alphabet with his arm. And Drew Miller, who used to pick his nose in recess when no one was looking. They were all sprinting as fast as they could, in a straight line, and it gave me the same feeling I got when my history teacher showed us that slideshow of all the Hitler

Youth, the brown uniforms that turned them all the same. Turned into killers overnight, just like that, my teacher said, and snapped his fingers. Like, Hey, boys, here's your uniform. Congratulations. You're a monster now.

It wasn't until I entered seventh grade when I truly realized how little my classmates spoke to me. If you walked by my locker, you might think I had a lot of friends, but I didn't. If you listened closely to what people were saying, it was always, "Wait, you used three different sources?" "Wait, our history test is *today*?"

It was a relief to get home from school and find you watching TV, swallowed up by the big couch.

"Come watch with me," you said.

We watched shows we could only watch when Mom and Dad were not home. Trashy talk shows. *Jillian Williams.* I snuggled against you on the couch and we sat there and listened to some woman onstage confess things to her husband.

"This whole time we've been married," the woman said, "I secretly had two vaginas."

The husband had no idea. "I'm not angry," the husband kept saying. "I'm not even upset. I'm just confused. Where's the other one?"

His wife slapped him across the face. The question was, apparently, very insulting if you had two vaginas. The audience gasped, but we didn't. We knew better. We watched these shows too much to find them wholly believable anymore, which we were learning was the only way to be entertained by them.

"Come on," you said. "How would he *not* notice that his wife had two vaginas?"

You seemed to be seriously asking me.

"There's no such *thing* as two vaginas," I said with the kind of angry confidence we once used to denounce Santa Claus after we found out it was just Dad who had been writing *Merry Christmas! Ho Ho Ho! Love, Santa* on the presents each year.

"Of course, there's such a thing," you said. "This is *America*. Don't be stupid, Sally."

I did not want to be stupid. I wanted to know everything you knew. So I considered the possibility that you were right—that anything was possible. That this was America, where some women had two vaginas and were proud of it.

That's exactly what I told everybody in the auditorium when the nurse called us down to tell us about our periods, which some girls still didn't know about. They were in a state of disbelief. Every twenty-eight days? For the rest of our lives? they asked each other. That couldn't be.

But I refused to act surprised. I knew better than that. I raised my hand. "What if you have two vaginas, though?" I asked. "Do you get two periods?"

I had expected my classmates to be impressed. I imagined girls crowding around me after, asking follow-up questions. But they just gave each other looks, raised their eyebrows, burst into hysterical laughter.

"I'm afraid I don't understand what that means, Sally," the nurse said. "People don't have two vaginas."

It was only Valerie Mitt who asked about it later on the bus.

"So if a person has two vaginas, do they pee out of both?" she asked, and I said, "I mean, probably?" and we laughed. Valerie was interested in strange things. In science. Her father, she told me, was a scientist who made the chemical that made white bread even softer.

But later that night, you were embarrassed for me. "I can't believe you asked that question," you said across our beds.

"The nurse told us to ask questions!"

"Listen, Sally, you're getting older. The number one rule in sex information sessions is to never ask questions, even if the nurse stands up there for twenty minutes and says, Please, girls, ask me questions."

You told me about Priscilla Mountain and how once she asked if having a longer index finger meant you were a lesbian, and everybody since has thought she was a lesbian.

"Is Priscilla a lesbian?" I asked.

"See? That's why you don't ask questions."

You were right. A few days later, I returned to school to see SALLY HOLT HAS TWO VAGINAS written on a bathroom stall. I stopped peeing as soon as I saw it—how long had this been written here? Who wrote it? I felt frantic as I failed to scribble it out with a pen.

I went to class, humiliated. Late. I felt everyone in the room looking at me and my two vaginas as I sat down. I didn't speak for the rest of the day, not even when Mr. Briggs called on me.

"Sally, what was a major invention that contributed to the Industrial Revolution?" he asked, because he always called on me when the room was entirely silent. He relied on me. He knew I knew the answer: the steam engine. We had learned about it a thousand times. But I just shrugged.

After a few weeks of not participating, I actually got in trouble for it. It was the only thing that I ever really got in trouble for during middle school. Teachers didn't like it when you didn't participate, even when you were a spelling bee champion who got 100s on all the exams. Silence made them uncomfortable. Silence was like a big watery void that reflected back whatever they feared the most.

"Mr. Briggs is worried that you don't like his class anymore," Mom said upon returning home from her parent-teacher conference with him. "He's says you've become quite shy. What's going on, Sally?"

Mom was a community leader. A member of the PTA. A crucial

number on the neighborhood phone chain. How could she have raised one daughter who sings proudly in front of hundreds of people and another who couldn't answer a simple question in class?

Dad didn't seem concerned. All during dinner, Dad kept citing past geniuses who were late to bloom. Einstein didn't speak until he was four, Dad said. Maybe five. Dad defended me and Einstein as if he were defending himself.

But Mom wouldn't have it.

"She's twelve, Richard," Mom said. "It's time."

Mom bought a book about how shy I was. I don't know if you ever noticed it, but the book was called *The Shy Child* and they stuck it on the bookshelf for all to see, and the only thing it did was remind me that I was problematically shy and so I became shier. I refused to audition for the school play. I blushed wildly anytime a teacher called on me, even if I knew the answer, and Mom and Dad were brought back into school to have more conferences about my shyness.

"You need to participate, Sally," Mom said over and over again that year, then called everybody she knew on the phone, as if she could participate the problem away.

"We've tried everything," she said to Aunt Beatrice.

"She's just so quiet, so unlike Kathy," she said to Priscilla's mom.

"I don't know how I ended up with two kids so different," she said to some woman at the grocery store.

It wasn't the first time in my life that I had suspected we were different, that we were opposite children, but it was the first time I had heard Mom concerned about it. I tucked Mom's comments away in my brain. I started watching you even more closely, to see how you did it. I sat in our room when Priscilla and Margaret came over, and I marveled at the way words just spilled out of your mouth when you rehearsed songs loudly or prank-called Stop & Shop.

"Uh hi," you said into the phone, with a French accent. "What is the cheese du jour?"

The three of you laughed hard as you hung up. Until, of course, you remembered I was in the room, watching.

"Sally," you said. "Go downstairs with Mom."

That year, I looked forward to our summer vacation with a zeal I never had before. Priscilla would be far away in Italy and Margaret would be up north at music camp and we would be where we always were that first week of July: together in Watch Hill, Rhode Island. Not a far drive—only forty minutes north on 95 and one tank of gas there and back, Dad said—yet it always felt like another world when we arrived.

"It *is* another world," you said. "It's the ocean."

We loved it by the ocean. There, Mom read her big novels under the umbrella and made her famous Baybreeze drink, though famous for what, she never made clear. Dad drank beer from a cooler and spent a lot of time trying to finish a crossword puzzle, and I felt proud whenever I got a word before him. You were writing your name in the sand, asking me if I'd rather be really rich or really funny, huge or teeny-tiny, a successful doctor or a famous writer, and I decided with a speed that impresses me now.

"Rich," I said.

"Huge."

"Doctor!"

After, we ran into the waves and looked back at the big houses along the sea.

"That's where I want to live one day," you said, and pointed to a mansion with dramatic geometric shapes. You liked the modern beach houses. But I didn't. They didn't seem to fit at the edge of a majestic bluff.

"And ocean houses are too much work, anyway," I said, which was what Dad had said after Grandma's house had started to grow mold all along the walls and she refused to move. The house is literally killing you, Dad said to her once. But Grandma didn't care. It was her house. She wanted to die there, she said, and she did.

"Oh my God, Sally." You laughed and started to make your way to shore. "I'm not talking about reality. It's just a dream house."

On the way home from vacation, Dad always stopped at the gas station in town to fill the car back up. "Girls, go give them forty dollars," Dad said, which excited me, because that meant we got to buy whatever we wanted with the change.

We ran inside the mini-mart, all the way to the potato chips in the back. We stood there for a moment, trying to decide between the different flavors, when Billy walked in with a girl I didn't recognize.

"Ugh," you whispered. "Shelby Meyers."

"Who is that?"

"Just some girl in my chem class," you said.

I was surprised by how different Billy looked when he was standing in the market with a girl. He looked like he was in some play, cast as Shelby's husband, reaching out for a can of beans, turning it over and over as if to ask himself, are these the ones that my mom buys? We watched as he walked to the register with his hand in Shelby's back pocket, and hers in his.

"Why do they walk like that?" I asked you. "Seems like it would get annoying."

"Because they're in looove," you said. "When you're in looove, you have to stick your fingers in each other's pockets."

"Mom and Dad never do that," I said.

"Mom and Dad are married," you said, as if married people couldn't be in love.

But when we got back to the car, I felt vindicated. Dad and Mom were kissing. "You caught us!" Mom said, but she clearly wasn't embarrassed. Just flushed from a week of sun.

"Gross!" you shouted.

"Get a room!" I added, because I knew I was supposed to be upset by such a sight. But Dad turned on the car and said, "You get a room! I bought this room. This is my room."

"Your father has a point, girls," Mom said.

Then, before he started driving, Dad leaned over to kiss Mom again, for dramatic effect. This time, Mom really did blush. Smiled as she turned to look out the window. And I don't know why this should have felt like a sudden realization, but it did: *Mom was Dad's wife*, I thought. *And Dad was Mom's husband. And they loved each other the way we loved Billy Barnes.*

A t the end of July, it got so hot, the air conditioner broke. "Well, that's it, folks," Dad said, patting it with his hand.

For some reason, Dad left it in the wall and refused to fix it. He walked around in his boxers before work, and Mom put cucumbers in her water as if that made it colder.

"This isn't so bad, is it?" Mom said, holding up her glass like it was a cocktail.

"This is living!" Dad said.

"I don't understand why we can't just have air-conditioning," you said.

"Air-conditioning!" Dad said. "Who needs air-conditioning?"

"People do," you said.

"Au contraire," Dad said. "People do not. Do you think the Egyptians had air-conditioning when they built the great pyramids?"

Dad did not yell to teach us our lessons; he went to graduate school, he often reminded us. He appealed to the history of other people's suffering to teach us our lessons.

"But we're not Egyptians," you said.

That wasn't Dad's point.

"What's your point?" you asked.

"The point is, you girls need to toughen up!"

Then Dad went to work (where there was air-conditioning, you pointed out), and Mom suggested we all get a grip.

"Your father works very hard," Mom said. "He deserves air-conditioning."

"What does he even do?" I asked.

I never understood this. Dad's job was so confusing, even though you had explained it a million times.

"He's a safety consultant," you said. "He keeps people safe."

"But what people?"

"Telephone people," you said.

"What are telephone people?"

"Those men, you know those men who climb all those cell towers everybody is building now? The ones that go really high up in the sky?"

No. I didn't. I didn't know what a cell tower was. And I had never heard about telephone people before. But you were done explaining.

"It's too hot to talk," you said.

So Mom suggested the pool. We put on our bathing suits, met in the garage.

"Can I drive?" you asked.

You were newly sixteen, with a learner's permit, and lately Mom had been letting you drive us places.

"Are you going to finish putting on your clothes?" Mom asked.

"Why do I need clothes?" you asked. "I'm wearing a bathing suit. We're just going to the pool."

"What if we get in an accident?" Mom asked. "And you're stuck in your bathing suit all day."

"I won't get in an accident, then," you said.

But Mom wouldn't let you drive until you went upstairs and put on a shirt and jean shorts. You didn't button them, though, and rolled the waist band over to show off the top of your bathing suit underneath. I prepared myself for the fight to begin again, but Mom didn't say anything. We just quietly watched as you drove us to the pool, and I became fixated by your hands, how they looked like Mom's on the steering wheel. Your nails, tipped the same color as hers: Like Linen.

You parked. "Are you going to finish putting on your shorts?" Mom asked, then locked the doors.

"They're on," you said.

"You haven't buttoned them."

"Nobody buttons their shorts anymore."

"Nobody buttons their shorts anymore?" Mom said. "Is that what you are really saying to me?"

"Yeah. It's a trend."

"Oh, is that so?" Mom asked. "And what is this trend called exactly?"

"I don't know what it's called," you said. "Trends don't have names. Trends just *are*."

"Sally," Mom said. "Please be honest with me. Is your sister making this up?"

"Maybe," I said. "Maybe not." Because that was the most honest answer I had. You had told me a lot about high school, but you never mentioned whether people were or were not buttoning their shorts, and I had not thought to ask. I looked out the window for the telephone people in the sky, but I didn't see them. Mom sighed.

"I refuse to ask my own daughter to button her own pants. That's supposed to be a given. That's supposed to be something your child just does."

By then, she didn't even sound like she was talking to us anymore. She sounded as if she was talking to the company who manufactured us.

"Fine," you said. "I'll button them."

You seemed annoyed until we opened the gate and walked onto the pool deck and saw him. Billy, at the edge of the high dive, just about to jump. You clutched my arm, pulled me closer to you. You didn't even have to say his name.

"Predictable, but perfect," you said, as if we were watching the Olympics. "What do you say, Sally?"

"A classic dive," I said, in my best announcer voice. "Nine for style, ten for technique."

At the pool, I wanted to swim the way we had in the ocean. I wanted to jump off the high dive like Billy and the other boys, fly through the air, but you didn't. You were different at the pool where Billy and the rest of the town could see us.

You wanted to lay out—far away from Mom's chair, you said—and I didn't see the point of being anywhere you were not, so I spread my towel next to yours. I sat heavy in my bulky one-piece, while you were sprawled out in your American flag bikini, with one eye always on Billy, who would swim laps so perfect they barely made any sound. When he was done, he floated on an inner tube, listening to his Walkman. And then, when his break was over, he returned to the snack bar, where he sold candies.

This was our chance.

"Come on, Sally," you said.

We walked up to the window.

"I'll have an ice-cream sandwich," you said to Billy.

"Sure thing," Billy said.

Billy's face—it had become wider and flatter since I last saw him. It reminded me of a prairie I once saw in my history book at school. It made me imagine building things on top of it.

"And what do you want?" Billy asked me.

"A Jolly Rancher," I said.

"What flavor?" he asked.

"Watermelon."

You didn't say anything as Billy handed you the goods. Your hand did not shake and you did not fidget with your ice-cream sandwich, and this steadiness surprised me. Reminded me of how calm you were before you sang the National Anthem, how you simply moved the hair off your shoulder and began.

"Hey, thanks," you said.

"No sweat," Billy said. "It's my job."

Billy tapped his thumb against the counter. He was listening to music on a boom box just loud enough so he could hear, but softly enough so he wouldn't get fired: Nirvana and then Ace of Base. Our favorite bands.

"Well, you're very good at it," you said.

He laughed. "I know. So talented," he said. He opened the register, and then dropped each quarter dramatically into your open palm. "Someone should give me an award."

"Not everybody can make change like that," you said.

Then we walked back to our towels, where you sat down and became yourself again.

"Sally, did you *see* that?" you asked.

"See what?"

"When Billy handed me the money, he winked at me."

I didn't see it. I had been very busy trying to unwrap my Jolly Rancher—notoriously difficult. Sometimes the plastic melted into the candy or the candy melted into the plastic. I couldn't tell, which Mom said was a reason I should not be eating it—you shouldn't be eating something that cannot be distinguished from plastic. But I ate it, because Dad said we were already doomed—our bodies were practically half-plastic now.

"But why would he wink at you?" I asked. I felt the sweet burst of candy in my mouth.

"My question exactly," you said.

I had never seen anybody wink before in real life, except Grandpa, but Grandpa only ever winked at our cat, the one we called Doctor, and only in those few months before Grandpa died, and Grandpa winking at Doctor was even more confusing than Billy winking at you, because it made me think that Doctor knew something about

Grandpa's looming death, that maybe Doctor was Death, and for years, I was too spooked to look Doctor in the eye, as if she would take me, too. But Doctor never did, of course—Doctor died. We found her curled up under the deck one day, and I felt so bad as Dad removed her. Cried for days until Mom said, "Sally, it's just a cat," which was exactly why I was crying. That whole time, it had just been a cat.

"Do people in high school wink a lot?" I asked.

"No," you said. "It's simply not done."

You explained that normally when a boy wanted a girl's attention in high school, he would nod in her general direction or make an obscene gesture with his hands or maybe just say "Wassup" and then completely ignore her response. It was important, you said, for boys to act like giant assholes.

But Billy winked at you. And no boy had ever dared wink at you before. It was nice, you said. Old-fashioned.

"What do you think it means?" I asked.

You licked the ice cream around the edges of your sandwich before you answered. You started doing this in high school a lot—made me wait for your big conclusion.

"I think it means he likes me," you said.

"But what about Shelby?"

"Oh, they broke up."

You had heard from Priscilla's brother that Billy had dumped Shelby last week. Billy wasn't ready for a serious relationship. Billy was just a boy and wanted to be a boy forever, or something like that. But Shelby was distraught, cried for nearly a week and dyed her hair blonder than her mother's and wrote terrible things about Billy in chat rooms online.

"I need a napkin," you said.

You were determined to get Billy's attention that day. You stood up and walked back to the snack bar window without waiting for me. I put on the hat you were wearing and cloaked my body in a

giant T-shirt and started to run after you, but I tripped. Stubbed
my toe. By the time I caught up with you, it was too late. You were
leaning over the bar into the window, laughing at something Billy
said, and you looked so different to me. Something to do with
your hair, how long it had gotten, and your breasts, which had
started to look like Mom's breasts, and I know that's a thing you
told me never to say again, but it's true. It all gave me the same
strange feeling I got after Billy jumped off the school roof, as if
you were someone I didn't know. As if you had drowned the real
Kathy—sticks and stones for bones—somewhere in the ocean in
Rhode Island.

But then he gave you the napkin, and we walked back to the towels, and there was another girl at the window. The lifeguard—she
kept blowing her whistle for Adult Swim and then leaned against the
counter to talk to Billy for much longer than it took to order fries.
Each time Billy spoke, she laughed, held her stomach, like it was all
just too funny.

"Ugh, Lisa Halloway," you said.

"Who is she?"

"According to legend, a slut."

I flinched. I had never heard you call anybody that before, and it
didn't sound right coming from you. "But she's the lifeguard."

"So?" you said. "You can be a slut and a lifeguard at the same time.
Do you even know what a slut is?"

I shrugged. I had heard the word before, but never understood what
it really meant since the boys used it to describe everybody they came
in contact with at school—the librarian, who taught us how to use the
Dewey decimal system. The bus driver, who gave us snap bracelets as we
walked off the bus. *Slut*, Rick Stevenson said, as she drove away.

"How can you be so smart and not know what a slut is?" you
asked.

"It wasn't on any of my vocab tests."

This was a joke, but you didn't laugh.

"Well, if you want to know, a slut is a girl who tries to sleep with anybody, even someone else's boyfriend," you said.

"But Billy isn't your boyfriend," I said.

You ignored my comment. You pulled out one of Mom's beauty magazines and we did a personality quiz that determined whether we were Yellow People, Green People, or Red People. I didn't know these were kinds of people, I said. But you acted like it was science. You scored our answers and then announced the results.

"You're a Red Person," you said.

Even before you read the description, I knew it was not good. A Red Person liked symmetrical shapes, place mats, and feedback. A Red Person was rational, sensible, reliable.

"What are you?"

"A Green Person," you said. A Green Person was chill. A Green Person was ready for anything. A Green Person liked dreams, open seas, and crystals. A Green Person wore a string bikini to the pool and said things like, "Nudity is what you make of it, you know. In Europe, people are naked all of the time and nobody cares."

And a Red Person felt upset by this. "They are?"

That couldn't be. An entire continent of naked people? But then again, Europeans were often naked in the paintings and sculptures we studied at school and our teachers acted like it was no big deal, pointed to their genitals with their fingers, and said, "What Michelangelo is doing here is celebrating the beauty of the human form."

"I just mean, Americans are such puritans," you said.

"You're American," I said.

"I know."

I sat there and felt the fuzz covering my legs, two hairs almost out of every follicle, which was an outrage to me, but apparently my fate, according to Mom. "You're half-Italian, half-German," Mom always said. "This is what life is going to be like for you, Sally." And yet she still wouldn't let me shave. Mom hid the razors on the top shelf, and then dragged me to the salon every six weeks, and I didn't understand—why did I have to keep my leg hair but was not allowed to keep the hair on my head?

You kept turning over, kept looking over at Billy to see if he was noticing you. But he wasn't. He was talking to Lisa the lifeguard and she was laughing, playfully swatting him away from her body.

"Lisa's not even pretty," you said. "Everybody just thinks she's pretty because she's the lifeguard."

I nodded.

"And Billy's not really that attractive, either," you said.

This made no sense. All summer, you had talked about how handsome Billy had become.

"What do you mean?" I asked.

"He's too handsome," you said. "He looks exactly like he's supposed to look."

"Isn't that a good thing?"

"Only a Red Person would say that," you said, and put your head on the towel and closed your eyes.

But I couldn't just lie there. I was too upset to nap. I felt deeply flawed. Ruined for life. I was a Red Person. I was boring. I knew it. Why did I worry about how much work it would be to take care of a dream house? Why couldn't I see the flaws in Billy's absolute perfection? Why did I like it so much when Mom cut my sandwich in neat symmetrical halves? Why did I, as a toddler, try to clean the backyard? I would go outside and separate the rocks from the twigs. Put the leaves in little piles. And then cry when the wind blew. You and Mom and Dad all laughed, like it was the funniest thing about me, but it wasn't. It was evidence that I was doomed.

I started to read my summer reading book, *Oedipus the King*. But when the chorus began to sing things I did not understand, I looked up to see Peter Heart sitting on the other side of the pool, also reading *Oedipus*. Peter was a Red Person, too. Peter clearly did not belong at the pool. He looked severe under the awning in a black T-shirt that was wet and slick like sealskin. I felt embarrassed each time Billy walked by him. Billy, who ran around the pool deck, shirtless and solid, a Greek statue coming to life under the sun.

"I can't believe he was my boyfriend," I said.

"When did you have a boyfriend?" you asked.

"You don't remember?" I asked. "In the first grade."

"Oh, the first grade?" You laughed. "That's not a real boyfriend."

I felt that flash of anger I got whenever you did not take my life seriously. I pointed to Peter, as if to prove something to you. "Him. See? He's real. He's right there!"

"Sally," you said. "Stop pointing at him. He's looking right at us."

I stopped. I picked up my book again.

"He's still looking at us," you said. "I bet he has a crush on you."

"No," I said. "Peter doesn't like anybody. He's incapable."

"Just because you don't like Peter, it doesn't mean that Peter doesn't like you."

You put on one of Mom's extra big hats to cover your face.

"I'm bored," you said. "Hot."

It always felt like my fault when you were bored, for some reason. "Let's go swim."

"No," you said. You looked at my book. "I remember that one. It's good. It's all about sex."

"No, it's not," I said. It was about a king who was murdered. Another king, who was trying to solve the murder. And a whole city that was sick with the plague. "It's for school."

"Exactly," you said. "School is all about sex."

I had no idea how someone could make such a claim. School had nothing to do with sex. School was all about who won World War II and how were amoebas different from paramecia and who can build the best roller coaster out of pipe cleaners? I looked at Mom, a former teacher, who would have backed me up on this, but she was too far away to help me. I had abandoned her for you, and now she looked asleep under her big hat.

"How is school about sex?" I asked, but you didn't answer. You were done with the conversation—and I hated that you got to decide things like that. You flipped up the floppy brim and you looked like one of those dogs with the big fluffy bangs. You were never the person I expected under the hat, different each time you met sunlight.

"Who cares?" you said.

You put your head down. But a few minutes later, you couldn't resist. "Is he still talking to Lisa?" you asked.

"Yes."

"What's she doing?"

Lisa was laughing at something he said. Then, she started walking away, through the pool gate.

"She's leaving," I said.

"Good," you said.

But Lisa didn't go to her car. She stood on the other side of the pool fence and pulled out a cigarette. And it looked wrong, smoking in a bikini.

"Actually, she's not leaving. She's just smoking."

"I feel like the lifeguard shouldn't be allowed to smoke," you said. "She's supposed to be saving lives."

I didn't know why anybody would smoke. Smoking was stupid. That's what we heard every year in the auditorium when the nurse wheeled out the black lung in the glass case and pointed at it. Kids, she said, this could be your lung one day.

"Yeah, well, Lisa is kind of stupid," you said.

Lisa was in your history class last year, and she didn't know who Gandhi was. After a week of your teacher talking about nothing but Gandhi, she was like, "I don't know. I heard of the guy. I just can't remember why."

Everybody in class laughed. You didn't understand why it was cool for some girls to be stupid and embarrassing for other girls to be stupid. You didn't understand why everybody made fun of Melissa Frank for being slow and not knowing how to spell her own name, but everybody applauded Lisa for not knowing who Gandhi was.

"There's a rumor," you said, "that Lisa gives all the guys on the swim team blow jobs after they win."

"What's a blow job?" I asked.

"Seriously?" you asked. "What are you even learning at school?"

Things I had been learning at school: The hottest place on earth was not Death Valley. Tigers are not native to Africa. And the water that fell from the sky gathered in lakes and puddles and pools and slowly, invisibly, evaporated back up into the sky to become rain again. And it was amazing to me that water disappeared from the ground and returned to us again and again. Open your mouths and taste the rain from two thousand years ago! Mrs. Felmore had commanded during science class.

Things I had not been learning at school: blow jobs.

"I'll tell you later," you said and put your head back on your towel.

I resumed watching Billy, who seemed to get busier as the day got hotter. But every once in a while, when he had no customers, when he was just sitting there eating M&M's tapping his thumb to the beat of the music, he glanced over at us on our towels.

"He's looking," I said.

"Stop looking at him then!"

"How'm I supposed to know if he's looking if I can't look at him?"

"You've got to be sneaky," you said. "Like a spy."

I liked the thought of being a spy for you. A soldier dressed in casual swimwear to fight the Queen's war. After you fell asleep, I made another trip to the snack bar.

"I'll take another Jolly Rancher, please," I said, with the seriousness of a woman much older than me. "Watermelon."

"One watermelon Jolly Rancher," Billy said. "Coming right up."

He leaned forward to give me the candy. But he held it in his hand for just a second before I could take it.

"Promise me that you won't sue me if you actually turn into a Jolly Rancher," he said.

"I promise," I said. It was then I would have swept the hair off my shoulders, if it touched my shoulders. He handed me the candy. "Thanks."

"No sweat," he said.

And then it happened. Billy Barnes winked at me.

H e did not wink at you," you said when you woke up. "Why would he do that?"

"Maybe he just winks at everybody," I said.

"No," you said. "Nobody winks at everybody. That'd be a creepy thing to do."

"Well, he winked at me."

"Why would he wink at you? You're just a child."

"I'm not a child," I said. "I'm thirteen."

Turning thirteen felt like a big deal when it happened in May. Mom made a birthday cake and you lit the candles and Dad said, "Speech, Sally! Speech!" and I didn't know what to say about being thirteen. I just turned thirteen. I had no thoughts or grand conclusions about it yet. And definitely no speech. Why hadn't I prepared a speech? I started to cry right there, over the cake, and you said, "He's just joking, Sally. You take everything so literally." Dad gave me a lecture after, about what it meant to be a teenager. About how I couldn't just go around crying over everything. The more the girl cried, he said, the more pitiable the girl became. He said he spent years watching his own mother shrink in this way. And I didn't know what this meant, but I knew I didn't ever want to be accused of shrinking.

"Exactly. You're thirteen. You're just a child," you said. "I'm hot. I'm going in the water."

Finally. I got up to join you, but you said, "Don't. Follow. Me."

So I just watched you walk into the water, and studied you, as if I were trying to figure out something crucial. When did your hair get so long? When did you get so pretty? And had you always been bowlegged? Your legs curved outward, like a warped table, making it so that your thighs never touched. Watching you walk in the water in your bikini was enough to reveal the errors of my morning outfit choices. It made me question every little thing I had ever done in my life. Like why was I wearing a swimsuit with a giant three on the back like I was a member of some sports team, when in reality I played no sports at all?

You sank under the water, and I felt silly sitting all alone, so I went over to Mom, who was no longer alone. She had been joined by some women I didn't recognize. Women, I was sure, from her various committees. Women with children scattered somewhere at the pool. They were drinking things out of red plastic cups. I could hear bits of their gossip in the wind as I approached.

"James Green is getting rid of his thyroid, you know."

"The Hamiltons are harboring an illegal chicken in their basement."

But it quieted as I neared. "Hi, Mom," I said.

Mom poked my shoulder. "You're getting pink," she said. "Sally, put on some more sunscreen."

No. I hated sunscreen. Sunscreen made me feel like a Red Person.

"The sun's not even out," I said.

The sun was setting and Billy had just closed up the snack bar window. Lisa blew her whistle. Adult Swim, she called, and went to smoke through the fence again.

"Can we go?" I asked.

"Not yet, honey," she said. "I'm just talking here with some friends and then we can go."

But I didn't want to sit back down next to Mom and her friends. I didn't want to pick up my book again, either, because it was upsetting. You were right—it was all about sex. It was all about how Oedipus had been sleeping with his mother, so he gouged his eyes out with his mother's hairpins.

I felt like I needed to do something drastic. Something a Red Person would never do. I walked over to the high dive. I climbed the stairs and walked to the edge and stood there like a Green Person. I felt good up there, and I looked around to see who was watching me, until I realized that nobody was watching me.

Lisa was looking at her cigarette. Billy was looking at Lisa's fingers, which he was touching through the fence. And you were looking at Billy. The only person who was watching me was Peter, which made me feel sad, for both me and Peter, and the next thing I knew, I lost my balance. I fell hard off the diving board. I hit the water, which is the last thing I remember.

When I woke, there was Billy's face.

"Sally!" Billy shouted, and it was amazing. Nobody, to this day, has ever looked at me directly in the eye and shouted my name like that. Not even you. "Sally!"

"She's alive!" you screamed, appearing behind him.

"Are you okay?" Mom asked.

I wasn't sure what had happened. I felt a crushing weight in my lungs and a rawness in the back of my throat. But I could breathe. I could see them all standing before me perfectly fine.

"I'm okay," I said.

But you cried. And Mom cried. "Thank God!" you said, and you and Mom took turns hugging me. Mom was so grateful, so grateful, thank you thank you thank you, she kept saying to Billy.

"Yeah, of course," Billy said.

"You're not even the lifeguard!" you exclaimed. "How did you *do* that?"

Do what? I wondered.

"Where *is* the lifeguard?" Mom asked.

"I'm right here," Lisa said. Lisa looked at me. "Sally, are you sure you're okay?"

Up close, I could smell the smoke on her breath. She didn't look like a slut at all. She looked concerned, and so I almost told her the truth: Actually, I have a splitting headache.

"I'm okay," I said again.

"We'll have to thank you somehow," Mom said to Billy before we left. "Let us have you over for dinner this week."

You blushed, but Billy shrugged like there was nothing embarrassing about it at all.

"Sure," Billy said. "I love dinner."

The veins on Billy's arm seemed full of blood. The water had beaded on his chest, and his skin looked thick and amphibious, a coat that could never tear.

The whole ride home from the pool you were upset.

"I can't *believe* you asked him over for dinner," you said. "It's so embarrassing."

"I don't see what's so embarrassing about it," Mom said.

"He's popular, Mom," you said.

"Do popular people not eat dinner?"

"I highly doubt it."

"They just survive off their own awesomeness," Mom said.

"Exactly."

"Oh, get over it," Mom said. "This isn't about you. We're thanking him for saving Sally's life."

"You've got a pretty high opinion of your potato salad," you said. "Thank you for saving my precious daughter's life. Your reward shall be potato salad."

Mom laughed. "It *is* good potato salad. I challenge you to find me a better recipe."

You kept looking over at me. My teeth were still chattering. I was cold.

"Hey, are you okay?" you asked me.

I nodded. "I could go for some potato salad," I said, and I meant it seriously, but you both laughed.

"See?" Mom said. "Sally likes it."

"Sally likes everything," you said, and I know you meant it as a compliment, but it felt like an insult, like the thing we'd say about our dog, if we had one.

We were antsy in the days leading up to the dinner with Billy. We thought only of Billy and of all the things Billy could be doing right now.

"He could be swimming," I said.

"That's boring," you said. "I think Billy should be doing something better."

"Like what?"

"He could be saving a small kitten. Or maybe a baby? From a tree?"

"Why is there a baby in a tree?"

"Because that's where it is."

Everybody was very nice to me that week I almost died, but nobody was nicer than you. You kept close by my side, and asked me so many questions about my near-death experience, I eventually felt proud of it. It was, I realized, something you had never experienced.

"Did you see the light?" you asked.

"No," I said.

"Did you see anybody? Grandpa?"

"I didn't see anything," I said. "I was just, like, not there. Like sleeping or something."

"That's boring," you said. You hoped for more from death. You wanted to believe there was something exciting waiting for us. You hoped we would all turn into ghosts because if you're a ghost, it's like you're not really dead. And as ghosts, we could do anything we wanted, you said. Go to Paris. Live in a beautiful mansion by the sea. And spy on Billy whenever we felt like it.

"Did you at least feel it when Billy gave you mouth-to-mouth?"

"No," I said. I couldn't even imagine it, Billy with his lips pressed to mine. "I couldn't feel him kiss me."

You laughed.

"Oh my God, it was definitely not a kiss," you said. "You have to be conscious for your first kiss to count. Pretty sure that's a rule."

"Says who?" I asked.

"Says the *law*."

Other requirements for a kiss to be real, according to you: It can't be because you're playing spin the bottle. And it can't be because you're in some play and a character has to kiss you.

"I'd never be in a play."

"Good. Because ever since Priscilla got kissed in *Les Mis* she acts like she's some expert," you said. "I don't count any of my stage kisses."

You stood up, walked to the bathroom, and stubbed your toe on the ottoman. "Fuck!" you said, and there was Mom as usual, appearing whenever we said a bad word.

"What did you just say?" Mom asked.

"I said 'fuck,'" you said.

And why? Why would you say that? Why would you say "fuck" when there are so many other words in the English language? Did we even know how many words there are in the English language?

We didn't.

"A thousand?"

"A million?"

"A lot of people think that," Mom said, "but they're wrong. Nobody actually knows."

"What's your point?"

"My point is, there are so many beautiful words out there."

"Like what?" I asked.

"Oh, let me think," Mom said, and then began to list them: Vermillion. Sibilance. Halcyon. Mom liked three-syllable words. "So why on earth would you choose an ugly word when you can choose a beautiful word?"

"Because I wanted to," you said. "It felt right."

"Yeah," Mom said. "We'll see how much you want to after you say it a hundred times."

O ur punishment: go outside and say the ugly word into each one of these little sandwich baggies. Don't come back in until all the ugly words are out of our systems and sealed up into these baggies where they belong!

"Mom is crazy," you said.

But we did what we were told. We went outside and we said "fuck" until it didn't even sound like a bad word anymore. It didn't sound like anything. It was just a sound. Fuck. Fuck. Fuck. And after a while, it was boring, which I guessed was the point of the punishment. To say a word so many times, you don't even want to say it anymore. So we tried other words. *Shit. Bitch. Dick*, which wasn't a swear, you said.

"What is it then?" I asked.

"It's just a body part."

When we went back inside, we handed our shits and fucks back to Mom, and she took them so seriously—Thank you, girls—that we couldn't help but laugh later up in our room. We couldn't help but wonder what she did with them all. You started to run around the room, opening drawers. "No shits and fucks in here!" you shouted, and so I opened the closet. "No shits and fucks in here, either!" I said, and by that time, we were laughing so hard, it all felt less like getting in trouble and more like winning a prize.

T wo days later, Billy came for dinner and the whole thing seemed to happen in slow motion. Maybe this had something to do with my concussion earlier in the week, but I think it was just the shock of Billy's presence in our house. There was Billy, in our living room.

Billy, at our kitchen table. Billy, eating our mother's potato salad. I couldn't make sense of it. Billy was so big at the dinner table, bigger than even Dad, and I wondered how this made Dad feel, to be smaller than a boy.

Mom and Dad were funny around Billy all night, too. They were nervous, like we were all on a date with Billy. It started as soon as he showed up, standing in the doorway with flowers.

"How did you know I loved tulips?" Mom laughed, like the flowers were for her.

"My father said I couldn't go wrong with tulips," Billy said, and then told us that his father was a florist, as if we didn't know everything about him already.

"Oh, we know Bill," Mom said. We had purchased hundreds of flowers from him when Grandpa died, and then, again, when Grandma died.

"Bill's a great guy," Dad said. He shook Billy's hand, which made Billy seem a hundred years older. "Gives me discounted marigolds every year. How's he doing, by the way?"

"He's doing really well," Billy said.

"Good," Dad said.

Billy put his hands in his pockets and started answering Dad's questions about the team. Were they planning on being champions this year?

"You bet!" Billy said.

Billy was an optimist. He believed in noble things, and he wore these beliefs literally printed down the sleeves of his shirts. That night, his sleeve said, ONE TEAM, ONE GOAL.

"Attaboy," Dad said. Then a slap on the back. "That new coach is really turning things around."

"He is," Billy said.

Then Billy said a lot of boring things about the new coach, who had been a player in college. He had a wife who was a CFO and so he didn't work.

"Which means his job is *us*," he explained. "He's crazy."

He made Billy practice all of the time, even on weekends, even on holidays, but it was worth it. They were getting better. PRACTICE MAKES PERFECT, it said on his other arm.

"We have a chance this year," Billy said.

"That's what all the papers say," Dad said.

That night, I noticed something about Dad: He spoke with Billy in a way he never spoke to us—like they were colleagues or something. Two men, just talking about a game together. When they finished, Billy looked at me.

"How are you doing?" Billy said.

But you answered before I could.

"She's still alive," you said. "Right, Sally?"

"Right," I said.

All through dinner, Mom kept thanking him for saving my life.

"There were a ton of people there," Mom said while Billy ate our potato salad, stabbing each cube whole and popping them into his mouth. "But you were the only one who reacted."

"Hey, it's no big deal," Billy said, as if he saved people all of the time, and, apparently, he did. Just punched his grandmother in the stomach earlier that year when she was choking on a piece of meat. The meat came flying out, and his grandmother would live another two weeks, only to die of a heart attack in her sleep.

"Oh, that's sad," Mom said.

"It's okay," Billy said. "She was really old."

"Wait, you really punched your grandmother?" you asked.

"I did," he said.

"Don't get any ideas," Dad said.

"It's not really what you're supposed to do. I found out later that I could have killed her," Billy said. "My dad kept saying, 'You could have killed her, Billy. What were you thinking?' But I wasn't thinking. I just did it. I just reacted."

"Everybody chew very slowly," you said. "So Billy won't punch us."

Billy laughed, a real laugh. Then he put up his hands and said, "I won't be punching anybody, I promise."

He relaxed.

"Mrs. Holt, can you please pass me the potato salad?" Billy was hungry. Billy was always hungry.

After dinner, you offered to help clean up, but Mom said, "Go walk Billy out," and she gave you a wink that made only me blush.

Through our kitchen window, I watched you talk to Billy by his car for a long time. Eventually you started leaning on his car. You laughed, like Shelby Meyers. Like Lisa the Lifeguard. You held your stomach the way they did when Billy said something too funny for them to take. I wondered what Billy could possibly be saying to make you laugh so hard. Could Billy really be that funny?

"Come on, Sally," Mom said, behind me. "Don't spy. Give your sister some room to breathe."

So I went up to our room, and I looked out our window, but I couldn't see you anymore. You must have gotten into his car. I got on my bed and couldn't believe any of it. What a strange few days. To have almost died. To have been brought back to life by Billy. To have sat next to Billy across our dinner table as he ate our mother's potato salad.

While you were in his car, I kept trying to picture the moment he saved me. Even though I hadn't seen it, I felt like I had seen it. You had described it to me so many times, as if you were proud of me for almost dying, like it wasn't something you had expected from a Red Person, and so after a while, I could see Billy running and jumping into the water. Pulling me up. Laying me on my back. Leaning down to kiss me while you watched.

But then you came in the room, face flushed, as if you had lived through something extraordinary.

"Billy kissed me," you said.

"He *kissed* you?" I asked.

"He kissed me."

I thought you were going to continue, but you stopped.

"How?" I asked.

"Like a gentleman," you said.

"I mean, how does a gentleman kiss?"

"He asks you."

"He asked you?" I said. "That's awkward."

"No. It was nice."

You said you were tired of all the boys who tried to get you drunk at Priscilla's theater parties, boys who, with no segue whatsoever, just leaned over and tried to kiss without you noticing.

"How do you not notice?" I asked.

"You know what I mean," you said, and I nodded, even though I didn't really.

"If anybody ever tried to kiss me, I'm pretty sure I'd notice," I said.

Then you set the scene: "I walked him out and we were talking for so long he was like, Why don't we get in the car? Then we listened to some music and before I got out, Billy said, If this is like a 'we're just hanging out kind of thing,' I wouldn't kiss you. But if this is a date, I would."

"What was it?"

"A date," you said. You turned off the light. "Obviously."

But I wasn't done. "What was it like?" I asked.

"Nice," you said. "Except maybe he used too much tongue. But that's what boys do. It's their way of trying to have sex with you before they can have sex with you, you know?"

I didn't know. I had never kissed anything but the back of my hand, and even that was embarrassing, practicing in the dark with nobody watching. Except for Jesus, Grandma said once, when she barged in on me doing it. You shouldn't do anything that you wouldn't do in front of Jesus, she scolded, which made no sense to me, because I wouldn't ever do anything in front of anyone. Especially not Jesus.

But I said, "Yeah, I know."

By the time we returned to the town pool, it was August, and everything was different. Lisa stayed seated on her lifeguard chair, stern and dutiful, looking out at the pool. Shelby Meyers was nowhere in sight. And you never stayed put on our towels. You spent all day at the snack bar, sitting on Billy's lap. Sometimes, he even let you sell candies.

I didn't know what to do with myself next to Mom.

"Can I have some change for the snack bar?" I asked.

"You've had enough," Mom said, without turning from her book.

"Just one more snack?"

"Leave your sister alone," Mom said, and turned the page.

But I couldn't help it. I watched as you sat on his lap, as he tickled your sides, as he threw you in the pool. I watched the way you laughed as you emerged out of the water, mouth opened wide and up to the sky, as if you had just been born. Mom watched, too—and I thought she might scold you for letting a boy touch you that way in public, but she didn't.

"He's a handsome boy, isn't he?" Mom said.

"Actually," I said. "Not really."

"What do you mean?"

"I mean, he's too good-looking to be good-looking."

"I don't follow," Mom said.

"He's so good-looking he's actually ugly," I said.

"That makes no sense, Sally," Mom said. "There's no such thing as someone being too good-looking."

"Well, *he* is."

Mom sighed. "It'll happen to you, you know. One day, you'll have a love like that."

I couldn't imagine it.

"I had a love like that once," Mom said. "In high school. He was very special to me, but then he died."

"How?"

"In Vietnam."

"Oh," I said. "Did Dad go to Vietnam?"

"No," Mom said. "He joined the National Guard so he wouldn't have to go to Vietnam."

Dad dug ditches for years, while Mom's boyfriend was blown up overseas. Mom was devastated when she heard the news about Fred—that was his name. Mom and Dad both went to his funeral, and that was how Mom and Dad started dating. Dad was kind to her. Took her out for a drink. Took her dancing. Anything to get her mind off her dead boyfriend. And it worked.

"But Dad's a terrible dancer," I said.

That's what Mom always said when Dad put on Frank Sinatra after dinner, twirled and dipped her so hard, she threw her head back and laughed. "Richard!" Mom said, as the laughter rolled out her mouth and hit the floor like a marble. "You're a terrible dancer!"

"That's what I liked about him," Mom said. "He dances anyway. To make me laugh."

Lisa blew the whistle. The sun was setting. It was time to go home. Thank God. But you weren't ready.

"Billy's going to drive me home," you said, dripping water all over my towel. "Is that okay?"

Of course, it was okay. Mom loved Billy. Billy saved my life. Mom would probably let Billy drive you to the moon, if you asked.

The whole way home, I kept picturing Mom's old boyfriend running through some field, running toward the end of his life, until Mom turned on the radio. The news report. The traffic report. The weather report about a hurricane that was heading our way.

"Shh," Mom said, even though I wasn't talking. "This sounds like a big one."

"Good," I said.

I loved listening to the weather report for the same reason I loved waiting for a hurricane. It felt like something big was about to happen to me for a change. But when I got home, nothing was different. The storm was late. So I turned on the TV to see where it was. I watched the weatherman as he stood on a beach in Jersey, picking up a fistful of sand, holding it up to the camera dramatically. I reenacted it for you when you finally got home.

"In a few hours, this beach will no longer be a normal beach!" I said, but you didn't say anything. You sat down and turned on the computer that Dad had bought a few months back. He had plopped it down on the desk in the living room and said, "Girls, this is the future," and I didn't understand what he meant at the time, until you started talking to Billy on it.

"And this sand!" I shouted, pretending to pick up a fistful. "It will become blinding!"

Then, the sound of Billy's instant message fluttering into the room like a bird. I tried to see what he wrote, but you covered it with your hand.

"Sally," you said. "You're so weird sometimes. Go away."

When the hurricane arrived the next night, the house shook you back into being yourself. We were all stuck inside together. We became sisters again. We played Scrabble. Dad drank a beer and Mom had a glass of wine. We all got silly. You spelled *penis* on the board, because it was the only thing you could do with your letters. "I swear!" you said. And we laughed hard as you spelled it on the board, until I realized this meant you won and said, "But swear words don't count?"

"Penis is just a body part," Mom declared.

And so it was official. "I win!" you said.

"Your sister is a champion," Dad said.

He actually seemed proud.

Dad went to set up the candles before the power went out, so it'd feel less like the power going out and more like a magic trick. Ta-da! Look at all the beautiful candles. He smiled, and I could tell he liked it when it stormed, too—he liked the TV off, the hum of the world silenced, the four of us in the kitchen.

"Our little family," he said, and kissed Mom on the lips.

Jee? They *are* in love," I said, when we got to our bedroom. "They just kissed."

"It's just for show," you said. "It's just to make us leave the room."

But that couldn't be, because soon after, they followed us upstairs. Dad came to tuck us in. On nights like this, he treated us like we were still little kids.

"Girls, there's no need to be afraid," he said. "The storm isn't going to kill you."

He paused.

"I mean, the only way it would kill you is if a tree fell on the house, which is always possible," he said. "But not likely."

He had been meaning, he said, to cut down some of the trees.

"Richard," Mom said, appearing in the doorway. "Girls, you'll be fine. The trees in our yard are very strong. They've been here since before we were."

"That's what worries me about them," Dad said. "Those trees are dying. Ready to topple."

"We *know*," I said. I did not want to be reminded of our dying trees on a night like this, when the sky was purple and ready to hurl things at us through the window. Neither did you. You looked at me. A gust of wind shook the glass.

"I'm not taking my chances," you said. "I don't want to die young! Come on, Sally."

We went downstairs. We built a tiny house made of blankets and couch cushions. We crawled in.

"I love forts," you said.

You were too old to love forts—you were sixteen, a girl with a learner's permit and a boyfriend now. But I didn't remind you of this, because that was the fun of being sisters. Sometimes, you got to be younger than you were, and I got to be older.

"Me, too," I said. "This is a really good one."

Then we began our favorite game. Would you rather get a massage from Satan or have all your hair ripped off by a loved one? Would you rather make out with a prince who has an STD or a very healthy serial killer? Would you rather be stuck in a box for all of eternity alone or in a box with a Nazi?

We didn't know. Agh. Life was hard.

"Give me death!" I joked.

You laughed, but no, no, you can't choose death, you said. "Death is no fun. Death is not an option."

"Okay, fine, I'd rather be with a Nazi," I said.

"You'd rather be with a Nazi?" you said. "Do you know what a Nazi even is?"

"Of course, I know what a Nazi is!"

"Being trapped with a Nazi would be the worst," you said.

"It's not my *preference*."

But at least if you were with the Nazi, you could ask him questions. You could pretend to be a journalist after the war, pretend like you were visiting his prison cell in very tall high heels, and say, "Tell me, when was it that you first realized you wanted to be a Nazi?" and make the Nazi think about his childhood and cry.

"I don't know," you said. "That sounds weird. I'd rather be alone."

But I knew then that anybody who chose to be alone had no idea what it really meant to be alone.

In the morning, Dad went outside to assess the situation with the trees. The storm didn't knock any of them over but ripped off enough branches to concern Dad. We followed him as he put his hand over each tree trunk to determine which ones were survivors and which ones were beyond repair.

"Survivor," he said. "Survivor. Survivor."

Then, he put his hand on the maple outside our bedroom. "Not a survivor."

"What are you going to do to it?" you asked.

"Maybe your boyfriend's father will come and cut it down," Dad said. It sounded weird to hear Dad call Billy your boyfriend. It sounded very official.

"I'll ask Billy," you said. "Maybe he'll give us a discount."

"Isn't his dad in a wheelchair?" I asked.

"Sally, that was years ago," you said. "He's fine now."

Dad dragged the broken branches to the center of the yard, and we used them to build a campfire that night. We roasted marshmallows and listened to your ghost stories. You loved ghost stories.

"Apparently, according to Billy, there's a ghost who haunts the town pool," you said.

"Ghosts can't haunt pools," I said. I didn't even know if I believed in ghosts, but I felt strongly that if ghosts existed, they wouldn't haunt municipal pools.

"Ghosts can haunt anything they want," you said with the same certainty you said everything.

"How do you even know ghosts exist?" I asked.

"How do you know they *don't* exist?" you said, and I couldn't explain.

"I've just never seen one," I said.

"Well, I've seen one," you said. "Sometimes, Grandma visits me in my sleep."

"Me, too, actually," Mom said.

I was shocked. What? I wanted to ask more questions about Grandma's ghost—How long had she been haunting you? And was I the only one not being haunted?—but you continued with your story.

"So Billy says there was this woman from the 1950s," you said. "She slit her wrists in the pool the first day it opened. People found her facedown in the water. And every year, somebody reports seeing her like that, floating in the bloody water. But when you jump in to save her, she disappears when you turn her over."

"That can't be true," I said.

"Of course it's true," you said. "Why would Billy lie about that?"

I didn't know. I didn't know anything.

When your junior year began, Billy drove you. He knocked on our door, of course, like a gentleman. But you weren't ready. You were never ready. Every morning, you tried on a million outfits until you slumped onto your bed like you didn't even know what an outfit was anymore.

"Tell Billy I'll be down in a minute," you said.

I opened the door to see Billy standing there with his hands in his pockets.

"Hey, Holt," he always said, and at first it bothered me that he addressed me using our last name, but after a few months, I grew to like it. Made me feel like we were on the same sports team, like we had some kind of an understanding.

But then we always fell silent as we walked into the kitchen. There was nothing to say. He put his hands back in his pockets, and I sat down at the table, pretended to be really busy taking notes for class. He didn't seem to mind the awkward silences, and maybe that's because it wasn't awkward for him. Maybe that's just how cool he was. He was above silence. Didn't even notice it.

But on the last day of the semester, the Friday before winter break, not even Billy could withstand the awkwardness anymore. He walked over to me as if something had to be done. He leaned over and looked at what I was writing in my notebook.

"What does *that* mean?" Billy asked.

He pointed to where I had written *Philomela: Rape –> Bird.*

"Oh." I blushed. "That's just the story of Philomela."

"Who's Philomela?" Billy asked.

The story of Philomela, according to my English teacher Mrs. Framer: Philomela was raped by her sister's husband, Tereus the king, who cut out her tongue after so she wouldn't tell her sister what happened. But then Philomela weaves the truth into a blanket and sends it to her sister, and when her sister reads it, she is so angry that she kills her own son, cooks him, and tries to feed him to Tereus. But before Tereus eats his son without realizing it, the gods miraculously show up and turn them all into birds.

"Man," Billy said. "That's pretty fucked up."

"It's just a myth," I said.

"Still," he said.

And then there was nothing to say again, so I did what I thought you would do. "What kind of bird would you want to be?"

His face lit up. "I wouldn't mind being an eagle or a hawk. You?"

"I'd definitely be a hummingbird," I said. It was something I had decided over the summer watching the pretty birds come up to Dad's feeder on the deck.

"Oh, you don't want to be a hummingbird. Trust me," Billy said. "Hummingbirds are insane."

"They are?"

"Big time," Billy said. "They're, like, extremely stressed out. Their hearts beat so fast and they flap their wings a thousand times a second. So fast you can barely see their wings."

"How do you know that?" I asked, but then you came down the stairs. You kissed as soon as you saw each other, like Mom and Dad. I looked away, but slowly, so I could see the beginning of it.

"What are you talking about?" you asked.

"About what kind of bird we'd want to be," Billy said.

"Why do you have to be birds?"

"The gods," Billy said. "They're going to make us."

You laughed. "I won't even ask."

Then you both left, without saying goodbye, and I was at the counter with Dad, who stirred Metamucil in his water with his finger.

"This, Sally, is the key to life," he said.

"How is that the key to life?" I asked. "It's just orange powder."

"One day, you'll understand."

I never wanted to understand anything like that. I walked out the door to the bus and saw you two still in the driveway. You were flipping through Billy's CD collection, as if the car wouldn't work without the right music.

I didn't wave as I passed you—it was too embarrassing. I just kept walking until I was standing at the end of our street with cold hair, with Rick Stevenson, who always wanted to play bloody knuckles that year. He pounded his fists into mine, and that's when you drove by me. The music was loud, and even louder when you rolled down the window. Billy drove fast down the street, as if you were driving toward something very important. Toward your future. Just before you disappeared out of sight, I saw you put your hand out into the breeze like the Green Person that you were.

"Your sister is hot," Rick said.

I blushed. I didn't know what to say. I felt the same way when people told us our cat had pretty eyes.

"Thanks," I said, as if it had something to do with me.

On the bus, the boys were especially restless, sticking pins in their fingertips and declaring everything in the world gay: the lunch ladies, the Dare Bear, and even the winter, the way it was going to keep them stuck inside every day over break.

Valerie and I made sure to avoid them. We sat up front, played Hangman in my notebook, until we pulled into the school parking lot and the boys crowded around us as we packed up our bags.

"Hey, Sally," Rick asked, hanging his head over my seat. "How are your two vaginas?"

I thought everybody had forgotten about that. I had almost forgotten.

"Yeah," another boy said. "Do you still have two vaginas?"

And what did I say?

"No."

But Rick said, "Prove it."

I looked at Valerie, but Valerie couldn't help me. I wanted to run, but that seemed foolish. That seemed like what a person with two vaginas would do. One of them was next to me and one of them held my arms above my head and one of them unhooked my overalls and lifted up my shirt. And I didn't know how many there were, but it felt like a million hands, a million boys, all who kept saying, We'll find out if you're lying. I screamed, as loud as I have ever screamed—I don't think I had ever really screamed until that moment—and everybody on the bus looked at me like I was a crazy animal, even Valerie, even the boys, who said, Chill, we weren't going to do it. Chill out. It was just a joke.

I kept my head down as I walked off the bus. Sally, what happened back there, the bus driver asked, the bus driver who always gave us free snap bracelets, which made me afraid of her for some reason. I flinched whenever she snapped the bracelet over my wrist, like it was going to hurt more than it did. But in that moment, I felt that maybe I loved the bus driver more than anybody in the world. Maybe she would make this all go away, cast a spell on the boys, turn them into frogs so I could smash them.

But she looked at me, like any concerned person would, and I knew she couldn't help, either.

"Nothing," I said. "I mean, it was just a joke."

I held out my hand for a bracelet.

I was going to tell you about it as soon as I got home from school, but you weren't there. Junior year, you were never home on Friday nights. You were out with Priscilla and Margaret, and if you weren't with them, you were at the mall with Billy or you were at the movies with Billy and you didn't come home until after we watched *20/20*. Your curfew was eleven on the weekends, which seemed late to me, but apparently not to you, since you came home even later than that sometimes. You came in with leaves in your hair. A glow on your face.

You didn't even ask how my day was. You just started talking about the movie you saw, and how *Bean* was kind of a hard movie to make out to, even though Billy tried his best. It was impossible though. Too many people, no privacy at all, which is why he drove you all the way to Watch Hill after.

"You went to make out in *Rhode Island*?" I asked.

"It's like, thirty minutes away," you said. "It's just across the border."

You told me how beautiful it was to be there in winter, when the parking lot was completely empty, covered in snow. It was there, in the back of Billy's car, where Billy slid his hand down your jeans and put his fingers inside you.

"You let him do that to you?" I asked.

"Yeah," you said. "I mean, he's my *boyfriend*."

"Still," I said. I was flustered. It felt wrong. To get fingered in the parking lot where we unloaded our beach chairs? "That's where we go on *vacation*."

"Well, where else are we supposed to go?" you said. "Teenagers have no place to fuck."

You said it with a long sigh, as if it were a national tragedy. As if it were something the president should address in a speech. And was I supposed to feel sorry for you?

"Is that what you and Billy did?" I asked.

"No," you said. "It's just an expression. God, you take everything so literally sometimes."

Then you leaned over to turn off the light, and I realized, in the sudden darkness, that I wasn't ever going to tell you what happened to me on the bus. It was too embarrassing. It was like you were in on the joke somehow. You couldn't save me from this world. From Rick Stevenson. You didn't even care. You rolled over to face the wall, and I listened to the tree branch *tap-tap-tap* against the window, and for the first time in my life, I wanted to hurt you. I wanted you to feel what I was always feeling. I wanted you to sit up the next morning and wonder where I was.

I n the morning, before anybody woke, I packed a bag. I slipped out of the house and into the dewy darkness of the garage where I hid in the back of Mom's van. Mom went to the library on Saturday mornings. Some kind of a book group. I didn't know where I'd go after Mom went into the library, but I would go somewhere. I would walk down the side of the highway until I felt certain you were worried about me. Until I could feel you out there, screaming for me.

But Mom kept driving and driving for so long, I realized she wasn't going to the library. Mom was listening to a tape called *Meditations on Madness* and the woman kept explaining that breathing was the antidote to madness. Mom was breathing very loudly, as if she couldn't quite remember how. As if she were practicing. She kept repeating certain phrases from the tape, like, "Remember yourself as a child," and then, "Visualize yourself giving that child a hug," and it must have been sad to think of hugging herself as a child, because Mom started crying, and her breathing became irregular, and it all made me feel so sick. I worried about vomiting every time she took a wide turn. I worried that Mom really was unhappy, and I tucked away this moment in my brain to tell you later that night, which was when I knew I wouldn't be running away. I would never leave you. I would always return to our bedroom at night to tell you what happened.

"Hi, Mom," I said, and popped my head up. Mom threw her tube of lipstick in the air.

"Jesus, Sally!" she said.

Mom had spent the whole car ride trying to relax, and now she was tense again. She was searching for her lipstick on the floor.

"Well," Mom said. "Now you know. Your mother is crazy."

"I already knew that," I said.

"You knew that?"

"Kathy told me," I said.

"That's good you know early," Mom said. "No illusions. I didn't find out my mother was crazy until I became a mother. Imagine that."

"Grandma was crazy?"

"Oh, Grandma was crazy all right. Grandma legally changed my birthday so I could drive earlier," Mom said. "She needed another driver in the house. When I became a mother, I thought, *That woman must have been really nuts.*"

"Maybe she just really needed another driver," I said.

"That's a nice way of thinking about it," Mom said. "You're very sweet, Sally."

Mom unbuckled her seat belt. She looked at herself in the mirror. She started applying lipstick so slowly, one half of her mouth at a time.

"You may have noticed, Sally, but I'm not going to ask what you were doing back there in the car," Mom said. "I'm not even going to ask."

Then she blotted her lips with a tissue, unlocked the car doors.

"So wait, how old are you really?"

"Who knows?"

She grabbed her purse.

"Come on," Mom said. "Inside."

I got out of the car, straightened out my legs, which were cramped from being curled up in the back for so long.

"Where are we going?" I asked.

We were in a giant parking lot. One of those parking lots that were so big, they always looked empty, the way I imagined parking lots will look at the end of the world.

"The mall," Mom said.

I had to go shopping all afternoon with Mom. That was my punishment, she said. She seemed to dawdle, just to make a point. She ran her hands along the Christmas trees on display at Macy's, marveled at the wreaths hanging from the ceilings. Picked up dish after dish to show me.

"Isn't this a nice dish?" she asked.

"Yes," I told her. It was a very nice dish.

"But do you love it?" she asked.

"No," I said. "But it's nothing against this dish. I've never loved a dish before."

Then, she put it back. We went through the whole store like that, Mom asking me how much I loved certain objects and me denying any past or potential connection with the object. No, I don't have any thoughts about the floor lamp, Mom.

"What did you actually *come* to the mall for?" I finally asked.

"Slippers," Mom said.

"Why'd you say you were going to the library then?"

"I changed my mind," Mom said.

"So you lied."

"I changed my mind."

"Do you *ever* go to the library when you say you're going to the library?"

"Sometimes," Mom said.

Then it was Mom's turn to ask questions.

"What were you doing in the back of the car, missy?"

"I thought you said you weren't going to ask."

"I'm your mother. I need to ask."

"I was trying to run away."

"But why?" Mom asked. She didn't sound mad or even surprised. She sounded curious, as if maybe I'd be allowed to run away if I had a good enough reason.

"I can't tell you," I said. "It's too embarrassing."

"The truth," Mom said. "Is it something we did, Sally? Are we that bad?"

I felt terrible, thinking that Mom thought I was running away because of something she did. It had nothing to do with her. Mom made us pancakes in the morning before school and she quit her job just to raise us and she played the piano on holidays so we could sing and last week, when I had asked her if I would gain weight from not going to the bathroom for four days, she didn't even laugh the way you had. Mom wrinkled her brow and said, Sally, why haven't you gone to the bathroom in four days? Then she made me an appointment to go see the doctor. Mom just wanted us to live forever and ever, which is why she demanded the truth. So I told her.

"Everybody at school thinks I have two vaginas," I said.

Mom laughed.

"Don't laugh!"

"I'm sorry," she said. "I shouldn't laugh. But that's not what I was expecting you to say. I mean, frankly, it's impossible."

"It's not, actually," I said. "Some women have two."

"Where did you get that idea?"

"*The Jillian Williams Show.*"

"Sally, that's exactly why you shouldn't be watching shows like that," Mom said. "They're fake. They're not real."

"It seemed real," I said.

"But wait," Mom said. "Why do people think *you* have two vaginas?"

"I *don't* have two vaginas."

"Of course not. I'm your mother. I know how many vaginas you have."

"Mom," I said. "Shh. We're at the mall."

"Oh, people at the mall don't care what we're saying. Do you think the people here care? No. Sally. Vagina vagina vagina! See? Nobody cares. And that's something you're going to have to learn. People don't care about things as much as you think. People will forget all about the two vaginas. People are people."

And that was that. Mom stopped dead in her tracks. She gasped. She put a hand over her heart. She walked over to the furniture section, ran her hand on a couch like it was a Persian cat she was petting.

"Isn't this a beautiful couch?" she asked. "I think we should get this couch."

"Do we need a new couch?"

"That's not the point," Mom said. "This couch is beautiful."

"I like our couch."

It was a great couch, which is what Dad said nearly every time he sat down on it.

"But what about this couch?" Mom said. "This is a *couch*. Look at it."

I looked at it. "It's very white."

"That's the point," Mom said.

Mom had always wanted a white couch, she said, like it was some big confession. Aunt Beatrice had a white couch, and she knew, even at a young age, that only a certain kind of woman could keep a white couch. A woman like Aunt Beatrice, who had no children and two hypoallergenic poodles.

I sat down on it. "I don't think Dad will like this."

"Trying to predict what your father will and will not like is no way to live, Sally."

But it was easy. Dad was very predictable. Dad was like me. He was a creature of routine.

"Okay," I said. "Well, I don't like the couch. It's not very comfortable."

"It's not supposed to be," Mom said.

Mom believed that we were growing up; it was time our furniture did, too.

"You know how your father is," Mom said, and I did, but she told me anyway. How when she was pregnant and they moved into our house all the furniture had to be child-friendly, spill-friendly—it had to pass Dad's safety code, Mom said. No furniture made out of glass, only edges that were peacefully rounded, and Mom just couldn't bear to look at it anymore. Mom needed a little beauty in her life. She said, "Just a little beauty is all I ask for."

"I'd like to buy this couch," Mom said to the man in the store.

"I'm afraid it's out of stock," the man said.

"But it's right here," Mom said, putting her hand on the couch.

"This is just the floor model," the man said.

The man ordered another one that would be delivered in three or four months. In April. Maybe May? Was that okay?

"That's a long time to wait," Mom said.

But Mom bought the couch.

"For this couch? That's nothing," Mom said to me as we walked to the car. "I'd wait forever for that couch."

Of course, walking out of Macy's, we couldn't imagine the way things would be different by the time the couch arrived. We couldn't imagine that by then, you would be dead.

How could we have ever imagined such a thing back then? When we got home, there you were, sitting in your winter parka, sunning your hair on the deck. Your hair was so thick, spread out over the back of the chaise lounge, and it seems impossible to me even now that a girl with hair like that could ever die. It looked like proof that you would always be here, lit up by the sun, lounging around, not worried about anything at all.

So I ignored you. I walked right by you and into the kitchen. I felt better as I wrote down the delivery date on the Big Calendar, as Mom always called it. I liked seeing our future spread out before me as it always had been, every week made up of tiny white squares. Every day, the same length as its width.

But six weeks later, you were dead.

I'm sorry if that seems sudden to you, but that's what it felt like to me. That's what it still feels like even now, fifteen years later. Like, poof! Sally, your sister is dead! Now, go to church.

There was no warning. No premonition. Not at all like the movies, where the sister always feels the bad thing that is about to happen. The sister notices a crooked painting on the wall or feels a chill up her spine or wakes in the middle of the night with a terrible feeling in her chest and clutches whoever is sitting next to her and says, Glen, something is wrong with my sister, and somehow Glen can feel it, too.

But I felt nothing. I thought it was just going to be another one of those school nights when nothing happened, when we did our homework and then ate dinner and then went upstairs to pick out our outfits for school in the morning.

But after dinner, when I went upstairs, I found you already in the bathroom brushing your teeth.

"Why are you brushing your teeth?" I asked. It was too early—normally, we didn't brush our teeth until just before bed.

I looked at the foam building in your mouth, and I thought, for a second, you might try to speak. I thought we might laugh the way we used to. But you were sensible. You spit in the sink, put your brush back on the holder, and said, "How's my breath?"

"Fine?" I said. "Toothpastey. Why?"

"I'm going out tonight with Billy."

"Going out?" I asked. I followed you into our bedroom. "You can't go out with Billy."

"Why not?"

"It's a school night."

School nights were sacred. The only nights when I was certain I would get to spend time with you.

"So?" you said. "Almost all nights are school nights. Statistically speaking, it means none of them can actually be that important."

This is what was important: Billy's semifinal game that night against Dalton. "Dalton, Sally!" you said, like it meant something to you, but I couldn't imagine what.

"If they win, they have a chance at being state champs," you said.

"Mom actually said you can go?"

It was rare for Mom to break her own rules. Mom ran a tight ship, which is something she liked to say a lot, just before she looked to Dad for confirmation about something. "What do you think? Richard?" And then Dad would take a sip of his beer. Dad didn't normally make the rules, but he had the power to veto them. Once canceled a trip to Hershey Park because we lied about cleaning our room.

"They said it was fine," you said, with less enthusiasm than I expected, as though you had negotiated a successful business deal with them. "I'm sixteen. I can do what I want. Why don't you mind your own business?"

You leaned close to our bedroom mirror to apply Mom's lipstick. Then, you blotted your lips with a tissue, which was something I had only ever seen Mom do, in the car, before we headed into the grocery store or the mall. A familiar gesture, but watching you do it gave me that strange feeling again, the same feeling I had earlier that morning before school when you leaned into Billy at our kitchen counter and said, "Congratulations, baby," because Billy showed us the 60 he got on his Global Civ quiz. And I was confused. When did you start calling him "baby"? And since when was 60 a good grade? I would have cried if I got a 60, even on a quiz, but Billy was pleased. All Billy needed was a passing grade, he said, because he had gotten into college that week—a scholarship to play ball at Villanova. But you were only a junior. You still needed to get As on your quizzes and tests, if you wanted to get into Villanova and join Billy one day.

"Sally, I need you to take notes on the State of the Union for me while I'm gone," you said, pulling away from the mirror. And suddenly, just like that, you were Kathy again. My sister, who always needed something from me, and what a relief. "There's going to be a quiz on it in history first thing in the morning."

Though I admit, I would have liked it to be something bigger than that. Something involving your boyfriend.

"What's the State of the Union have to do with history, though?" I asked. "It hasn't even happened yet."

"But it will happen," you said. "One day, it will be history. You don't know what's history as it's happening. That's what Mrs. Klausterman said."

You leaned forward to sweep shadow across your lid.

"But how do I know what to take notes on?" I asked. "I'm not even in the class."

"Just write down everything that sounds important," you said.

"But how do I *know* what's important?"

This had been a problem for me lately. Everything I thought was important was turning out not to be important. Like school nights. Like the myth of Philomela, which I had taken two pages of notes on because Mrs. Framer had talked about it for nearly twenty minutes, and then it wasn't even on the test.

But you weren't concerned. "You'll figure it out," you said to me. "You're smart."

You plucked two gold hoop earrings from your jewelry box—real gold, a Christmas gift from Billy. As you slid one through your ear, I picked up the other.

I was surprised by how heavy it was. It felt real in my hand, like the weight of the world you were about to enter with Billy. I couldn't bear the thought: soon, Billy would be at college, and then a year later, you would join him. And what would happen to me?

"I can't believe Billy is going to college next year," I said.

"Why not?" you asked.

Because it was Billy, the boy who was so stupid, he jumped off the school roof. The boy who was so stupid, he always dove headfirst to get a ball. The boy who got the first question wrong on his Global Civ quiz: *Who was Socrates?* And Billy had no idea. Billy wrote, "Socrates was a man of his time."

"Because," I said, "he doesn't even know who Socrates is."

"What does that have to do with anything?" you asked.

"It just seems like if you're going to college, you should know who Socrates is."

"What, is that some kind of admissions test? You think the basketball coach cares about that? Is that how you're going to pick a husband?"

You looked back at yourself in the mirror.

"I take you, Billy, to be my husband, for richer or poorer, in sickness and health," you said, dramatically to yourself. "Assuming you know who Socrates is, of course."

I laughed. I swallowed.

"Are you going to marry Billy?" I asked.

You were too young to get married. But you had already done things with Billy that I couldn't have ever imagined you doing, and so what did I know?

"Maybe," you said. "Now give me the other earring."

You started to slide in the other gold earring when the doorbell rang. Your hand shook, as if you could feel whatever your boyfriend did with his hands, and you dropped it on the desk.

"Tell Billy I'll be down in a minute," you said. "Oh, and Sally, don't tell Mom and Dad you're taking notes for me. Mom won't let me go out if she knows I've got homework to do."

I didn't like lying to Mom. Mom always knew. Mom said that lies showed up as white spots on our fingernails. Mom made us put our hands on the table whenever she suspected we were lying, and, of course, we always had a ton of white spots on our nails. We confessed—yes, we were watching *Jillian Williams*. Yes, we were making prank phone calls. Sorry, Mom, so sorry, but apologies were never enough. "Up to your room," she would say, "and don't come out until you're ready to respect the truth."

But I was willing to risk it that night. I loved keeping your secrets more than anything. It was the only thing that made me feel like I was still your sister.

"I won't tell anyone," I said, and then ran down the stairs, so excited to greet Billy.

B illy!" Dad said.
"Hi, Billy," Mom said.

Billy had brought flowers, as usual.

"What's the occasion?" Mom asked, as she put them in a vase.

"My dad likes to say that there shouldn't need to be an occasion," Billy said.

"A smart man," Mom said.

You rushed down, grabbed Billy's arm. It was a quick exit, over as soon as it began. "Bye!" you shouted at us, like we were all the same person, and then you slammed the door. Mom poured herself a glass of wine and Dad poured himself a beer, and they clinked glasses.

"To us!" Mom said.

"Everything really has gone according to plan, hasn't it?" Dad said, and then provided evidence: We've got two beautiful daughters, we take vacations twice a year, we even had a deck with a water feature, not to mention a new car that tested well in mock safety crashes. That was actually Dad's toast.

"And Billy," Dad said. "He's not too bad."

"I like Billy a lot," Mom said.

"He's a really great ball player," Dad said, because that was how Dad complimented Billy. "A tall kid who can actually handle the ball."

Mom stuck her nose in the flowers he brought.

"On a *Tuesday*," Mom said. "So sweet."

"His dad is a florist," I finally said, because I couldn't take it. "He gets them for free."

"Oh Sally," Mom said, "don't be like that."

She patted me on the head, like I said something embarrassing, but she was the one with orange pollen on the tip of her nose.

"You've got something on your nose," I said.

Mom went to the mirror and Dad put his arm around me.

"Let's go watch a movie," he said, and I followed him into the living room.

Dad started flipping through the channels, until he stopped on a western. I don't remember which one, but I remember it was a western because the screen was very yellow and everything always looked very yellow in a western, as if the world had been left outside for too long and gone bad.

"Ah! John Wayne," Dad said. "This is a good one, Sally."

"What's it about?" I asked.

Dad didn't remember. On-screen, cowboys started shooting Native Americans, for no reason that I could understand. There was a lot of death, but never any blood. People shot dead like milk bottles off the wall. And a blue-eyed girl who had been abandoned by her man in Apache territory, which was all anybody knew about her, but enough to make us, and John Wayne, fall in love with her. I remember worrying for her, as various men approached her cabin, I remember wondering if she would live or die, and that's when the president came on TV and interrupted our regularly scheduled program.

"Aw, come on!" Dad exclaimed. "This man won't leave us alone."

"It's the State of the Union," I said. "All the presidents do it."

"But this one enjoys it too much, don't you think?" Dad asked.

I didn't know. I didn't know much about Bill Clinton. I almost never thought about him. All I knew was that now it was my duty to watch him speak.

"I have to take notes," I said.

"Take notes on what?"

"Everything the president says that's important," I said.

Dad laughed. "Ha! Good luck with that," he said. He changed the channel, started searching for something else.

"I have to watch it," I said, more firmly this time. I sat on my hands so Mom couldn't see my fingernails, just in case. But Mom didn't turn around. She was curled up on the floor.

"Richard," Mom said. "Put the president back on."

Mom was no longer a teacher, but she still had that voice, the kind that convinces people it's very important to do whatever it is they don't want to do. That's how she got Dad to put the president on. But he wouldn't go down quietly.

"You want to know a secret, Sally?" Dad asked.

"Yeah," I said.

"The only reason your mother wants to watch the State of the Union is because she thinks the president is handsome," Dad said. I waited for Mom to disagree, to get embarrassed, but she didn't. Only I got embarrassed. Mom was on her second glass of wine. Mom just shrugged and said, "He's got very nice features."

"Ladies and gentlemen," the president said on TV. "The state of our union is strong."

Everybody in the audience stood up and started clapping for a long time.

"Are you jotting this down, Sally?" Dad joked. "This is very important. A bunch of people are clapping."

"I am," I said. I knew Dad was joking, but I wasn't. We couldn't possibly know what was important yet—not until after the test was taken, not until after the State of the Union was over. That's what I was learning. So I had decided to write down everything the president said, just in case.

The president was wearing a black suit.

The president had bags under his eyes.

The president seemed very tired.

But this was not a time to rest.

It was a time to:

Build a new America!

Cure diabetes!

Not to mention AIDS!

The president wanted to save a lot of things, like Social Security. The national parks. Not to mention, all of the children. Everybody was invited to the discussion about how to save the children. The circle of opportunity here was very wide.

"This is a new world," the president said.

"It certainly is," Dad agreed.

He took a sip of his beer. Then he cleared his throat, which meant he was about to give a public service announcement. "This is a great time to be alive, you know. Life used to be hard."

Reasons life used to be hard, according to Dad: If we lived "way back when," I would already have two kids, and you would be pregnant with your third, walking across some endless prairie, searching for water in the night. If we ever found it, which we wouldn't obviously, that's when we'd step on the rattlesnake.

"Okay, Richard," Mom said. "Let's just watch the show."

"It's not a show, Mom," I said. "It's the State of the Union."

"Oh, it's a show all right," Dad said. "Look at all those people clapping."

And that's what we were doing when the phone rang. We were so committed to watching the show that nobody answered it.

"Well, isn't somebody going to answer it?" Mom finally asked.

"I'm taking notes!" I said.

"I thought we were supposed to be *watching the show!*" Dad said.

"Well, somebody should answer it," Mom said. "Why am I the only one in this house who answers the phone?"

"Why would *I* answer it?" Dad said. "It's never for me."

"How do you know that, Richard?"

"Because I don't have any friends."

Mom thought this was funny. "Of course you have friends, Richard."

"Name one," Dad said, and now he was laughing, too. "Name one friend that I have."

But Mom couldn't name one. She started to look concerned, until she remembered John. From the club!

"You mean, Frank? From the gym?" Dad said. "Frank and I aren't friends. We're just people who go to the gym. We do sit-ups together. Frank holds my feet."

Mom laughed. Mom was a little drunk.

"Well, that's something, Richard," Mom said. "That's something."

Now Mom seemed upset by the fact that Dad didn't have any friends. Mom had a lot of friends. Having friends was important, she was always telling me. Mom had once gone backpacking through Europe with some of her friends, bought a marble chess set, and ran through the empty town square of Amsterdam at three in the morning, and wanted these things for me, too. Mom believed we were put on this earth to *be together*, which is why she was always talking on the phone with Mrs. Mitt or Mrs. Mountain, always coordinating group trips to the grocery store so nobody would have to go it alone.

But Dad was like me. Dad was always alone. Because when he was alone, he could get things done. He could work in his wood shop or sit out on the deck with a big thick book and a smoky-looking beer and enjoy the silence. Being totally friendless, Dad said, was what being a father was all about.

"What do I need friends for anyway?" Dad said. "I have you guys."

That's how I always felt. But suddenly, I felt embarrassed of it. To have no friends. To be like Dad.

"Fine, I'll get it!" I said, because when our parents refused to do something, it became your job, unless you weren't there, and then it became my job. "It's probably for me anyway."

I left the living room, walked through the kitchen, and as soon as I put my hand on it, it stopped ringing.

"Hello?" I said, but there was nothing. Just a dial tone. I put it back on the hook, and in that moment of silence, I could hear Mom and Dad from the TV room.

"Admit it!" Dad said. "You think the president is handsome."

Mom laughed. I loved Mom's laugh. Mom's laugh was your laugh, and it made things sound funnier than they were.

"Richard!" Mom said. "You're being ridiculous."

"Only if you admit it," Dad said. Then he whispered, so low I could barely hear it, but I heard it. "Admit that you want to fuck the president of the United States."

"Fine," Mom said. "Yes. Okay. I want to fuck the president. Are you happy now?"

"Very," Dad said.

I seized with panic in the kitchen. I had no idea there were people in this world that wanted to fuck the president of the United States. It didn't sound right. It sounded like a crime. Like something I should tell Mom about, but Mom already knew. Mom was fine with it and Dad was even happy about it.

What?

If you were there, the whole thing would have been funny. We would have looked at each other and laughed until we were crumbly messes on the kitchen floor. But you weren't there—you were out. Probably done with Billy's game now, driving to Watch Hill. The music was probably loud and his hand was probably on your thigh. Or maybe you were already there. Maybe you were already surrounded by the beautiful snow, in the parking lot, kissing. Maybe you were on your back and your boyfriend was on top, undressing you, sucking on your tits, which is what you said Billy called them once, and I was horrified. "*Tits?*" I asked. I couldn't picture Billy saying the word. But you said, "Yeah. That's what they are, Sally. Tits."

I felt sick.

I wanted to go upstairs, crawl into our bed. But I returned to the TV room. I had to finish taking notes. I sat down and couldn't even look at Mom and Dad, because they didn't seem like Mom and Dad anymore.

"Who was it?" Mom asked.

"Nobody," I said. "No message."

"Telemarketer," Mom said. "They never leave messages. That's how you know."

I shrugged. I knew nothing about telemarketers. But I knew that Mom wanted to believe it was a telemarketer for some reason. She continued eating her popcorn and drinking her wine and seemed satisfied about her decision to not pick up the phone. To not be the maid, for once.

"You still getting down the important stuff?" Dad asked.

"Yes," I said.

The president continued: This is the information age. We must not use disease as a weapon. We must work with other countries. But none of this sounded important anymore. Now the only thing that seemed important about the president was the fact that Mom wanted to fuck him. And that Dad, for some reason, wasn't even bothered by it. Dad was just sitting there, drinking beer and munching on pretzels.

"Want some?" Dad asked.

"No," I said.

I felt a weird kind of pain, spreading across my torso. Mom moved closer to the TV, as if she was on some kind of date with the president.

This is America.

This is planet earth.

And that was the State of the Union.

"Thank God," Dad said, and the western came back on again. But it was ten now, and the western was mostly over, which meant all the Native Americans were dead.

I went upstairs and I waited in the dark for you. I kept rehearsing what I was going to tell you when you came home, and how I was going to say it. I decided I would blurt it out right away, before you could take off your earrings, before you could utter one word about Billy and all the amazing places he touched you at the beach. I was going to say, in a comically low and solemn voice, "I don't know how to tell you this, Kathy, but Mom wants to fuck the president of the United States."

And you were going to be shocked. "No!" you were going to say.

"It's true!" I would say, and then we would laugh and laugh and laugh, the way we did when we were on the side of the curb, saying fuck fuck fuck fuck fuck until all the bad things of this world were like a joke between us.

But you were late. And I got tired. I opened your notebook and I wrote in all capitals, MOM WANTS TO FUCK THE PRESIDENT so you would see it as soon as you came home.

I n the morning, we all slept in by accident. We didn't wake up until Billy knocked on the door.

"Shit," you said. You ran to the bathroom. You brushed your teeth while you peed, combed your hair while you ate an apple. Then, before you left, you looked at me. "Sally, where are those notes on the State of the Union?"

The notebook was still in my bed, under my covers. "I have them," I said.

"Can I have them?" you asked.

And maybe if you had said please.

Maybe if you had asked nicely.

Maybe if you had said thank you, Sally, for taking notes on the State of the Union while I was out fooling around with my boyfriend. But you didn't.

"Only if Billy takes me to school," I said.

"What? That wasn't part of the deal."

"Yeah, well the deal was not good."

"Sally, you're my sister," you said. "Sisters do each other favors."

"When was the last time you did me a favor?"

"Honestly, I can't think of it. But he can't take you to school. Hendrick is in the opposite direction. We'll be late for the quiz!"

"So?" I said, and I made sure to say it exactly like you. "It's just a quiz. Who cares?"

"I do," you said. "I need to get a good grade."

You begged. You said something about Villanova. Something about needing to be in the top 10 percent of your class.

"This is my *future*, Sally," you said.

But I was unmoved. I didn't want to think about your future with Billy at Villanova. I wanted you to stay here, in our house, forever.

"Then maybe you should have stayed home last night," I said.

"Sally! Come on. Why are you being like this?"

I could have told you. I could have explained what this year had been like for me, what the boys did to me on the bus, what it felt like to lose you a little bit each day.

But you were in a rush. And I was silent, spiteful. I held the notes firmly behind my back. I was tired of you getting all the things you wanted. You lunged for them, and you missed, and I was glad.

"Fine," you said. You grabbed your coat. "Come on."

You didn't talk to me on the drive. I didn't know if this was because you were annoyed with me or if you were just busy trying to absorb all the things the president said before your quiz. But at the time, I didn't care. I got what I wanted. I was in Billy's back seat, and I felt like a queen as we drove by Rick Stevenson and Billy turned up the music. Counting Crows.

"Here we go," Billy said.

"Drive fast," you said. "I can't be late for this quiz."

"Yes, ma'am," Billy said.

You returned to your notebook, and Billy drove faster. He put his hand on your thigh. He stopped at the red light on Main and started speaking to me through the mirror.

"So what do you think, Holt?" he asked.

"What do I think?" I asked.

"About the car."

Nobody had ever asked me what I thought about a car.

"I don't think anything about cars," I said.

"Of course, you do," he said. "You're always thinking, Holt. It's what you do."

"How do you know that?" I asked, confused that Billy had, at some point, drawn conclusions about me.

"Because you always look like you want to say something, but then you don't."

I wanted to ask him to keep going, to talk about me some more, but I blushed. Looked out the window. This whole time, I had no idea that Billy had real thoughts about me. "Well, I don't think much about cars," I said.

Then I told him all I knew about cars, which was everything I learned from listening to Dad try to buy a new one for himself all year: a good car is a Subaru, because every other car is a death trap. No exceptions.

He laughed. "Oh, great," he said.

"But I mean, it's nice. It's really clean."

I ran my hand over the leather of the back seat. "Yeah," he said, as if this was his only complaint about the car. "Sometimes, I think it's *too* clean. It feels like a rental."

Your boyfriend said he preferred his cars to be a bit more disgusting, like his old one, which was so disgusting it was awesome. Once, he found an entire stick of butter in the back seat and he couldn't remember why it was ever there in the first place. He sounded proud of this, like these were the things that real cars are made of. Butter.

The new car was automatic. Another problem with the car, Billy said. He liked shifting gears. He said it kept you connected to the car. Like it was a part of your body.

I agreed, though I had never driven. Except when Dad used to let us drive down the street while sitting on his lap. Mom used to get so mad about this, but Dad didn't understand what the big deal was. "I'm in control, Susan," he'd say.

When the light turned green, Billy sped down the quiet part of Main Street, away from the stores. That's when you finally looked up from your notebook.

"Mom wants to fuck the president?" you said.

"What'd you just say?" Billy asked. He turned down the music. I blushed again. I had completely forgotten what I had written in your notebook. I had forgotten all about Mom and the president.

"Oh my God," you said. You turned around to look at me. You started to laugh, just as I wanted. "Sally, why did you write this in my notebook? I have to give these notes to Mrs. Klausterman."

"Wait, who wants to fuck the president?" Billy asked. "Your mom?"

"Look," you said, holding up the notebook. "Look at what Sally wrote."

And Billy looked.

That's how quickly it happens. That's what Dad has always said about accidents. All it takes is one second, one glance, girls, one moment of not paying attention, and all of a sudden, there's a wrench falling a thousand feet from a cell phone tower. And Jesus Christ, this time it fell on Jim's head, and Jim wasn't wearing a hard hat, and now poor Jim is going to be dribbling oatmeal out his mouth for the rest of his life because some jackass didn't keep his wrench secured to his belt.

"Fuck!" Billy said.

There was a deer in the middle of the road. A stupid deer. And Billy didn't want to hit it. Billy didn't see it coming. It was just standing there in the middle of the road, not even moving, as if it had been waiting for us. Billy swerved hard to the right, toward a tree.

"Billy!" you shouted.

And that was it—your very last word. That's what I told the police. That's what I put in the official report. It seemed important to document for some reason. It seemed like something people ought to know, how you called out for Billy even in that final moment, even as he killed you. Because that was how much you loved him.

THE FRENCH REVOLUTION

(AND OTHER VERY IMPORTANT MOMENTS IN HISTORY)

At this point, I'm not sure what to tell you about your own death. The people at the morgue, they stood in front of Mom and Dad, and they said, It all happened so fast—blunt trauma to the head—you wouldn't have even felt it. They somehow made this sound like a good thing, as if you were spared the knowledge of your own death.

But I wasn't fooled. I was over in the blue chairs at the morgue, and I knew you'd want to know everything about your death, the same way you wanted to know if Billy was talking to Lisa at the pool or if you had spinach in your teeth or if your hair had become frizzy after a summer storm.

I knew it was my job to tell you the truth, because when I didn't, you would look in the mirror and say, "Sally, why didn't you tell me my hair was so frizzy today?" which is exactly why I didn't tell you. You sounded mad at me, as if I was your hair—I was your ugliness—following you around, haunting you from all sides.

But I am much older now. I am twenty-eight. I know a lot of things I did not know when I was sitting on those blue chairs, waiting to identify your body. I know there are some things people are better off not knowing, which is why Billy kept ordering me not to look at your face after we hit the tree. "Don't look!" he kept shouting, and yet I looked, because you were my sister, and not looking felt wrong, as if I were leaving you all alone in your own death.

But now sometimes when I am combing my hair in the mirror,

when I am brushing my teeth, when I am smoothing cream on my face at night, when I am laughing with my fiancé on a balcony in New York City and I forget, for one moment, that you ever existed (amazing that this kind of thing can even happen), I close my eyes and see your teeth. They were hemorrhagic, the autopsy report documented. So bloody, it makes me feel faint.

So that is all I am going to say about it for now. Because there are other things—better things—I know you'd want to hear. Like the fact that Billy leaned close to you, hovered over your body, shouting "Kathy!" with such purpose and determination that I believed he loved you. I believed that the louder Billy shouted, the more you'd come alive. Like one of those clap-o-meters on *The Price Is Right*, the louder your boyfriend shouted, the more the red thing on TV would rise, and you would win. You would stand up and reclaim your life. Your prize.

But you didn't move. You were clearly dead. And yet, I kept asking, "Is she dead?" as if only Billy knew the truth about death. But Billy wouldn't answer. Billy just continued to shout, "Sally, don't look at your sister!" and then added, "Go get help!"

It was the first time Billy had called me Sally since the day he saved me at the pool. It made things feel very serious again—too serious— like this was a thing that was actually happening. You were actually dead. So I got out of the car, and the whole time I ran for help, I kept thinking, Was that really my sister? Was that *Kathy*?

I knocked on a house with a red door, but the woman inside was already in the process of opening it. The children, already at the windows. She had heard the crash. She had called 911. And yet this didn't feel like enough. She didn't understand. She hadn't seen you. "You have to help my sister!" I shouted at her, and in the silence that followed, I noticed the white sweatband wrapped around her head. I heard the TV in the background. I saw the woman on screen, lifting her thigh to the beat of Gloria Estefan. Aerobics.

By the time I returned to the scene, it felt like the accident had nothing to do with me anymore. It looked like a scene out of some terrible movie Dad might make us watch. The cops kept going, "Come on, son, you have to leave her," and the boyfriend—much bloodier than I remember Billy being—kept saying, "No, I won't leave her!" And then the cops said, "You have to leave her, son. We need to clear the scene," in their deepest, most cop-like voices, as if it was in everybody's manly interests to comply, but the boyfriend didn't see it that way. The boyfriend was bleeding from nearly every part of his face—his jaw, broken in three places, I would learn later—and yet his only duty, as boyfriend, was to stay with you. He shrugged off the cops and ran back to the car to hold his girlfriend one last time because he has just realized something important. He realized, at the very end, how in love he was. He realized this was his last chance to tell you, and what an idiot he had been. Why didn't he tell you earlier? What a stupid boy he was. "I love you, Kathy," Billy shouted, over and over again. And then he put his hands to his face and cried between the spaces of his fingers because that was how, I learned, your boyfriend cried.

"I was in the accident!" I told the officers. "That's my sister! Let me back in!"

But this only made them concerned for me. They brought me to the back of an ambulance so I could get my vitals checked. I was fine, an EMT said, which disappointed me greatly. I was perfectly fine. Emerged from the car without a scratch.

"Are you sure?" I asked.

As I sat there, I kept waiting for someone to tell me that I was dead. To put a stethoscope to my heart and say, She's not working. But then I saw myself in the glare of the ambulance window. I saw my ponytail, still high up on my head just as I liked it. My snap bracelets, all four of them, latched to my wrist. Mom and Dad, running toward me like I was still alive.

I was fine. But Billy was not. Billy was bleeding from his head. Billy's face slammed into the steering wheel when we hit the tree. Billy needed to get into the ambulance right now. Come on, son, the police said one more time, and finally Billy was too tired or too bloody to refuse. He got into the ambulance, and then he was gone.

None of us even said goodbye. But that was okay. I kept thinking I would see you both again very soon. So I just sat there, by the ambulance, watching the cops take photos of you in the car.

While I waited, the cop asked me questions. How did the accident happen? Did Billy swerve on purpose? Was he driving recklessly? Did he mean to drive that fast into the tree? What kind of boyfriend was he? And why were they asking me? Did they think Billy did this on purpose? Did they think this was Billy's fault? This was my fault. I was the one who made Billy drive me to school, and he did because he was a good boyfriend.

"He is a very good boyfriend," I said to them. He always rang the doorbell. He brought us tulips. He ate Mom's potato salad with a gusto we could never muster up. "He really loves my mom's potato salad."

But the cop just said, "I think she might be in shock," to another policeman I was surprised to recognize. He volunteered as the girl's middle school soccer coach and all the kids called him Jelly Roll for some reason. I never understood this. He wasn't fat. He was never seen eating doughnuts. He was always walking around with a green smoothie in his water bottle. But whenever the cool girls like Lia McGree saw him in the hallway, they would go Jel-lyyyy Roll and Jelly Roll would high-five them.

But he did not high-five me. He looked at me like I was not the kind of girl you could ever high-five, like I was the kind of girl you just felt sorry for, and I hated him for how real he made everything feel that morning.

"Where is my *sister*?" I finally asked. "Is she okay? Is she still in the car?"

"Why don't you have some water?" Jelly Roll said. "I think you're very confused right now."

And maybe he was right. Maybe I was confused. Because I remember feeling like I had something very important to tell you when I got home later that night. I kept picturing you on your bed, saying, "Now tell me everything. Was it exciting? Was Billy upset? Did he try to save me?"

But it took forever to get home. We had to go to the police station. And then the morgue. And did you know we had a morgue in our town? I didn't. But we had one, of course. Every town needs a place to put its dead people, and ours was right between the McDonald's and the highway. This didn't seem like the right place, but so it was.

I was surprised to realize that the morgue was just like any other building in the world. It was almost like a hospital, except all the people in it were dead and downstairs.

"Let me see my daughter!" Mom said, when a doctor emerged from the door.

Mom and Dad, needless to say, were distraught. Ever since they arrived at the scene, they kept alternating between screaming and crying. And now here, at the morgue, they were still screaming. Or, well, Mom was. Mom wanted to see you. But the doctor wouldn't allow it. The doctor was eerily calm, wearing his white coat, standing in front of his door, like a bouncer to the underworld.

"I'm sorry, I can't let you see her," he said.

In his palm, he held two gold hoop earrings.

"Are these your daughter's?"

"I don't know," Dad said. Dad rubbed his cheeks. Dad was upset. Dad pinched the bridge of his nose the way he did when he wanted to travel back in time to the moment before he rear-ended the mayor, before he spilled his coffee on the rug. "I don't recognize them. I mean, they look like anybody's earrings."

And Mom wasn't even listening to the doctor. Wasn't even looking at the earrings. Mom wanted to see more than a pair of earrings.

"Let me see my daughter!" Mom shouted.

But the doctor was a professional. He stood there in his white coat with his pen, khakis, and gelled brown hair—and to think that he actually gelled his hair. To think people spent their whole lives at the morgue. People like this doctor got up every morning and showered and put on cologne and did their hair to be attractive at the morgue.

"I can't let you see her," he said. "I'm sorry. She's not Kathy anymore."

I'm sure this was another thing he was trained to say, something that was supposed to make us feel better, but it sounded like the worst thing I ever heard. You were not Kathy anymore. And if you weren't Kathy, what were you?

That's when they all looked at me.

"Yes," I finally said. "Those are her earrings."

And in that moment, as Mom screamed and collapsed into Dad's chest, it felt as if I had finally killed you.

It was over. Mom and Dad signed some papers. The doctor gave me your earrings. They sat heavy in my palm, like two fossils dug up from the ruins. I didn't know what to do with them, so I put them in my pocket. The bouncer put his clipboard under his arm. Dad put his arm around Mom. And then we did the craziest thing: We just walked out of the building and left you there. We walked through the door, back into the world, and the doctor descended into the basement, where he'd spend the beautiful day with your body.

On the way home, there was no more screaming. Mom and Dad were just quiet in an awful way. It was certain—you were dead, and we were just people in a car again. How could this be? The world was over, but we still had to do things like obey street signs and traffic lights. Dad held tightly to the wheel, and Mom kept looking back at me with a teary face, squeezing my hand. But then she faced forward, and it became really quiet, and it was still possible to pretend like none of this was happening. Like maybe we were on our way to the movies. Maybe we were going to the mall to buy you a dress for Billy's prom.

But then we were on Main Street and the red light wouldn't turn green. We were stopped at the red light for so long it seemed like somebody should turn on a radio or something, but nobody did. Music was already irrelevant.

In the silence of the red light, Dad gripped the wheel. Mom stared out the window like she might see you out there. A movement in the woods. A dog running across the street. I felt like somebody should speak, like if somebody didn't speak now, there would never again be another thing to say.

"Is the light broken?" I asked.

Nobody knew. Nobody knew anything about the light. Nobody knew anything at all, except Mom, apparently.

"It sometimes takes this long," Mom said.

Remember that Mom was connected to the town in a way Dad was not. A PTA member. A member of the Nutrition Committee. The Parks Committee. This would be important in the coming months— Mom would always be surrounded by a ring of women, everywhere she went, while Dad would grieve alone, like a dying wolf. Always inside. In his car. In his office. Dad, I would realize, didn't belong to anything in this town, except to us.

"Does it?" Dad asked.

"Yes."

"I don't remember this light ever taking so long," Dad said.

I waited. Please turn green, I thought. Please turn green. But it didn't turn green. There was no mercy. Dad banged on the wheel. The horn half honked. Like we were in a clown car.

"Where did they take Billy?" I asked.

"The hospital," Mom said.

"Is he going to be okay?"

"We don't know," Dad said.

"Can we go see him?"

"Sally," Dad said. "Please stop asking about Billy."

"I just want to know if he's going to be okay."

"We don't know, honey," Mom said.

"He better hope not," Dad says. "If that boy is alive, I'll kill him. I really will."

Then the car was quiet again. The light was still red.

"This is ridiculous," Dad said.

He couldn't wait anymore. He stepped on the gas, and he drove through a red light for probably the first time in his life, and Mom shrieked and asked him to please drive like a normal person because *our other daughter is still in the car*, which he apparently had forgotten.

"I know our daughter is in the car!" Dad shouted.

Remember that this was our father, the same father who yelled "Eye on task" whenever we were carrying too many grocery bags into the house. Our father, who still wouldn't let our mother buy furniture with glass edges despite the fact that we were teenagers. Our father, who put yellow masking tape at the top of the stairs so we would never forget that it was the top of the stairs. Our Father, Who art in Heaven, hallowed be Thy name. That's what I repeated as we drove home, as I walked the stairs to our bedroom and put your gold earrings back in the tiny drawer of your jewelry box, so you'd know exactly where to find them.

After you died, we went to church. That's how it always was in our family—never religious until we had to be. Never prayed, until we lost our keys. Never went to church, until Mrs. Mitt called and asked if I was getting my first Communion like Valerie.

"Of course, Sally is getting her Communion," Mom had said.

We were Catholics, weren't we? We were baptized. Held above a basin of water and welcomed into the Church. Mom made me try on the same beautiful white dress that you wore for your first Communion, and I felt like I was getting sized for a costume, cast in a play about becoming a good Catholic. And you know I hated being in plays, especially plays that involved me confessing things. To a priest! But you promised me it would be easy.

"All you have to do is go in the little room and tell the priest the worst thing you ever did," you said.

"But why?"

"So he can forgive you."

"For what though?"

"For the terrible thing you've done."

"But what if I haven't done anything terrible?"

You laughed. "Everybody does terrible things. Even you, Sally."

The trick was, you said, not to overthink it. If you overthought it, you'd never be able to choose between all the horrible things you did.

And so I tried not to overthink it. I got in the car, where Dad put on the baseball game. Mom put on her lipstick in the mirror. I decided I'd say whatever you said for your first confession.

"What'd you tell the priest?" I asked.

"I kept it pretty simple," you said. "I apologized for pinching the boys in my class."

But I would never pinch a boy. I would never talk back to the teacher or harass the lunch ladies or pour milk on anybody's head. I was a good student. I was quiet. *A natural sharer*, the teachers wrote. A spelling bee champ who cleaned the chalkboards before lunch.

"It doesn't have to be pinching," you said. "Could be anything you did wrong. What have you done wrong lately?"

It was too terrible to admit: After Grandpa's funeral, I waited for everybody to leave the living room, walked over to the mantle, opened the urn, and looked inside. If this was actually Grandpa, I was going to take some of him home with me. I stuck my hand in, grabbed a fistful of ash, and the next thing I knew, Grandma was at my side. Grandma slapped me hard across the face.

"What do you think you're doing?" she asked. "This isn't some stupid cookie jar you stick your hand in! This is my *husband*."

I didn't know, after, whether to wash my hand or not. It seemed wrong, to wash Grandma's husband down the drain. So I just kept it in my pocket all the way home. I was so ashamed, I didn't even tell you about it.

"I honestly can't think of anything," I said to you all in the car.

"You don't always have to *do* something," Mom said. "It could also be something you feel. What's the worst thing you've felt recently?"

"Okay," I said. "Well. If I'm going to be honest, I don't really like Grandma all that much."

"I'm glad someone finally said it," Dad said.

But Mom got mad. "Sally! That's a terrible thing to say about your only living grandparent."

"I thought saying something terrible was the point?" I asked.

"Well, you can't say *that*," Mom said. "Your grandmother loves you. She's driving all the way from the ocean, just to watch you be a sinner. Right, Richard?"

Mom always talked about Grandma coming straight from the ocean, which didn't help things. It made her sound as if she lived in the ocean, like Ursula from *The Little Mermaid* who could drown people in her wild storms.

"Your mother is right, Sally," Dad said.

"She's kind of mean, sometimes," you admitted.

"Your grandmother had a hard life, girls," Dad said. "Try to imagine what it was like to be her, growing up during the Great Depression."

I felt terrible when I saw Grandma at the church for my Communion, all done up in her orange suit, her blue lids, and the pearls around her neck. I hung my head and tried to picture her suffering, on a small boat, as a little girl, shivering in the wind. But after the ceremony, in the parking lot, I felt giddy in my white dress. I felt cleansed! Free of something terrible. Of myself.

We drove home with our parents, to the tiny party awaiting us in our backyard, to the mini hot dogs and the lemon cakes that we would feast on, because that's what our parties were like then, so small, took place on one card table and one patch of grass between houses, and yet they felt huge. By the end of the night, I was full again. I felt like myself again. Weighted to the earth. Eating candy. Afraid to look at Grandma, who was just sitting at the card table, watching me.

"Sally," Grandma said. "Come here. Show us what you did to your beautiful dress."

I went. I showed them my white dress, tinged with mud from playing tag with Rick Stevenson and Peter Heart. But Mom didn't care about the dress. "Oh, who cares about the dress?" Mom said. "I'm not having another kid. As far as I'm concerned, Sally can ruin it."

Dad didn't care, either. Dad said, "What are you going to do? That's what kids do. They ruin things," which upset Mom.

"That's a terrible thing to say about children, Richard," Mom said.

But Grandma just looked at me. Grandma could see the truth about me, all the way down to my rotten heart.

"Sally, what do you have to say for yourself?"

I didn't know.

"Cat got your tongue?" Grandma said.

Grandma was always saying this to me. But I didn't understand. Didn't she remember that our cat was dead? That we had buried Doctor in the yard?

"What's wrong with you, Sally? Why won't you speak?" Grandma said. "What's wrong with her, Susan? She's getting too shy."

Was I getting too shy?

"Sally's not shy," you said.

But this didn't convince Grandma. I avoided Grandma for the rest of the night. For the rest of her life. Didn't see her again until she was dead, laid out in the funeral home. She looked shockingly small, not like a sea monster at all. Grandma had just been a woman, I realized, and now she was dead, and I felt so ashamed of having been scared of her that I refused to speak at her funeral. I was too shy, I told Mom. Grandma was right. And what could I even say by that point, except I'm sorry?

I declined to speak at your funeral, too. The thought of standing up in front of our whole town made me too nervous. So, I sat quietly in the first pew between Mom and Dad and I made a mental list of all the things other people said about you:

You are a beautiful angel.

A candle blowing in the wind.

The warmth of the sun on our faces.

The reasons that the sunflowers grow tall.

And it amazed me how easily people said these things about you, how confident they sounded that you were better off now.

Then it was over and all the people came to our house and ate apple pie and swirled around our mother at the kitchen table, who was catatonic in her chair. They were still talking:

"What a terrible thing," Mrs. Mountain said. "A terrible accident."

"A stupid accident," Aunt Beatrice said. "Stupid for that boy to be driving so fast."

"He should be arrested," Mrs. Mitt said.

Arrested?

"But Kathy told him to speed!" I finally said, because that was the truth. But the whole room looked at me as if I were crazy, even Mom and Dad. "She actually begged him to speed."

"Sally," Dad ordered. "Be quiet."

Billy had just been doing me a favor, driving me to school when you told me there was absolutely no time to drive me to school. If it was Billy's fault that you were dead, then it was also my fault—I knew this for certain. "It's true!" I said. But nobody wanted to hear it. They refused to blame this on you.

"Sally, go up to your room!" Dad yelled, without even looking at me. Ever since you died, he seemed pained when he looked at me, as though it was too difficult to stare at one girl while trying to remember another.

For the rest of the night, I didn't speak again. I felt weirdly unwelcome in our house. I went up to our bedroom, where I belonged. I turned off the lights and stared up at our ceiling and there we still were. KATHY and SALLY, glowing in the dark.

"What do you think Billy is doing, *right now*?" I asked, but you were silent.

Billy didn't go to your funeral. For that, he was very sorry. He was sick over it. Wrote us a letter after he got out of the ICU, apologizing, and when he got home from the hospital, he apologized to me again online.

Yes, I was on your screen name. But I only went on once, and after, I deleted it forever, because some of your friends frantically messaged to see if you had virtually come back from the dead. Even Billy was spooked by it.

Who is this? Billy messaged, as soon as I logged on.

It's just Sally, I wrote.

Oh, he wrote.

Sorry for confusing you.

Don't apologize, he wrote. I'm the one who should be sorry.

There was a long pause.

I'm sorry I couldn't come to the funeral, too, he wrote.

You were in the hospital, I wrote to him. Nobody blames you for that.

Your parents must hate me.

They don't hate you, I wrote.

Our parents were divided on the issue of Billy. At night, they fought a lot about what they were going to do. To sue for reckless driving or not to sue? That was the question.

Dad wanted to sue. Dad wanted to press charges.

"That boy should be punished," he said. "What was he thinking driving so fast on Main Street?"

But Mom wasn't so sure that suing Billy was going to accomplish anything. Mom had driven fifty before on Main Street. Mom had become a good Catholic again ever since you died. Mom didn't see how punishing Billy was going to help us feel better. Mom suggested we pray for him instead.

"*Pray* for him?" Dad laughed.

"Mrs. Barnes says that Billy's not doing well," Mom said. She told us how his broken jaw had been wired shut for weeks. "She said he can't even speak. Or eat. He just cries all night long and makes himself sick."

"Why are you telling me this, Susan?"

"Because she asked if we would have a meeting of the families," Mom said. "She thinks it might help things if Billy could apologize to us in person."

"Why do I need to be worried about what will help Billy?" Dad said. "Cry me a river. We've got enough to deal with."

"Maybe it would be good for us," Mom said. "It could be healing."

"No," Dad said. "There's no healing from this, Susan."

Dad rubbed his chin, which was stubbled with the beginnings of a beard now. Ever since you died, he stopped shaving and going to work. He stopped putting Metamucil in his cup—didn't seem to care when or how often he took a shit. He had started to look strange to me, like a wild animal who was always growing hair around his mouth, always angry.

"That woman just wants to parade him around our house so we feel bad for him," Dad said. "So we don't sue them for all they have. We could, you know. We could sue them for all they have."

"It was an accident, Richard," Mom said. "You of all people should understand that."

"Yes, it was an accident," Dad said. "But do you know why accidents happen? Because people are careless. Because people aren't paying attention to what they're doing. And, I'm sorry, but people need to be punished for that."

But I didn't want to punish Billy. I felt no anger toward Billy. All I wanted in those months after you died was to talk to Billy. While Mom and Dad fought about Billy's fate in the kitchen, I talked to Billy in secret, online. The angrier Dad got at Billy in the kitchen, the quicker I typed.

I don't hate you, I wrote. I know it was an accident. I know you were speeding because she told you to. And you were just trying not to kill the deer.

That stupid fucking deer, Billy wrote. I should have just killed it.

He couldn't stop seeing that deer. He saw the deer in his nightmares. In his dreams. And there, even in his dreams, he couldn't kill it. The deer always got away. The deer was too fast in the woods for Billy to catch.

Because it's a deer, I wrote. Because you didn't know what was going to happen. You couldn't see the future. You weren't a prophet.

Well, that's definitely true, Billy wrote. Now we know that for sure. Billy Barnes: definitely not a prophet.

Nearly every night that February, Billy had questions for me. Can you talk? How are you? How *was* the funeral anyway? Is that a weird question to ask?

Maybe.

But I was glad he asked.

Nobody had yet asked me this, because everybody I knew was at the funeral. And I liked talking about the funeral. I wish I could have stayed at the funeral forever. At the funeral, you were still with us, right there in the middle of the church. And everybody else we knew was there, too. Priscilla. Valerie. Our cousins. People who did sit-ups with you during gym. Old elementary school teachers. Geno from down the street. The old lady who gave us whole Snickers bars on Halloween. Even Shelby and Lisa the Lifeguard came. They wore tight black dresses, Lisa's with two tiny triangle holes cut out of the sides. I stared at the holes, as she hugged me and told me about her fondest memory of you: that time you guys had to do a scavenger hunt in bio, how the teacher made you collect the weirdest things in your bags, like caterpillars and deer scat, which is just a fancy word for poop, Lisa said, and it was really weird, but really funny.

"Anyway," Lisa said. "I'm so sorry."

Everybody had a story about you I hadn't heard before. Everybody but me, it seemed, had something to say about your death, and how was this possible since I was the only person there who witnessed it? Yet they went up to the pulpit and declared you an angel, a shining star, and then Priscilla leaned in real close to the mic and said, "I know Kathy is now the light of the sun and in the songs of the birds," and I didn't even realize how much this all bothered me until I described it to Billy online.

It just makes no sense, I wrote to Billy. I mean, you can't be an angel and a shining star and a bird all at the same time.

That's true, he wrote. Three completely different things.

And I forgot what I was supposed to say when the priest said, The Body of Christ, I wrote. It had been so long since my Communion, and I forgot if it was Amen or Thank you, if I was supposed to be holy or polite, and it seemed strange to have to choose between the two.

What'd you end up saying? Billy asked.

I said thank you.

But then walking back to the pew, I didn't know if I was supposed to chew it or let it absorb into my tongue. Because if it really was the body of Jesus Christ, it seemed wrong to chew it. So I looked to see what Dad was doing but his mouth was a straight line. I looked at Mom, but she had her face in her hands. And then I looked at you, but you were in your box, completely unknowable. I couldn't tell what you were doing.

So I just chewed it.

I don't think you're supposed to chew it, Billy said.

Well, too late, I wrote.

After, we walked out of the church to Celine Dion's "Because You Loved Me," which was a little embarrassing, because it was an embarrassing song, and you'd think it'd be impossible to be embarrassed on the day of your own sister's funeral, but it turns out, I can literally be embarrassed anywhere.

In your defense, Kathy didn't even like that song, Billy wrote.

That's what I just kept wanting to tell people, I wrote. I wanted to go up to the microphone and say, Actually, Kathy preferred Ace of Base.

Haha, Billy wrote. Not to mention, Janet Jackson.

But I guess you can't play those songs at a funeral.

No, Billy wrote. It probably wouldn't be appropriate, no.

So we all filed out of the church to Celine Dion, and then there was the burial, and did you know that they don't actually bury the person while the family is still there? I didn't know that.

I only knew what I knew from people dying in Dad's movies, and in movies they always lower the body dramatically as the family weeps.

But in real life, they just suspend the body over the grave (that's what they call it, the body) and then everyone throws in roses and walks away and gets in the limo and trusts that the two random employees standing nearby will bury it before dark.

And Billy was like, I actually knew that.

He went to a funeral last year. His grandmother. And it was surprising to me that Billy had a grandmother, but of course he did. Billy was a boy and his grandmother was Polish. A really impressive lady. Came to America at the age of fourteen, was smuggled through Canada in a giant trunk. She made very good pierogi, he said.

I've never had pierogi before, I wrote.

What? he wrote. How is this possible?

I've just never encountered it.

But it's everywhere? he wrote. Oh my God. Sally. You need to have pierogi. Stop everything you are doing right now and go eat some pierogi.

But I couldn't. I had to get ready for school in the morning.

"Sally, are you ready for school?" Mom had been asking me for the last hour.

No. I was not. School seemed absurd. How could people expect me to go to school at a time like this? But I had to. I had to, as Dad ordered, return to life.

Can we talk again? Billy asked. It's been really nice talking to you.

Yeah, I wrote. I'll be on tomorrow.

I only missed three weeks of school after you died, but in history, two thousand years had passed.

"After you left, the Holy Roman Empire fell," Peter Heart told me. Peter had taken notes for me on everything I missed, and he sounded excited about it all. "Now, it's 1806 and we are in France, just after the French Revolution. The king and queen are dead. The people have risen. And here comes Napoleon, swooping in from out of nowhere. From Corsica! Which wasn't even really France, by the way."

Then, he handed me a notebook. "Anyway, it's all in here."

"Thanks," I said.

He looked unsatisfied by my response, as though he expected more than a thanks. But I had nothing else to say, and Mr. Klein clapped, said, "Take your seats," and wrote NAPOLEON on the board. "Kids, the first thing you must know about Napoleon is that he was not as short as everybody believed."

There was a misunderstanding, apparently. Something about the French measurement system. Something about Americans not understanding anything except for America.

After class, Mr. Klein said to me, "While you were gone, we all picked parts of the French Revolution out of my hat and everybody gave a report on their part."

He cheated and saved me the best part. The part all the boys wanted.

"Can you guess what it is?"

I really couldn't.

"The guillotine," he said. "Now, take your time researching it. Whenever you're ready to give your report, let me know."

I went to health class, where I was also very behind. I had missed all the STDs, Valerie told me. Valerie had taken notes for me. Gave me a handout that our teacher had given us. An STD chart that Mrs. Klusspuss had drawn herself. The lines were so straight, it was actually impressive.

AIDS can happen to anyone. Even people in love! AIDS does not care if you're in love. Neither does HIV.

"But wait," I said. "What's HIV?"

"It's AIDS," Valerie said.

"How is that different from AIDS?"

"It comes before AIDS," Valerie said.

"Does something come after AIDS?"

"In all instances, death."

In all of my classes, someone had taken notes for me and I couldn't help but be touched. I hadn't realized my classmates could be so nice. Before you died, people had been mostly indifferent to me, if not a little mean. But now, even Rick Stevenson was being kind. Actually apologized to me at the bus stop that first morning.

"I'm sorry about your sister," he said.

At first, I didn't know how to react. I wasn't used to being looked at by people, or being pitied by teachers, or getting high-fived by Jelly Roll in the parking lot on my way out of school. I wasn't used to the popular girls like Lia McGree tilting their heads during gym class to say, "I can't believe you actually survived that accident. It looked so bad in the paper."

I was famous now. Like Billy was after he jumped off the roof, so many years ago. I was a survivor—at least, according to Lia McGree and the *Aldan Times*. I had lived through a terrible car accident. I had seen the flesh and blood and bones. I had proof that we were all, in the end, exactly the same and that anybody who pretends differently is lying. When Lia McGree acted better than all of us just because she was in a commercial for the Olive Garden, I knew she was being a fool. Yes, Lia might have long flowing blond hair and a perfect face. But Lia was going to die one day, Lia was going to lose all that hair and all that beauty, and so was Rick Stevenson, and thinking of this—Rick in his coffin—made me feel like I could say or do anything to him at the bus stop.

"Fuck you, Rick," I said.

But even that didn't feel like enough. I wanted to punish Rick. That's who I was angry at in those months after you died. Not Billy.

But Rick didn't get it. Rick was like, Huh?

"What the hell, Sally?" Rick said. "I was just trying to be nice."

But Rick would never be nice the way Billy was nice. Rick fed the fish in class like he was peppering them. Flirted with Valerie in computer class by trying to squeeze her and make her fart.

But Billy was different. Billy was in mourning. Billy was suddenly full of a love for you that was so deep, all he wanted to do at night was talk very earnestly about this love.

I don't know what I am going to do, Billy wrote. I just love her so much, Sally.

These were the things Billy loved about you: Your face. Your hair. The way you laughed. The way you sang, sometimes, in the car. How you stroked the back of his neck and chewed gum. How excited you got when a song you liked came on the radio.

I've never felt this way about anybody, Billy wrote. Never loved a girl like this before. Not really.

Not even Shelby? I asked. Or Lisa?

Shelby? Lisa? Oh. No. That was nothing.

Billy admitted that he had been a little in love with you ever since you sang the National Anthem at his game. Looking at you, with your hair, with your voice filling the gym, it made him feel like things were possible. You made him feel the way he felt when he was a kid and he used to draw pictures of his family so big, their faces hardly fit on the page.

You draw? I asked.

(Did you know this about your boyfriend?)

Yeah, he said. I used to be kind of good at it.

Why'd you stop? I asked.

I don't really remember, he said. I think I just started playing basketball, and that was that.

Basketball took up all his time. And what a waste of time it all was, Billy said. All of those nights he spent running suicides, up and down the court. The family vacations he missed. The classes he slept through. The ankles he twisted and the knees he scraped by diving for the ball. Billy used to always dive for the ball. Billy gave it everything he had. That's what people were always saying about Billy in the papers, that he was going to be a star. He was going to make some college very happy one day.

That's all over now, Billy wrote.

Billy couldn't play on the basketball team at Villanova anymore. He wasn't ever going to run the way he used to run—now, he had two steel rods in his right leg. Now, he was just an ordinary person who was going to be in pain for the rest of his life.

Some nights, Billy wrote, I just sit in the dark, and I'm like, who the fuck was I?

Do you want me to answer that? I wrote.

Sure, he said. Go for it.

I stuck to the facts.

You were the president of Students Against Smoking, I wrote. You were the boy who worked the snack bar. You were a basketball player.

I was, he wrote.

You were very good.

I was the best in the state, he wrote.

That's what he used to say about himself in the shower after practice. He'd sit there on the tile, his ankles blue at the base, and he would say, "I am the best basketball player in the state," and it scared him that he did this, this compulsion to brag about himself to himself, and so he never did it again. He started taking shorter showers. He could hardly look at himself in the mirror some nights.

I understood what he meant. I was having a hard time looking at myself in the mirror after I talked to Billy.

Did you know that in the eighteenth century, kids used to play with tiny toy guillotines? They'd use them to chop off their dolls' heads.

That's pretty fucked up, Billy wrote.

And sometimes they'd use them on mice.

Can I ask how you know these things? Billy asked. And why would anybody give their kid a tiny toy guillotine?

Because I have to give a report, I wrote. Because life used to be terrible.

Yeah, well, life is pretty terrible now, too, Billy wrote. Try drinking a hamburger smoothie every night of your life and not killing yourself.

Billy could see why the guillotine would be considered humane. Most nights, Billy wished the accident had finished him. Wished it had sliced his head off his body. It took him two months to admit this to me.

I don't deserve to live, he wrote. I feel like a monster.

He looked like one, too, he said; he had scars all over his body, and plastic surgery didn't really help much. The surgeons tried; they took skin from different body parts and grafted them onto his face.

But all that means now is that my ass is on my face, he wrote. Because that's a thing.

Wait, really?

Yes. They put my ass on my face. Apparently, the ass is good for that kind of thing. The ass can literally be applied anywhere.

So does your face look like an ass now?

Lol. That might be the first thing that has made me laugh in a long time. Thanks.

You're welcome.

Would be kind of funny. But no. It doesn't actually look like my ass.

Well that's good.

It's just normal skin. It's just my face. Except not really. Because it looks nothing like my face.

I don't get it.

You will, when you see.

B ut when would I see Billy again? That spring, this was the only question that mattered to me, which was not good, because it was still traitorous in our house to express concern or any kind of affection for Billy. Anytime Mom started to feel slightly bad for Billy, Dad was like, NO.

And Mom was like, Maybe?

And Dad was like, How could you?

And Mom was like, How could you not even?

And then Dad saw me enter the kitchen, and was like, What's for dinner?

I got the silver tray from the bottom of the freezer. That's what dinner was now. A silver tray, delivered by our neighbors or relatives or whoever else felt sorry for us. We got so many after you died, we just started putting them in the freezer, and now we were always pulling them out of the freezer, standing over the counter, eating directly from the silver trays, forks in hand, like barbarians, Dad said. We're barbarians. But apparently, he didn't mind this, because we continued being barbarians.

Mom opened the lid.

"What is it?" I asked.

"I think it's fajitas," Mom said.

"Fajitas?" Dad said.

Apparently, Dad didn't know what fajitas were. He was like, I swear I never heard the word before, and Mom said, Richard, in the way that Mom does, don't tell me I married a man who doesn't know what a fajita is, and Dad said, I'm afraid you did. He repeated it twice, and by the second time, it sounded ominous, like we were all doomed because we knew him.

I explained how they're basically like tacos, except you have to assemble them yourself, which Dad didn't get because why would you want to assemble the meal yourself if you don't have to? Wasn't the whole point of the silver tray so that we didn't have to do any work?

And Mom went, "Richard, I know we had fajitas before. I just know it. We went on our honeymoon to Mexico."

"You expect me to remember what we ate on our honeymoon?" Dad asked.

And that's what dinner was like until Dad finally said, "Enough. Let's eat at the table tonight. Let's be civilized."

But I didn't want to set the table. I didn't want to be civilized. Civilization, I was learning, was not all it was cracked up to be. "Man's attempt to be civilized," Mr. Klein had said, "has produced more massacres, holocausts, and genocides than any barbarians ever did." This upset a lot of the kids at school—especially Valerie. Valerie didn't like to hear that simply by sitting there, wearing the shoes and the shirts and the socks that she was wearing, she was oppressing children in Indonesia. Valerie was like, "I'm just, like, sitting here. I'm not doing anything. I didn't even *buy* these sneakers. If you want to point fingers at the oppressor, point them at my mother. She's the one who buys this stuff for me." Valerie just wanted to wear shoes and shirts and socks and not have to feel bad about it. Who could blame her, really.

But I was starting to believe in the things that upset me; I was starting to realize that it was much more likely that all the bad things were true. That civilization was the worst. Because whenever we sat around the table, eating on place mats, like a *goddamned family*, Dad said, "So how was school?" and I said, "School was good," and Dad didn't believe me for some reason.

"Good, huh?" Dad said. "School is always good. You'd think one of these days, school might just be something else, no?"

"What do you mean?" I asked.

Dad had always accepted "Good" as a response before, when school was not good, when boys were holding me down in my seat and accusing me of having two vaginas. But now that people were actually friendly to me, now that people wanted to be my lab partner and sit with me at lunch, he was acting suspicious, as if school could not possibly be good.

"It was good," I said. "I don't know what else you want me to say about it."

Dad rested the vodka on the table. Dad was drinking a lot of vodka now. Stuffing grapes in it at four in the afternoon, as if that made it less like vodka.

"I went to school once," Dad said. "And what I remember about school was that it was either the best day of my life or the worst day of my life. Either I got asked to the pep rally by Cindy Lee or I shat my pants in gym class."

And Mom didn't even scold him. Mom didn't even say, *Richard!* Because now that you were dead, we could say anything we wanted. No swear word was ever going to be as terrible as the word *dead*.

"Who was Cindy Lee?" I asked.

"A girl I used to have a big crush on."

"You didn't have a crush on Mom?"

"Mom was dating Fred Hopper," he said.

"The Vietnam guy?"

Dad took a sip of his vodka.

"The guy who rode his motorcycle and walked around all tough. A bully."

I looked at Mom. I thought Mom might like talking about her old boyfriend, the way she had at the pool. But she wasn't even paying attention.

"Sally, is that your sister's shirt?" she asked.

Yes. Of course it was. I started to grow fast after you died, and your shirts were starting to fit me better than my own. But Mom wouldn't have it.

"We'll have to take you to the mall," Mom said. "Get you some new shirts."

But I didn't want to get new shirts. I wanted to wear your shirts, for the same reason I wanted to sleep in your bed and wear your two gold hoop earrings. I had always planned on inheriting your things. Mom had been a big champion of perfectly good hand-me-downs.

But now she was acting like I had committed a crime, desecrated our bedroom, which was starting to feel less like a bedroom and more like a sacred site, the ancient ruins of your past.

So, I didn't sleep in your bed. I didn't wear your earrings. But I did get my ears pierced. I asked Valerie to do it after school in her giant bathroom. She was an expert. "Stay still," she said, and it bled more than I thought it would. My ears were red and infected for days, and I couldn't sleep on my left side. But Valerie wasn't concerned. "So sleep on your right," she said in health class.

"Can I be excused?" I asked Mom and Dad. I kept waiting for them to notice the earrings, to punish me for something, but they didn't. "I need to use the computer."

The computer. It was where I lived that spring. It was where I sat and talked to Billy on school nights, because Mom didn't care what time I went to bed now. Mom felt bad for me. Mom kept her distance most nights, silently circling around me, looking concerned, until she came over to say good night. Leaned in to kiss me on the cheek and said something like, "I know this must be hard for you."

"It's fine," I said, trying to cover Billy's messages on the computer screen with my body.

"I can't imagine having to go to school at a time like this," Mom said.

"It's really okay," I said.

By the time she left, Billy had signed off without saying goodbye. It didn't feel like that big of a deal at the time, because I knew he'd be on the next night. His online presence had become as reliable to me as the sunset.

But he wasn't online the next night. Or the night after that. Or the night after that. Weeks passed in his silence, and by the end of April, when he still hadn't returned, I was confused.

I felt sick.

But I went to school. Gave my report on the guillotine, which was reserved mostly for the nobility. A humane achievement by eighteenth-century-people standards. Its benefits included a quick, painless death as opposed to being drawn and quartered, which means that you are literally ripped at the seams by four horses, and maybe not even dead for a long while after that.

Marie Antoinette and her husband—

"You mean the king?" Mr. Klein said.

"Yes," I said. "Marie Antoinette and King Louis XVI were executed by the guillotine. They had their heads chopped off by the people. Even though Louis XVI wasn't a bad guy. But the people had to do it. It was symbolic."

"Thank you, Sally," Mr. Klein said. "That was very good."

Everybody clapped.

But I didn't care.

Where was Billy?

Billy tried to kill himself," Priscilla finally explained on your seventeenth birthday.

"*What?*" I asked.

"You didn't hear?"

Priscilla had come over to sit on your bedspread. That's where she wanted to celebrate. To mourn. To feel the seams of her old life. To sit around and talk about Billy like the good old days.

"I mean, he took all of his painkillers, blended them into a smoothie, and drank the whole thing."

His mother found him, in the nick of time. Cut the wires in his mouth with her sewing scissors and stuck her finger down his throat and made him puke it all up in the toilet.

And, at first, I thought Priscilla was lying.

"Billy wouldn't do that," I said.

Billy was a survivor. Billy was an optimist. Billy believed that you could win simply by visualizing the win.

"Why would I lie about something like that?" Priscilla asked.

"Well, I don't know," I said. "I just can't imagine Billy doing something like that."

I still could only imagine Billy accomplishing things.

"I'm not lying," Priscilla said. "It's very obvious that boy's got a death wish. That's what my mom said, anyway. His life is *ruined*."

"It's not ruined."

"Of course it's ruined. And he deserves it. It was stupid," Priscilla said, "to be driving fifty miles per hour on Main Street."

"It didn't actually feel that fast," I said again. "You don't know. You weren't there."

And she wasn't. So she shut up. She ran her hand on your bedspread.

"I still can't believe Kathy's gone," she kept saying. "I can't believe I'll never be in this room again."

"You can come back whenever," I said, but I knew, as time went on, she wouldn't.

After she left, I went downstairs to have dinner with Mom and Dad, and I told them right away about Billy.

"Billy tried to kill himself," I said.

"Who told you that, honey?" Mom said.

"Priscilla," I said.

And Dad just put his face in his hands. "Christ," he said.

"I think we should have the family over," Mom said. "Something needs to be done."

A week later, when Billy came back online, I didn't say anything about his suicide attempt. It seemed rude to remind somebody of how they tried to die. So I was just like, Oh hey.

But he brought it up right away. He said, I'm sorry if I scared you.

He had just been so upset, he explained. And so lonely. Nobody ever spoke to him anymore except for me, and it was so weird, walking the halls with his mouth wired shut. Without saying hello to a single person.

People act like I'm a murderer, he wrote. And maybe I am.

You're not a murderer, I said. I was *there*.

On the plus side, he wrote, not playing basketball or having any friends means I can actually do my homework now.

He had started doing all his homework for the first time in his life. He read all the books he was supposed to read for school, and then he started reading books off a summer reading list sent by Villanova, read more than he ever had in his entire life, which was ironic because now his right eye was so fucked up.

Which is, I'll have you know, he wrote, the surgeon's official diagnosis.

It turned out that Billy kind of liked reading. He liked *Paradise Lost*, and could identify with Satan, who was kicked out of Heaven by God. That's how Billy felt. As if he was on the other side of life now. Where people didn't high-five you just for walking down the hallway. Where girls looked away from you, because your face was too hideous.

Have you ever read *Beowulf*? he wrote.

No, I said.

You got to read *Beowulf*, he said.

What's it about? I asked.

It's basically about a bunch of guys drinking beer and getting into fights with a monster. Who was not really a monster.

Why do people think he's a monster then?

Because he's terrorizing a town.

Sounds like maybe he's a monster though?

Yeah, until you realize how horribly they treated him.

A few weeks later, Billy finally came over with his parents. All day long, I admit I was nervous. I spent hours in the bathroom. I shaved myself for the first time, all the way up to the thigh. I put on your lipstick, blotted my lips with a tissue. I straightened my hair, too, the way you did, but it didn't end up looking like your hair. My hair was still too short, and with too much heat, I looked like an overbrushed dog.

"Sally," Mom said, knocking as she entered.

"Don't come in!"

In Mom's presence, I felt embarrassed by the lipstick. I wiped it with my arm, but it didn't come off easily. It smudged around the corners. And I could tell Mom was going to say something about it but then the doorbell rang.

"Oh," Mom said. "Guess Billy's here."

Mom went downstairs, but it wasn't Billy. It was the delivery people.

"Someone ordered a couch?" one of the men asked.

"The couch," Mom said.

Even Mom had forgotten about the white couch. I ran downstairs to see it. It looked strange. An artifact from long ago. We all just stared at it after the delivery men left.

"What is this?" Dad said. "Susan, why did these men bring us a couch?"

"Because I bought a couch," Mom said, as if remembering a wonderful vacation.

"When?"

"In another lifetime."

"Susan, you're not helping me understand this. Did we need a new couch?"

Mom didn't answer. She just sat down on it.

"No," I said. "She bought it because it was beautiful. Look at it. Isn't it beautiful?"

"It's very white," Dad said.

"It's supposed to be white," I said.

"It's too white," Mom said. Then Mom looked at me. "Sally. Why are you wearing lipstick?"

I didn't know.

"Go wipe it off," she said.

But it was too late. Billy and his parents were in the doorway.

"Hello," Mr. and Mrs. Barnes said.

Billy stood between them in the doorway, and it was shocking to see him. He was extremely thin, as if his parents had put a nozzle up to his mouth and vacuumed the life out of him. And he had these two deep scars across his forehead—thick red raised lines that made me cringe. But the worst part was the wires locking his teeth together— they made it impossible for him to speak clearly, so he waved at us, which made him seem farther away than he was, as if he were across the street, trying to say hello.

"Hello," Dad said, but did not shake their hands.

"Come sit," Mom said.

Billy and his parents sat down on the new white couch. I kept look-ing expectantly at Billy, as if he might say something to me. As if he might start bleeding from his wounds at any moment. Or maybe that was how the white couch made everybody look—like everybody was just mere moments away from ruining it.

"Thank you for having us," Mr. Barnes said, and then nobody wasted any time after that.

Nobody commented on how beautiful the couch was or how lovely the marigolds looked by the mailbox, because there were no marigolds by the mailbox this spring. Mr. Barnes just cleared his throat and said, "My son has something he wants to say to you all."

Billy held a whiteboard and a marker ready in his hand to communicate with us. As he wrote something on it, Dad said to me, "Go upstairs."

I resented this, how they tried to keep your death from me, how they acted like Billy was some rated-R movie I couldn't watch. Billy was ours. Billy had always been ours. Billy was a secret we shared in the dead of night. I didn't budge. I sat there as Billy held up his whiteboard. I'M SO SORRY, he wrote.

Mom and Dad nodded.

"We know this isn't easy for you," Mrs. Barnes said.

"It's not," Dad said.

"And that's why we thank you so much for seeing us," Mr. Barnes said.

"Of course," Mom said.

They talked for a bit about how Billy was doing (not well, but he would get his wires off soon enough), and how Mom and Dad were doing (not well, but they were trying their best to hang on), and then Billy's mother started apologizing for Billy, started crying, and saying things like, "He's just so sorry, words can't express," and then Billy held up the whiteboard again, which still said I'M SO SORRY. Then he started to cry, which his mother said wasn't a good idea. She said, No, Billy, no, like he was a dog. We talked about this. You could choke.

This made Mom start to cry.

And it was all so terrible. You wouldn't have believed any of it—I could hardly believe it, how pitiable Billy looked. I suddenly felt foolish for straightening my hair, sitting there with a red mouth when Billy's was still wired shut. What did I think would happen? That Billy would see me and fall in love with me? By the end of the meeting, I couldn't bear to look at Billy. Not even Dad could look at him for long, Dad who had once pulled his own tooth from his mouth.

Dad kept putting his hands over his face, saying, "Oh God. This is just terrible."

PLEASE DON'T FEEL BAD FOR ME I AM OKAY, Billy wrote.

Eventually, Dad told them what they wanted to know.

"We won't press charges," Dad finally said. "But please do us a favor and don't ever contact us again. Please just let us mourn in peace."

Billy nodded. His father nodded. His mother nodded. A cascade of agreement, and then, everybody stood up.

"It's just too hard for us to speak with you," Mom said. "We don't mean to be cruel."

"We understand," Mrs. Barnes said. "You're so kind."

At the door, as we said goodbye, Billy looked at me for what felt like the first time that evening. It was just a quick glance, but it was weird. It was like making eye contact with an animal trapped in a cage. Like I could see the old Billy for just a moment, and this old Billy was trying to communicate something to me. But then Mr. Barnes said, "Thank you for meeting with us," and Billy left our house soundlessly. I went to the window, watched him walk away as I always did, but this time, he got into his mother's car instead of his own. This time, I knew he was never coming back.

Billy was online every night that week. I was, too. I waited at the computer with the hope that he would message me, even though I knew deep down he wasn't going to. I knew he wasn't going to reach out to me again; he would honor Dad's request. And the thought of never talking to Billy again was sickening.

I started to lose my appetite. I started to avoid dinner as much as I could, but it was hard, because Mom and Dad insisted I eat. Eat. Sally. Eat.

So I ate a bite of pizza.

"Good, huh?" Dad said.

It was. It was very good. And how strange was that—you were

dead, you were no longer in the universe, but pizza was still good. I
went to swallow, but I couldn't. To eat when my sister had no working mouth? It seemed wrong. Felt like betrayal. I opened my mouth,
let the pizza fall into a napkin.

"Something wrong with the pizza?" Mom asked.

"Just not hungry," I said.

"Are you okay?" Mom asked. "Are you sick?"

I didn't know. I felt sick. But Mom got the thermometer and I
didn't have a temperature. I was fine.

"You're fine," she said, smoothing over my forehead. Always so fine.

"But I don't feel fine," I said.

"I know you don't," Mom said. She pulled the covers back from my
bed. "That's why your father and I have decided that you should see
a therapist."

B y the last day of school, it felt like the world had ended. Maybe
because that's how Mr. Klein kept describing it.

"That's it, kids," Mr. Klein said. "That's the end of history."

This is how history ends: with us. With the American empire. With
Bill Clinton, who most certainly got a blow job from someone he
should not have gotten a blow job from. But what was the big deal?
That's what Mr. Klein wondered. "What that man did was nothing!
Do you know what the emperors used to do in Ancient Rome?"

And it was true what you said.

Everything really was about sex.

Even school. Especially school. In English class, when Mrs. Forster
quoted from *Tess of the d'Urbervilles* to prove how charming Angel
Clare the rancher was, she was really just talking about how she liked
to fuck men who wore flannel, and in social studies, Mrs. Hoyt was
talking about how the men and women of Borneo only came together
for a weekly fornication, and in biology it was all sex as common
denominator, mammals birds plants unite! And in history, Mr. Klein

said, "The emperor Caligula turned the palace into a brothel just so he could raise extra tax revenue!"

And was this going to be on the test? That's what Peter wanted to know.

"No," Mr. Klein said. "No, that won't be on the test."

But, of course, I messaged Billy again. I messaged him in the middle of that first summer after you died. I'm sorry, but I couldn't help myself. I was bored, lonely, sitting at the computer with one leg up on the desk, while Mom and Dad watched the news. That's what we had been doing on summer nights: watching the news. It was the only thing Mom and Dad could agree to watch together, as if they had both agreed they were no longer allowed to be entertained by movies. No longer allowed to have any fun at all, and I admit, I didn't mind learning about all of the awful things happening around the country. It was hard to feel sorry for myself when I watched some woman on TV talk about her beloved sister who had been decapitated by her husband "for no reason at all."

"As if there's a reason to chop your wife's head off?" Mom said, sipping on her tea. "As if there would ever be a reason for doing something like that."

That's when I heard the sound of Billy coming online, and it felt like a miracle. It felt like he had shown up to save me from Mom and Dad. From the long summer without you. And, honestly, what did I have to lose by messaging him? I had already lost him.

Hi, I wrote.

Hi, he wrote back right away, as if no time at all had passed.

Can you talk? I wrote.

I can, he said. Like for real. I can actually talk now. My wires are off.

Oh, I wrote. Congratulations.

Want to hear? he asked.

Your voice?

Yeah, I could call you. I could use the practice.

Okay, I wrote. Later tonight, after my parents go to sleep.

We continued sitting in the living room, watching the news together, but everything had shifted for me. I was going to talk to Billy on the phone. I felt energized for the first time in months. I was suddenly very interested in everything, including the interview on TV that Jane Mills was conducting with some homicidal dictator of some foreign country. We sat there and listened to the interviewer ask the homicidal dictator a lot of questions, including what his favorite book was. Dad got all upset, didn't believe dictators deserved a platform for sharing things like their favorite books, but I was very curious about what a homicidal dictator might read before bed.

"Shh," I said. "I want to hear."

"*Huckleberry Finn*," the homicidal dictator said. "I am a sucker for a great adventure story."

Eventually they took their little white pills (this is the only way they could sleep now) and went to bed. I went to bed, too, but I didn't fall asleep. I waited until the house settled, until it was silent. Then, I went downstairs, got the phone (it's cordless now), and called your boyfriend.

ally," Billy said, when he picked up. "It's good to hear your voice."

"This is me," I said. "This is my voice."

"Not a bad voice."

"Thanks. I've been using it my whole life."

"It shows." He laughed. "How's my voice?"

"A little different. Raspier, I think. But then again, I don't know. It's hard to remember."

"It's actually weird talking again. I'm not really used to it."

Billy said that it was nice to have the wires off. It was amazing to eat solid foods again. But talking came with its downsides.

"Now that I can talk, my mom is making me do it all the time," he said. "I have to go to a therapist."

His therapist's name was Barbara.

"And today she was like, here, Billy, why don't you take this bat and hit a tree, and I'm like, you really want me to hit this tree?"

"I'm going to a therapist, too," I said.

I hadn't even told Valerie this. It was embarrassing to spend the summer seeing a therapist when Valerie was going to spend it at her cousin's condo in Disney Safari.

But I could tell Billy about Lydia, because nobody was sadder than Billy. I told him all about Lydia and her beige chair and how she sat below a painting of a big yacht.

"I told her I didn't think it was a good idea to be hanging up pictures of yachts when her clients were probably depressed people who were never on yachts."

And she said: "Are you depressed, Sally?"

"*No*," I said to Lydia.

Lydia asked me why I was here then, and so I said, "My sister's dead."

"And how do you feel about that?"

"Not good," I said. "That's why they sent me to a therapist."

Lydia clarified: she is not a therapist.

"So what is she then?" Billy asked.

"She's just a person," I said.

That's what she said.

"I am just a person," I said. "A person who is here to help you with your problems, Sally."

Billy laughed.

"I like how you do voices," he said.

I hadn't realized I had been doing voices.

"And I was like, I don't really have any problems," I said. "I mean, something terrible happened. But it didn't happen to me. It happened to my sister. And I don't have problems. Or well, everyone has problems. And so I don't know what there is to talk about right now really. And Lydia was like, Well, here, in this space, you don't need to talk."

"Isn't that the whole point though?" Billy asked. "That you have to talk?"

"That's what I said."

"What'd Lydia say?" Billy asked.

"When you are ready, Sally, you can talk."

It was forty-eight minutes later when I felt ready.

"I was like, goodbye, Lydia. Have a great day."

B efore Valerie left for Disney, she invited me over to swim in her pool. We sat by the pool and ate the softest whitest loaves of bread that said C on the blank plastic packaging.

"C," I said, picking up the loaf on the counter. "Like, for Cancer?"

"For Control," Valerie said. "That'd be funny though. If it said cancer."

Valerie's laugh was short and thrust into the atmosphere like a gunshot. A hollow noise that sounded like a laugh and looked like a laugh, but did not feel like one. Like the white bread itself, which looked like food and claimed to be food, but did not taste or feel like food inside me.

"Oh hello, Sally," Mrs. Mitt said. She was drinking a red drink, holding a dog on a leash.

"We got a new dog," Valerie said.

"What's his name?"

"We couldn't decide on a name, so we just called him The Dog for a while, and now it just sounds like his name," Valerie said.

I bent down to pet him, but he snarled.

"The Dog likes to be scratched behind the ear," Mrs. Mitt said, as she leaned over so much it looked like she was going to give The Dog a sip of her drink.

"It's a cross between a poodle and a Shih Tzu," Valerie said. "So sometimes we call it the ShitPu."

"That's not nice, Valerie," her mother said.

"That's his name," Valerie said.

We went upstairs to her room, where Valerie wanted to talk about boys.

"Who do you like?" Valerie asked.

But I didn't want to talk about boys anymore. It was no fun when I couldn't be honest about boys, and I couldn't be honest with anybody that summer. Not even Valerie, who would soon become my best friend, the girl I would tell everything to. But back then, at the very start, I didn't fully trust her. So when she asked, "Do you like Chris Miller? He likes you," I said, "Yeah sure. He's okay."

I looked down at my nails. I had started painting them all kinds of funky colors. Silver and then gold and then blue. I was lying all of the time now. Lying to Valerie, lying to Mom, when she said, "Hey, where's the phone?" in the morning. I always forgot to bring the phone down after talking to Billy, and Mom never knew where it was. "I'm starting to see why it had a cord!" she said. And then: "Were you on the phone last night, Sally?"

"No," I lied.

But this is the truth: Billy and I, we had watched you die together. And now, nobody understood me the way Billy did. Billy understood that my real life was over, and that his real life was over, and now we were living in some alternative universe where nothing mattered except each other. It was a strangely liberating feeling. We could say anything.

"Do you think our parents ever regret having kids?" Billy asked.

We talked a lot about our parents, like they were the villains of our lives. We talked about his friends, too, who were officially not his friends anymore—Billy had suspected this for a while, but now that he had his wires off, now that it was summer, he knew this for sure. They didn't call him, and he didn't call them. They went to the pool every day, and he didn't care. He didn't even feel like talking to them. He didn't feel like talking to anyone.

"You're talking to me," I said.

"That's different," he said. "I always want to talk to you."

"You do?"

"You're easy to talk with," he said. "But everybody else expects me to be the same person. My dad is always like, Son, just be who you always were. Then he slaps me on the back and says, Remember, you're Billy Barnes."

But Billy was like, "I'm not. I'm not Billy Barnes anymore. I don't know who I am."

Billy no longer cared about basketball. He didn't care about the summer parties and which ones were going to be the sickest, which ones were going to have the keg. He didn't care that Lisa the Lifeguard had anal on the golf course with Ryan Ronald. He didn't care about prom, either—totally skipped it—because why would he go to prom? His girlfriend was dead.

"I don't even know why anyone goes to prom, to be honest," he said. "If you really think about it, prom is just a bunch of people in a room, in nice clothes, rubbing their genitals together."

"I never thought about it that way," I said.

I had only been to one school dance before and that dance wasn't really a dance. It was more like a session of game-playing in the cafeteria. Potato sack races and scooter tag and then a short square dance before we left.

I danced with Chris Miller, who kept telling me he had warts on his hands. That they were contagious.

"Why did he keep telling me that?" I asked Billy. "I mean, wasn't he embarrassed of them?"

"Well, it's the right thing to do, I guess," Billy said. "If they're contagious."

"I guess so," I said.

"And it's not like anyone would have gone to prom with me," Billy said.

"I bet Shelby would have gone with you. Or Lisa, maybe?"

"Not even Shelby," he said. "Not even Lisa. I told you. I'm a monster now."

"You did look a bit gruesome."

"Thanks for not lying to me," he said. "Really, I mean it. It's annoying when people lie. I'm like, I know my ass is on my face now. It's okay."

I laughed. He sighed.

"Fuck," he said. "Life is weird."

"Yeah," I said. "So fucking weird."

I waited for Mom to hear me swear, waited for her to appear. To send us out to the curb with our punishment. But Mom was asleep. Mom had no idea who I was becoming late at night, on the phone, while she slept.

"Do you know the only thing that ever makes me feel better?" he said.

"What?"

"Knowing you didn't get hurt," he said. "Knowing you came out without a scratch. And thank fucking God for that."

"That's funny," I said. "That's the thing that makes me feel the worst, sometimes."

Some nights, Billy and I talked until the sun rose. I didn't care if I was tired in the morning. It was the summer. You were dead. What did I have to get up early for?

"This is crazy," Billy said. "We should get some sleep."

But then he stayed on the phone.

"You know, our eyelids are just thick enough so that they let in enough light to wake us up in the morning," he said.

"I didn't know that."

When it got really late like this, I don't even know what we talked about. We didn't even have to talk about anything in particular. Mostly, we talked about nothing. That was the most fun. He agreed.

"I like talking about nothing with you," he said. "It's my favorite subject these days. Nothing with Sally Holt."

"Is that an honors class?" I asked.

"AP," he said. "Which is good. Will get me ready for college."

"Oh," I said. I was surprised. I had forgotten all about college. "You're still going to Villanova?"

"Well yeah," he said. "They'll still let me go. I just don't get the money anymore."

He was worried about it. He knew he was behind academically. He knew the only reason he got in was for basketball. He was at least smart enough to know how stupid he was.

"You're not stupid," I said.

"Well, I'm not smart like you," he said. But he was trying to be. He wanted to be. He said I was his role model. He confessed to being impressed by me, the way I used to take notes in the kitchen those mornings, the way I seemed to give myself over to my studies. "I want to be more like that."

He wanted a whole new life, he kept repeating. "In college, I can become anybody."

"Do you know what you want to study?" I asked.

No, he didn't know what he wanted to study. He'd just started studying, for the first time in his life, and everything was interesting to him, especially art. And poetry. He had been reading a lot of poetry lately.

"Robert Frost," he said. "It's really sad stuff. Have you ever read Robert Frost, Sally?"

That whole summer we talked on the phone, Billy and I never suggested meeting up. It was not, as Grandma used to say, in the cards. Mom and Dad never would have allowed it. And I don't even know if we would have known what to do when in the same room. So we just talked on the phone. It helped me get through the night. Helped me fall sleep. I'd wake up with the phone next to my ear, and Mom downstairs watching TV. Mom never went anywhere anymore. Didn't even drag me to the hair salon, which was fine by me, because my hair was now down to my shoulders. It had started to look nice. Softened into waves instead of frizzing around my ears.

Not that it mattered what I looked like anymore. That summer, I hardly saw anybody but Mom and Dad and the mailman. I stayed inside, where at least there was A/C. That's what Mom kept saying all summer. We may be in hell, but at least it's nice and cool in here.

"Yeah," I said.

Mom's show of choice that summer was your favorite show: *Jillian Williams*. Mom was obsessed with it. She watched it openly and did not seem to remember that just a year ago, she had punished us for watching it.

We sat there and listened to the women on TV talk about how they didn't want to have sex with their husbands anymore, all for different reasons. That was the theme of the show: Why Don't I Want Sex with My Husband?

"I just can't bear it," one of the women confessed. "What's wrong with me?"

It was the job of Jillian Williams and the TV doctor to figure it out. The doctor came out onstage and said, There's nothing wrong with you women. There's something wrong with your vaginas. There was so much, I learned, that could be wrong with a vagina. You could have a dry vagina. You could have no vagina. You could have a tense vagina that clamps shut when you least want it to. These were the reasons, the doctor explained, that many women never wanted to have sex, and he said it was okay to never want to have sex, just as it was okay to want sex all of the time. Unless you were addicted to sex, he said, and no longer enjoyed it; that was the marker of addiction, the doctor explained. When you become a slave to the thing that used to liberate you. When you pumped your body full of heroin and cried over the needle and then did it again.

"That is addiction," he said in the next segment, which was about mothers and daughters who did drugs together. "It's the addiction that keeps you from knowing you are addicted."

At four, Mom would get up, make herself a cocktail, and then begin dinner. She would turn the TV up even louder, so she could hear it from the kitchen.

"I'm seeing the letter *K*," the TV psychic said. "Does anybody have a deceased loved one whose name begins with *K*?"

Yes. A lot of people did.

I went up to our bedroom. On nights that Billy and I didn't talk—some nights, Billy fell asleep early or had to go away for a few days with his parents—I couldn't sleep. I didn't know what was keeping me up. If it was the heat of the room or the stars on our ceiling, which at some point in the night started to seem too bright. I called Billy and the phone just rang and rang. When his mother answered, I hung up right away. I was nervous. I didn't know what to do with myself. I worried Mrs. Barnes might call me back, accuse me of something, but she didn't. Our bedroom was silent. Too silent. And I knew that if Billy never called me back, I would be alone like this for the rest of my life.

So I said, "Kathy?" Just once, into the darkness. It was all I could bear. "Are you there?"

Of course, you weren't there. You were over in the cemetery where we had buried you. Why did I keep forgetting this? I stood on your bed, and I took your name off the ceiling, ripped off each star one by one, and stripped some of the paint. But I didn't care. At a certain point that summer, I just couldn't look at your name anymore.

At the end of July, Mom and I finally had to leave the house. We had a dentist appointment, which surprised me the same way it surprised me to see Dad putting on a tie to go to work a few weeks after you died.

Grief doesn't pay the bills, a thing he literally said as he looked into the mirror.

Our lives were over and yet we still had to do things like go to the dentist. We had put this cleaning off long enough, Mom said. And Mom needed a mouth guard to wear at night. She had been grinding her teeth lately, and her back tooth was starting to crack.

On our way to the dentist, Mom stopped for gas. She handed me the money and said, "Sally, would you be a dear?" and so I went inside to give the guy cash and that's when I saw him.

Your boyfriend was standing by the fridge, looking at the sodas with some girl I had never seen before. He and the girl stood there for a long time, because the girl couldn't decide on a soda. Your boyfriend was like, "What do you want?" and the girl kept saying, "I don't know. I just don't know."

The girl was torn. The girl was wearing Sketchers. The girl had a thousand bracelets on. The girl was experiencing a major problem, she said: she really liked orange soda, and she also liked grape, and Sprite was what she drank just before dance competitions, but Coke was good, too. Coke had its place in the world. Sunday mornings, that's when she always snuck a Coke with her brother.

"Hmmm, this is hard," she said again, and at this point, I almost yelled at her, the way Dad always yelled at us when we couldn't decide what ice cream flavor we wanted. Just choose! Dad said. This isn't a strategic military decision. This is ice cream, girls. And we laughed, because Dad was right. It was just ice cream. And Dad was never really angry. Dad was like the Dad in sitcoms who only got angry for laughs.

Well, I didn't yell at the girl, of course. That would have been weird. That would have been what Lydia the therapist called *acting on an impulse.* I just stood there and consoled myself with the fact that she had terrible hair, nothing at all like yours. And I'm not just saying that because you're my sister or because you're dead now. It was a fact. Determined by the end-of-the-year poll. *Kathy Holt: Best Hair,* it said in the yearbook. Priscilla showed us, and it was nice, Mom said. Very nice. Even though you were dead, your classmates still voted for you. What good classmates. They must have really loved your hair.

But this girl's hair, it was not the best. It was no waterfall. It was brown and short and ugly. It sat just above her shoulders like mine used to. It was so hair-sprayed that it hardly even moved as she leaned on her right leg, then her left leg, and then her right leg again. And it was so ridiculous how long it was taking her that I will now present it to you as a one-act play:

YOUR BOYFRIEND AND THE GIRL BUYING SODA:
A DRAMA IN TWO ACTS

The girl: I don't know why this decision is so hard for me.

Your boyfriend: Maybe we should consult an expert.

Your boyfriend: Or maybe you can blindfold me and I'll just stick out my hand and let the random hand of fate decide for us?

The girl: Good idea. I love the random hand of fate.

The girl blindfolded your boyfriend with her hands. She spun him around three times. Then your boyfriend stuck out his random hand and grabbed two sodas, and the girl laughed really hard until she realized what he chose.

The girl: Oh. Root beer. I don't actually like root beer.

Your boyfriend: That's fate, I guess. Can't fight fate.

And isn't that weird that at some point, your boyfriend was driving you toward your death, toward a tree, and we were all screaming, and we were all bloody, but now he was here, at the mini-mart, with some girl who was not you, unable to decide on a soda? And you would never drink a soda again, I realized. You were dead, buried in a field under a hundred roses, and your boyfriend was here, in the mini-mart, with another girl, surrounded by soda. By opportunity. And I could just tell by looking at them, the way they leaned into each other on the way to the cash register, that they were going to go drink their root beers and have sex somewhere. Probably in your boyfriend's car. Probably on the beach somewhere.

I could tell that kind of thing about people now. And not just because I had watched a lot of *Jillian Williams* that summer. I was fourteen now—not that I allowed anybody to celebrate my birthday this year. But even so, I felt older. Wiser. I had aged a thousand years overnight, Mom liked to say. That's what death does to a person. Death destroys people, splits them open. Reveals who we really are inside, and it's not a pretty sight. It's quite bloody, actually. And your teeth—

I'm not supposed to think about your teeth. Lydia the therapist told me not to dwell on things like that. She said it was not productive. But sometimes, I thought about your teeth. Sometimes, the sight of your bloody teeth returned to me when I least expected it, like there, in the brightly lit chip aisle of the mini-mart where your boyfriend said, "Oh hey, Sally," like I was nobody. Like he was running into a teacher from school or his mother's friend. And so I was like, "Oh, hey, Billy."

As if I didn't see him until that moment.

As if he did not have a giant scar running all the way down his cheek.

As if his ass were not on his face.

That's what I wanted to tell the girl. Did you know that his ass is on his face? But that was not a thing to say. And so we just stood there, as if all the conversation in the world had dried up like a beach just before a tidal wave. All of the beautiful words, sucked out to sea.

"Well, see you later," he said.

He left with the sodas. The door dinged, and I looked around the store, as if you might materialize, as if your love for your boyfriend was so strong it could bring you back from the dead, and I half expected it to.

But you didn't appear. And Billy walked to his car with some other girl. I was left standing alone in the mini-mart, and the guy behind the register was like, "Um, can I help you?"

"No," I said. "You can't. You really can't."

I threw up all over the floor. The guy behind the register wasn't even mad. He just sighed. Like this was always his fate. Like his life was a bad movie and he had seen the vomit coming from the very first scene. No matter what he did, he could never keep this gas station clean.

I offered to help, but he just said, No, please, like it'd be better if I just left. I paid for the gas, and some gum to get the bad taste out of my mouth. And then one of those waffles wrapped in plastic. Your favorite.

Back in the car, Mom was annoyed. "What took you so long?" she asked.

I didn't dare tell Mom about throwing up or seeing your boyfriend.

Both things would have upset her, and I didn't want to upset Mom. At the moment, Mom wasn't upset. And these were precious moments, when Mom was listening to the radio, putting on her lipstick, opening up her checkbook, or making a sandwich. It would only be a matter of seconds before she started up the car and began crying again.

"There was a line," I said.

"Were you talking to Billy in the store?" Mom said. "I saw Billy come out of the store."

"No," I said. "We didn't talk."

"He looks better," Mom said, and she did not sound pleased about this. Mom looked like this might make her cry. And maybe she would. Mom could cry while doing just about anything. She was a champion weeper. I don't know who gives out awards for this kind of thing, but Mom could win awards. I have seen her weep while vacuuming. I have seen her sob while standing in front of the microwave waiting for peas to defrost. I have seen her break down in the mailman's arms. She even cried once while eating ice cream at Sunny Daes. We had gone on your birthday, because we didn't know what else to do after Priscilla left—it felt wrong to celebrate, wrong not to celebrate—so Dad said, "How about ice cream?" as if we could replace you with an ice-cream cone, as if Mom were a child, and I'll admit that sometimes when Mom cried, she looked like our little cousin when he wanted candy, and she said, Okay, sure, in this tiny soft voice. But then she just stared at the cone and said, "Kathy used to love ice cream," and I wanted to say, "Everybody loves ice cream," but I just watched the cream drip down her hand.

That was how Mom was staring at the waffle in my hands. I opened it up, tried to eat it before it could have any effect on her, but it was no use.

"Kathy used to love those waffles," Mom said, and then she got so teary-eyed, I felt angry.

"It's just a waffle! Everybody likes these waffles," I said. "That's why they keep them up front by the register. It's not a specific thing to Kathy."

Mom looked at me.

"Sally, don't be like that," she said.

I tried not to be like that, whatever that was. I just finished the waffle while we listened to the music on the radio, which was a sad song about children getting older. Mom was always listening to sad shit like this. Gone were the days of driving through town while listening to the Beach Boys or Ace of Base or whatever song it was that you were currently obsessed with. Now, it was just:

MOM AND ME AND THE CAR: ANOTHER DRAMA IN TWO ACTS

Me: Why do you listen to such sad songs?

Mom: They're not sad, Sally. They're beautiful.

But they sounded pretty sad to me. I turned the radio off, before the song could fill up our car and destroy us. Not that silence was much better. Silence made my gum chewing very loud.

Mom: I really wish you wouldn't chew gum just before the dentist.

Me: This gum is actually recommended by dentists.

Silence again. But not even that helped, because the silence made me wish you were here. It made me want to tell you how I saw Billy flirting with the girl in the mini-mart, even though I know it would have made you jealous. Jealousy turned you mean. Jealousy turned you against me sometimes, on perfectly fun car rides to Grandma's house—Why does Sally get the front seat? I'm the older one, shouldn't I get the front seat? Jealousy made you talk shit about your very own best friend, Priscilla, when she went to faraway places on holidays with her family and sent you postcards—a perfectly nice thing for a friend to do—but you thought it was sinister. "I don't get the point of postcards," you said to me, throwing Pricilla's cards into the trash. "They basically exist just to be like, Ha ha! I am in Europe and you are not."

We were never in Europe. Always in Watch Hill, and that one time, Amish Country, which we loved. We had no complaints in Amish Country.

Remember how much we loved Amish Country?

"I wish I could be Amish," I told you, after we toured an Amish house.

"Me, too," you said.

I was fascinated that the Amish were allowed to drink Coke, and you were more interested in the coffin on display in the other room. I remember you saying, Sally, check it out, and we checked it out. A simple thing. Not a big box like the ones on TV. The corners were cut, to save space in the ground, to be economical, practical, and the insides were lined in white. Everybody gets the same coffin, the tour guide said, so nobody has to worry about what kind to choose, and we thought this was silly. How hard could it be to pick out a coffin? I asked you on the way out.

But this was actually a problem for Mom and Dad. There were so many different kinds. Some were even on sale, which upset Dad. Dad was like, Who would do that? Who would buy their daughter a casket on sale? And Mom was like, Richard, these kinds of things get very pricey. And then they stared at the coffins again. It was a surprisingly difficult decision, it felt like picking out a home for you forever. It *was* picking out a home for you forever.

This was what I mean about getting older. Once, I stood in front of a hundred coffins, and Dad said, "What do you think, Sally?" and I had no idea what made one coffin better than another, so I pointed to the shiniest one and said, "I like that coffin," and Mom got upset, because apparently we weren't supposed to say "coffin." It was "casket." Caskets were for people. Coffins were for vampires.

But whatever. How was I supposed to know that? Mom was always getting mad at me, about weird things now. For example: Why did I buy a sugary waffle just before we went to see the dentist? Mom didn't understand. Didn't that defeat the point of going to the dentist?

Me: I bought the waffle *because* we're on our way to the dentist.

Mom: You're acting like this is your last meal.

Me: Maybe it is.

It was supposed to be a joke but didn't feel like one because Mom started crying. There was only Mom now, Mom and her tears and her blinker, keeping time, as we turned onto Main Street. We passed the spot where you died, and Mom started crying so hard, she had to pull over. Right up next to the tree and the memorial of teddy bears and crucifixes. Not like you were very religious. But now it was like, poof! Kathy is dead! Fold your hands and pray for the repose of her soul.

"In the name of the Father, the Son, and the Holy Spirit," Mom said. "Amen."

Mom said a little prayer every time we passed the spot, which was nearly every day, because it was Main Street, and we had to drive on Main Street to get anywhere in our town, so we were always driving by the spot, always praying to the Lord.

By the time the prayer was over, Mom was weeping hard. Mom bent over the seat, put her hand against the steering wheel, and started howling, like her guts were being shoveled out of her, and I knew that was how death was supposed to make a person feel, like your insides were on your outsides.

But I just sat there.

"Yep. This is where it happened," I eventually said. It felt like I was in class, looking at slides of some sacred and historic site that meant nothing to me. Like Mr. Klein was pointing at the houses ancient people used to live in.

This is where the people slept.

This is where the people went to the bathroom.

This is where they ate. Just imagine.

But I couldn't.

"Mom," I said. "We're going to be late for the dentist."

"I'm sorry, Sally," Mom said, wiping her tears. "I'm really sorry you have to see your mother like this."

I nodded. I was sorry, too. But I knew it wasn't her fault. I knew nothing was worse than a mother's grief, because that's what people kept reminding me, even Mom herself, late at night when she couldn't sleep. Nothing is worse than a mother's grief, Sally, she said into her tea (Mom drank a lot of tea now), and I nodded. I agreed. It sounded profound. True. But then she said it again on the way to the bank and again on the way to the dentist, and I started to become skeptical. These are the kinds of statements teachers were always warning us about using in our papers, bold declarations that include words like *never*, or *always*, or *since the beginning of time*. Mrs. Framer said, be very suspicious of these kinds of sentences, because there are always exceptions. "Nothing is always true," Mrs. Framer said. "Which is exactly the kind of sentence I'm talking about!"

"Actually," I said. "There are more terrible things than a mother's grief."

"Oh?" Mom asked.

I told her about all the people who were drawn and quartered throughout history. Their bodies were ripped at the seams and then dragged through town on horses. Not to mention, the millions of people who died from the plague. And the Romans!

"What about the Romans?" Mom asked.

"They used to wipe their butts with shit sticks."

"I don't know what a shit stick is," Mom said. "But I don't like the sound of it."

"It's a communal stick the Romans kept in the bathhouses," I said. "Everybody used the same one. Can you even imagine?"

Mom couldn't imagine.

"You mean to tell me that everybody in the ancient world had to wipe their butts with the same stick?"

"Imagine everybody in Aldan sharing the same toilet paper."

"Sally," Mom said. "Stop it."

But I could see her begin to smile, which meant she was about to laugh in that crazy way she always laughed just after she cried. I didn't care if it was somewhat crazy. I loved Mom's laugh. I would say anything to hear it (though it was true about the shit stick).

"Well, thank God for modern plumbing," Mom said.

Mom dabbed at her eyes. Turned the car back on. No matter how upset Mom was, no matter how many of her children she buried, she would not be late to the dentist. That was just rude.

"Okay," Mom said. "Off we go."

Five hundred dollars?" Mom said, when the dentist told her how much the mouth guard would cost. "Are there any other alternatives?"

"Well," he said. "You could relax."

This was a joke, but Mom was humorless again. "Not possible," she said. Then she looked at me. "Let me think it over. You go first, Sally."

The dentist stocked the room with all of his watercolor artwork. In his paintings, green and red people were always sitting on a white rooftop drinking coffee or wine, which was even more sad, because his office was in the middle of the strip mall, right between the One Hop Pleasure Stop and the painting store Where Art and Animals Come Together.

Mom, who had been taking us here our entire lives and never once commented on the paintings, went on and on about his paintings while the dentist worked on my teeth. He poked and prodded until I bled, kept wiping the tool thing on the napkin and there'd be a streak of blood.

"You've got the light just right," Mom said, and tossed her hair off her shoulder.

Was Mom flirting with the dentist? Or did she just really like the paintings? Were they good paintings? I couldn't tell.

"Are you a painter?" the dentist asked and then wiped the tool on the napkin again. "Sally, your teeth, they keep bleeding. Are you flossing?"

I nodded. I wasn't flossing. Did anybody really floss?

"I almost went to art school once," Mom said.

"What happened?"

"I had kids," Mom said.

I knew Mom had been a teacher, but I didn't know Mom almost went to art school. Did you know this? Mom had submitted a drawing once to a contest and won a free summer of art school in Paris. She didn't go, of course, because she was pregnant with you.

"You make sacrifices," Mom said. "It's what you do."

"Okay," the dentist said. "Mom's up."

Mom climbed into the seat.

"But why'd you even apply if you were pregnant?" I asked.

Mom didn't answer. Mom opened her mouth for the dentist so he could make the mold, and her silence made my question sound more like an accusation. I got a strange feeling that I didn't really understand Mom, either. Who was this woman, opening her mouth, as the dentist filled it with plaster? This woman who wanted to fuck the president. Who gave up art school for us. Who liked the dentist's paintings. I watched her clamp down and the plaster billow out around her teeth and I worried her mouth might get cemented shut forever, like yours. I felt bad for snapping at her. I looked around at the green and red people in the paintings having the time of their lives. I felt compelled to say something about his paintings all of a sudden, maybe to remind the dentist that there was a better version of himself, or maybe a better version of myself who could one day talk confidently about art as I strolled the streets of Paris.

But the truth was, I never knew what to say about art; I was terrible in museums, stood there and looked at the statues and couldn't speak. Amazing things always dulled me into nothingness.

But it was my job, I knew, to fill the silence now. You were dead and Mom's mouth was full of plaster, and so I stared and sighed at the paintings, and said, "Well, I really like your art."

After, Mom was embarrassed, told me it was insulting to lump all the paintings together as though they were indistinct or something, like you could buy the man's art in bulk at BJ's.

"What's wrong with BJ's? We buy everything at BJ's."

"Exactly. You can buy *anything* at BJ's."

I felt sorry for all of us as we walked out and the bell above the door dinged, but not sorry enough to run back and do something about it. According to Mom, that's not being sorry at all.

"Let me see those pretty white teeth," Mom said in the car, but I wouldn't show her. I refused. It felt like bragging or something. Like, my sister's teeth are *hemorrhagic* but look how white my teeth are!

So, it was silence again, all the way back home, until Mom pulled into our driveway and locked the doors. "Who are you talking to at night, Sally?"

"Nobody," I said.

I made sure to sound angry, because that was how you always got away with lying. You sounded angry when you were lying, as if you were the one being betrayed.

But this was our new mother: She lit candles in her nightgown and prayed with Rosary beads. She was always saying something I didn't expect. She asked questions that embarrassed me: Had I been speaking with you at night?

"If you're talking to Kathy, it's okay," Mom said. "I do, too, sometimes."

"You do? What do you say?"

"I just tell her about our day. I tell her about the things I think she might want to know."

"But why?" I asked. "It's not like she can hear you."

"Of course, she can," Mom said. "Of course, she can hear me. Don't ever say a thing like that again."

It was becoming increasingly hard to predict what Dad would be doing when we got home. Once, Dad had spread out photos of you on the kitchen table and was weeping over them. But when we returned from the dentist, Dad was assessing the fridge. Dad had come to the conclusion that the fridge needed to be two inches higher.

"Why?" I asked.

"Because the fridge is too short," he said. "Look at it. It's an outrage!"

"Seems normal to me."

"Well, you're little. I'm a big man," he said. "I'm tired of having to bend down for the trays in the freezer."

"Maybe one of us should start cooking then," I said.

We cooked that night. We cleaned. Mom and Dad went to bed, and I took the phone to my room. I dialed Billy's number, and he picked up. I felt nervous as it rang, as if something might be different between us now, but it wasn't.

"Sorry if that was awkward earlier at the deli," Billy said. "I was just surprised to see you."

"I was surprised to see you, too," I said. "I couldn't really talk anyway. I was late to the dentist."

"Oh, that sucks. I hate going to the dentist," he said. "He's always poking my teeth, telling me I need to brush better, and that's why they're bleeding. And I'm like, I think they're bleeding because you keep stabbing them with tiny metal spears."

I laughed. "Yeah," I said. "That's true. Good point. That's exactly what my dentist does."

"Do we have the same dentist?"

"Dr. Kurn?"

"Yeah. I see Dr. Kurn, too."

"The painter."

"He's a painter? I didn't know Dr. Kurn painted," he said.

"All those paintings, in his office. He did those."

"No shit," your boyfriend said. He sounded really impressed. Like maybe he didn't hate the dentist after all. "Those are pretty good."

"How do you know what a good painting is?" I asked.

"I don't know," Billy said. "I think you just like it or you don't like it. I think it's as simple as that."

I pulled the bedspread over my head and pressed my mouth closer to the phone. I told him about Mom, about how she had to choose between the life of an artist in Paris or her life here, as Mom.

"I bet she thinks she made the wrong decision now," I said.

Billy told me about his mother and how unhappy she had been lately, too. She had dreams of divorcing his father—he heard them fight about it all of the time. The accident, the guilt, Billy's medical care—it had all been hard on them. His father had to re-mortgage the Tree and Garden. Worked overtime on the weekends just to pay off some of the bills, while his mother spent her weekends at the racquet club, playing tennis with people who were not Billy's father. And it all made sense even as it surprised me—it never occurred to me to feel bad for Billy's parents. But of course. Something like this was hard for everybody.

We talked for so long that night, Billy actually fell asleep. And whenever Billy fell asleep on the phone, I knew right away. Your boyfriend, he snored. I don't know if you knew this about your boyfriend, but it was kind of loud.

"Billy," I said. "Wake up!"

He woke up.

"Who were you with today?" I asked. "Who was that girl?"

The girl, your boyfriend said, was nobody. She was just some girl. From high school. From his bio class. Her name was Karen. They had dissected a frog together in May. And she was kind of funny. Kind of pretty. She seemed to like him, but he didn't know. He was still a mess. A big fucking mess.

"I just keep thinking about Kathy in the car that day," he said. "Sometimes, when I close my eyes, that's all I see."

"I know," I said. "Me, too."

Sometimes, I fell asleep on the phone, too. It was always a deep sleep, the kind I would only get when I fell asleep on our towels at the beach—I'd wake up suddenly, so confused to see the ocean. I felt as if I had traveled from very far away and had no idea where I was or who I was until you looked at me. And that's when I'd remember: You were my sister. And we were just at the beach.

"Sally," Billy said. "You fell asleep."

And then we'd just start talking again.

"You guys going anywhere this summer?" Billy asked. "I mean, other than to the dentist."

"I only ever go to the dentist," I said.

"Well, let's just say you happened to be going somewhere else besides the dentist's," he said. "Where would you go?"

"Amish Country," I said.

"Amish Country?" he said. "That's random. Amish Country freaks me out."

"Why?"

"All those buggies," he said. "They're so dark inside. I remember passing one on the road, and not being able to see the woman's face next to the man, and I remember thinking, What the fuck happens to women in those buggies?"

"I never thought about that. What do you think happens?"

"I don't know. That's what weirds me out."

"Are you going on vacation?" I asked.

Billy was going on too many vacations, actually. He was going to Disney World and then Long Island and then California to see his cousins. His mother's idea. His mother was concerned. Billy was not doing the normal things a boy was supposed to be doing at his age. He was never out with his friends. He was never in the yard playing. He was not having the best summer of his life before he went to college.

"Every day it's like, Are you depressed, Billy? I honestly think my mom would be relieved if I went to a party and got arrested for being drunk."

Billy laughed at the thought.

"So Disney World it is."

"Because it's the happiest place on earth?"

"Exactly," he said. "And do you want to know why Disney World is the happiest place on earth?"

"Because Mickey Mouse is there?"

"Because it's the sluttiest place on earth."

"That doesn't sound true to me."

"It is. Everybody who works there fucks everybody else who works there."

"That just can't be true."

"It is. My cousin, she used to work there, at Epcot. And she said it's just a bunch of people having sex all the time."

"You mean, like the characters in the costumes?"

"Everybody, she said."

We laughed, thinking about it all. Mickey Mouse having sex. Donald Duck getting to third.

"Cinderella getting a rim job," he said.

"What's a rim job?

"Oh God. I probably shouldn't tell you this."

"Tell me."

"It's when someone licks someone else's asshole."

"But why?"

"For fun."

"For fun?"

"Some people like that, I guess."

"No way," I said. "Nobody likes that!"

"I bet you even Cinderella likes that," he said.

I laughed. I didn't even realize how loud I was talking or how late it was, how we were both basically asleep, talking with our eyes closed, until Dad burst into the room.

"Who are you talking to?" Dad asked.

"Nobody," I said.

Dad knew better than to reprimand me. He was a longtime admirer of John Locke and Benjamin Franklin. Read biographies of the great American presidents every night before bed now. He believed we were all innocent until proven guilty.

So he grabbed the phone.

"Who is this?" Dad said.

I don't know what Billy said.

"Billy," he said. "I told you to never contact us again. I suggest you never call back here again, unless you want to wind up in court."

Then Dad looked at me.

"Meet me downstairs, now," he said.

We met on the white couch. There, Dad was mad. He was Mad Dad. I don't think you know this man. I didn't meet him until you died. This father yelled, so loudly, it was like his voice was coming from the center of the earth. His words like liquid magma, bubbling up and spewing all over our room.

Who knows what he said.

Something about our family.

Something about respect.

Something about Billy, being too old for me.

And I told him it wasn't like that.

But Dad insisted that it was always like that.

I reminded him that Billy was just your boyfriend, but he didn't understand.

He just looked at me, and said, "Sally, your sister doesn't have a boyfriend anymore."

It was the worst thing he could have said. It made me start to cry, harder than I cried when we buried you in St. Martin's field, or when Mom finally pulled the sheets from your bed, because even then, I didn't understand what it meant for you to be dead. I didn't understand that everything you had, everything we shared, would just disappear.

"Billy has nothing to do with us anymore," Dad said.

He was right. Billy was going to go off to college in the fall to study poetry and art, and you were going to stay buried in the dirt. Billy was going to move into his dorm and meet new people and make a whole new life for himself, while you were going to rot. You were going to still be in that casket, and the thought made me cry so hard that Dad stopped yelling. Dad put his arm around me, tried to calm me down, but it was too late. I was too upset. I was heaving, near hyperventilation, when it happened again: I threw up all over the white couch.

"Oh no," I said, looking at the vomit drip down the beautiful fabric. "The white couch."

"Don't worry about the couch," Dad said, going to get the towels. "The couch will be just fine. The couch doesn't even know what happened to it."

But Mom did. Mom came in the room.

"Sally, did something happen to the couch?" Mom said. "Did you vomit on the couch?"

Mom got the club soda and some paper towels. She started scrubbing the couch. Took some bleach to it. Then started apologizing to the couch about the state of the couch.

"What a crazy woman I was," she said, "thinking I could have two kids and a white couch."

At the end of summer, cats started to appear at our back door at night. Or maybe I was so lonely that I just started to notice them. Either way, it was hard to know what to make of them.

"It must mean something," Mom said.

Dad agreed.

"It means they're hungry," he said, but of course this was not what Mom meant. Mom fed the cats, which she was not supposed to do, because the cats could have rabies or ticks. The cats could kill us—Dad was very afraid of this happening, of us dying from some stupid avoidable thing, and I suppose that was his job.

But I liked them. I liked stepping onto the deck, feeling the cats curl around my legs.

"Get!" Dad said. He came out with a broom like he was some old witch. "Get out of here."

The cats scattered and Dad sat down on his porch chair.

Dad was still angry at me, it seemed. He was angry for the rest of the year like this. Angry at taxes, angry at the shows about sex on TV, angry at the doctors who weren't making Mom happier, angry that I left my sneakers at the top of the stairs where anybody could trip over them and break a leg or worse. Dad got so angry about my carelessness, my messy room, which he described as a danger to us all. It gave him heart palpitations to see me run around corners in socks, and if I fell down the stairs one more time, he quasi-jokingly threatened to put me through his summer safety school.

"Being safe," he explained to me, "requires eliminating all the potential for risk."

Being safe requires keeping your eye always on task; it requires you to think ahead and be organized and pay attention to where all of your tools are, because when you are a thousand feet in the air on a cell phone tower and your hammer is falling to the ground, well, that's no good. People die because of that, he said.

Dad taught men how to see the bad things before they happened: To look at a table and see the four sharp corners that any small child could run into. To look out at the deck and see the nail sticking out of the wood and the black ice on the driveway before it formed. Dad could see all of this, and you'd think this kind of thing would make a person a hero, but it didn't. When nothing bad happened, nobody even noticed. When nothing bad happened, it was just an ordinary day. Sometimes, when Dad was yelling his loudest at me, this was what he seemed to be saying: Do you people know how many ordinary days I've provided for you?

But Dad would never say this. Dad just looked out at the yard. The stone wall that lined the property. The three maple trees.

"Those trees need to be cut down, don't you think, Sally?" he said.

"Yeah," I said, because it felt important to agree.

"At the very least, I should cut off some of the branches," he said.

The next day, Dad went to Home Depot to get a ladder and a chain saw. But instead, he came back with a red leather chair and plopped it down in the living room next to the white couch. He sat and slept in it so much, I started to call it the Man Chair in my head, because Dad was a man and that was where he lived now.

A t night, when I couldn't sleep, I tried to think of the good times. That's what Lydia the therapist suggested. Don't think about your sister's teeth. Think about the good times. Maybe make a list of all the good times?

That time we boogie-boarded in Rhode Island.

That time we had to say "fuck" outside on the curb.

That time we drank an entire bottle of Mountain Dew at the ocean. Laughed so hard, spit the Mountain Dew out into the water.

But eventually, I thought of Billy. I wondered what he was doing. I wondered if I should call him. It was very hard not to call him. Even harder imagining him at Disney World, on roller coasters, his mouth wide open as he laughed. On the worst of nights, I could see him so clearly, having sex with all the Disney princesses. Giving a rim job to Cinderella. By the end of summer, I could even picture her asshole, lined with fairy dust.

"I can't sleep," I said to Mom.

Mom patted the bed and I curled up next to her. Dad was always sleeping downstairs on the Man Chair, and Mom was always eating clementines in bed.

"Good," she said. "I don't trust sound sleepers."

I got in bed.

"Your father," she said. "I don't know how he does it. He just passes out on that chair. I don't know how anybody can sleep on a chair. But he does. He's just like, Goodbye, world! It's sick! Really."

I slept a lot in Mom's bedroom after that. I liked it in there. Mom hung fancy golden curtains and had someone paint flowers on her wall. She peeled oranges and watched TV and stroked my hair while we listened to the news, which was usually about the president. The president was getting impeached not because of his blow job, but because he lied about his blow job. That seemed to be the consensus: if he had just been honest about the blow job from the very beginning—if he had raised his hand in court and swore that yes, I was the recipient of said blow job, people wouldn't be so angry. Some people would have even been proud of him. And it should have been embarrassing to be sitting there with Mom learning details about the president's official White House blow job, but it wasn't.

"The world is a very strange place, Sally," Mom said.

"I know," I said.

Things Dad said at dinner in August:

Did you know that Lewis and Clark had to build their own canoes when they were *already on* their expedition? Can you imagine?

Did you know that John Adams and Thomas Jefferson died on the same exact day? July 4, 1826!

"Richard, please," Mom said, as if it was rude to talk about America during dinner.

But America was something to talk about. Mom rarely talked about anything but you, and then she started to cry, which was awkward. It was awkward to eat potatoes and listen to someone cry. To swallow and think, Hmm, this is a good potato, while your mother is weeping.

"What'd they die of?" I asked.

Mom got up, started putting the dishes in the sink. She washed them by hand. She insisted the dishwasher was broken, and Dad insisted he fixed it, and I didn't know how they could disagree on something like that, but they did.

"Who knows?" Dad said. "Could have been a million things."

"*Richard*, stop," Mom said, and that was that.

I started to take long baths after dinner. I began a quest to become hairless. I plucked the hairs all over my body and used a waxing strip on my armpit, but all it did was strip bits of skin off.

"Ow!" I said, and thought of how hard it must have been for Lewis and Clark to make a canoe in the middle of nowhere. I pulled another strip off, and Mom walked in.

"Mom!" I said. "I'm half-naked!"

"Oh, who cares, I'm your mother," Mom said. "I know what you look like fully naked." Which is the worst thing any mother can say to a child. I didn't want to know that Mom could picture me naked any time she wanted.

"What are you doing to yourself?" Mom asked.

I didn't know.

So I stopped taking baths and starting writing stories at my desk. The first one was about a girl who stayed in her bathtub for too long. She wrinkled so much that everyone in her house thought she aged eighty years. She started to go on elderly adventures. She discovered she was good at Bingo and made a lot of nut rolls. But then the bath wore off and she de-wrinkled and returned to being young again, with a newfound appreciation for the elderly.

"This is good," Mom said, after I read it at dinner.

"This is very good," Dad said. "A nice lesson at the end."

"I think I'll dedicate it to Grandma," I said.

When it stormed, I wrote a story about a hurricane sweeping away a farm girl into a river, where she was happy, because there she could cry as hard as she wanted. There, in the river, nobody noticed. In the river, she was surrounded by tears. But then the tears kept filling up the river and the river flooded the town until the whole world was underwater.

"You could try scaling down the drama a bit," Dad suggested, after I read it aloud at dinner. "Why don't you try seeing what happens to the girl when she *returns* to the farm after the giant flood. Now *that's* interesting."

"And why don't you call Valerie?" Mom said.

"She's still at Disney," I said.

"What about Priscilla?" Mom said.

"Priscilla was Kathy's friend," I remind her. "And Kathy is dead."

By the end of summer, I had written so many stories about girls returning to the ruins of their homes, I knew what I wanted to be when I grew up.

"I want to be a Victorian novelist," I announced at dinner. I wanted to be like Thomas Hardy.

"Not to be discouraging," Dad said, "but the Victorians are dead."

Of course. Everybody was dead.

"You can be a regular novelist though," Mom said. "A living one."

"Unfortunately," Dad said, "that kind doesn't make as much money."

Mom must have called Priscilla, because why else would Priscilla have called me? She wanted to know if I wanted to come hang out with everybody at the Aldan Day Carnival at the end of August. I didn't ask who "everybody" was. I knew better than that.

"Can I invite someone?" I asked.

"Of course," Priscilla said. "Invite anybody you want. Everybody's going."

When I invited Valerie, she was impressed. "To the carnival, with Priscilla?" she asked. "But isn't Priscilla a senior?"

"Yes," I said.

Valerie was excited. She had heard things about the carnival. "Like what?" I asked.

"Like people go to the carnival to make out," she said.

"Make out with whom?" I asked.

Valerie laughed. "Make out with *whom*," she repeated. "Only you would say that, Sally."

"It's how you say it," I said. "Everybody should say it like that."

"The point is, you can make out with anybody you want," Valerie said. "I don't think it matters. I think the point is just to make out."

"But how do you make out at the carnival? Aren't there a lot of people there?"

"Exactly," Valerie said. "I don't know about you, but I plan on making out with a person."

"Right," I agreed. I laughed. "People. No squirrels."

"You can even sleep over after," Valerie said. "My mom said it was okay."

I told Mom about the carnival and the sleepover and she was thrilled. She deemed it My First Big Outing of the Summer, which made me suddenly not want to go.

But I was going. "Get in the car," she said. She drove me to Valerie's herself. When she pulled into the driveway, I could tell she wanted to come with me. I could see how Mom wanted everything to be different. Mom wanted to be a young girl again. Start her life over. Choose Paris.

But she couldn't.

She chose us and now she was stuck. Stuck in the house like those Greek women in the attics. (That's what Mr. Klein had said—that the Greeks may have invented democracy, but they were no heroes! They still kept their wives in the attics.) Mom was going to drive home and sit by herself and watch *Jillian Williams*.

"Be careful," Mom said. "Call me if you need anything."

By the time we pulled into Valerie's driveway, I felt as if I was going off to war, as if this was goodbye forever, as if we all knew I would not return home as the same person, or maybe I'd never return. This was what I was always worried about. When Mom left for the store, I looked at her longingly, as if she was already dead. I loved her so much, it made me want to cry sometimes.

But then Mom said, "Sally, you've got to do something with your hair," as if my hair was my own fault. She licked her thumb, pressed my hair down, tucked a piece behind my ears, and I felt like I hated her.

"Hey," Mom said. "Your ears are pierced."

I waited for her to get angry. To say something about how I defied her orders. To ask me who in God's name pierced my ears? But all she said was, "They look nice. You look really pretty, Sally," and a deep well of sadness opened up within me as I walked to Valerie's door.

D o you have any earrings I can wear?" I asked Valerie in her bedroom. I was tired of the two metal dots I had been wearing for months. Subtle enough so Mom wouldn't notice. But now that she knew, I wanted something bigger. "Anything funky?"

"You can wear these," Valerie said. Two triangle earrings that she bought in Florida. They hung downward into a point. "They're made of bone. Real bone, Sally."

I was confused. "Whose bone?"

"What do you mean, whose bone?"

"Like, human bone?"

Valerie laughed. "No! I don't know what kind of bone," she said. "But it's not human bone."

"How do you know though?"

"I don't know. Because why would someone want earrings made out of human bone?"

All she knew was that the guy who sold them to her kept saying, "Three dollars, real bone, real bone!" and she thought it sounded like a good deal. Like that might be pretty cheap for bone. But now, she admitted, it sounded weird.

"I don't know what kind of bone they are." She shrugged, and so I shrugged and put them in anyway. I leaned close to the mirror the way you always did when you got ready to leave the house, and thought of how you once told me there were only two kinds of faces in this world: hearts and ovals.

"Did you know that my sister's face used to be shaped like a heart?" I asked Valerie.

She didn't. "Is mine a heart?"

"No. You're an oval."

Valerie looked disappointed, the way I had been when you announced that God had made me an oval. "Why can't I be a heart?"

"Because God didn't make you that way, I guess."

"But that's stupid. Why wouldn't God just make everybody a heart?"

A good question, one I hadn't thought to ask you at the time. "I guess that's not how God does things."

When the earrings were in, I looked at myself in the mirror and smiled.

"They look cool," Valerie said. "Bone really works for you."

We laughed.

We were ready.

We walked downstairs, through the kitchen, and out the door. We passed Valerie's ShitPu. The dog barked at us as we walked down the street. As if he were trying to warn the world about us. Or maybe he just thought we were strangers, unrecognizable with all that makeup, and our jean shorts, now split up the seams. It felt better that way.

It wasn't a long walk to the high school. But longer than Valerie had made it sound on the phone. I secretly understood why her mother kept insisting on dropping us off at the carnival. It's no big deal, Mrs. Mitt said, we're happy to drop you off, but it seemed weirdly important to Valerie that no one's parents dropped us off, important that we were not caught sliding out the dark minivan of our mother's love.

We were teenagers now, and we preferred, when given the opportunity, to suffer.

We walked in silence down Main Street. We passed the mini-mart. Bill's Tree and Garden. The abandoned parking lot. The tree that

killed you. We didn't say a word until I saw the empty brick buildings called "Professional Buildings," which always made us laugh,
because whenever we saw them, you said, "They must be really good
at being buildings," and I said, "They're the best."

But when I said it to Valerie, it sounded wrong, not funny for some
reason, and we both pretended that I hadn't said it. We walked in
silence again until we approached the high school.

"Wait," Valerie said. "We can't go in looking like this."

What did we look like?

We looked like girls in blue jeans and striped shirts. Valerie passed
me a tube of lipstick. A green tube. Clinique. We put it on. We drew
circles around our mouths.

"We're here!" Valerie said.

We walked up to the entrance. It cost ten bucks to get into the carnival. Funny how we could walk onto this field at all points of the year
for free, but for three days in August, someone tied orange CAUTION
tape to two trees, and suddenly we had to pay to cross the line.

Inside, the carnival was not as full of people making out as Valerie
led me to believe. Some rock band was on a stage, apologizing,
asking the audience to please understand how everything sounds so
much better at night and under really dramatic lighting. I understood. I was no good in this light. I couldn't believe Valerie would
consider making out with someone at four in the afternoon.

"Where are we meeting Priscilla?" Valerie asked.

"She didn't say," I said.

I looked around the carnival for Priscilla, but I didn't see anybody I
knew, even though everybody looked familiar in some way. Who were
all these people? And how were we going to make out with them?

I didn't know.

"Want to go on the Ferris wheel?" I asked.

"No," Valerie said, and we immediately agreed that we both hated the Ferris wheel. It was too slow. Made us feel like we should be having a really meaningful conversation or getting engaged at the top. So we went on the Slingshot, which I loved. I loved the feeling of being flung into the air and dropping so fast that we left ourselves behind.

We passed by the simple games: Keep-A-Critter, Touch-a-Duck. Guess-How-Much-You-Weigh! We considered guessing our weight, but Valerie said, "How is that a game? Why would anybody pay a dollar to find out how much they weigh? I already *know* how much I weigh."

Valerie's mother weighed her every day. And Valerie weighed too much, apparently. She was getting put on Weight Watchers when school started. She bought Big League Chew and dangled it dramatically over her mouth, right before she bit. Then, she looked down and said, "Hey! Rick Stevenson."

Rick was working at one of the game booths.

"What are you doing here?" Valerie asked him.

"I have to be here," Rick said.

Rick said all the high school sports teams were volunteering to work the rides—for charity.

"Since when are you on the high school basketball team?" I asked.

"Since last week," he said.

"So, what is this booth?" Valerie asked.

Rick shrugged. He barely knew. Behind him was a giant cardboard school bus with the windows cut out. Valerie leaned on the counter of the booth toward Rick. "Just throw that ball in one of the holes," he said.

"How's that any fun?" Valerie asked.

"You'll find out once you throw the ball through a hole," Rick said.

Valerie picked up a white ball on the counter and threw it through one of the giant holes cut out of the bus.

"Welp," Rick said. "That's a dollar."

"A dollar?" I asked. We looked at each other. No way were we giving Rick a dollar for that.

"Run!" Valerie said.

We sprinted away before paying, and exploded into one giant laugh, because that was the only way we knew how to laugh. We held our stomachs and crumbled against the popcorn machine and waited for Rick to chase after us and demand the dollar, but he didn't. Rick didn't care, either. The money from the carnival was only going to us, anyway. To be used to build a new computer room at the high school, Valerie explained.

"And what do we really need computers for at school?" Valerie asked.

I had no idea. All we ever did in computer class was type out our name and then play *Oregon Trail*. We had spent a lot of time trying to get our wagons across some river, but I never could. The river was always too big. The water too strong. Someone always died, each time a different girl with a name that Valerie and I had spent way too much time choosing.

We began to wander through the booths again, where it was loud. That's what I liked most about the carnival, I decided. There was no pressure to speak and fill the silence like there was at dinner with Mom and Dad. Here, there were so many noises: sirens and whistles and children screaming for things. Valerie and I watched in total silence as an elderly man got dunked in a tub of water. As a goat stood on top of a horse. As a woman in a cowboy hat sang a song about broken hearts. Then, we ate fried dough and watched the people swinging around and around on the swings.

"Where's Priscilla?" Valerie asked.

I didn't know.

"But oh my God, look," I said. "There's Mr. Klein."

I couldn't bear to watch, but we did. There he was. Mr. Klein, alone on the swings. A fate I wouldn't wish upon my greatest enemy, if I had such things. We watched and marveled as his jowls set into orbit.

"Come on," I said, "Let's keep walking," as if it were indecent, like staring at a wreck on the side of the road.

The sun began to set and the heat at the carnival grew. I started seeing more people I knew. Peter and his sister. Our math teacher. But no Priscilla. And no Billy—not like I expected to see him there. I had no idea where Billy was by that point in August.

I could tell Valerie was getting bored with the carnival by the way she looked at her pink watch that hadn't told the time in three years. She didn't care; she liked the way the leather straps had browned on the edges, like it was slowly becoming a part of her. And suddenly, there was Priscilla.

"Hey, there's Priscilla," I said.

She was walking toward us with a bunch of girls I didn't recognize. I wondered if they knew you well, if they had come to your funeral, if they wept over your casket. But, I admit, it was hard to picture them being sad as they shared a giant stick of cotton candy. Not even Priscilla looked sad at the carnival. She smiled as soon as she saw me.

"Sally, oh my goodness, so nice to see you!" Priscilla said.

She hugged us, as if we were her long-lost relatives.

"Come with us," Priscilla said. "We're going to go on the Hurricane. It's the best ride here."

At the Hurricane, the girls started to pair off, which was a problem, because there were seven of us. We all knew a person was going to be shaved off, left to stand and wait alone, and I knew it was going to be Valerie, because nobody knew Valerie. So, I said, Valerie, why don't you go on the ride with Priscilla, and for some reason, I was surprised when she did. I was left just standing there on the grass, and that's when I heard him.

"Hey, Sally."

I didn't have to turn around to know it was Billy. But I turned around and I saw him, sitting in the ride's operating booth. He was wearing a baseball hat, so I couldn't really see his scars. All I could see was a giant lip ring, a silver band on the left side of his mouth. It looked odd, not at all like something Billy would want on his face. But there it was, shining in the sun.

"You work here?" I asked.

"Volunteering," he said.

"But you're not on the basketball team anymore," I said.

"Oh," he said. "Sometimes, I think I'll always be on the basketball team."

"What does that mean?" I asked.

"Why don't you come in here," he said. "Sit with me for a second." It was quiet in the booth, but Billy didn't seem to notice.

"So, how's the job?" I asked.

The question felt wrong and made Billy smile for some reason.

"Pretty riveting," he said. He told me that the most exciting part about the job was hearing the metal hit against metal. "Cah-lick-ah."

I could see inside his mouth when he did this.

"The rest of the job," he said, "is me moving my fingers on this thing right here."

"Oh," I said. I imagined what I'd say to someone else. To Dad. "That's very interesting."

"Is it?" he said. "I was really just joking."

I wish I hadn't come in there, in this tiny booth, where there wasn't really enough room for both of us. It was hard to talk to any boy, let alone Billy in sunglasses. I didn't have access to his eyes. He was completely unknowable. I made a mental note to start wearing sunglasses more.

"Want to do it?" he asked.

I stopped breathing for a moment. "Do what?"

"Run the ride," he said.

"Oh," I said. I didn't want to run the ride. Could he really be asking me this question? If we were on the ride, I wouldn't want me running it, either. What do I know about running a carnival ride? "It doesn't feel right. I mean, I don't know how."

"Suit yourself," he said.

The light left his face. I made a mistake. I suddenly felt awkward, the way I used to feel in our kitchen before school when there was nothing for Billy and me to say. I should have said yes. I should be more open to things now, ready for anything. Like a Green Person.

"Well, is it safe?" I asked.

He smiled.

"Yeah," he said. "A baby could do it."

I put my hand on the stick. Billy smiled, like he was proud of me.

"Yeah, like that," he said. "But don't start the ride until the doors are locked."

He put his hand over mine. This was a first of many. The first time I ever broke the law. The first time Billy had ever touched my hand. I breathed my first deep breath of the afternoon. Of maybe my entire life.

"All right, now," he said. "Here we go."

He gave the guy the thumbs-up from afar. He hit a button that said On.

"I'll get them in the air for you," he said, "but once they're there, it's all yours."

I watched as he lifted the cages in the air and that's when the screaming started. Or the laughing. From far away, it was hard to tell if the people on the ride were terrified or having the time of their lives or both.

"Are they okay?" I asked.

"They're just laughing," he said. "That's what laughing looks like from far away."

"It looks kind of weird. Sort of demonic."

I started noticing specific people on the ride, people we knew. Mr. Beers, the high school principal. The librarian. Valerie and Priscilla. But soon, everyone else was just whirls of ponytails. A red Slurpee flew out. The ride went faster and faster, and I couldn't believe I was the one running it.

"This is fun!" I said, and laughed.

I was in charge of all these lives. I don't think I had ever been in charge of anything before that moment. And it was an amazing feeling.

"You really don't even have to move it much," he said. "Just go around in little circles like this and don't stop."

"Okay."

"Now, we've got to lower it," Billy said. "Slowly get them all to the ground."

I watched as the cages descended until they hit the grass. Billy and I, we had accomplished something together. And your friends looked so small on the other side of the ride, suddenly seemed so irrelevant to me and Billy.

Me and Billy.

But then people got off the ride, and Priscilla and the girls started running back to us in the booth. That's when I recognized her: the girl from the mini-mart—the girl with the brown triangle of hair. Karen. She looked at me, and then at Billy, and then back at me.

"Who are you?" Karen asked, like I had taken her place.

"Oh," Billy said. "This is Sally. Kathy Holt's sister."

"Oh, I'm so sorry about what happened to your sister, Sally," Karen said. "We all really miss her."

"Yeah," I said.

Billy rested back in the seat, and I watched as he put his hands behind his head. Jealousy was dark, made everything look like night instead of day, the view became narrow and finite and so focused on one particular thing: your boyfriend's face. His arms. His chin.

"Did you show her the trick?" Karen asked.

"What trick?" I asked.

A gnat stuck to her sweaty cheek like fly paper. "If you hold the stick just right," Karen said, "if you jam it at the right time, you can make all the girls' tits fall out."

"Oh," I said.

"*Karen*," Billy said. He looked horrified. "She's little. Don't teach her that."

But I wasn't little, I wanted to scream. I was fourteen!

"Let me try this now," Karen said, and scooted me out of the booth so she could sit down and Billy didn't stop her.

I got out of the booth. I didn't look back to see Karen sit on Billy's lap. I walked away fast, passed the American Diabetes booth, where a woman was licking cotton candy. The Breast Cancer Association, where they were selling lollipops. I stopped in front of a booth that sold hamsters for ninety-nine cents.

"What's *wrong*?" Valerie asked, catching up.

"Ninety-nine cents?" I asked. "Hamsters are only ninety-nine cents?"

"We could get a hundred!"

I had no idea hamsters were this cheap. Why this should surprise me, I'm not sure, why this should affect me, I did not know. Ninety-nine cents.

"A fish, yeah, a hermit crab, okay, but a hamster?" I said.

The more I said it, the sadder it sounded.

"It's less than a hamburger at McDonald's," Valerie said.

"Cheaper than a pack of gum," I said.

"A pencil costs more."

I wanted to keel over and cry on the street. But I peered through the cages. The hamsters looked at me through the wires, sniffing, woodchips dotting their fur. They were not even trying to escape. It's like they knew they were worth nothing. Like they agreed to this price.

"Come on," Priscilla said, when she found me. "We're meeting some boys in the field."

N otice how I didn't even ask, "What boys?" I just went. Because that was how you became a Girl Who Meets Boys in the Field.

That's how you go from one thing to another thing. I don't know why I thought it was going to be so hard. I don't know why it seemed so magical when you did it. In reality, when you're actually on the field, there wasn't much to it at all. It was as easy as breathing.

The boys were all around us, in different T-shirts, but the same exact T-shirt. T-shirts proudly proclaiming where they last went on vacation (St. John's), and what they wanted to drink (Sprite) or wherever their dad worked (Lenny's Landscaping).

"I've got booze," Priscilla said.

The bottle was clear, majestic, like something brewed under the sea. Exactly what her mother would drink. Parrot Bay. Coconut Rum. It was sickening. It was sweet. But I held on to the bottle like it was some kind of elixir.

"Is Karen Billy's new girlfriend?" I said to Priscilla.

"Yeah," Priscilla said. "They've been dating all summer."

Priscilla must have seen the sadness come over me, so she said, "Here. Drink this. Forget about them."

And I did. The rum made the night a little less everything. The heat was not so hot and the people seemed less like people, or more like the watercolor people, like I was in one of our dentist's paintings. The red and green people having the time of their lives on a field. The red and green people, dancing in circles under the stars.

"What's your name?" Sprite finally asked me. He caught me by the arm, mid-twirl.

"Sally," I said.

"Nice," Sprite said. Like, solid choice. He took my hand and twirled me around and around until I got dizzy and crashed into him. He put his arms around my waist. "So, what's your deal, Sally?"

"I don't have a deal," I said.

And then he turned his face to me, and I opened my mouth, tilted my head up, and took in his tongue.

"He used so much tongue," I told Valerie on the way back.

"Mine, too," Valerie said. "Like he was cleaning my mouth."

We laughed on the walk back to Valerie's, laughed about how kissing actually was not a big deal at all. We pressed our fingers to our lips all the way home. I kept trying to feel it, because I couldn't feel it. Maybe I was drunk. Or maybe it just didn't feel the way you had always made it out to feel. In all of your talk about kissing, you had never mentioned that it might feel like nothing. You had never described the sadness that would follow me, all the way into the bright lights of Valerie's bedroom.

Thankfully, Valerie turned on a tape recording of her dishwasher before bed.

"I hope you don't mind," Valerie said. "I'm addicted."

Valerie had recorded the sound of her own dishwasher before she went to Disney, so she could listen to it in the hotel. And I'll admit, it was nice. Easy falling asleep like that, right next to Valerie, knowing that all her mother's dishes would be clean by morning.

WATCH HILL

That winter before I graduated high school, you started haunting us.

It began in the living room, where we were gathered to watch the State of the Union.

"We last met in an hour of shock and suffering," President Bush began, and then the TV shut off.

"That was weird," Mom said, and looked at me.

It was—all the other lights in the room were still on.

"I'll go check the fuse box," Dad said, and went down to the basement.

In his absence, Mom whispered, "Do you think that was Kathy?"

"I think that was just a fuse," I said.

And it must have been. Because Dad emerged from the basement and the TV turned back on and he sat back down in the Man Chair and said, "There. It's back on."

But then, as we tried to listen to the president, a bird—a cardinal—started flying into the window. Each time, the bird hit it with such a loud smack that it startled Mom. She finally spilled her drink into her lap, and said, "Okay, *that's* Kathy! Kathy is trying to get back into the house."

Which made no sense to me. How Mom could believe the bird was you, and then just sit there, wiping the drink off her lap? I looked to Dad, but he was plopping peanuts into his mouth. Dad was just doing what Mom had always asked—he was just watching the show.

"If it's Kathy trying to get back into the house, then maybe we should open the window?" I said.

"Sally, what would we do with a bird in the house?" Mom said.

Mom stood up to make herself another cocktail. Mom drank vodka, too, now. She poured cranberry juice and seltzer in it and the ice jingled loudly every time she took a sip. Dad turned up the TV.

The state of the union was not good.

The twin towers had been attacked.

Our nation was on the brink of war.

The economy was in a recession.

Not to mention, Mom hadn't gone to the bathroom in a week and Dad had lost his job.

But Dad wasn't worried. It'd be fine, he had decreed from the depths of the Man Chair. He was going to start his own business.

In the weeks after the State of the Union, Mom went to see a psychic. She confessed this to me as we drove to the mall to get a prom dress. Prom wasn't for months, but Mom was worried about finding a dress that would fit me. So, she started the car, drove down our street, and with no shame at all, said, "Sally, I've been seeing this woman who talks to Kathy."

"You're seeing a *psychic*?" I asked.

"She actually doesn't prefer to be called a psychic," Mom said.

"What does she want to be called then?"

"Jan," Mom said.

"Jan? Why Jan?"

"Because that's her name."

She was already in our Rolodex, Mom said, the first entry under *J*. But I was confused.

"Her name is *Jan*?"

"What's wrong with Jan?" Mom said. Mom turned the corner onto Main Street. Mom drove all the way down without stopping. She no longer stopped at the site of your death anymore to say a prayer. "It's a perfectly nice name."

"I guess," I said. "Just kind of a normal name for a psychic."

It was the name of a very normal girl from *The Brady Bunch*. The name of the librarian at school.

"Well, Jan is a very normal woman."

"She doesn't sound like it."

"She has a gift," Mom said.

Jan was just a normal woman with a gift, according to Mom. Jan didn't even charge. Why charge? She had too much money already, Mom said. She and her husband were extremely wealthy—both of them lawyers who lived on the beach in Watch Hill.

"Wait, Jan lives in Watch Hill?" I asked.

"Yes," Mom said. "Her house is beautiful. Just beautiful. Right on the beach. Remember how Kathy used to love it there?"

Mom was telling me all this about Jan like it was some kind of proof. Proof that Jan really did see the dead, because why would a lawyer from Watch Hill with two honors-student daughters and a blond bob and a minivan pretend to see the dead when she obviously had so many other things to do?

"Jan knows there is a child missing," Mom said. "That's the first thing she said when I walked in. She said, There's a child missing."

I felt the hairs rise on my arm. Mom pulled into the mall parking lot.

"Of course, Jan knows," I said. "Kathy's death was in the paper for weeks!"

"Jan doesn't know our last name," Mom said. "And Kathy died five years ago, Sally. Those articles were from so long ago. And apparently she just sees Kathy, standing right next to her."

"Doesn't that scare her?" I asked.

"Why would that scare her?" Mom asked. "It's just Kathy."

Yes. But whenever I saw you in my dreams—whenever I walked into our room and found you lying on your bed, your eyes stitched shut—I woke in a panic. Ever since the State of the Union, that's what my nightmares had been like: Your dead body was always surfacing in places I didn't expect. One time, your casket was even lying in the middle of the kitchen floor.

But when I woke, in the middle of the night, there was no one to tell. You were gone. And who knows where Billy was. I hadn't talked to Billy since I saw him at the Aldan Day Carnival. He left for Villanova, and I began high school, and I never saw him again. I kept thinking I would run into him somewhere—at the carnival each summer, on the basketball court next to the town pool where the guys always played, or maybe at a party at Rick Stevenson's house, because that's where we were always partying senior year. That's where the basketball team drank their fathers' beers. And each time I went, each time I leaned against Rick's fence, took a sip of my beer, a drag of my cigarette, I looked around, as if Billy might walk in at any moment.

But he didn't come. And I didn't really smoke. Smoking was stupid—that's what I told the entire auditorium of people during the annual assemblies when I wheeled out the black lung in the glass case. I was president of Students Against Smoking senior year. Member of the school newspaper. Secretary of the Key Club. President of Latin Club, not like there was much competition for that role. Not many people in high school were interested in learning Latin, except Peter, who wanted to learn all the medical terminology for when he was a doctor. Most people didn't see the point. "Why learn a language you can never use in real life?" Valerie asked me, which is exactly what I liked about it. Finally. A language I'd never have to speak aloud. "A language that, in some sense, allows you to speak with the dead," Mr. Prim said on the first day of class, which actually did sound practical to me. You were the only person I wanted to talk to then. And the sentences we had to translate for homework became increasingly archaic over the years; they were funny to me and Peter.

"Please translate, *insidias nautae heri non tolerabas*," he said.

"Yesterday, you did not tolerate the treachery of the sailor," I said.

"Please translate, *stultus vir mala belli laudat.*"

"The dumb man praises the evils of war."

"Please translate, *populus multam pecuniam filiis Romanorum dat.*"

"You don't have to say please translate each time, Peter," I said.

"Huh?"

"You say please, like you're actually the teacher."

"I'm just being polite," Peter said.

"Fine. The people gives much money to the sons of the Romans."

"Correct," Peter said. "And why does the verb in Latin come at the very end of the sentence?"

"Because it makes it more suspenseful," I said. "Because you don't know what the subject is doing until the very end."

And then, we closed the books, and Peter and I made out on his bed. Yes, Peter. Peter was my boyfriend senior year—but I didn't call him in the middle of the night to talk about my nightmares. Peter was a student athlete. Captain of the tennis team. Homecoming king. Student body president. Vice president of Latin Club. President of the Honor Society. He had a lot to do tomorrow, Peter always said before we got off the phone at ten. He always had a lot to do tomorrow. He needed his sleep.

So, most nights, I woke up and sat alone in our room, staring up at the dark ceiling. I heard the tree branch tap against the window. I heard the creak of the radiators. I translated Roman myths into my notebook, stories about terrible things happening to nondescript girls. I stayed up so late, translating, which was ironic, because then I overslept for school. "You're late again," Mr. Prim would say—and then continued his slideshow on the ruins and excavations of ancient cities. The city of Pompeii, he said, destroyed by a sudden volcanic eruption in 79 AD. The people died fast—"Thermal shock" is how Mr. Prim described it—killed in the middle of whatever they were doing. He showed us slide after slide of the things found in the ruins—a pair of earrings, a bronze lamp, and the dead bodies, which were not really bodies, just casts of bodies. Impressions of the dead in their final positions: A couple, kissing. A child, kneeling to pray. "A complete city scene, a vision of Ancient Rome in motion, a historian's dream!" Mr. Prim said. But my nightmare.

"Seeing the dead just seems scary," I said to Mom.

"It's just Kathy, golfing," Mom said.

"Golfing?" I said. "But Kathy didn't golf."

Mom turned off the car.

"Well, I guess she golfs now," Mom said. "Jan said Kathy was swinging a golf club. She wanted Dad to know that his swing would be okay. It would get better. And how would Jan know that Dad likes to golf?"

"Everybody in Connecticut likes to golf," I said. "That's what people do here. They golf."

"Now that's just not true," Mom said. "I don't like to golf. Grandma didn't like to golf. And when was the last time you golfed, huh?"

She waited, as if I would actually answer that.

"That's what she saw, Sally. She saw a young girl swinging a golf club."

"Dad's swing is always off," I said. "And why would Kathy come back all the way from the dead only to talk about Dad's golf swing? I mean, really, who cares? She definitely didn't care."

"She liked to joke," Mom said. "Maybe she was joking. Teasing Dad. Jan said she had a silly grin on her face when she said it. Remember her silly grin?"

Mom did a "silly grin," and when I didn't laugh, she said, "See, Jan knows you're like this."

"Like what?"

"Angry. Unwilling to laugh."

"Maybe that's because I don't find this very funny," I said.

"Maybe you're just hungry."

We got food from Sbarro. Pizza and salad. And some of those garlic knots. Mom watched me eat. Mom said, "Eat, eat." Jan was worried I was not eating.

"How does Jan know if I'm eating?" I asked.

"Jan says it has something to do with a boy."

"What boy?" I asked.

"She didn't say."

"Peter?"

Mom didn't say anything.

"What's wrong with my boyfriend?"

"Sally, nothing is wrong with Peter. But you're too young for boyfriends."

"I'm almost eighteen!" I said. "Kathy was sixteen when she had her first boyfriend."

"My point exactly."

"I'm an adult," I said.

"Not yet."

"In two months, I could actually marry Peter if I wanted to."

"Do you want to marry Peter?"

"No!"

"Well, if you don't want to marry Peter, then why are you dating him?"

"I'm just saying . . ."

"What are you saying, Sally? Are you and Peter thinking about marriage?"

I started to laugh, right there, over my pizza at the food court of the mall. No, Peter and I were not thinking about marriage. Peter and I were just starting to think about different ways to touch each other. Peter was always suggesting something new—why don't you take off your pants? Why don't you spread your legs a little more? And I was the one saying, Like this? Like this?

"If I were a seventeen-year-old back in Ancient Rome, I'd have two kids by now," I told Mom.

"You sound like your father."

"Well, it's true."

"Then aren't you glad you don't live in Ancient Rome? Aren't you glad we spared you that?" Mom sighed. "You've got your whole life ahead of you."

When you start applying for college senior year, people start saying this to you a lot. Mom and Dad said it during dinner, guidance counselors said it at the end of meetings, and the doctor said it when he put a stethoscope up to my heart during my last physical. "You've got a long life ahead of you," he said, like it was good news, and it was. I had a normal heartbeat, clear lungs, a spine as straight as a pencil. There was no excuse not to start thinking about my future, so Valerie and I spent the fall visiting colleges and taking quizzes during lunch to see what we should become. A nurse. A doctor. A farmer!

"A farmer?" Valerie said, and we laughed. "No offense, but I really can't see you as a farmer."

"None taken."

But then I sent in my college application for Villanova, and felt guilty, like I was running a race that was over, stomping over your body to cross the finish line and go to Villanova.

And Peter! That felt wrong sometimes, too. We did things we shouldn't late at night on Mom's white couch. Peter put his hands up my shirt, his face in my breasts, and said, "I just want to bury my face in them and die there," and it was still funny to me that Peter (Peter!) could say these kinds of things to me now. And that I could say these kinds of things now: "I feel like that'd make for an awkward obituary. Peter Heart, age eighteen, died facedown in some girl's breasts."

"Oh, is that all you are to me?" Peter asked. "Just some girl?"

"Are you being serious?" I asked.

"I'm very serious."

But he was joking. He knew what he was to me.

"You're my boyfriend," I said, and I loved saying it. Peter loved hearing it. I was his first real girlfriend, and Peter was my first real boyfriend. But Mom didn't understand.

I pushed my pizza around the plate.

"See?" Mom said. "You aren't touching your food."

Mom was like a detective that year. Like we were on *Jillian Williams* and the theme was What Is Wrong with My Daughter?

"This isn't food," I said. "We're at the mall. And for the record, I *am* eating."

"But *what* are you eating?" Mom said. "Pizza! Oreos! Which is exactly why Jan says you should be taking vitamins."

Jan had suggested zinc. Iron. B_6. Omega-3 fatty acids.

"Is Jan a doctor, too?" I asked.

"No," Mom said. "She's just very smart."

Mom pulled out a tape recorder from her purse. Apparently, Jan let Mom record their sessions. "That's how authentic she is."

"Right," I said.

"I'll play you the tape if you don't believe me," Mom said. She held it up, put her finger on the Play button.

"No!" I shouted.

I didn't believe Mom. I didn't believe Jan. I really didn't. And yet, still, I couldn't bear to listen to it.

"We're at the *mall*," I said.

After, we went from store to store, from nice dress to nice dress—now that's very nice, Mom said, but then she tugged at the fabric. She pulled out a measuring strip from her purse and wrapped them around my boobies. That's what Mom kept calling them, as if that made them smaller.

"Sally, we're going to have to do something about your boobies," she said.

"Like what?" I asked. "Cut them off?"

Mom laughed.

"Don't be ridiculous," she said.

I looked at myself in the mirror. I thought about how surprised you'd be to see me this way.

Sally? Is that really you? Jesus. What happened to your tits?

They had grown. They were like yours now. And my hips—they

were more like Mom's than Mom's, heavy and wide like a boat. Most days, walking down the halls at school, I felt like a boat. Like everything inside the boat was real and everything outside of it was a mirage. Every time I thought I was getting close to something real, every time I saw land, and approached Peter's body, felt his hands all over me, the boat, it wasn't enough. His hands didn't change me. They didn't pierce through the walls. The walls were thick, built to keep out an entire ocean.

"Harder," I was always saying to Peter. "Bite them harder."

But Peter moved his mouth away. "That really doesn't hurt?" he asked. "I feel like I'm hurting you." He was worried. And I was worried. Because when Peter left the house, when he took his hands with him, I was alone with myself again.

"We'll just have to go somewhere else," Mom said. "Special order a dress. There's nothing here for you."

"Right," I said.

I could have told her this.

There had been other boys before Peter.

There was Alex from freshman chem with the lip ring, which was the only thing Mom could ever remember about him. But this was what I remember: He felt my tits for the first time under the bleachers after school and it felt good. It was the first time I didn't feel embarrassed about them. During the day, at school, people stared at them as if they were inappropriate, like, what was I thinking, bringing these breasts to school! Girls looked at them as I changed during gym, like I was oversharing. And in the hallways, they were always in the way. Sorry, I said, sorry when we were caught in traffic jams at the corners of the hallway. When we were all pressed up against each other, trying to get to class. Sorry my tits are so fucking big. Sorry they're full of so much tissue and fat and blood. Sorry I'm alive. But there, under the bleachers with Alex, they seemed to be the best part about me.

Then there was Jake, who taught me how to make out at the movies, who kept his wallet chained to his belt loop, something Mom didn't understand. What's he got in that wallet that's so important? Mom asked, after he dropped me off the last time.

"Money?" I asked.

"How much money does he keep in there?"

I didn't know. That wasn't a normal question to ask another person, not like Mom would understand such a thing. Mom would ask any-body anything. ("Do you have any dresses for large-chested women?" Mom asked the cashier at Macy's.)

And then, there was Peter, my first real boyfriend. I know it sounds childish to put it that way, but it's how I thought of him when he rang our doorbell for the first time senior year. I thought, *Here is my first real boyfriend, coming to have dinner with my parents like Billy.*

"Hello, Mr. and Mrs. Holt," Peter said.

Peter stood in the hallway, shaking Dad's hand.

"So, Sally tells me you're headed off to Michigan in the fall?" Dad asked.

"Yes sir," Peter said.

"Good school," Dad said.

"It is," Peter said.

"They have a great football team," Dad said.

And then it was like neither of them knew what to say.

"How's the team this year?" Dad asked.

"Which team?"

"Which team are you on again?"

So many teams.

"Track," Peter said. "And chess. And tennis."

"Oh, you play tennis?" Mom asked.

Once upon a time, before you were dead, Mom played tennis. Once upon a time, Mom put on earrings and lipstick and a white tennis skirt and drove to the town racquet club to play tennis with other women. But now, she only left the house to contact you.

"Not really," Peter said.

Then he explained: His mother was the manager at the racquet club.

"Oh," Mom said. "Really? Wow. That must be a big job."

Mom didn't seem interested, but Peter kept talking. Peter explained how he got free lessons there his whole life. I don't know why he always added that last part. It would have been better if he just said,

"Yes, I am on the tennis team." But it seemed important to Peter that everybody knew he got free lessons. That he didn't pay anybody in order to become great.

"Well, come sit," Mom said. "Dinner is ready."

That first night she met Peter, Mom was on her best behavior. She even cooked. Mom almost never cooked anymore. Mom ate a lot of Lean Cuisines. But it was nice to see her preparing the salad while Dad was outside grilling burgers. Even though I told Dad not to grill burgers. Peter was a vegetarian, something Dad refused to accept as a fact.

"No boy is a vegetarian," he said.

"But Peter is," I insisted.

Peter turned down the burger Dad had grilled (just as I warned), but Dad acted surprised. Horrified. And I could see Peter in that moment through Dad's eyes and I, too, was horrified. Was this really my boyfriend? This is the one I choose to give my only body to? The vegetarian who doesn't eat meat not because he cares about animals, but because of inflammation? That's what Peter said at dinner. He said it wasn't because he cared about animals.

"I do believe we're meant to eat them," Peter said, as if he were giving a public speech. "But I eat less meat and I feel less pain."

Mom was confused.

"But how do you get all your vitamins?"

Dad was annoyed. Dad said something about meat and cavemen and evolution and our growing brains. Dad said, "Our brains are twice as big as they used to be."

And Peter said, "Well, there are other factors."

Dad ate a big bite of burger.

Mom poured herself more wine.

I tried to float elsewhere, detach from my body like the stoics I had learned about in school.

"So, how'd you two meet?" Mom asked, as if there might be some other answer besides "school."

"We met a long time ago," I joked. "In fifth grade."

Peter once put Band-Aids over my wounded lips, remember? Peter once said, Show me your wounds.

"It's a funny story," Peter said. "Sally and I have actually been *dating* since the fifth grade."

My stomach clenched.

"Oh," Mom said. She looked confused. "Have you?"

"It's just a joke," I said.

"I asked Sally out in fifth grade," Peter said. "And she said yes."

But after, Peter and I didn't speak for years. Not even in Latin class. We mostly just translated sentences together, and then went our separate ways when the bell rang.

But then I joined the school paper senior year and started spending a lot of time interviewing Peter in the cafeteria, because Peter was always doing the most impressive thing. Peter was always thinking of quick and efficient ways he could become a hero to the other guys at school, which is why he ran for student body president: The guys wanted soda machines in the cafeteria. And now, finally, we had them. And everybody loved Peter for it. Clapped when he walked into the cafeteria during lunch. I covered the story for our school newspaper. "How'd you do it?" I asked Peter. "How'd you cut through the red tape and actually make something happen in this godforsaken place?" And Peter just looked at me, confused, like, it was easy. Like, don't you know who I am? I am the student body president. I am the president of the Honor Society. I am the homecoming king, which surprised me. I didn't expect the president of the Honor Society to be the same person as the homecoming king. One thing meant you were cool, and the other thing meant you were not.

"Is Peter Heart cool now?" I asked Valerie at lunch.

"I don't think you have to be cool to be homecoming king," she said. "I think that's just a myth."

The point is: It didn't really matter who was cool anymore. Senior year was different from all the other years in high school. Everybody started getting invited to all of the parties at Rick Stevenson's house, because who cares? As soon as senior year started, it felt like we were no longer in high school, because sometimes, on weekends, I was literally at college, visiting with Mom and Dad, walking through the halls of Villanova, with Dad going, "Oh, nice, this is nice." And Mom going, "A Catholic college? I didn't think you wanted that."

I tensed. I waited for her to accuse me of something. Waited for her to remember that Billy was a senior there. But maybe she didn't know?

"I'm a Catholic, aren't I?" I said, which seemed to satisfy her.

I admit, at first I wanted to visit Villanova because I thought I might run into Billy. I kept searching for him in every room. I kept scanning the rows of students, the rows of beards and baseball caps to see if he was among them, but he wasn't. It was just random strangers, sitting in tiny wooden desks, deeply engrossed in each other's conversations. They looked like they were talking about the meaning of life. But then I heard one girl laugh real loudly and say, "Okay, dolphins so do not gang-rape each other. That's total bullshit." I waited for the professor to yell at her, but the professor was just stacking papers on top of papers. The professor didn't care. And that's when I knew it must be okay to do things like that in college—talk about dolphin gang rape, and things like dolphin gang rape, that maybe it was even on the syllabus.

"This is where I want to go," I told Mom and Dad on the ride home.

When I returned to high school, it felt so small. All the things that had seemed so important to me before I visited Villanova were no longer important. In a year, I wouldn't even know these people. In a year, I would be in Philadelphia, talking about dolphin gang rape with bearded strangers. Valerie would be in California. Rick Stevenson would be at NYU. And who was cool and who was not cool was no longer a cool question to be asking. The only people who thought they were cool were actually no longer cool, like Lia McGree, homecoming queen.

"So you two are dating?" I asked, when I interviewed Lia and Peter for the school paper that fall.

"No," Peter said.

"*Definitely not*," Lia said. "I actually have a boyfriend. Derek Simms. Double *m*. He's in college."

"But aren't the homecoming king and queen supposed to be dating?" I said. "I thought that was a rule."

It was just a joke. But Peter and Lia both looked at each other and blushed, as if they were suddenly embarrassed to not be dating. Homecoming king and queen failures.

"We hardly know each other," Lia said.

"I mean, we're in calc together," Peter said.

Lia looked at her watch. Lia really was as beautiful as a model. I mean, she was a model. She had been signed to an agency she called John Casablancas. She had been in an L.L.Bean catalog that winter wearing a skort. But that didn't make her popular the way it would have in a movie. It just made her a little boring and somewhat deranged-seeming. It made Valerie go, "Lia's actually wearing the skort today," and then laugh.

"Are we done here?" Lia said. "I have a test."

Lia left, but Peter remained seated, as if he had expected more from the interview. As if he had blocked out an hour, which he had.

"Well, this is awkward," Peter said.

"What's awkward?" I asked.

"Should I remind you that you and I are dating?" Peter said.

"Excuse me?" I asked.

"We never broke up," Peter said. "We were going out in the fifth grade, remember?"

"I remember."

"And you never actually dumped me."

"Oh. I guess I assumed the breakup was implied," I said. "The whole not-speaking-to-each-other thing for seven years."

"Seven years?" Peter said. "That's a long time."

"I guess this is our seven-year anniversary," I said.

"A big milestone."

"I hope you got me something nice," I said, and he said, "Sadly, all I have is this pen," and so I took the pen, because I thought we were just joking around. I said, "This is an excellent pen," and I was surprised by how quickly I blushed. Surprised by how quickly I suddenly liked Peter—this was Peter, who used to ask for his Latin homework days in advance. Captain of the track and tennis teams. On his way to the University of Michigan, where he was going to be premed. All-around good guy. That's what people were always saying about Peter senior year.

Good guy. Good guy. Good guy.

But Mom and Dad didn't see it that way.

Mom and Dad didn't believe in good guys. All boyfriends were bad boyfriends. Even Peter, who parted his hair directly down the middle and hung posters of famous astronauts in his room. Peter, who was just trying to tell them a funny little story about how we met. But they didn't find it funny. They were confused.

"Wait, you've been dating for seven years?" Mom said.

I hated how this happened, how certain audiences could turn something wonderful into something humiliating. How they can make you look at someone and suddenly, for no reason, hate them.

"It's just a funny story," I said.

"Interesting," Dad said.

Dad shifted in his chair. Dad didn't say anything in response to Peter's story. And it was excruciating to live in his cold silence. Dad was very quiet now. The loudest he ever got was when the computer froze or the remote control was not where it was supposed to be.

At least Mom tried to be nice to Peter. She ate a tomato.

"That's a cute story," Mom said. "So, Sally says you want to be a doctor?"

"Why does everybody think I want to be a doctor?" Peter asked.

"Because you tell people you want to be a doctor," I said.

"Ever since 9/11, I've become very interested in politics," Peter said.

What he wanted to be now was the president of the United States. But he understood that was a long shot, so if that didn't work out, he'd shoot for senator. Of Connecticut.

"You know what they always say about the people who run for office?" Dad said, when he finally spoke. "The best people never do."

When dinner with Peter was over, Mom went upstairs to her bedroom. She put her fan on so high, she couldn't hear the rest of the house. Sometimes, Dad went out to the porch to read his book about Abraham Lincoln (he was really into Abraham Lincoln now) or eat cereal in the kitchen (Dad believed in cereal for dessert now), and Peter and I slipped into the living room to claim the white couch.

"I'm sorry about the couch," I said, as if Peter might stop liking me because of my couch. It was uncomfortable to sit on the white couch and watch as many movies as Peter and I did. But Peter didn't care.

"You know, I hear Lia McGree has an amazing couch," he said. "Maybe I should just go there."

I laughed. I swatted him.

"Is it suede? I hear it's suede."

"Of course."

At first, in those early days with Peter, we didn't touch. I didn't think it bothered him, because he took film very seriously. That's what he called it—film. And I figured he couldn't make out while watching film, the way Dad couldn't hold conversation when a golf tournament was on TV.

But eventually, he slid his hand under the blanket. He put it on my thigh. And I understood that watching the movie was not really about watching the movie. It was always about Peter touching my thigh under the blanket.

This was when Dad would walk in, of course.

"What are you kids watching?" he said, and sat in the Man Chair. He sliced an apple with a paring knife, because that was the only way you were allowed to eat fruit in the Man Chair: with a weapon.

"*Alien*," I said.

"What's it about?" Dad asked.

"An alien," I said.

Dad settled in his chair. "Does the alien have a name?"

"I don't think so," I said. "Everybody just calls it the alien."

Dad watched in silence for a bit. Until one of the aliens popped out of a woman's womb.

"These aliens are kind of dumb-looking, don't you think?" Dad said.

"What do you mean, they're dumb-looking?" Peter said.

"They just don't look like aliens are supposed to look," Dad said.

They did not look like any aliens that Dad knew.

"But how do you know what aliens are supposed to look like?" Peter asked.

"I just know," Dad said.

"But isn't that the whole point of aliens?" Peter said. "That they challenge the status quo? They make us question the incidentals of our evolutionary history?"

I felt proud of Peter. How much he knew.

Until Dad said, "Okay, why don't we just watch the movie, Peter."

So, the three of us just sat there and watched the movie, and I understood why you and Billy literally crossed the border into Rhode Island just to touch each other. But when I suggested the same to Peter, he didn't get the point of driving so far. "And I'm not really much of a beach person," he said.

After nine, TV movies always descended into madness. Like the one about the misogynistic ghost who haunted a hotel and pulled the bedsheets from only the women while they were sleeping.

"This doesn't make sense," I said. "How can the ghost turn door-knobs but then also float through walls?"

"Because it's a shitty movie," Peter said. "Anything can happen in shitty movies. That's why they're so shitty."

I loved making fun of movies with Peter. But I could tell that when Peter was done making fun of the movie, he was ready to make out. He put his hand on my thigh under the blanket, and I was like, Peter, my dad is upstairs right now reading about Abraham Lincoln, and Peter said, "What? You don't think Abraham Lincoln would approve? Is that what you're trying to tell me?"

I laughed. For the first time, I felt like maybe I loved Peter. We started to kiss, right there on Mom's white couch, with the television blaring in the background to cover up any noise we might make. Fooling around was so new to us that it trumped any other thing happening in the universe, except the informercial about dirty catheters.

Attention catheter users!

Peter and I stopped. We looked at each other. We laughed. But then he just shrugged and slid his tongue back into my mouth.

Stop using dirty catheters!

Eventually, Peter went for my pants. He unbuttoned them with one hand—something he seemed very proud of—and then slipped his hand down. Slid his fingers into me, and at first it felt strange. It felt wrong to be doing this in our house, to become the kind of girl who gets fingered on this couch, of all the couches, but it felt so good to be touched like that by another human being, I completely forgot about the couch. There was only me and Peter and our hands.

And then, footsteps.

Mom always woke up whenever we started getting serious, as if she could feel the terrible things that were happening to her couch.

We paused. Looked at each other and hung in the silence, waiting to see what would happen to us. But nothing happened. Mom just flushed the toilet and never came down.

If you or a loved one are using dirty catheters . . .

We really started to get into things. We kissed until our lips were raw. I wondered how long we were going to do this, kiss until our lips just fell off our bodies. We both wanted more, I knew. But sometimes, we were too polite. Too careful. So nervous.

I'm sorry, Peter said. Does that feel okay?

Yeah, I said. That feels okay. I mean, good.

But every night, the footsteps. We retreated to opposite sides of the couch. Peter always kept his speech for graduation on the ottoman. The student body president had to give a speech, and Peter had been working on it ever since April. Kept it close by his side so he could pick it up and pretend like that's what we were doing, just going over Peter's speech at midnight. One second he would be sucking on my tits—that's what Peter called them, too—and the next, he'd be reading from his speech so quickly and so formally, it made us laugh.

"China is an emerging super-economy and we must begin to take it seriously," Peter said.

"Good," I said, "that was very good. The best speech about China that I heard today."

"Why, thank you," Peter said. "I've only been working on it my entire life. I mean, China could crush us, just like that! Like that, Sally!!"

He snapped his fingers, and I could see in this moment what would happen to us in the fall, when he went to Michigan and I went to Villanova, and we became different people. Peter was going to major in political science and work for the government and one day try to abolish the death penalty. One day, Peter was going to sit behind a mahogany desk and sign all the bills. And who was I going to become?

The footsteps upstairs stopped. But we just returned to watching TV. China had killed the mood. We watched some terrible show about serial killers who loved their mothers too much, and we watched it in such utter silence, it disturbed me. Eventually, Peter reached over, tried to start things up again. But a woman on-screen was getting her throat slit. Her blood squirted out of her neck, and Peter slid his hand over my breasts.

"Your tits look so good in the glow of the TV," he said.

I pulled the blanket over them.

"It's late," I said. "Maybe you should go."

"But I can't go," Peter said, sliding his hand down my shirt. Removing the blanket. "I don't know who killed her yet."

"It's obviously the boyfriend," I said.

Two weeks before prom, on what would have been your twenty-first birthday, Peter and I almost had sex for the first time.

It was late in the night, and I was upset. Your birthday had been a mess, so I called Peter. I said, "Come over," and he came over. He sat on our white couch, and said, "What's wrong?" but I didn't tell him.

The whole day was too weird, and Peter was not weird. I had been suspecting this about Peter ever since he told me that the last time he ever cried was when he was eleven and watched *Field of Dreams* with his dad.

"It's very sad," Peter had explained. "But also incredibly moving. He has a catch with his dad, but his dad is dead and, oh my God, I think I might start crying just explaining the plot."

I knew, in that moment, with one single tear running down Peter's cheek, that Peter was Very Normal. And Peter came from a Very Normal Family. He was always reminding me of this, how his mother served dinner every night at six, meat and three vegetables as a side, even though she worked, and also volunteered, because the Hearts were not criers. They were doers. The first and last time he ever saw his mother cry was when she had to give him cereal for dinner that one night, because she was late coming home from decorating the gym for the eighth-grade dance.

But Mom was not Normal. Mom didn't work. Mom didn't even

have any friends anymore, and I didn't know what had happened to them. For a short while after you died, there had been this woman Wendy, an obese woman down the road who had become Mom's best friend. They used to get together and smoke weed that Wendy's brother got for them in Puerto Rico. They didn't care how it looked, two middle-aged women with joints in their mouths, in their porch chairs, facing the cruel neighborhood. We don't care! they would say, and laugh. And I didn't care, either. Because it would make them laugh, deep hearty laughs that I hadn't heard from Mom since you died. Wendy and Mom were both extremely depressed, and if there was anything that depression gave you, I learned, it was the freedom of not giving a shit.

For the whole of my sophomore year, Wendy and Mom laughed and got high and made big elaborate dinners that we feasted on all night. Those were the days. The only ones after you died that Mom seemed somewhat happy, but then Wendy joined a weight-loss program and she shrunk until we could barely see her. She rarely even said hello to Mom anymore when she walked around the neighborhood with her new husband, a sports medicine guy.

Now Mom smoked cigarettes alone on the porch. She watched TV all day in her pajamas. She only left the house to see the psychic or the dentist or to buy a cake for your twenty-first birthday.

"Let's go to the store and get cake mix for Kathy," Mom said that morning.

I didn't say what I should have. I didn't say, But Kathy is dead. And how do you think Kathy is going to eat the cake if she's dead? Because Mom knew you were dead, and it seemed cruel to remind her of this. I just got in the car. I was a dutiful daughter. It made me feel good to do things like this for Mom, after doing such bad things on her couch. I just shut up and went for the ride.

At first, the grocery store trip was fine. I liked going to the store with Mom. It seemed to be the only place where Mom seemed like Mom again. I liked watching her push the cart and reach for the things we needed.

But then we ran into someone. At the store, we always ran into someone—someone she hadn't seen for a long time. Billy's mother.

"Hello," Billy's mother said.

"Hello," Mom said.

"How are you?" Billy's mother asked, and if you were the old man with the mustache walking past us to get the peppers, you'd have no idea by her tone that her son had driven you to your death. You'd think they were just regular women, friends, standing by their grocery carts. Billy's mother, in her little white tennis skirt and alarmingly large gold earrings (how did she play tennis with such large earrings?).

"Okay, just doing a little shopping," Mom said. "I see you're doing a lot of shopping."

You should have seen Mrs. Barnes's cart. Full of so much food, as if she were bragging. I could see things that only a hungry boy liked to eat: Tang, Pop-Tarts, frozen pizzas, Gatorade. Things Billy ate. Billy loved Eggos—sometimes late at night, on the phone, Billy used to take all eight out of the package, stack them on top of each other, and then cut into them. He said it was like cutting into a couch. And did the Eggos mean that Billy was home? I couldn't imagine Mrs. Barnes ever eating Eggos. She wasn't the type—she was a woman always dressed for tennis.

I didn't ask, of course. I just looked at our cart. Tea and blueberry jam and cake mix for a dead person. Confetti cake, obviously. Because everybody, even dead people, likes confetti cake.

"Yes." Mrs. Barnes laughed. "I'm stocking up. Billy just got back from Villanova."

I tensed.

"Villanova?" Mom asked. She looked at me. In that one glance, I knew she understood.

"Yes. He just graduated," Mrs. Barnes said. "We're throwing him a little party tonight, actually."

"Oh," Mom said. "That's nice. Very nice. And how did Billy like . . . Villanova?"

"He just loved it," Mrs. Barnes said.

"Well, that's nice," Mom said. "Good for him."

"And how are you doing?" Billy's mother asked me. "You must be headed to college soon, no?"

"Yes," I said, and paused. Normally, I would have told her where I was headed, but I couldn't. "And I'm good."

"Good. Well, that's great."

"Yes, we're doing okay," Mom said.

I was impressed by Mom and her restraint.

Things Mom did not say, but could have said:

Oh, you know. I've been thinking of killing myself.

Oh, I've been thinking of smashing the mirror with my fist and dragging the pieces along my wrist.

I've been thinking of that cemetery, where we buried my daughter.

Remember how your son killed my daughter? That son you're having a party for tonight?

He drove her pretty little face straight into a tree. Enjoy your Eggos!

"I really should get going," Mrs. Barnes said. She was already faced in the direction she would soon turn, back to her life, as if looking at Mom for too long might be dangerous. As if the sorrow was contagious.

"Yes," Mom said.

"It was so nice to see you, Susan," Mrs. Barnes said. "You look well. Good to see you surviving this."

"I'm trying," Mom said.

"That's good, that's all you can do," Mrs. Barnes said. "Well, have a nice day."

She gave us each hugs. Up close, I could see she had thick foundation all over her face. I could smell the spray she used to harden her hair into place. I imagined Billy's mother, walking into the tennis club, and someone like Peter's mother, signing her in.

"Why women put on makeup just to go play tennis is beyond me," Mom said by the register.

I wanted to remind her that she used to do this. She used to wear makeup while gardening. She used to wear gold earrings to bed. But I knew enough by then to know that it was unfair to use a woman's past self against her. So we quietly paid for the groceries, and Mom kept it together until we tried loading them into the car. Mom picked up a bag, and the bottom was wet—the food broke through and onto the ground and she started to cry. The old man with the mustache, the one I had seen earlier in the store, came up and offered to help us.

That was the first weird thing, Mom said after, when we got into the car.

The second weird thing: "How many other kids do you have?" the old man asked.

"None," Mom said.

Then she corrected herself. She said, "Two. I have two daughters."

"That's right," he said. "You have two daughters."

"And why did he say that? That was strange," Mom said. "It's like the old man knew."

"Knew what?" I asked.

"He knew Kathy wanted to be included. It was like he *was* Kathy."

"You think that Kathy was the old man?" I asked.

"I think Kathy was speaking through the old man," Mom said.

I laughed. I couldn't help it.

"You heard him! He knew. He knew I had two kids."

"That just means he's probably stalking you," I said.

"Well," Mom said. "If he's stalking me, I certainly feel bad for him. It's not like I go anywhere or do anything interesting."

"That's true," I said. "Though he gets to watch a lot of good TV."

"Maybe that's why the stalker does it," Mom said.

"Right," I said. "Stalks you because he doesn't have cable."

"We've got all the good channels now," Mom said.

And we laughed, for the first time in a long time.

But then we were back at home and we made a cake and we went to the cemetery and stood over your grave, which had a full covering of grass now. Mom said, Someone should say a prayer, and Dad said, Why don't you say the prayer? And Mom said, Sally, would you like to say the prayer? And I said, I don't know any prayers, and Mom said, What do you mean, you don't know any prayers, you're the one who wants to go to a Catholic college, aren't you? And that whole time we were standing over your bones. Did you hear any of it? Did you roll your eyes? I half expected you to sit upright in the grass and say, *You guys. Stop. Please.*

But it was Dad who said something.

"Dear Lord," Dad said. "Please continue watching over our daughter Kathy."

Then Mom started crying, and this time she didn't stop. She cried all the way home and all the way through dinner, and even while she cut the cake.

"This is excellent cake," Dad said.

I agreed.

But I did not eat the cake.

"Do you not like the cake, Sally?" Mom asked.

"The cake is good," I said.

"You haven't even tried it!"

Because it felt wrong to be eating your birthday cake without you. "May I be excused?" I asked.

"Richard, did you know that Billy Barnes went to Villanova?" Mom asked.

"I did not know that," Dad said.

"What do you think about that?"

"I'm not sure I have any thoughts about it," Dad said.

"I just think it's a strange coincidence," Mom said.

Dad took a long sip of his beer. Dad was refusing to engage. "It's a great school," Dad said.

"I got a scholarship," I reminded them. "May I be excused now?"

They said yes. Mom went upstairs, defeated. Dad poured a beer and went outside. And I called Peter. The only thing that would make the day better was telling Peter about the day, but then he was on the couch, asking me what was wrong, and it didn't feel right to tell him anything about it. It wouldn't translate. And Peter had just gotten home from his cousin's baptism. Peter was the godfather.

"I just renounced Satan," he said. "And it was weird. Not like I'm into Satan. It's just weird to renounce something you don't believe in."

"I don't want to talk about Satan right now," I said. "Is that okay?"

"What do you want to do?"

I just wanted to make out. I wanted to feel Peter's hands on me.

"Let's have sex tonight," I said.

"Tonight?"

"Yes," I said. "Right now."

I wanted to fuck all over Mom's white couch. I wanted to ruin it.

We started making out. Really making out. But it wasn't enough. Sometimes, I felt this incredible itch to be closer to Peter. To kiss him, but then when I was kissing him, it wasn't enough. I wanted more.

"Touch my tits," I said to Peter.

Peter did what he was asked. But it wasn't enough. "Harder," I said.

"Like that?"

"Yes. Except harder."

I wanted Peter to grab me, make me feel something. Take me out of my life and to his dinner table, where his mother would make us dinner every night. But he unbuttoned my pants and slid them around my ankles (not off, just in case), and he touched me, the way I touched myself some nights, until it felt so good that I opened my mouth wide, pressed it into the floral pillow Grandma once stitched.

"Kathy!" Mom shouted from upstairs.

Mom was awake. The footsteps were heavy this time. Peter and I looked at each other. Peter searched for his graduation speech (where did that thing go?) and I tried pulling up my pants, but my jeans were too tight (they were always so tight then). I pulled the blanket over me. Peter sat straight against the couch, gripping the speech.

"China is an emerging super-economy," Peter said, while Mom ran down the stairs screaming.

"Kathy was here!" she shouted.

It's hard to describe Mom in this moment. Her face was red and raw with tears, but her eyes wide, like a child who had seen something amazing.

"Kathy was here!"

"What do you mean, Kathy was here?" I asked.

"Kathy was here," Mom kept saying. "Kathy was here!"

Then Dad was here, too, holding Mom's head in his lap, saying, Shhh, Susan, come on now, it was just a dream. And Mom kept saying, "No, Kathy was here." Mom was getting angry. "It was not just a dream, do not tell me it was just a dream," she said.

"Sally, go make Mom some tea," Dad said.

But my pants.

And my shirt.

It was inside out.

Holy shit.

I looked at Peter, who was almost shaking by this point. "Peter will make her some tea."

Did Peter even know how to make tea? Did Peter know where our tea was?

"I'll take care of it," Peter said, like he was already the president.

He left, and we just sat there, the three of us, listening to the commercials on TV and Peter in the kitchen, opening the cabinets. Peter seemed so random in that moment, alone in our kitchen making Mom tea, while Mom talked about you being an angel.

"If Kathy is really an angel, what did she look like?" I asked.

"Sally," Dad said. "Let your mother rest."

But Mom didn't want to rest. Mom was wired.

"Oh, she was a beautiful angel," Mom said. "Just beautiful. You know your sister. She'd be beautiful with a paper bag over her head!"

"Did she have a paper bag over her head?" I asked.

"No. Sally. Why would she have a paper bag over her head?"

I didn't know. Who knew what happened after you died? We were not allowed to talk about these things at school. We just counted up the number of all the people who died in all the wars and expressed shock and shame over how large the number was.

"She looked like Grace Kelly," Mom said.

"Grace Kelly?"

"Except with dreadlocks."

"But why would she have dreadlocks?"

"Who knows?" Mom said. "But they were these white long dreadlocks down to her knees."

I was skeptical. I couldn't imagine anyone convincing you to dye your hair white and grow dreadlocks, not even God.

"Her hair was so big, so wild," Mom said. "You know how it is. When she's not torturing it."

Mom hated when you tortured your hair. When you ironed it and brushed it and bleached it—bleached the personality right out of it, Kathy! Something you had done with Priscilla one night in the bathroom, because your hair was no longer blond toward the end, not really—it was turning darker every year, and one day, we both knew, it would be like Mom's hair.

"Enough," Dad said.

Mom started to cry again. Peter returned and handed her a cup of her tea like it was the Holy Grail.

"Careful," he said. "It's hot."

"Thank you," Mom said.

Mom drank a lot of tea. Teas that promised her things like SLEEP NOW and RELAX, but I didn't think they were working. She was never relaxed. She was never sleeping through the night. But she sipped the tea slowly, like one day it might work, like at the very least, she was still a woman who believed in things.

"It's getting late. I should probably go," Peter said, even before he looked at his watch.

I s your mom, like, okay?" Peter asked by his car, and I hated his soft tone, the way he tilted his head sideways.

"Yeah," I said. "She's fine."

I could tell that Peter thought she was not fine. Peter had never seen a mother behave like Mom, except maybe on TV.

"She's just having a hard time," I said.

I told him how Mom believed almost everything that people told her at the funeral: Yes, Kathy is an angel now. Yes, Kathy is a shooting star. Kathy is the reason the curtains mysteriously blow when the windows are closed.

"She's been seeing this psychic," I said, "who is not really a psychic."

And Peter got mad on my behalf.

"Women like that should be arrested," he said.

"That seems a bit harsh."

"Not really," he said.

Peter reminded me that it happened all the time. All throughout history, he said, false prophets have been condemned to death. And he sort of understood that now, because what is crueler, more sadistic than playing with people's fears for glory? Even worse—for money?

"Jan actually doesn't charge," I said.

But Peter frowned. "If your mom needs professional help," Peter said, "my dad knows a lot of psychiatrists."

"Thanks," I said. "But we don't believe in that stuff."

"It's not stuff," Peter said. "It's science."

Then Peter kissed me goodbye. Tongue. Always so much tongue.

"I'll call you tomorrow," Peter said.

P eter didn't call. And I refused to call him. Because if you say, I'll call you tomorrow, then you should call a person tomorrow. So I stayed up late Sunday night watching TV in bed with Mom.

Reruns of *Jillian Williams*, but I secretly knew Mom was waiting for you to return. We sat there in silence as we watched women on TV confess things.

"I have a leaky anus," a woman said. "It's been too embarrassing to admit to anyone. Which is why I haven't sought help. The stigma is literally killing me."

The audience clapped, in support, in solidarity. Many of the audience members had leaky anuses, too. The doctor asked the audience members with leaky anuses to please stand up. Half the room rose, and then they all clapped for themselves, for their anuses.

"Did you know that millions of Americans suffer from anal leakage?" the TV doctor said. "No. You probably didn't."

The doctor explained that 50 percent of all women were too embarrassed to say the word *anus*. Let's all say it together now, he chanted. Then the doctor suggested people experiencing anal leakage immediately cut out chocolate, coffee, and alcohol from their diet. If it continued, they should go see a doctor who was not him.

"Anus, anus, anus," the women said.

I looked over at Mom. Mom was wide-eyed. It alarmed me, so I looked out the window and imagined Mom's poor stalker, having to watch this with us.

"Anus, anus, anus," I said, and Mom burst into laughter. The hysterical kind that only came when she was most sad.

"Sally. You're funny," she said.

"This makes no sense," I said. "If you're too embarrassed to tell your doctor in the privacy of an appointment, why would you go on national TV to tell the world?"

"I think people do it for the community," Mom said.

"The leaky anus community?"

Mom started howling, crying so hard tears ran down her cheeks. Then she took my hand and said, "Why don't you come with me to Jan's tomorrow after school?"

"No," I said.

"We can stop and look for a prom dress after," Mom added, as if that would make it more tempting.

"I actually don't feel well," I said.

"Are you sick?"

"Maybe," I said. "Probably."

I stayed home for four days. Each morning, Mom put out milk and vitamins on a place mat, and then went back to sleep, as though her job was done for the day. But I wouldn't take them. I refused to listen to Jan. I flicked them off the counter and our new cat Bear ate them—a stray Mom had adopted two years ago. Bear ran around the room, coughing up green powder, and I laughed, and so Dad laughed, and Mom came out of her bedroom only to scold me.

"You take these vitamins now!" she said. "Your hands, they're so cold!"

This was true. My hands were cold all the time now.

"Does Jan know how cold my hands are?" I asked.

"She didn't mention it."

I spent most of those four days sleeping in our bedroom, which still very much looked like our bedroom. All of your things had hardly been touched since you died. And I almost never wore clothes from your side of the closet anymore—it felt wrong disturbing them.

But Mom kept reminding me—you need a dress, Sally! So one afternoon, while I was home sick and Mom was downstairs watching TV, I tried on your green dress, the one that you bought for Billy's Winter Dance weeks before you died. You had looked so old to me in that dress, so mature and regal standing next to Billy, and how strange that I couldn't even get it over my chest. Senior year, I was bigger—and older—than you ever were. I stuffed the dress all the way in the back of the closet so I'd never have to look at it again and went downstairs.

"I think I'm feeling better enough to go to school," I said to Mom.

By the time I returned to school on Friday, Peter liked me again. He found me between classes, and he said, "Why don't you come over to my house tonight?" and so I started going to Peter's on weekends, but Peter's house wasn't much better. Peter's mother had mounted the letters F-U-N, made from steel, above the mantle, which was something I stared at a lot while Peter and I made out on his couch. It confused me. Was the sign supposed to make everything more fun? Was it supposed to remind us to have fun, in case we forgot to have fun?

"I think she just likes the colors," Peter said.

At Peter's house, his mother was always in the other room, typing away on the computer or knitting a sock for one of Peter's sisters. She was always saying, Kids, do you want a snack? And don't get me wrong—I loved her snacks. I wanted to eat her tomato-basil soup until I died. And the banana bread. Oh God. But Peter was antsy around her. Sick of snacks. Peter thought snacks were what was wrong with America. They made us lazy. He was like, Hey, can we take Dad's car out? And we drove around until I felt sick.

"What's wrong?" Peter asked.

"I think it's the leather," I said.

"It's genuine leather," Peter said.

"I know. I don't think I like that."

"How can you not like that?"

"I just don't like it, apparently."

He parked the car in the dark empty mall parking lot. He opened the windows. He started to kiss me. He started to lift up my shirt. He said, Maybe we should get in the back seat? And I said, Why? And he said, Because I love you.

"Because you love me we should get in the back seat?"

"Sally, don't make me do this."

"Do what?"

"Tell you how much I love you."

"Why wouldn't you want to do that?"

"It's embarrassing," he said.

"I'm sorry your love for me embarrasses you."

"It's only embarrassing if you don't love me."

Did I love Peter? I didn't know. Because what was love? Was it what you had felt for Billy? Was it what I had felt for Billy? Or was that just obsession? Was that just wanting something I could never have? A desire too easily confused for love, Jillian Williams said to her guests one night—a man who only wanted to fuck his wife's sister, a woman who stalked her married boss, and a girl from Idaho who had sex with her boyfriend only once, with a condom, while she was on the pill, and somehow ended up having a baby, which she was holding for the first time on national television. I love it very much, she told Jillian Williams, but kept calling the baby *it*, which Mom said did not sound like love at all. And I remember feeling very sad for this girl who could not love the beautiful thing sitting in her arms.

"I love you, too," I finally said to Peter.

Until that point it had all been hand stuff. Under the table stuff. But that night, he laid out a blanket his mother had stitched, cloth napkins from all their old vacations. He went down on me first (that was the deal), and then I went down on him, and he let out a grunt that embarrassed me, which I knew meant he was close, too close. Please, not inside my mouth, and so I pulled away; Peter was a good boy, he put his toys back in the chest without his mother having to ask, *Plays well with others*, his first-grade teacher wrote on his report card. He went on a little red square that said NIAGARA FALLS STATE PARK and then looked up to the ceiling and sighed a big relief.

"That was really great," he said, like we had just done a workout class together.

"Yeah," I said.

Though to be honest, I thought it would feel a little better than it did; it felt good, but I had expected more. I always expected more. Maybe this was because of how you used to describe these things to me at night or maybe I had become desensitized by all those years I spent touching myself in bed with the back of a hairbrush (a tip from one of Mom's magazines); maybe I hadn't counted on the breeze through the trees that left us both a little colder. Maybe I had expected it to make me actually fall in love with Peter, that I'd look over at him and there'd be something to say, something that was absolute and necessary, something other than, *Wow, I can't believe I just sucked on your penis*, but there wasn't. It was the only thing I could think of to say, the only true conclusion to be made about the event.

"Gee," Peter said. "You really are so romantic."

We laughed, because I knew he liked this about me, how unromantic I insisted on being. Not like his sister at all, who pasted pictures of handsome movie stars from magazines in her bedroom. Peter was like, She's so boy crazy. But you're different.

"Different how?" I asked.

"Sometimes I just feel like you're the guy," he always said. Then he pulled me into him. "I've been thinking."

Peter was always thinking. Always making a plan.

"Maybe we should have sex on prom night," he said.

"Now who sounds like the guy?" I said.

When I got home, I thought Mom would be mad at me for being late, but she was in a good mood. She was always in a good mood a few days after going to Jan's, like Jan was some kind of a drug.

"Jan thinks there might be something off with your thyroid," Mom said.

"How would Jan know things about my thyroid?"

"She has a gift," Mom said.

Have you checked your daughter's thyroid? Jan asked Mom. Maybe that's why she's been so sleepy? Jan said my sudden sluggishness, my unwillingness to do anything, is a reason to see the doctor. She said that sometimes grief manifests itself on the body, that a lot of doctors see underactive thyroids after a trauma.

"That's a very specific thing for Jan to say," I said.

"Jan is very thorough."

The next morning, Mom went to the phone and scheduled an appointment for me with a doctor. I watched her write it down on the Big Calendar.

The day of prom, everybody at school acted like they were on drugs. And maybe they were. Maybe they started early in the parking lot like Peter said people might. But I was sober and felt sick all day and maybe it was because of a thyroid problem, or maybe it was because Peter kept giving me weird smiles during Latin.

"I need to go to the nurse," I finally said.

"*Latine!*" Mr. Prim said.

"*Guttur mihi dolet,*" I said. My throat hurts.

But Mr. Prim wanted to use this moment as a teaching lesson.

"Interesting. You could say that. But you could also say, *Fauces mihi dolent,*" he said to the class. "*Fauces* is strictly the back of the mouth. More commonly used for 'throat' in ancient medical writings. *Guttur* is lower down, the esophagus proper."

He looked at me.

"So what is it?"

"*Fauces,*" I said.

I went to the nurse. The nurse said she had been seeing a lot of sore throats lately. She said, "Have you ever given oral sex, Sally?"

"Huh?"

"Sometimes, we see a lot of girls with gonorrhea in their throats."

"I'm feeling much better, thanks," I said to the nurse.

* * *

Instead of going back to Latin, I went to the mall. I cut school for the second time in my life because it felt good to break through the double doors at the end of the hallway. To hit sunlight. Besides, I still didn't have a dress. Mom forgot about special ordering me one, and I didn't remind her. I didn't want to go anywhere with Mom that I didn't have to. So I drove to the mall and walked into Macy's and there, standing by a rack of men's shirts, was your boyfriend.

"Sally," he said.

"Billy," I said.

After four years of waiting to see him again, of hoping to see him around every corner, I was somehow surprised to see him. I hadn't expected it to be like this, the two of us standing there in the brightly lit world of Macy's. Me, with a glittery dress on my arm, and him, with a huge tattoo on his neck. A series of green vines crawling up to his ear. I couldn't stop looking at it.

"I know," he said. "I have a neck tattoo."

"Did it hurt?" I asked.

"That's why I got it."

"Interesting," I said, as if I understood.

"What are you doing here?" Billy asked. "Shouldn't you be at school?"

"I'm looking for a dress."

"For what?"

"Prom," I said.

"Prom," he said. "Wow."

The other changes in Billy came slowly. Like when we were little and you'd pull the prickers out of my legs and the cuts were so deep, the blood wouldn't come out right away. His face was smoother. The accident, not so visible anymore. Still there in some places, by his ear, where there was a deep, pink scar. But the rest was covered by the tattoo.

"I know, I know," I said. "I know your feelings on prom."

"I have feelings on prom?"

NOTES ON YOUR SUDDEN DISAPPEARANCE

"Yes."

"Oh. Well. What are they?"

"You said, and I quote, prom is just a place where people go to dress up really nicely and then rub their genitals together."

"That does sound like something I would have said," he said. "But now that I've lived longer, I can confidently say, I'm sure there's more to it than that."

"I don't know," I said. "I'm skeptical."

"Well, I shouldn't keep you," Billy said. "You look like you're in the middle of something important."

But it wasn't important. Not anymore. Prom seemed so stupid, standing in front of Billy. It felt as if Billy were the only thing that was real, and everything else was a fake. The mall just an elaborate set. The dress on my arm, a prop. These breasts and this long hair—part of the costume. And Billy, somehow, was the truth about my life.

"What are you doing here?" I asked.

"Looking for a nice shirt," he said.

"What do you need a nice shirt for?"

"What do I need a nice shirt for? she says. Like why would this dirtbag ever need a nice shirt."

I laughed. He did look like a dirtbag though. Between the neck tattoo and the snap-up pants and the stubble on his chin.

"I've got a job interview in a few weeks," he said. "Got to present myself as a respectable human being. Psychologically healthy, the application said."

"Hmm," I said. "I've seen my dad wear that shirt before. It's blue."

He looked around, as if somebody might be watching us.

"A good tip," he said. "I'll be on the lookout for blue."

"Do you want some help?" I asked.

"Sure," he said. He looked at my shirt. "You look like you know what you're doing. That's a pretty nice shirt."

Of course, it was. It was actually one of yours. Found it after I put the green dress back in your closet. It was too tight across the chest, according to Mom, but I didn't care. I liked it too much to ever throw it away.

B illy and I looked for nice shirts in Macy's. JCPenney. Express for men. He said, "What do you think, Sally?"

Do the sleeves fit right?

Does the collar look too tight?

Does this shirt make me look psychologically healthy or what?

Yes, that shirt is so psychologically healthy.

"I would never know," I said, "that you are secretly in love with all the Disney princesses."

He laughed. He looked at himself in the mirror. And it was all so fun. I loved the feeling of deciding these things for Billy. Of passing judgment. I felt like his mother. His sister. His lover.

"Yes," I said. "The sleeves are a little short."

"Fuck," he said. "The sleeves are always so fucking short."

Billy was bigger now.

"Still growing," he said. "Everybody at holidays, they're always like, Billy, are you getting taller? And I'm like, Ha ha ha, good one, Aunt Barbara. But now I'm like, Maybe I do have a gland disorder or something?"

"Maybe you should go to the doctor."

Finally, a lady in the store came up to him and said, "Well that's a nice shirt," and we both looked at each other and laughed.

"It's settled then," he said.

I watched him turn and look at himself in the mirror. The woman got him a tie, too, just to try on. I felt the floor open up beneath me. Your boyfriend was going to leave the mall soon. He was going to leave the mall and put on his nice shirt and get a job. And I would have to actually go to prom with Peter and live the rest of my life without either of you.

"What do you mean, you got the tattoo just because it hurt?" I asked.

"That's just what I was like in college," he said.

Billy told me that he did all kinds of fucked-up things in college to hurt himself. Drugs. Alcohol. Even lit his hand on fire once. But his body healed. His body always healed. And he didn't want it to. He couldn't stand the thought that he got to heal and you did not, so one night, he went out and marked it permanently with this tattoo.

"My mother cried for about a month," Billy said. "She said, You'll never get a real job now. And I said, Good. I don't want a real job. But you know. Time passes. And here I am, trying to get a real job."

I stared at a single red tulip growing out of a vine on his jugular.

"Well, good thing you have this nice shirt," I said.

"Good thing." He bought the shirt. We stepped into the glow of the mall hallway.

"What next?" he asked.

"What next?"

It was three in the afternoon. I was supposed to go home. I was supposed to be at Valerie's for pictures at five, because her mother had already bought the carrot snacks and the onion dip. We were going to stand on her giant stairwell and take photographs with our handsome boyfriends in tuxedos. Peter bought a flask, and we were going to drink out of it in the limo and then maybe in the bathroom and dance all night and then, after, go to Rick Stevenson's house, where he was throwing a giant party. And there, in some dark corner of Rick's house, Peter and I were supposed to have sex.

"Want a coffee?" Billy asked.

"I don't drink coffee."

"That's impressive. The only reason I'm standing up right now is coffee."

"Billy Barnes, brought to us by Folgers."

He laughed.

"Something like that," he said. "How about ice cream?"

He pointed to the Dippin' Dots.

"Sure," I said. "If you call that ice cream."

"It's ice cream of the future," he said, reading from the sign.

"Ice cream of the future," I said, holding up my cup. "But it doesn't make any sense. It's ice cream now. It's in my hand."

"Yeah, it's fucking stupid," he said, digging into his.

"I wonder what these dots from the future know," I said. "If only they could tell us."

"Maybe in the future, ice cream can talk," he said.

"Probably."

"What do you think the ice cream would say?"

"Hello, I am ice cream," I said, and we laughed harder than I expected.

"That's a bit disappointing, I got to be honest. I expected more from ice cream."

"What does the future hold?" I asked, stupidly, to the dots. I tried not to laugh again; I didn't want to be the one who was always finding things too funny, but I was. "Nobody knows! Except for maybe Jan."

"Jan?"

"Oh," I said. "My mom. She's been seeing a psychic. Well, I guess she's not really a psychic."

"What is she then?"

"My question exactly. She's a woman," I said. "With a gift."

"A gift of what?"

"Seeing dead people."

"Like the kid from *The Sixth Sense*?"

"Yes. Exactly. Except she's not a kid. She's a rich woman who lives in Watch Hill."

"So not at all like *The Sixth Sense*."

"No. She's a lawyer."

"I thought she was a psychic?"

"Not a real one," I said.

"This is confusing."

We laughed again.

"I think it's just a hobby," I said. "I don't know. Apparently, she only sees a few dead people. She's very selective. And one of them happens to be Kathy."

"She sees *Kathy*?"

"Yeah," I said. "I mean. It's crazy, of course. It's total bullshit."

But Billy looked more intrigued than skeptical. He leaned back, ate a spoonful of his ice cream from the future.

"Maybe," Billy said. "Maybe."

"You believe that stuff?"

"All I know is that I don't know what I know."

It was a nice thought.

"That's what college taught me," he said. "That I know absolutely fucking nothing."

I looked down at my cup. My ice cream of the future was gone.

"We should go see her," Billy said.

"Go see who?"

"Jan," he said.

"Jan?" I asked. "Right."

"I'm serious."

"Well, I don't know which house is hers. Her address is at home."

"Maybe we'll know," Billy said. "Maybe we're psychics, too. Maybe we'll just be driving around, and we'll feel it."

So we left the mall, walked to the parking lot, where Billy looked at me. "You drive," he said. "I insist."

I could feel the ocean before I saw it. That's always how it worked with the ocean—I could taste it as soon as I opened the car door.

It had been so long since I had been here, yet the ocean looked exactly the same. We walked up the familiar staircase and over the weathered deck and on to the sand. I looked out at the water and then at the sky beyond it. I looked as if I might see you somewhere in the distance, but the truth was, I couldn't feel you there. You seemed so small in comparison to the ocean, to the history of water.

"So, where to?" Billy asked.

"All I know is that Jan lives in a mansion along the beach," I said.

We walked along the beach for hours, pointing at different houses, trying to imagine if any of them was Jan's.

"The castle?" I said. "Nah. That doesn't seem like Jan. She's a lawyer, remember?"

He laughed. "Are lawyers not allowed to live in castles?"

"No," I said. "Not their style."

We kept walking. We kept talking. Eventually, I found myself saying things I didn't know I believed, like, "Honestly, I would never want to live in a castle."

"Why not?"

"I'd get too scared at night."

"Even with the guards that you order to stand at your door?"

"They'd be the worst part," I said. "Who are they? What are their motives? Why so many swords? I like small houses. Grapefruit spoons. Where all you need is one good dog."

I didn't really expect to find Jan's house. There were miles of beach houses, and besides, I thought we were just joking about finding Jan. I thought we were just trying to get out of the mall. And I'm glad we did, because it was nice, being back at the ocean, along the edge of the country. It felt like I was being returned to something. To an old, ancient version of myself. But then Billy stopped.

"You smell that?" he asked.

"I do."

"It smells like something dead," he said.

An awful, rotting smell. But we ignored it. Kept walking along the beach and I told Billy about our old vacations here, how Dad used to bring us to the lighthouse because it was one of the oldest lighthouses in New England. He asked us to imagine how dark it must have been before electricity, how terrifying the ocean must have seemed.

"The Ancient Greeks were sort of terrified by it," Billy said.

"You know things about the Ancient Greeks?"

"I was a philosophy major," he said. "Studied a shit ton about them. And I remember that in Greek mythology, at least, there's usually nothing on the other side of the ocean. It's usually portrayed as an uncrossable, eternal river."

"I guess I can see why," I said. "Sort of how it looks."

We paused for a moment to consider the uncrossable, eternal river.

"It's funny running into you today," Billy said.

"Why?"

"Last night, I actually had a dream about Kathy. First dream about her in years."

"You did? What about?"

"All I really remember was that I was in a black room playing the piano."

"I didn't know you played the piano."

"In my dreams, I do," he said. "So I was playing the piano, and then I looked out a window and saw Kathy dancing at the sea. She was in some kind of a tutu and it was soaking wet."

"And then what?"

"And that's pretty much the end of it. I thought nothing of it when I woke up this morning. But then I ran into you today at the mall, and I thought it was really weird to see you today, of all days. Kind of spooked me, actually."

"I've been dreaming about her, too," I said.

"What are your dreams like?"

"You really want to hear about my dreams? Dreams are boring."

That's what Peter said one night. Dreams are boring because dreams are nonsense. Just neurons firing.

"Dreams are absolutely not boring," Billy said. "Dreams are crazy. The fact that we're not constantly mystified by our own dreams is crazy to me."

"Okay, well, in this dream, I'm coming down the stairs," I said. "And

Kathy's casket is in the middle of the kitchen. But it's no big deal, because Kathy is at the table, eating breakfast before school. But then my mom comes in and she gets mad. She's like, Kathy, why'd you leave your casket in the middle of the kitchen floor! But Kathy won't do anything about it. She's just like, Calm down, Mom. So I have to move it. I go to pick it up, but it's too heavy, and then it slams back down on my foot."

"Shit," he said.

The smell was getting worse.

"What *is* that?" I asked.

"I don't know," he said. He squinted, as if he saw something up ahead in the dark. And then I saw something: A man. A shovel. He was digging something. "Look. Do you see that?"

We walked toward the man until we could see he was hacking into something with his shovel. A body.

"Billy," I said, and it was weird to call your boyfriend by his name. Weird to call him anything at all. "I think we should turn back. This is kind of weird."

But it was too late. The man saw us. He looked unfriendly until he waved.

"Hey!" he called out to us.

"Come on," your boyfriend said.

Your boyfriend was never afraid. That's what the newspapers always said about him. He's a fearless captain—trusted his body to take the team where they ought to be going.

"What are you kids doing out here so late?" the man asked.

The man was wearing big brown boots that Dad used for shoveling the driveway after it snowed.

"What are *you* doing?" Billy asked.

We all stood over what looked like a massacred animal.

"Hacking up this seal," he said. "Or what was a seal."

"Why?" your boyfriend asked.

"Had to," he said. "Got to get this thing out of here by morning.

It's stinking up the whole neighborhood. And the owners got people coming to look at this house."

I looked up to see a giant house overlooking the water. It was one of those geometric ones that didn't seem to belong to the beach. The kind you always liked. The kind you wanted to live in.

"Is this your house?" I asked.

"No," he said. The man was a real estate agent. "I just work for the couple trying to sell it."

The couple wanted to move far, far away from here, he said. Beach life wasn't what they expected. And who could blame them? Every week, they had a seal washing up on their shore, getting beached when the tide went out.

"Then the poor things just starve to death and rot," he said. "It's awful. It's got to go. Nothing says welcome to your new multimillion-dollar home like a big bloated seal carcass."

So we helped the man get rid of the seal. Your boyfriend picked up one of the big black bags as the man dumped seal parts in them. I watched and I looked at the body and I waited for it to look like a seal, waited to see if I could notice anything important inside it, any sealness, but it just looked like raw meat.

After, we each carried a bag up the long staircase to the house. We stood in the driveway and the man threw the bags in the back of his truck.

"Need a ride?" the man said.

Before we got in his car, I got a glimpse of the house number: 38 Lindell Drive. He drove us back to the parking lot, where my car waited for us.

"Thanks," the man said, then shook our hands, like we just did something great together.

"No problem," your boyfriend said.

Your boyfriend's cheeks were flushed, like a boy on Christmas morning. Like this was exactly what we had been called to the sea to do. Like maybe his dream did mean something after all.

"That was weird," Billy said, back in the car. "Very weird."

"Do you think that was Jan's house?" I asked. I was joking. But Billy shrugged.

"Maybe," he said.

My purse started to shake.

"What the fuck is happening to your purse?" Billy asked.

"It's my cell phone," I said. "It vibrates."

It spooked me, too, for a second—it was the first time my cell phone had ever rung.

"Look at you," he said. "You and your cell phone."

"A graduation gift," I said. "So they can track me."

Dad presented the phone to me as an early graduation gift that might be useful for prom night. To be used as a lifesaving tool only. A thing to pull out in case I should ever find myself being chased down a long alleyway by a murderer. But the only thing that happened on it yet was that Mom called. Mom was the only person who knew the number.

"Hi, Mom," I said.

"Where are you?" she said. "Don't you have prom tonight?"

"Tell Peter I'll call him when I get back. Tell Peter to calm down. Tell him it's only prom."

After I hung up, we were quiet for a bit, until Billy spoke.

"Your prom was tonight?" he asked.

"Yeah," I said.

"I didn't think it was tonight. Weren't you just trying to buy a dress today?"

"I was," I said. "But I couldn't find one. So it worked out."

"I'm sorry. Sorry I made you miss your prom."

I shrugged. "A wise man once said that prom is just . . ."

"A wise man indeed," he said.

"Someone give that guy a PhD."

"Will your date be mad?"

"He'll get over it."

I was less interested in Peter at the moment, and more interested in the dead seal.

"What do you think he's going to do with the body?" I asked.

"Probably bring it to the dump," your boyfriend said.

"You can do that? Just drop off a seal at the dump?" I asked.

"Yeah," your boyfriend said. "I mean, it's a dump. You can put anything there. We throw out animals all the time. Have you ever thrown out a cheeseburger? I mean, same thing really."

Your boyfriend rolled down the window. He started to smoke.

"Since when do you smoke?" I asked.

"It's been a few years now," he said. "Like I said. The whole self-destruction thing."

He lit up his stick and took in a deep breath. He didn't cough once on our way back to the mall. A pro.

"So this Peter guy," Billy said. "A good guy?"

"Yeah," I said. "Peter's a good guy."

"What's Peter like?"

"Hard to explain," I said. "He's very Peter-like."

"Ah. Peter-like. Yes. Say no more . . ."

"I don't know what to say. He's very normal. He wants to be president. He wears stripes a lot."

"That tells me nothing. All boys want to be the president. All boys wear stripes."

"You're not wearing stripes."

"Men don't wear stripes," he said. "But I used to wear stripes. All kinds of stripes."

"When you wanted to look like a boy."

"Exactly."

I laughed.

The heat was on high.

I suddenly felt bad for Peter and his stripes. I liked his stripes. So I added, "He's smart."

"You're smart," Billy said.

"I know. But he's actually smarter than me."

"You were smarter than me when you were twelve. I'd argue that nobody is smarter than you, Sally."

"I appreciate the compliment. But we have to take into consideration the fact that Bill Gates exists. Not to mention all those guys who got us to the moon."

"Yeah, pretty fucking incredible, huh?"

"Can you imagine what it's like to be an astronaut?"

"I can't imagine a less desirable job," he said.

Billy couldn't imagine surviving in a spaceship for that long. Such close quarters. I mean, how do they even have sex up there? Do they even have sex up there? And we decided that no, they couldn't have sex up there. Because what if you had sex and someone got pregnant? What would happen then?

"They have to masturbate," I said.

It was something Peter told me.

"But how?" Billy asked.

"What do you mean, how?" I asked.

How do they do it? Where does it go? Wasn't that awkward? These were our questions all the way back to the mall.

"Which car is yours?" I asked.

He pointed me to a black Ford Explorer.

"Hey, you should call me sometime on that fancy phone of yours," Billy said. He gave me his number. "If you ever have another bad dream."

"Assuming this thing really is a phone," I said.

Billy took it from my hand, held it up to the light.

"It is suspiciously small," Billy said.

"Pocket-size," I said. "For a doll, really."

He flipped it open, pretended to dial a number, and pressed it to his ear.

"Hello?" he asked. "God? Is that you?"

I laughed. I dropped the phone back in my purse.

"Well?" I asked. "Was it God?"

"Yes," he said. "But he was very busy. Said he'd call me back."

At home, I went to the Rolodex and looked up Jan's address right away. She was not hard to find. The first entry under *J*: Jan New-man, 38 Lindell Drive.

Peter was very upset on the phone," Mom said the next morning. And suddenly, she was on Peter's side. Upset on his behalf.

"I'm sorry," I said.

"He came over in his little tux," Mom said. "It was very sweet. Very sad."

"I'm sorry," I said again.

"And I didn't even know what to tell him when he asked where you were! I said, Peter, your guess is as good as mine."

I hung my head.

"That was a very mean thing you did," Mom said. "You should have called. What did we get you that phone for if you aren't going to use it?"

"I don't know," I said. "I'm sorry."

But then Dad came home with a six-pack and a carton of strawberries and all conversation about Peter stopped. Dad had just been golfing. Dad put down the beer and said, "Don't ask," not like anybody was about to ask.

We didn't have to, really.

"My swing is all off," he said. "Last week, my swing was great. This week, it's all off."

Mom raised her eyebrow at me. She wanted to tell him about Jan, and you, and how he shouldn't worry; his swing will be fine. Just fine. These were the comforts that you brought us from heaven, small and shortsighted assurances.

But she didn't say anything; she did not bring up Jan in front of Dad because she knew there was no point. Dad would never believe in Jan. Dad believed in computers, in carpets, in cell phone towers. Dad cut the strawberry stems off, put the berries in a silver bowl, and we sat there, spreading whipped cream on each one.

It was quiet for a while.

"But you know what? These strawberries are good," Dad said. "Too damn good."

"Yeah," I said. It was true. I didn't know why these things still sometimes took me by surprise.

After Mom and Dad left the room, I called Billy right away. He didn't pick up, so I left a message.

"You were right," I said. "We found it. We actually found it. Jan's house."

And then I hung up and called Peter.

"You made me miss my own prom, Sally," Peter said.

"I'm sorry," I said. "I know."

"I'm the homecoming king! I should have been there."

"You could have still gone."

"I did go," he said.

"Oh. You went?"

"I'm the homecoming king," he said. "I had to go. But that's not the point."

"What's the point? That the homecoming king shouldn't have to go to prom alone?"

"The point is you've been extremely weird lately."

"Since when have I been weird?"

He lowered his voice. "Ever since that night your mom had the psychotic episode."

"It wasn't a psychotic episode."

"Whatever it was. You've been a little distant."

"I don't know what's going on with me," I said.

And I really didn't. I was confused.

I wanted to see Peter.

Peter was my first real boyfriend.

"Do you want to come over?" I asked.

"Why don't you come here?" Peter asked.

By the time I got to Peter's, he had forgiven me. Mostly because he wanted to complain about how much prom sucked. Prom was actually a shit show, Peter said. Everybody got too drunk, way too quickly. And then Valerie's heel broke. And then Rick dumped her.

"Because her heel broke?"

"No," Peter said.

Apparently, Rick was in love with someone he met at NYU, which was confusing because he wasn't even at NYU yet.

"How did it happen then?" I asked.

"Some internet group," Peter said. "I guess he's been chatting with some girl who is going to be in his dorm. They've already had cybersex."

"That's fast," I said. "We haven't even had cybersex yet."

"I prefer real sex to cybersex, thanks," he said.

"How would you know, if you haven't done either?"

"It's just a guess," he said. Peter pulled me into him, on his couch. He started to kiss me, but then pulled away. "So, *do* you want to have sex?"

"One day," I said.

"I mean, with me."

"Oh, with *you*," I joked. "I thought you meant, with Bill Nye the Science Guy."

"You're so random, sometimes," he said. "Be serious with me."

"Okay. Yes. I would."

"I was thinking graduation."

"You want to do it in our robes?"

"Sally. No. I want to do it on graduation night," he said. "It'll be special. I'll get a hotel room."

"Okay," I said, because it sounded special. Because I always liked hotels. The little soaps. The white robes hanging on the back of the bathroom door. We used to always put those on before we went to bed.

"It's a plan then," he said, because Peter liked plans.

B ut then Billy called me back.

"I had a feeling we'd find Jan," he said. "I can't explain it other than to say I had a feeling."

Then I told him about my bad dreams. There were so many bad dreams that week before graduation. In one of them, you were standing alongside the road. You were wearing a princess dress. The bottom was wet. Like you had just washed up to shore, but there was no water in sight. You were like, Sally, why didn't you guys tell me I was dead? Do you know how embarrassing it's been to walk around for hours, looking for our house? Where's our house, by the way?

In another dream, you are sitting next to me in the car. You are alive! We're all thrilled. Dad is driving and Mom turns up the radio, but then I see something in the corner of your eye. A gray spot that spreads like blood. And I know the truth: You're still dead. You're just pretending to be alive so Mom doesn't get upset. And that is very stressful because then I have to pretend for the rest of the car ride.

"In mine, we went to the movies," Billy said.

He didn't remember which movie, just some stupid movie she didn't want to watch.

"But when it's over, I can't get her to leave," Billy said. "I say, Kathy, we've got to go now. The movie is over. And she's like, No. Just let me sit here. And I go to pick her up but I can't. She's like a statue. Fixed to the ground. And then she becomes a statue. Actually turns into rock."

And that's how we began to talk again—every night, on the phone, like old times.

It was nice to see Mom dressed up for my graduation. She was wearing lipstick again. She had on her gold earrings again. She looked like Mom. Even sounded like Mom. "Honey, I'm so proud of you," she kept saying.

She was proud of all of us.

Proud of Peter, too, who gave his big speech about self-acceptance as it related to the rising cost of oil and China's super-economy.

"But I must say, I did not understand the valedictorian's speech," she said.

Oh yeah. Our valedictorian was the worst. He was this guy Jim Kravitz. A stoner anarchist pothead who was also a genius. He stood up at the podium and pretended to have a hamster in his hand. Then he pretended to crush the hamster with two little fingers. He shouted, "Crush the hamster!" and half the crowd went wild, like it was some kind of strange joke he had with the universe.

I didn't understand it, either.

The police escorted him offstage.

I looked at Valerie. We shrugged.

And then we graduated. I took the diploma. I was a little disappointed that graduating didn't feel like anything. I had expected a kind of feeling, a noise maybe. The click of a camera to make it feel official. I was done with high school. I looked down at my hands, my body, entirely encased in a blue sheen. I felt uncomfortably large in my robe. The diploma wasn't even really my diploma. It was a fake, so none of us would ruin the original on the way home or something.

I n the parking lot, I hugged Valerie and her parents. They were headed to the Cheesecake Factory at the mall. Was I?

No.

"What are you doing then?" Valerie asked.

"I'm waiting for Peter," I said.

Oh, yes, Peter, the class president.

"What a great job he did," Valerie's parents said. "Where is he?"

We got to the parking lot before him; it took the student body president two times as long to get off the football field as it did for a regular person. I could still hear him, hours before the graduation on the phone: "It will take me longer to get to the parking lot than it will take you. Wait for me."

No, I was not the class president, but still. I was president of Latin Club, president of Students Against Smoking, not to mention, secretary of the Key Club, not like anybody really knew what that was, not even me. We take attendance, I told Mom and Dad. The club was the largest one at school, because it didn't require anything from its members, so all we really had time for in a thirty-minute meeting was attendance. There were seventy-nine of us.

So why had it not taken me long at all to get to the parking lot? Did nobody stop me, and did I stop nobody? Did I have nothing to say at all to Key Club's seventy-nine members, after four years?

I didn't.

"I'll see you later tonight at home," I said to Mom and Dad.

"We're so proud of you," Mom said, and Dad agreed.

There was Peter, headed off the field and toward the parking lot, searching for me. He was walking through crowds of blue, with his yellow cords around his neck, and for a second, I felt proud. Look at my boyfriend. My first real boyfriend.

But even from this distance, I could see his smile. It was his *how'd I do?* smile. What did you think about my speech on the rising cost of oil as it related to China's economy as it related to surmounting personal obstacles in my preadult life? By the time I hugged Peter, I was certain he had nothing at all to do with me anymore.

The hotel Peter got was really a motel. There was a lamp on top of the microwave and the painting of a woman looking out at the moon and I told him that this was the kind of motel where people got shot, people died, and nobody even cared. Not that I minded. I was just saying. I had seen a lot of exposés on TV about people like this, and it really made you think about the bedspread, not to mention the energy of the place.

"What do you think happens to us after we die?" I asked Peter.

"Wow. This is some pretty good sexy talk," Peter said.

"I know," I said. "I should probably start a hotline."

But Peter didn't laugh. Peter was confused. "Why are you asking me this?"

"I just want to know," I said.

"If you really want to know, nothing," he said. "I think it's just nothing."

"Nothing?"

He turned to me. "You're being weird."

"Sometimes, I'm weird."

"Don't be weird tonight."

"I'm weird every night."

He sighed. "I just thought."

"You thought what?"

I knew what he thought. He thought we were going to have sex. But if he couldn't say the words, I didn't want to do it with him. That seemed only right. If a man cannot say, Will you have sex with me, then you shouldn't have sex with him. If a man cannot say, Will you have sex with me, then he is probably just a boy, and he will probably stay a boy, wearing stripes, forever—that's what you would have said, isn't it? Or maybe this is something Jillian Williams would have said. Either way, it made me want to leave.

"I want to give you something," Peter said. He pulled a necklace out of his pocket. "I was going to give it to you at prom. But you know, you kind of ditched me."

"I said I was sorry."

He handed me the necklace. "It's my mother's. She wants you to have it."

"She wants me to have it? Why?"

"She likes you," he said. "You're my girlfriend. She knows we're serious."

I put it around my neck. It was a heart made out of gold.

"Yeah, it looks good like that," he said. He positioned the heart so it fell down my chest. He took off his pants. His shirt. I took off my pants. My shirt. We lay down on the bed. He kept staring at the necklace. He kept repositioning it, making sure it was between my breasts.

"Looks kind of hot like that, right between your tits."

I backed away. "Why would you say something like that about your mother's necklace?"

"I didn't say it about my mother's necklace," he said. "I was saying it about your tits. It was a compliment."

"That is not a compliment. And these are not tits!" I said. "They're my breasts."

"I thought that's what you wanted me to call them," he said. "I thought you thought it was hot. You said—"

"Never mind," I said.

"Sally, what's *wrong* with you?"

I stared at him. "I don't want to go out with you anymore."

Peter looked angry. "Are you serious?"

"Yes," I said. "Very serious."

"You can't be serious," he said. "I love you, Sally."

"I don't love you, Peter."

He put his head in his hands.

"Why not?"

"I'm in love with someone else," I said.

"Who?"

There was no point in telling him. Except that it would finally feel so good to tell someone.

"Billy Barnes," I said.

Peter laughed a little. "Are you serious? The guy who killed your sister?"

"It was an accident," I said.

"Still," Peter said. "That's fucked up, Sally."

"Fuck you," I said. "You don't know anything about it."

I started to pack my things.

"Where are you going?" he asked.

"Home," I said.

"And how do you think you're going to get home if I don't take you?"

"I'll figure it out," I said.

I would be fine. This, I realized, was exactly what cell phones were for.

"Please, Sally. Don't go," Peter said. "I'm sorry. Let's just talk some more."

"No," I said. "I'm leaving."

"You can't just leave! It's graduation night! And we have concert tickets for Dave Matthews next week!"

"We do?" I asked.

"Yes!" he said.

"Well, I didn't know that."

"It was a surprise," he said. "I was going to surprise you."

"I'm sorry," I said. "You'll have to go with someone else."

I opened the door. I could hear the trucks on the highway.

"Fine," he said. "Fine. I will. Just leave. You fucked-up bitch."

I walked down the main road for a bit before I called Billy. He picked up right away. He said, "Stay there. Don't move."

He pulled up in his black car. He rolled down the window.

"You understand this makes me very nervous, right?" he asked. "Driving you."

"I understand," I said.

"Get in," he said.

I got in.

"May I ask what happened?" Billy said.

"We got in a fight," I said.

"What about?"

"He gave me a necklace," I said.

That's when I realized I was still wearing his mother's necklace. I pulled it out from under my shirt.

"What a fucking asshole," Billy said. "Buying you a necklace."

"He didn't buy it for me," I said. "It's his mother's. I mean, look at it. Can't you tell? It's a heart made out of gold."

"True," he said.

Billy put his two fingers on the heart, as if to feel how ugly it was.

"But it was more about the way he was staring at it," I said, "like he wanted me to be his mother or something. Like that's why he gave it to me."

"Some guys are actually kind of weird like that," Billy said.

"Are you weird like that?"

"I don't think so," Billy said. "But hey, you never know."

"I just felt like he wanted me to be this exact kind of person," I said. "He's just got a life plan. He just wants to go to prom and parties and concerts and never talk about anything real until we die. And maybe not even then."

I imagined Peter, on his deathbed, just blinking. Saying, Okay, I guess it's time now. And then . . . eternal darkness.

"And you?" Billy said.

"I think I actually hate going to concerts," I said.

"You hate concerts?" Billy asked.

"I know, I know, everybody likes concerts."

"What do you hate about them?"

"I just hate having to pay all that money to hear what I could hear from the comforts of my own room. And live music is never what you want it to be."

"Now I know I will never get you concert tickets for your birthday."

"Please don't."

Suddenly, it was the ease of the conversation that made everything so uncomfortable. The awareness that talking had become too easy between two people it was supposed to be difficult between. We had admitted our possible coexistence in some near future, where we might be buying each other gifts; he would never get me concert tickets and what would I never get him?

"A sweater from Gap," he said. "I once broke up with a girl sophomore year in college for buying me a sweater from the Gap. It was just so sad. I was like, We're only in college and we're already buying each other sweaters? Of course, I wore it all the time. A great sweater."

He looked at my necklace.

"I definitely won't be wearing this," I said.

"If you don't like the necklace," he said, "take it off."

I took it off. He looked at me, and for a moment I thought he might kiss me, but he didn't. He pulled out a cigarette.

"Can I have one?" I said. I was curious. I was no longer the president of Students Against Smoking. I was free.

"No," Billy said.

"Just one."

"Trust me," he said. "There's no such thing as one."

"I think you're confusing that with heroin."

"And potato chips," he said.

But he didn't give me one. He smoked two cigarettes right in front of me.

"We should go," he said. "I should get you home."

"No," I said. "I never want to go home."

He started up the car.

"You know I don't like this, driving you," he said again.

"I know," I said. "I understand. I really appreciate it."

He took me home. He drove so slowly, it took an hour.

B efore I left for college, there were many things to do. I had to sort through my belongings, decide which ones I wanted to keep as my belongings. Then I had to go to new stores and buy more belongings.

"How about this Swiffer?" Mom asked at Bed Bath & Beyond. "You'll need a Swiffer."

"I will?"

"Of course, you will!"

And then I was like, Mom, I really don't think I'll need a Swiffer in college, nobody else will have a Swiffer, and she insisted, said, "How are you supposed to clean without a Swiffer? Do you expect they give each of you a mop and broom?" And I said, Mom, I think what I mean is, I don't plan on cleaning, and she said, "You mean to say you're going to go a whole year without cleaning your room?" and I said, I have gone an entire year without cleaning my room, and this got her so upset she could barely speak. But then she did speak and said, "What kind of daughter did I raise?"

I didn't know. "A daughter like you, I guess," I said.

But she wasn't deterred. She kept going: "I've seen those dorm rooms, you have plenty of storage space for a Swiffer, you have ridiculous amounts of storage space. Who even needs that much storage space?" like she was angry about all of my future storage space.

"The sad thing is, I know she is," I said to Valerie, later at her house.

"That's the thing. It's like my mother wants my storage space or something, or like I don't deserve to have it. It all just makes me so sad. The storage space, the Swiffer. I should have just taken the Swiffer."

Valerie nodded.

"I know what you mean," she said. Then she lowered her voice and pretended like she was in therapy. "It took me a long time to accept my parents' mortality and the fact that they actually do love me."

We laughed.

Downstairs, we made sandwiches and sat at her new kitchen counter, something Valerie's mother was very proud of.

"It's medicinal," Mrs. Mitt said. "It's made of pink granite, sourced from the top of a mountain."

I was confused.

"Do you have to eat the countertop in order to be enriched by it?" I asked, and even Mrs. Mitt laughed.

"Yes, we eat the countertop!" she howled.

The countertop thing felt funny until I went home and saw the filth of our bedroom with a new kind of clarity. Your snow globe, your dance trophies, the tiny Bible Grandma gave you for your First Communion—all of it was sitting on your desk, covered in a layer of dust so thick, it reminded me of the awful pictures Mr. Prim showed us of Pompeii, the layers of volcanic ash and dust that fell on everything— the people, their houses, their jewelry—and hardened into a shell.

I didn't want to wind up like that. Like Mom. I didn't want to sit in our bedroom forever and collect dust upon my head like I was your snow globe. I had a whole life ahead of me, I realized, for maybe the first time since you died. I was going to Villanova. I put the acceptance letter out on my desk, where I could always be reminded of it.

I needed to move—I got a box of garbage bags. I started to throw things away indiscriminately. I worked for hours, late into the night, and heard Mom in the hallway saying, "I hear good things happening in there," but in the morning, when Mom saw my work, she gasped.

"What have you done with Kathy's things?" she asked.

"Put them in the bags," I said. I had destroyed the ancient and untouched site that was your desk and your side of the closet. I felt satisfied. "Look how clean it is."

"*Why did you do that?*"

"Do you know how dusty her things were?" I asked. "Did you ever think to bring a Swiffer in here? That's probably why I've been sick all year."

Mom sighed. "Well, let me just go through her things before you put the bags in the van. See what I can save."

I was already wearing what I wanted to save: the two gold earrings Billy gave you just before you died. When I found them in the bottom of the jewelry box, exactly where I put them four years ago, I was shocked to see them there, waiting. As if it were somehow you, curled up and sleeping at the bottom of the tiny felt box.

At first, I just wanted to try them on. Just to see how they would look. But once they were in my ears, I liked it, the way they framed my face and hung heavy at my ears. The way they hurt just a tiny bit.

M y, you're dressed up for the doctor," Mom said, when she saw me come down the stairs in the gold earrings. I waited for her to recognize them, but if she did, she didn't say anything. She looked traumatized after a day of going through your things.

"They're just earrings," I said.

The doctor checked my body, took my blood. He said, "Everything is fine. But actually, your mother was right. Your thyroid levels are a bit off."

"See?" Mom said after in the car. "Jan was right. She knew it. I told you she knew it."

After Mom had dumped the bags off at the Goodwill, she made an emergency appointment with Jan, but that hadn't helped her feel much better, because all Jan wanted to do was talk about Grandpa.

"What about Grandpa?" I asked. "Jan's being haunted by Grandpa now, too?"

"It seems so. She mentioned him yesterday," Mom said. "She said she saw an older man, who put a hand across his heart. And how would she have known about his heart attack?"

"Older men have heart attacks," I said. "Everybody knows that."

"How would she have known he was overweight though?"

"I mean, it *is* America."

"Sally," Mom said. "Don't be like that."

"Be like what?"

"So negative."

"Maybe I'm just negative."

M elancholic, is what Dad called me at dinner. "Like Abraham Lincoln," Dad said. "He was melancholic."

"Gee thanks," I said.

"Don't say that to Sally," Mom said. "No woman wants to be compared to Abraham Lincoln."

It was the first time I ever heard Mom refer to me as a woman.

"Why not?" Dad said. He looked genuinely confused. "I don't understand why that's an insult. Abraham Lincoln was a great man."

"He supported colonization," I said.

"Right," Dad said. "There's that."

T he next day, I went to Valerie's to say goodbye. Valerie was headed out to California early, to be an orientation leader.

"I cannot wait to get out of here," Valerie said. "My mom is driving me crazy."

"*Your* mother is driving you crazy?" I asked.

"Yes," Valerie said, and reminded me that her mother had taken away her bedroom door all summer for getting so drunk at prom (she'll get it back when she deserves privacy) and then put her on Weight Watchers again.

"Can mothers do that?" I asked.

"They can do anything they want," Valerie said.

Valerie was always counting her points now. She was like, This chicken finger is twenty-two points. This is an entire day of points. And I would point to things around the room, like, How many points is this pen? How many points is a bed? And she said, Oh. So many points. That many points could kill a person.

Back at home, Mom was drinking a cocktail. She was upset. She had called Jan to schedule another appointment, and Jan delivered the bad news.

"Jan is moving," Mom said. "I can't believe it. She's moving to California! Just like that."

For a second I thought Mom might suggest we move, too. Follow Jan and you out to California.

"That makes sense," I said. "California is supposed to be nice."

Mom nodded. Mom started to cry. "I know. It's really beautiful there."

The news of Jan's departure was hard on Mom. She started acting as if you had died all over again—started going to her room at the brightest parts of the afternoons. When she came to join us for dinner, she sat there and cried over her pasta.

"Mom," I said. "Come on. We're trying to eat dinner here."

"I'm sorry," she said. "I'm sorry, but I just can't stop."

The crying seemed worse than usual, maybe because it was summer. Every day was just another goddamned day in paradise, Dad said in a jokey monotone voice when we had a long stretch of good weather like this—and it suddenly made sense to me why more people would become suicidal in the spring and summer. Every day, the sun shone high in the sky and asked Mom the same question: Why don't you take off those sweatpants and comb your hair and come outside? Every day, Mom has the same answer: No. My daughter is still dead.

"Susan, you have to stop," Dad said eventually. "You just have to stop crying."

I didn't like hearing myself through Dad. It was only when Dad ordered Mom to stop crying that I understood we were bullies. We ordered her to be happy as if we knew what it meant to be happy. As if a person was not happy because they simply forgot to write it on their to-do list. We knew from experience that nothing we said or did would work, but we couldn't help ourselves; it was our job as the slightly happier people to make her happier. We were like corrupt policemen at the dinner table. We applied blunt force. We did not listen very well, and often spoke in commands. Go outside. Get a job. Do some gardening. Take a walk. Try harder. Don't give up. Don't be depressed. Stop crying. Which was exactly the kind of instruction that made a crying person cry harder.

"I'll be right back," I said.

I was a child again, sneaking to the bathroom to spit out my carrots. I sat on the toilet and I listened to our parents downstairs. They didn't think I could hear them, but I could. I heard everything in this house. The wood was so thin that nobody was ever really alone. I couldn't believe Peter and I fooled around downstairs, thinking nobody heard us.

"I can leave, you know," Dad said. "I can just get up and drive to California, too, if I want to. I don't *have* to be here. It's like you don't realize that."

Mom did not realize this. To be fair, I had not realized this, either. Dad never went anywhere, unless it was for work. And then, he only traveled to places like Appleton, Wisconsin; Joliet, Illinois. Small places known for the enormity of their prisons. Cities defined by high-rises and highways. He came home and talked about how uncomfortable the plane was, which was why he still refused to go to Europe. He liked being comfortable; he liked his house, his Man Chair.

"So why don't you?" Mom asked. "Why don't you just leave?"

She did not even sound angry. She sounded curious, as if she would have left herself, too.

"Because we can still look each other in the eye," Dad said. "Because after a child dies, people stop being able to look at each other. That's why they get divorced. But we can still look each other in the eye. We still have that."

I don't know what Mom said. I didn't hear anything, so maybe she said nothing at all. Maybe she agreed so completely that all she had to do was nod her head. Or maybe she disagreed so completely that she couldn't bring herself to speak. Maybe she put a hand to his shoulder and maybe he leaned and kissed her on the forehead. Maybe they still loved each other the way they had before you died. Or maybe they didn't. Maybe she knew that if she opened her mouth, she would cry, and Dad would put down his fork, get in his car, drive to California with Jan and you, and never return.

I don't know.

All I know is that I returned to the table and we continued eating pasta like nothing happened. Maybe nothing did happen. Maybe this was just life. What did I know about life? I was only eighteen. This was what our parents and people in their thirties liked to say to me as soon as I turned eighteen.

Dad handed me a spoon. "I don't need a spoon," I said, which upset him more than it should have.

"You can't eat pasta without a spoon," he said.

He was a German who insisted on eating pasta the correct way: like an Italian! I took the spoon, because it seemed like the least I could do. I would be gone soon, too—I would be leaving Mom and Dad to start a new life, just like Jan.

'm actually going to Villanova," I finally confessed to Billy one night at a diner.

But he didn't act weird about it. He just said, "That's where I went," like it was a total coincidence and told me about his freshman-year roommate.

"He was the worst," Billy said. "He was always playing the ukulele. And it's kinda cool, yeah, I get it, but there's only so much ukulele one can take. After a while it all sounds the same. Doot doot doo-doot."

"Doot?"

"Oh God. Not you, too."

"Doot."

"And then, of course, the pedal effects. Waa waaa. And such."

"Sounds miserable. I hope my roommate is extremely musically untalented. I hope she's never once strummed a guitar."

"That's the dream."

I had already spoken twice on the phone with my roommate. Her name was Nicole. She went to a Catholic school. She was very excited to be an English major. She was also very excited to drink and join the peace corps one day. And no, I didn't know what I was going to major in. But I was probably going to take some history courses. A few journalism courses. I liked reporting for the school paper.

"I can see you being a reporter actually," Billy said. "You're a good listener. Very observant. I used to always feel like you were watching me."

"I was," I said, and we laughed.

I had always been studying your boyfriend from afar, like some distant painting. So much so, that it still sometimes overwhelmed me when I found myself just sitting across the table from him, with his hands wrapped around a Coke, but there's where I was all July. We went to the movies a lot, then got pizza at Famous Joe's, where we debated whether any of the famous Joes out there were real people. Then, we talked about college.

"Did you like college?" I asked him.

"College was important to me," he said. "But I wouldn't say that I liked it. I was too unstable."

Billy showed up to Villanova and fell in with the art kids. He hung out with them, partied with them, did drugs with them, but never got too close to them. What was the point? He had a pretty nihilistic view of things then, often found himself alone at the end of the night, painting something in the art studio, high off too many shrooms. He thought he could paint away his pain. He thought he could make something beautiful out of it, until one morning, he woke up, covered in sweat and booze and paint, and looked over at his canvas and saw it for what it was.

"What was it?" I asked.

"A mushroom," he said. "I had spent all night painting a still life of my drugs."

I laughed.

"That's when I knew it was bad," he said. "I knew I had to change or I would die."

He moved off campus junior year to live alone. He started taking different classes, philosophy classes that promised to help him understand the meaning of life. He studied every night in the chapel basement. He felt comfortable there. He liked the priests who were always hanging around, suggesting books for him to read. He found that it felt good, to work hard at something again, to exhaust himself by the end of the night. After studying, he would go up to the pews and pray.

"What'd you pray for?" I asked.

"Everything," Billy said. "But mostly, forgiveness. You know. The usual."

"Oh yeah," I joked. "That's what I do. I just walk into the church and say, Give me the usual!"

"One order of absolution, coming right up."

It was getting late. It was always getting late. The days were passing quickly. There was this feeling that we were running out of time. Soon, I would have to leave for college. Soon, I would be living with a girl named Nicole who would be drinking heavily. Soon, Billy would start his job. Whatever that was. Wherever that was.

"Where are you moving again?" I asked. I had no memory of him telling me for some reason.

"D.C.," he said.

"Oh," I said.

We ended the night with the ocean water always at our feet, a sadness creeping up my leg. We stood in the foam and Billy told me how he used to stand in rivers like this with his dad.

"My dad loved to fish in Maine before he broke his neck," he said. "We used to go up there for two weeks during mayfly season."

"What's that?"

"When all the mayflies breed in June. It's crazy. The mayflies are born, fuck for two days, and then they die and the fish and the birds go crazy."

He looked over at me.

"What?" he said. "What are you thinking?"

Billy always wanted to know what I was thinking. He asked me all of the time. And I often considered lying, as I usually did when people asked me because what I was thinking was strange. That is what Peter taught me. But pretending to be normal in front of Billy suddenly seemed like a giant waste of time. I was tired of lying. There's no point in lying. The truth always rises, like a bloated body in the water.

"Tell me, exactly what you are thinking right now," Billy said. "Don't hesitate."

I was thinking that there was nothing better in this world than to discover someone who was weird in exactly the same way I was weird. To be weird and then loved for it.

"I'm thinking about how strange it is that flies have to have sex in the air," I said. "Can you imagine flying and fucking at the same time?"

"No," he said.

There was silence.

"Sorry, were you expecting a different answer?" I asked.

"Yes, actually."

"Are you disappointed by my answer?"

"No. I think it was the perfect answer."

"So what are you thinking about then?"

"Well, now I'm thinking about fucking and flying," he said. "Can you imagine getting eaten by a bird in the middle of fucking? That's what happens to a lot of the mayflies."

"It wouldn't be the ideal way to go," I said.

"It would be the perfect way to go," he said. "To die doing something like that."

Billy would rather go out doing something extreme. Like maybe jump out of an airplane. Or get eaten alive by a tiger. If he had to die, he'd want to make a big production out of it. He'd want to be prepared. Settle the big ol' estate.

"Right," I said. "Get your affairs in order."

"Figure out what to do with the dog."

"Do you have a dog?"

"One day, I'll have a dog," he said. "You want the dog? I think I'd want you to have my dog."

"Sure," I said.

It was the nicest thing anyone had ever said to me. He took my hand.

"I feel like I can say anything to you, Sally," he said. "What is that? Why is that?"

I didn't know. I felt it, too, and I didn't know if this was a good thing or a bad thing. If it was the way I felt around the cat, to whom I could say anything, because it was just a cat. Or if this was what real love felt like. If this is what it meant to be close to another human being. To actually trust someone with your weirdest and worst thoughts. He pulled out a cigarette. But he didn't smoke it. He just twirled it in his hands.

"This right here is my second-to-last cigarette ever," he said.

"Why are you quitting?"

He laughed. "Oh, have you not heard? Smoking is bad for you."

"It kills, they say."

"I've got to quit, before I move to D.C."

"Do they not let you smoke in D.C.?"

"They let you smoke in D.C.," he said. "But they don't let you smoke in the seminary."

"In the seminary?" I asked.

"I'm going to enter the seminary, Sally."

I laughed. What?

"Are you joking?" I asked.

"No. This is not a joke," he said. "I've been trying to decide all summer."

"Decide what?"

"Whether or not I wanted to become a friar."

"You have to be joking."

"No."

"This whole summer we've been hanging out, and you've been deciding whether or not you should become a priest?"

"Well," he said. "A friar. It's different."

"Like a monk?"

"Sort of. Except friars don't live in isolation."

"Why would you ever become a friar?"

"You say it like it'd be better if I were joining the Mafia."

"I mean, I guess I never realized you were that religious."

"I wasn't," he said. "That's the problem. I was a little shit."

"You weren't a little shit."

"Oh, I was a little shit."

"That's not exactly how I would have described you."

"Well," he said. "Trust me. I was."

It bothered him to think about how ungrateful he was as a boy. How proud. Even when his parents took him to church, he just pretended to pray because why did he need to pray? Everything always came to him, so naturally. He barely had to try; he could make a three-pointer with his eyes closed. He could sit at the snack bar and watch the girls come up to him. He could never do his homework and still somehow get a scholarship to a great school like Villanova. And that's how he thought life would always be—easy, uninterrupted, always a team surrounding him, pumping their fists with glee, always a basketball in his palm, always a body that would achieve things for him. He wanted to be a college basketball star. And then one day, maybe a coach. But then he held your bleeding head to his chest, and he understood what could be done to the body. He saw that the body was nothing. *He* was nothing. He was a little shit—a careless, reckless little shit who thought he could speed down Main Street without consequences. He was the reason you were dead, and for years after, his only wish was that he would die, too. He should have been the one to die. It was the only thing he truly believed during college, that he did not deserve the life that he—for some unknown reason—still had.

"So I tried to kill myself again," he said. "That's the part of the story of college that I left out."

It wasn't a premeditated decision. He just woke up and saw his mushroom painting and felt like shit. He had a throbbing headache. He took some of the pain medication he always kept in his nightstand. But the headache didn't go away, so he took more. And then more. He just wanted the pain to go away. So finally, he took all of it. He walked to the chapel on campus, a place he hadn't thought to enter before, because he felt ashamed. But now that he was dying, it seemed like the right place to be. He laid down on one of the pews and prepared to go to sleep forever.

"It was a miracle one of the friars found me," he said. "It really was."

Father Thomas—that was his name—came to visit Billy in the hospital every day until Billy was released. When he returned to campus junior year, he began to go to daily mass. He read the New Testament and then the Old Testament and started to go to confession, where he asked for God's forgiveness, and as the year went on, he really did start to feel better. He felt himself come alive again. He volunteered for Habitat for Humanity, and then, senior year, he started a program delivering the leftover dining hall food to the neighboring Pennsylvania farms that were struggling. By the time he graduated college, he was an entirely different person. A philosophy grad. A name on the dean's list. He knew the only path forward for him was the one he was on: the path that led to God.

"But what about me?" I asked. "You don't want to be with me?"

I was so stupid. I was like the seal. Returning to shore over and over and over again.

"I can't be with you," Billy said.

"Why not?" I asked.

"Why not?" Billy asked. "Are you seriously asking me that?"

"You can't be my boyfriend, but you can be a *friar*?"

"Sally, no," he said. "Of course I can't be your boyfriend. I killed your sister."

"You did not kill my sister," I said.

"I literally drove my car into a tree and she died," he said. "If I didn't kill her, then who did?"

"*I* made you take me to school that day," I said. "If you hadn't taken me to school that day, she'd be alive."

"No," he said. "Stop. Sally, this has nothing to do with you. I was driving the car. I was careless. I was speeding. I shouldn't have been speeding, even if she told me to."

"Well, I shouldn't have been in the car," I said. "If I hadn't been so in love with you, if I had just given her the notebook and let her go to school, she'd be here with you right now."

Billy was quiet. "You were in love with me?"

"Of course I was in love with you. You were my older sister's handsome boyfriend. I had no choice."

He laughed a little. "Do you still . . . love me?"

"Does it even matter? You're becoming a priest."

"It matters a lot," he said. "It matters to me."

"Why?" I asked. I was determined to make him say it.

"Because I love you."

It was something I had been waiting to hear my whole life, and even as he said it, it didn't sound possible. Billy Barnes, your boyfriend. Billy Barnes, the boy who once sucked on your tits. He loved me.

"Then why are you becoming a priest?"

"Because it's the only thing that feels possible for me," he said. "I can't explain it any other way."

I stared out at the water.

"You were just a kid, Sally," he said. "You know that, right? You're not to blame."

It was nice of him to say. But I didn't want to be a kid. Not when I was with him. So I took the cigarette from his hands.

"If you're not going to smoke this," I said, "then I will."

I put the cigarette in my mouth.

"You're really going to steal my second-to-last cigarette?"

"It doesn't have to be your second-to-last cigarette, if you don't want it to be."

He nodded. Billy, he would have given me anything, I knew. He would have given me his skin if I were cold. If I asked for it. But he couldn't ever give me the one thing I wanted, which was him.

"Do you have a lighter?" I asked.

Billy leaned in close to light it up for me, and then he stopped. Pulled the stick out of my mouth, turned it around, and put it back in.

"Can't smoke it out the ass, Holt," he said.

"Oh," I said.

We started laughing. I laughed so hard, in that hysterical way that Mom always laughed when she was most sad. I couldn't catch my breath.

"Whoa," he said. "You okay?"

He put his hand on my chest. Pressed his palm over my heart like he was already a priest, healing me. I closed my eyes.

"This isn't an easy decision," he said. "I do want you, you know."

"I know."

"I think about you a lot," he said. "I mean, all of the time."

I put my hand on his chest. On his nice shirt. The only one he had, I guess, because he wore it nearly every day.

"What do you think about?" I asked.

"I think about what it would feel like to kiss you," he said.

"You should try it," I said.

Then, he leaned in to kiss me and I know I don't have to describe what it's like to kiss Billy Barnes. I know you know what it's like to feel him inside your mouth, searching for something with his tongue. But he tasted smokier than I had imagined. A little metallic. After, I looked into his eyes and said, "Hello," and he laughed. A strangely formal greeting at this late stage. But it was nice.

"Hello," he said. "Hello, Sally."

We stayed like that for a while. I laid in the nook of his arm the way girls always do in movies. I looked up at the moon. But maybe you know all this already. Maybe you were there, watching us from Jan's big window.

D o you remember that photograph of Mom on our kitchen wall? It's Mom's favorite photograph of herself, she told me one night at the end of summer.

In it she is twenty-five, young and sexy—she is Michelle Pfeiffer; her thin legs crossed over each other, her blond hair long and straight, her dress white. It is summertime. She is laughing about something the photographer must have said. The photographer was Dad, Mom explained—a photo he took before they were engaged. Before she knew they would get married and have two children together. Before she knew what it would feel like to walk away from her daughter's grave. In the photo, all this woman knows is that she is a sixth-grade teacher who puts on plays for her students and she dates a handsome man in the National Guard who takes her dancing after work. And when she's too tired from work, she doesn't wash her hair and just wears a wig.

"He couldn't tell the difference between the wig and my real hair," Mom said.

"I bet Jan would be able to tell," I said.

"Maybe," Mom said. "But I'm telling you, your father had no idea when he came to my apartment on our first date. And we sat right next to each other, playing piano."

"You and Dad played the piano on your first date?"

"Yeah, why?"

"I don't know," I said. "Just surprising, is all."

I tried to imagine Billy and me playing the piano together. Something like this would never happen, I knew. We were not piano players. I had told Billy I thought concerts and plays were a waste of money, but I wished I didn't, because I wanted to be someone who went to plays and concerts with Billy. I wanted to wear my beautiful black peacoat in the closet, but it felt too extravagant for anything we did. Even on our last night together, when we could have gone anywhere, Billy and I had sat in his childhood bedroom, which looked very much like a childhood bedroom.

"Are you sure your parents are gone?" I had asked.

"Yes, trust me. They're out of town," he had assured me. "Thank God for Disney World."

"Yes. That's what I say every day when I wake up," I said, and he laughed so hard, he squirted water out his nose.

"Fuck," he said. "Give me some warning, Sally. That burns."

"I can't believe they still go, even without kids?"

"They say it's better without kids," he said. "I don't know. Don't ask me. I think they get tanked at Epcot."

I had never been to Billy's house before. Had you? I had never heard you talk about it. Maybe because it was unremarkable—just a regular house, like ours, with pictures on the wall. Pictures of Billy at Disney World. Pictures of Billy in California. Billy through the years. It surprised me to see how young he looked in some of the photos from high school. He had seemed so old to me then—so big. Such a hero. But that whole time we knew him, what he'd really been was a boy. He had acne along his jawline. He had neon blue walls. A plaid bedspread. Basketball trophies studding his desk. I ran my hand over his bedspread, trying to feel all the years that Billy slept here.

"It was always kind of a fantasy of mine to have a girl up here," he said.

"Oh yeah?" I asked.

In Billy's fantasy, the one he had over and over again as a teenager, he comes home from basketball practice to find a girl waiting for him in his room. She is just standing there in the dark, and when he closes the door, she starts to slowly undress. He watches her until she is entirely naked . . .

"Sally," Mom said in the kitchen, "are you even listening to me?"

I moved away from Mom and went to sit on top of the kitchen counter, like if I got farther away, I could hide myself from Mom. From Jan. I looked at the photo of her on the wall instead. I looked to it for proof of something, but I was not sure what. I was always looking to the past as evidence of something. Always looking to Mom to learn something, because Mom had secret ways of making people love her. I'm not sure what it was, but I think it's how she smiled before she said anything—that was how she did it. She reacted to what she said before she even said it.

"Are you having sex? Jan—"

"Mom," I said. "Stop. If you say *Jan* one more time, I'm going to lose it."

"I'm just asking. I'm your mother. If you're having sex, I should know. Jan says—"

"Who cares what Jan says? Jan is crazy and so are you!"

Mom looked down at the table. I hurt her. Or I embarrassed her. She was ashamed of herself. She was ashamed of me. I no longer understood boundaries. This was what your death did to me. It made life feel like death, love feel like hate.

I hated Mom. I loved Mom.

I waited for Mom to speak. I was desperate for her to speak. She didn't speak. We swallowed at unnecessary moments. She took a sip of tea. RELAX NOW.

"Jan knows that I'm not wearing my mother's necklace anymore," Mom said. She draped her hand across her neck. "I mean, how could she possibly know that?"

"Your neck is bare," I said.

Mom picked up her tea.

"She says my mother has forgiven me for taking it off. Which is nice to know. It was just so ugly, silver and gold hearts. I just couldn't wear it anymore, Sally."

And it really was starting to seem as if Jan knew everything. She knew I was not taking my vitamins. She knew my thyroid was slow. She knew I was still not eating, not anything besides string cheese and waffles and pretzels and soda. She was worried about me: I was listening to my music too loudly in the car, staying up too late at night, having sex with some boy I shouldn't be having sex with, and how did she possibly know all of these things about me?

Why would you be haunting some random lawyer named Jan, and not me?

"Jan's a fraud," I said to Mom. "Women like that used to be dragged through the streets. They used to be executed."

"Sally!" Mom said. "That's a terrible thing to say."

"Jan's a terrible person," I said. "Only a terrible person could do what she does."

Mom stood up. Mom wasn't in the mood for tea anymore. Mom wanted to sleep.

"Have some faith," she said.

I did have faith. I had so much faith. I had stood there in the middle of Billy's bedroom, completely naked, and I waited for just a moment before I kissed him. I waited, to see if you might finally show your face, to see if you would swing open Billy's door and see me reaching out for your boyfriend and say, *Slut. What are you doing with my boyfriend?* I would have understood, you know. I would have let you grab my hair. I would have let you drag me back to your grave. Down there, I would have lit a candle and told you things about life—about your boyfriend—that you wouldn't believe.

That was my fantasy.

But you didn't come. So I kissed Billy and he kissed me back. He put his hands through my hair and he spread my legs with his hand

and it all felt so good when he put himself inside of me. Please, come inside of me, I begged him, and he did.

"Oh, Sally," he said.

After, in the morning, I had watched him smoke his last cigarette out his bedroom window. I had watched him pack his bag. But then he said, "Goodbye, Sally," with such a finality, such a seriousness, I felt like he was departing for the moon.

And now I was here, at the kitchen table, with Mom. How did I end up here? I wanted to ask Mom. I wanted to tell Mom about what happened with Billy and how much I had always loved him. I wanted her to know me. I wanted to cry into her chest the way I used to when I stubbed a toe. Mom used to know about every single one of our cuts. Imagine that? Mom used to put Band-Aids on our fingers and IcyHot on our backs and stroke our hair and hum songs until we fell asleep.

But I said, "Good night," and Mom said, "Good night."

Mom kissed me on the forehead and went up to her room. I waited for her door to close. For the house to settle. Then, I grabbed my keys, and I went to Jan's.

I really liked driving. Especially at night, when the sky and the ocean all looked like the same thing. As I got closer to Watch Hill, the houses started to look like the sea, too. Most of them were quaint-looking houses, all built so long ago.

But then there was Jan's modern monstrosity. A geometric prison, spread along the ocean. I parked in front of the FOR SALE sign that now had an X over it.

I got out of the car and could smell it right away: the dead seal, somewhere in the distance. I walked to Jan's front door. I didn't even hesitate. I felt very aware of my feet, of myself moving toward something.

Knocking seemed like the right thing to do. The door was solid. An expensive door. One that obviously didn't come with the house.

It must have been special ordered by Jan. You couldn't break that door down with three axes. Nothing, except maybe a ghost, could get through that wood.

"Hello," Jan said.

I knew it was Jan because of the hair. It was a blond helmet. Two pearl earrings underneath. She looked like the women at school who lectured us on how there were nine teaspoons of sugar in a can of Coke. She looked like Mom, once upon a time, and maybe this is why Mom trusted her. It was like consulting her former self.

"Hi," I said.

I knew I was supposed to introduce myself, but I didn't. I stood in the doorway, and I waited for her to extract the truth, because this was Jan; she already knew everything about me. I wanted her to prove it, to remark on the familiarity of my arms, the malnutrition of my face, to finger my thyroid and check for nodules and say, Sweet girl, please! Why did you sleep with your sister's boyfriend? I wanted her to put an arm around me, to usher me into the bright light of her house, where we would summon you.

"Can I help you?" Jan said.

"Yes," I said.

In the silence that followed, Jan laughed a little, but a worried kind of laugh, the kind I did when Peter used to put my hand over the crotch of his jeans. I laughed because it felt like the only alternative.

"Okay, how can I help you?" Jan asked.

"I'm here to see Kathy," I said.

Jan did not even twitch. "I'm afraid you have the wrong house," she said. "There's no Kathy here."

Still, I waited. For what? For anything. For her to comment on the sharp line of eyebrows that I shared with you, to lean in and trace them with her finger and say, "Wow, you two have the same eyebrows." Because we did.

But Jan began to close the door, backing away so that only her face and shoulder were visible. I pushed the door open and shouted

"Kathy!" like a crazy person. It was amazing how quickly this made me feel like a crazy person. In here, in Jan's foyer, I was nobody I knew. And how was this even possible?

"Excuse me!" Jan said.

Her voice was loud and aggressive, but her body language was reluctant. She moved farther away from me as I called for you. Jan looked up the stairs, as though somebody should be coming to help her, but nobody did. Jan was not the type to push or shove, I could tell by the pearls laced around her neck. This was my only advantage.

"Kathy!" I shouted. "Where *are* you?"

I walked into the kitchen. There was a wooden table, with the leftover remains of a big dinner. Chicken thighs and drumsticks. A blue decorative vase in the foyer. And the smell of it all—the woody newness. It was not a dark, spooky house. There were no incense or candles or anything else you'd think one would need to contact the dead. It was so big and open, every room was every room. The kitchen was the living room was the foyer, lit up with strong overhead fluorescent lighting, like the kind we had at school, and I wondered if this was why you came. For the good lighting. For the pool. For the air-conditioning. For the mother who keeps her pearls on all through dinner. Maybe life was just better here.

"Please," Jan said. "What are you doing?"

I was waiting for something to happen. For the clock to fall off the wall. For the blue vase on the table to burst. For the chandelier to come crashing around my head like a wave. I was waiting for my nails to thicken, for my hair to grow and snake down my back like yours. For Billy to call my phone and say, "I'm sorry. I've changed my mind. I love you." But nothing happened—nothing miraculous ever happened—so I picked up the blue vase and I threw it to the floor and we watched in shock as the blue pieces spread like water.

The weirdest part was that Jan didn't even get angry. She said, "Please, my family is *sleeping*." She stared at me pleadingly, like she was the victim of my sudden appearance, which, I guess, she was. It is late, Jan's eyes were saying. Let me go to bed. And why wasn't Jan angry? Did Jan think I was a ghost? Is that why she wasn't calling the police? Did she think I was you?

"I'm not a ghost," I said. I felt a sudden and desperate need to make her understand this. "I'm alive!"

"I know, I can see that you're alive, sweetheart," Jan said, and put her arms around me.

And this is what I liked about Jan: She didn't even hesitate. Jan was a good mother, I could tell. She held me firmly to her chest, like I was one of her daughters, and it was there where I could finally cry.

THE WEATHER REPORT

Hurricane Kathy. No matter how many times the weatherman says it, it doesn't sound right. A Kathy does not flood canals. A Kathy does not, would not, flip over a tractor-trailer on 95. It's like a Mildred shooting up a convenience store. An Edith severing heads. An Adelaide snorting coke. It's a joke. That's what it still feels like, like the violence of it all is just a joke.

And who is pulling this joke on me?

This is a question my therapist likes to ask.

"I don't know," I say.

Sometimes, it feels like Mom. Mom wants to keep me trapped in your death. As if your death is a birthday cake we all must eat until we die. But Mom hasn't mentioned the hurricane or your name once since the storm formed south of the Caribbean days ago.

"I don't know what I know anymore," I say.

The therapist nods.

"That's good. All we can ever know is that we know nothing," the therapist says. "Do you know who said that?"

Billy? A long time ago, Billy once said that.

"Socrates," she says. "Socrates said that."

My therapist is always quoting important people of antiquity during our session, people like Ovid and Horace, and this doesn't bother me as much as you might think. I like knowing that my problems exist within a large and respected tradition of problems. That ever since the beginning of civilization, humans have been very upset.

"Though who can even say what Socrates really said?" my therapist adds. "We basically just have to take Plato's word for it."

My phone rings.

"Sorry," I say, reaching into my purse.

At some point during the therapy session, my phone always rings. At first, I don't pick up. It seems rude. But then it rings again—the sound of two bamboo sticks rubbing together because that is what phones sound like in 2013.

"Feel free to answer," the therapist says.

"No," I say. "It's just my mother."

"How do you know that?"

"Because I know."

I know it isn't my fiancé, Ray—he never calls during a workday. And I know it's not my college friends from Villanova, because we rarely talk on the phone anymore. We text and then meet up once a year somewhere mountainous and drink the beers we drank in college and say things like, "I am realizing now that one has to be in a *mood* to drink Natty Light."

The only friend I regularly talk to on the phone now is Valerie, because sometimes, being older is like being young again. Don't get me wrong, life is very different now—I am twenty-eight and I live in New York City and have a wonderful fiancé—yet I am back to wearing leggings and giant flannel shirts and talking to Valerie on the phone about the fanny pack she bought. "*What?*" she says. "It's Gucci. It helps me hold my things."

But Valerie doesn't randomly call. Valerie likes to plan our phone conversations weeks in advance, only to push it off to a later day, because Valerie is tired. Valerie is a packaging specialist. She packages things for Nestlé. Snapple. All day long, she thinks about how to put things in other things, and this doesn't seem to bother her. I mean, she loves it.

"My mother is the only person I know who calls twice in a row with no shame," I explain to my therapist.

And then, sometimes, Mom will call a third or a fourth time. My therapist and I will just stare at the phone and wait as if there's been some earthquake. We sit quietly and brace ourselves for each predictable aftershock.

"Is that your mother *again*?" the therapist asks.

Mom used to call so many times because she forgot that she called me—did I call you today already? Oh, I'm sorry. What did we talk about? But lately, her memory has been better and I'm not sure what her excuse is.

"Yes," I say to the therapist.

I used to be afraid there was some emergency—maybe Mom was about to kill herself and she was calling to say goodbye. Or maybe Dad was dead. But now I know that Dad will never die. Dad has given himself over to life. He drinks superfood every morning, a green vitamin shake that he swears isn't a scam. And Mom will call a hundred times just to ask what I'm eating for dinner. Or if I've been taking a multivitamin. And has Ray been taking one, too? Of course. Ray loves multivitamins. He swallows them whole, without water. Something I didn't know until I moved in with him.

"You don't have to pick up just because someone calls you again and again," the therapist says. "You are freer than you think you are."

My therapist is always giving me permission to stop loving Mom. That is why I go to her—she is always reminding me that Mom has damaged me, stunted my grieving process. She says things like, "Two people can't throw up in the toilet at the same time," and I can't argue differently. It's true. But then the therapist goes too far, says something like, "If another woman was calling you this much, what would you say to her?" and I get angry at the therapist for saying exactly the thing I am paying her to say.

"But she's not just another woman," I say. "She's my *mother*."

I end the session early and call Mom back.

Sally, you need to come home right away," Mom says when I call. "Your father has lost his mind."

I wasn't expecting that. I was expecting Mom to say something crazy about Hurricane Kathy. About how the storm is your ghost that has come to ominously hover over us. I had already prepared a speech: Mom, these names are picked out seven years in advance by scientists. It means nothing. It's just a name. A very common name. I'm sure one of the scientists has a daughter or a niece or an aunt named Kathy. Calm down.

"What'd Dad do?" I ask.

"Nothing yet," Mom says. "But your father wants the Norwegian maples gone before the hurricane. And he's about to start cutting them all down himself."

"Why?"

"He says they're long overdue. He says they're going to topple during the storm and kill us both."

"Does he know how to cut down trees?"

"No! Of course not," Mom says. "That's why I'm calling. Very soon, your father will be dead. I thought you should know."

"Shouldn't you call a tree guy though?"

"You know your father. He's crazy. He thinks he can do it by himself. He thinks he's still Superman. I said, Richard, do you know how old you are? And he says, No, Susan. I make it a point not to keep track. And I say, Do you even know how to cut down a tree? And he says, Men have been cutting down trees since the beginning of time."

"Well, you need to stop him," I say.

"I can't," Mom says. "He never listens to me anymore."

This is true. Over the years, Dad has slowly stopped listening to Mom. Dad blames his bad hearing, but it's more than that. He has learned to tune her out. Last time I was home for your birthday, I listened to an entire conversation between them that went like this:

Mom: "Did you eat the chicken?"

Dad: "Everything's electronic now."

Mom: "No, did you eat the chicken?"

Dad: "Everything is electronic now."

Mom: "Huh?"

Dad: "What did you say?"

Mom: "I said, Did you eat the chicken?"

Dad: "I thought you said, Did you hand in your application?"

Mom: "What application?"

Dad: "For the Golf Commission."

Mom: "No. I wanted to know if you ate the chicken."

Dad: "No. I didn't eat the chicken."

Mom: "Well, I didn't hear you."

And so on.

"Come home tonight," Mom says. "Talk some sense into him."

"I can't," I say. "Ray and I have a thing tomorrow."

"What thing?"

"An important thing," I say. "A lawyer work boat thing."

"How could that be more important than your father not falling off a ladder and breaking his neck?"

"Why don't you just call a tree removal service? There are people who do this kind of thing professionally."

"There are," Mom says. "But Dad refuses to call."

"Why?"

"You know why."

"I don't know why."

"The only place in town who does that kind of thing is Bill's Tree and Garden. And your sister's old boyfriend runs it."

"Excuse me?"

"Billy Barnes," Mom says. "Your sister's old boyfriend. You don't remember him?"

"Yes, of course I remember him. I just don't understand what you mean when you say he runs the Tree and Garden."

"It means what it means! He took over the place after his father died."

"Can friars *do* that?" I ask.

"How do I know?" Mom asks. "What on earth are you talking about, Sally?"

"Billy's a friar."

"Billy is not a friar."

"Yes, Mom, he's a friar."

It had taken me all of college to accept that statement as a fact. Billy was a friar. Billy had entered the seminary! I told my new college roommate, Nicole, but it didn't have the effect that I wanted. Nicole was not impressed. She had no idea who Billy was, and no idea what the seminary really was. "To be honest, I don't even know what that means," she said, and we never talked about Billy again because I didn't know what it meant, either. When I tried to imagine Billy in the seminary, I couldn't. I could only see him in flashes, in my dreams, in a poorly lit cave, with a single candle burning. On a shabby cot, flipping through a Bible. But then I woke up late for class, and I sat down in Nineteenth-Century Novel, where I learned about the socioeconomics of the Victorian era aristocracy, and by the end of class, Billy seemed completely irrelevant to me.

"I'm telling you, Billy runs the Tree and Garden," Mom says.

"Are you sure? Sometimes you get confused. You forget things."

Mom's had some memory problems for the past few years—she forgets that she forgets.

"I think I know a friar when I see one," Mom says. "Trust me, he had this awful neck tattoo. I said, Billy, why on earth would you do that to yourself?"

"You *asked* him about his neck tattoo?" I ask.

It was impossible to imagine Mom, after all these years, talking to Billy.

"How could I not ask him about it? It's all over his neck!" Mom says. "That's why people get neck tattoos, isn't it? They clearly want to be asked about them."

"I thought you hated him," I say.

I hated him. At least that's what it felt like in college, where I spent four years thinking only about the worst parts of Billy. Billy, in the back seat of his car, sucking on your tits. Billy, looking so proud as he climbed the stairs to the diving board. Billy, OD'ing in the pews of the chapel at Villanova, which is really beautiful, by the way. Built to let in as much light as possible. When I sat in it on Sunday nights with Nicole (she sang the mass sometimes), I felt embarrassed thinking of Billy, curled in the fetal position, drooling out his mouth onto the beautiful mahogany bench.

"Well, what am I supposed to do, just ignore the boy when I see him?" Mom asks. "I see him at the Tree and Garden all the time! It's the only place to get flowers in this town. Sheesh. You make it sound like I spoke with the devil, Sally. Billy's a person, you know."

"I know that."

I know that more than ever now that I am older. In my mind, Billy has become so small. When I'm with Ray, I can't even remember what I had loved about Billy. I watch Ray put on his leather belt to go to work each morning and think about Billy, who used to eat waffles wrapped in plastic. Three pieces of gum at the same time. A boy who wore practice shirts every day and got a neck tattoo just because it hurts.

"Well, sometimes, I think your father forgets that he was just a boy. I think your father is going to stay mad at him until he dies. And it's ridiculous, him going all the way to Groton just for mulch," Mom says.

"I can't believe it," I say.

"I know!" Mom says. "Groton is thirty minutes away. It's absurd."

"I mean, I can't believe Billy is not a friar."

"Well, if you came home more than once a year, you might know that," Mom says.

Now, I only go home for major holidays. In and out before the sadness can touch me. That's what Valerie advised. Valerie's not a therapist, but she's smart. Studied bio. Has her own mother problems. Sets a two-day limit. You've got to set boundaries, she said. You've got to be smart. Treat your mother like she has a disease. These were things Valerie did with her own mother, and they had a wonderful relationship now. They went to casinos together sometimes and actually won money from the slots. "Make active suggestions," Valerie said, "like, Let's go for a walk. Let's go to a movie. Let's get our nails done." But I hated getting my nails done. That makes me depressed, when the ladies at the salon called Mom Sabrina and she didn't correct them. She just sat down and chose the same color she wore when you were alive—Like Linen—while the women tried to convince her into something new. Something new, Sabrina! Something bright! Red! Even total strangers could feel her sadness. They painted her nails red, and for a moment, while she dried her nails under the blower, I truly believed the nail salon might fix her.

But when we returned to the house, she was the same except now her nails were red. Her fingernails were dazzling as she heated up soup in the microwave. They were the hands of a happy woman who was in control of her life. But I knew better than that. I was like a geologist who studied Mom's body for many years; from a distance, the landscape looked still and calm. A lovely day out. But I could see the earthquake begin in her shoulder, the slow curve of her back. When she turned around, her mouth cracked and her face crumbled. And then, of course, the flood.

"Mom," I say. "I should go. I'm already late for dinner."

"Oh," Mom says. "What are you and Ray having for dinner?"

We are having Lemon Chicken. Something Ray makes once a week. He puts chicken and vegetables in a pan, squeezes lemon on it, and calls it Lemon Chicken.

"So the man cooks," Mom says. "That's wonderful. Your father never cooked. He'll cut down all the trees in our yard by himself, but he won't make himself a proper meal. Would it have killed him to just make himself a meal?"

"Mom," I say. "He's not dead. You're talking about him in the past tense."

"Well, if you don't get here soon, Sally, he will be dead!"

I hang up the phone and take a breath and practice the truth aloud—that is something the therapist makes me do. She believes we can recite the truth over and over again until we believe it.

"My sister, Kathy, is dead," I say, to myself, to nobody, to my feet. "And Billy is not a friar."

Then, I let the truth go. I walk home through the crowded city streets to have Lemon Chicken with my fiancé.

haven't told Ray that I started seeing a therapist, even though it was his idea.

Ray thought the therapist might help me figure out if I want to have children or not. Ray wants to have children. He wants to be with a woman who wants children. At night, in bed, Ray says things no man has ever said to me before, like, "I want to have a family with you, Sally," and he says them very easily, as if they come naturally to him and maybe they do.

But then I say things like, "Okay. But what if they die?" which Ray finds concerning. Ray says, "Maybe these are things to ask a therapist."

"How would the therapist know if my children are going to die?" I ask. I'm only joking. But this is the one thing Ray doesn't like to joke about.

So I found a therapist. But I didn't tell Ray, because I knew that every time I came home, he would expect me to know whether or not I wanted to have kids. Every time I walked through the door, I was supposed to have more clarity about who I was and what I wanted from the world. But so far, the therapist hasn't helped me figure much out. Mostly, she just spews awful truths about the world.

"Sometimes, children die," the therapist says. "It happens."

"That's very comforting," I say.

"I'm not here to comfort you, Sally," she says. "If you want comfort, there are big pillows you can buy on Amazon for that. I'm here to help you navigate reality. And reality can be quite painful."

I nod.

"In reality, children sometimes die. And as Americans, we don't have a great way of dealing with this. Other cultures, they do. They understand this reality. In Ancient Greece, so many children died in infancy, people were advised not to love them until they turned seven."

She said it was too painful—dangerous, really—to love children before you knew they would live. And I didn't bother asking the obvious question: Can a person really do that? Withhold love from a person they truly love?

I already knew the answer. If I have learned anything in the years since I've seen Billy, it's that you can stop loving someone if you need to. You can stamp love out of your brain like a tiny fire.

O ver the years, Mom taught me how to do this. Mom did it herself. First, she started with those little white pills that helped her sleep, and then she moved on to the little white pills that helped her get through the day, and then there were the little white pills that counteracted the effects of all the other little white pills, not to mention the cocktails at four. That's when she would call me. I could hear the ice jingling in her glass. It was clearer than her words.

"Hi, Sthally," Mom said.

This was what Mom sounded like when I was in college. This was why I found ways to get off the phone. I was busy—taking more classes than I should. But mostly, I couldn't bear the sound of Mom's voice, how one word slipped into another. I couldn't bear to answer the same questions over again: What classes are you taking, Sally? What are you majoring in? Since when do you do the school paper?

Modern Poetry. English. Since sophomore year.

And then: "I have to go, Mom. Sorry, I have a thing."

On weekends, I went to parties. During snowstorms, I sledded down the quad hill. During summers, I went kayaking. I spent long hours in the newsroom, debating obscure things (does "people problems" have a hyphen?) and reporting on stupid things with gusto, like the arrival of Dunkin' Donuts to the student center or the group of boys who refused to wear anything but shorts during the winter. They claimed they didn't feel the cold. There was a scientific name for this, which I forget now.

"Interesting," I said. "Very interesting."

I interviewed a girl in my Latin class who was raised by bears in Alaska. A girl in my bio class who had once been in a cult.

"Mostly, I have fond memories of the cult," June said. She remembered feeling a real sense of community. Like everyone in the cult was her mother or father. "I remember painting a lot. I remember building fences. I remember being surrounded by people I loved all the time. Everything was communal. Even parenting."

Interviewing people for the paper, I learned, was not so different from our conversations at night across our beds. I was good at it—trained since birth to be curious about the lives of others. And in college, my questions won me a lot of friends. People loved telling me their stories for the same reason you loved telling me your stories. I gave people the space—literally five hundred words on the front page of the paper—to celebrate who they were. To listen to the things about them that nobody else would listen to.

By senior year, for the first time in my life, I had more friends than I could count on my hand, and Nicole and June and I went out with these friends nearly every weekend. We stood around kegs in their basements. We got high with them for the first time. We went to nightclubs downtown, where I learned how to dance in the dark. Sometimes, I brought a guy home, and when I was drunk like that, when I was in bed with a boy from my fiction class, I thought about how confused you'd be to see me there—my face pressed against a bedsheet of pizza crumbs. A random boy on top of me. A body I could hardly feel. And that's always when I started to cry. I cried hard—deep, heaving sobs, the way I had started crying ever since that night at Jan's.

"What's wrong?" the guy asked. "Am I doing something wrong?"

I tried to explain. I tried to tell him my story. I tried to tell him about my beautiful older sister, who loved me so much, who told me secret things late at night, but my pants were off, and he was hovering above me, and all I could bring myself to say was, "I don't know, my sister is dead," and then I pressed my face into the pillow and cried some more. The guy was always very understanding, whoever he was. But in the morning, as he put on his jeans, I hated him for all that he had seen.

I went through a lot of guys like this in college. A soccer player from Georgia who impressed me by adding Coke to his red wine. A guy from Iowa who kept trick boxes on his bookshelves. A guy in my Modern Poetry class just because he agreed with me that the grieving woman in Robert Frost's poem "Home Burial" had no right to be upset with her husband, even if her baby was dead.

"I don't understand why the woman is so upset," he said to the whole class. "He's just trying to help out."

Neither did I. The woman just sits in the house all day and watches her husband from the window as he digs a tiny grave in the ground. The woman can't stand it—the way her husband makes the gravel "leap up! Like that, like that, and land so lightly." And the way he comes in the house after to say, "Three foggy mornings and one rainy day will rot the best birch fence a man can build."

The woman doesn't understand: How can you talk like that, at a time like this?

And no, it didn't seem like the right time for spewing agricultural proverbs. But I remember wondering what else she thought the man was supposed to be doing? I mean, at least he is doing something!

"Somebody had to bury the baby, no?" I said.

We both hated the woman, and the baby needed to be buried. That was the last thing we agreed on before he came to my room and we did everything-but.

Nicole thought I was a slut but was careful never to say so. Nicole knew she had her own problems. As we got ready to go out at night, she always turned the lights off. She didn't want to see herself in the mirror, and I didn't understand. How can you see yourself then? I asked. She pressed her nose up very close to the mirror, put on her mascara.

"I can see all I need to see," I told Valerie. "That's what she says."

"I knew she couldn't be normal," Valerie said.

And I was glad for it. I loved Nicole, and I loved college, and felt depressed when I had to go home for some holiday. But I went home, and I walked into our old house, which no longer felt like our house. Said hello to Mom, who seemed less and less like Mom.

"Your mother is not herself," Dad always warned as we drove home from the train station.

I understood. Her memory was bad from the medication. What medication? I didn't even ask after a certain point. I just sat on the deck with Mom, while Mom said things like this: "They were going to put me in an institution, Sally. I just about had it. But I wanted to be here for you when you got home from college. I just wanted to see you."

Who is they? Dad?

Dad was always doing something then. Walking around the lawn, moving dead branches from the woods into a pile. Mom was on the porch, smoking a cigarette. Mom was a smoker now.

"But how can you want to *die*?" I asked her.

"I don't know," she said. "I'm a bad mother."

"Don't you want to be at my wedding one day?"

"I didn't think you wanted to get married," she said, and her eyes lit up for a second, like maybe she would just stick around after all!

"Why did you think I didn't want to get married?"

"Because you said, and I quote, 'Mom, I don't ever want to get married,'" Mom said.

"Well, that's not the point! I just mean, don't you want to be here with me for the rest of my life? Don't you want to know your grandchildren?"

"How are you going to have children if you don't get married, Sally?"

"I could have one out of wedlock," I said. "People do it all the time."

"Don't you dare," Mom said.

"Well, if you're dead, you won't be able to stop me," I said.

The thought of missing the rest of my life, of not being able to hold my bastard child, made Mom cry.

"If you die, you're dead. That's it."

"I know that. But I can't explain it," she said. "But I'm trying. I'm just trying to be honest, Sally."

Then Mom went inside to take a nap, and Dad sat down next to me in the chair, legs spread wide, admiring his work.

"Do you think she'll do it?" I asked Dad.

"Do what?"

"Kill herself," I said.

"Nah," Dad said.

"How do you know?"

"When she says that, I say, go ahead!" Dad said. "Do it!"

"You tell her to do it?"

"Because she won't do it. She won't. If she really wanted to do it, she would have done it."

Dad still spoke with the confidence of a man who had been alive forever, as though he shook hands with Jesus on his way to the cross. When I read my history texts at school, it was still sometimes Dad I imagined signing the Declaration of Independence. It was Dad, fighting in the Civil War. Dad claimed he was born in the wrong century. I could have been a Spanish fisherman, he said once. Or a cowboy. I would have been a great cowboy. Which we all agreed was true, because sometimes he sat out on the deck with a dark drink and just stared through the trees like he was waiting for a message arriving on horseback.

"I don't think that's true," I said. "I really don't think you should say that to her."

Dad kissed me on the head. He told me he loved me. He told me he loved me a lot. He knew it was important to say this to children and so he did it. It made me feel better. Like things might be okay, as long as we loved each other deeply.

But then I woke up the next morning to a pamphlet on the kitchen counter that said "Electroconvulsive Shock Therapy."

"What is this?" I asked Mom.

"Oh," Mom said. "That's just something I've been thinking about." As if it were yoga. A new yogurt flavor from the store.

"You've been thinking about *this*?"

"A little."

"Why?"

"Because it sounds like a good idea."

"A good idea? How is this a good idea?"

I read from the sheet. ECT: a treatment for severely depressed patients who have exhausted all their other options. It was used sometimes for patients who were imminently suicidal.

"They attach electrodes to your brain," I read.

"Honey, that was fifty years ago," she said. "It's much safer now."

That's what it said on the sheet of information. That the procedure was completely safe now because they used muscle relaxants to paralyze the patient and calm the jerking motions, because it's the wild jerking that broke the patients' bones.

"Grandma had this done. She was catatonic and she had a real improvement."

"She was?" I asked. "And you aren't catatonic."

"I swear. If I didn't have to feel like this, I wouldn't."

I did my research. ECT.

It was used to treat mania, catatonia, and schizophrenia.

Side effects: confusion, memory loss, cognitive impairment.

Famous people who had done it: Kitty Dukakis. Lou Reed. Sylvia Plath. Ernest Hemingway. I printed out the information for Mom. Two out of four killed themselves. Plath put her head in the oven. Ernest Hemingway shot himself after his treatments. "It was a brilliant cure, but we lost the patient," Hemingway said.

But most days, a mother's grief was a child that could not be reasoned with. At some point, it could only be put to bed.

"Good night," she said.

It was only noon.

D o you think this is a good idea?" I asked Dad.

"Something has to be done," he said. "It can't go on like this."

"How do you deal with all of this?"

I wanted to learn from Dad.

"I compartmentalize it," he said. "I put it in a box, in some tiny corner of my brain."

I imagined this little box, a tiny, practical coffin. One the Amish might use.

"Because you have to go on," he said. "You have to find a way."

He went into his office, where he sat under a photograph of a famous golf course in Scotland. It's the most beautiful golf course in the world, he said, but he would never visit because he still insisted he was too tall to go to Europe.

"Dad, you have to stop saying that," I said. "You have to just go to Europe."

"No way!" he said. "I can't sit on a plane like that for six hours. No way."

"Will you go when you get old and shrink?" I ask.

"I *am* old," he says. "That's what I keep trying to tell your mother. I say, Susan, we're getting old. It's time to live, before we're dead."

D uring my senior year in college, Mom went to the hospital a lot. Mom had repeated doctor visits to get clearance. The tests and tests and tests. They needed to know if she was sane enough to undergo this therapy.

Some doctors thought she was *too* sane. Some suggested estrogen pills, because they might make her happy, but all they did, Mom claimed, was make her cry, then give her a period.

"No fifty-eight-year-old woman should still be having monthly periods, should they?" she asked.

"I don't know," I said. And I didn't.

She began her first ECT treatments just after I graduated, and before I took off for Europe. I was scared to go home for a month. I was afraid of all the progress that going home would erase. I arrived armed with facts about very sad people who did very impressive things.

"Robert Frost," I told Mom and Dad at the dinner table. "He lost all his children. And then he won a Pulitzer."

"Is that so?" Dad said. Dad was always impressed. But Mom was never listening. Mom had the TV on very loud.

"John Edwards, too," I said. "He lost a son and now he's running for president. What are you doing?"

"I'm running for the Golf Commission," Dad said.

"What's that?" I asked.

"Run budget stuff for the course," Dad said.

Dad was doing okay. Dad had new knees. Dad was getting involved in things for the first time in his life—he wanted to move, too. Somewhere warm. Somewhere he could play golf every day. He kept asking Mom about it, but Mom refused to even have a discussion about it.

"Are you listening, Susan?" Dad said. "I just asked you a question."

But Mom was not responsive.

"I can't say weal world," Mom said.

"What?" Dad said.

"Why do you need to say 'real world'?" I asked.

"It just seems like a thing I should be able to say," Mom said. "Weal world. Weal world. Weal world. See?"

After her third treatment, everything hurt. She could pick up the remote, but she couldn't hold it above her head.

"Why do you have to lift the remote above your head?" I asked.

"Well, I don't," she said. "It's just good to be able to do a thing like that."

After the fourth treatment, she had stopped crying. But she was skeptical.

"I don't think it's working," Mom said. "I feel the same."

"Give it some time," Dad said.

"I just don't feel any different. I feel the same, but I just can't remember anything anymore," Mom said.

"Give it time."

"I'm going to call the doctor."

As the days went by, she forgot more and more.

"How do I get to the Stop and Shop?" she asked.

"It's just down Main Street."

"I know, but I don't know if I'll be able to remember that."

So many questions. What did we do last weekend? she asked.

Mall, movies, and dinner, I said.

Mom couldn't hold on to memories, and I wondered if this was how ECT worked. She couldn't be sad if she couldn't remember what was making her sad. She wouldn't cry through dinner if her mind wasn't flooded with images of you. Though the literature said it's more complicated than that. The electricity sparks the building of brain cells. These new brain cells, as I understood it, become happier than other brain cells.

"I'll go to Stop and Shop," I said.

"Can you get some prosciutto?" Mom asked.

"And some wine?" Dad asked.

And that's where I finally saw him again: Billy, walking out of the liquor store with a box full of wine. It stunned me to see him like that, in his bright white robes, outside the tiny coffin I had built for him in my head.

"Sally," he said.

And isn't this how it always happens with Billy? I try not to think about him. I try not to wonder what he is doing or who he is with and how he is touching her. I manage to decide that he is nothing, just a figment of my imagination. A mythological creature from our past. But then he appears.

"Billy," I said. He was standing there, in front of a liquor store, holding a giant box of liquor, as real as anything. "A priest robs a liquor store. Isn't there a joke about that?"

"If there's not, there probably should be," Billy said.

For a moment, I wanted to cry. I wanted to hug him. But then I stamped out the fire in my head. I put Billy back in his tiny coffin.

"I didn't know you could drink booze as a friar," I said.

"It's about the only thing you can still do," he said. "And technically, I'm not a friar yet."

He was going to take his final vows at the end of that year.

"What are final vows?" I asked.

"They're final," he said. "You make them and voilà. You're a friar forever."

"But what if you change your mind?"

"You can't. I mean. It's forever."

"But not if you change your mind."

"That's not really how it works . . ."

"Well," I said. "That all sounds nerve-racking. No wonder you need so much booze."

He laughed. "Oh no," he said. "The booze is for my father. I mean. He just died. We've got a bunch of people at the house."

"Oh," I said. "I'm sorry to hear that."

"Thanks," he said. "It's hard. But it's been coming for a few years now. Lung cancer. Diagnosed just after I left for the seminary."

We paused. "Oh," I said. "Still sad though."

"Yeah. But the good thing is, he had a long time to make peace with it."

"Right," I said. "Good for him then."

He cleared his throat. "What about you? How are your parents?"

"My dad is alive," I said, which suddenly sounded like bragging. So I told him about Mom. "My mom is not well."

"What do you mean?" he asked.

"It's a long story," I said.

"Why don't we get a drink?" he said. "You can tell me your long story."

"I guess it's not that long a story," I said.

In the parking lot, I told him all about Mom. About the ECT. About how Mom couldn't lift up her arms anymore. About how she fell the other day holding a laundry basket, all the way down the stairs. Because Billy was a friar now. I could tell Billy all the worst things.

"I'll say a prayer for her," Billy said.

"One prayer for Mom, coming right up!" I said. But he didn't get the joke. He wasn't joking. Billy was really going to go home and say a prayer for Mom. "Well. I should go."

But we stood there. Even though there wasn't anything to say. For the first time since you died, I had nothing to say to Billy.

"Hey," he said. "Maybe sometime, if you're around, we can grab a coffee."

"Oh," I said. "I won't be around. I'm leaving for London in a few days."

"Oh, wow," he said. "London. That's great. What for?"

"Just traveling," I said. "With my college roommate."

"Sounds fun."

"Should be," I said. "Well, I need to be off. Good luck with your final vows, Billy."

"It's actually not Billy anymore," he said.

Billy didn't have things anymore. He didn't have a phone or a car or a computer. He didn't even keep his name. He had taken a new name his first year. Gabriel Thomas.

But I refused to use it.

"See ya," I said, and I hope it hurt him as much as it hurt me.

W hen I got back from the grocery store, Mom couldn't remember what prosciutto was. She swore she never heard of it before. I said, You told me to get it at the store. I reminded Mom of its ham-like texture. How she used to wrap it around cantaloupe and we all sat around the kitchen counter and ate it.

"Oh, okay, now it's coming back to me," she said.

Everything was always suddenly coming back to Mom, and I felt jealous of her memory loss.

"How does it feel?" I asked Mom.

"Like you think you might be happy but then you remember something you are forgetting," she said. "And you know it's important but can't remember why or if that's supposed to make you sad. Does that make sense?"

I n those final days before I left for Europe, Dad was excited for me. Dad said, "Go! Get out of here. We're fine!"

Mom made grand proclamations from her bed about how dangerous Europe was going to be. She told me about her time in Europe after college—how she carried an Italian marble chess set across three countries. How she got chased down the street by Australians.

"I'll be fine, Mom," I said.

And I was fine. I was better than fine. I was in London. Paris. Germany. I was everywhere. In a new city each weekend. "Where are you again?" Mom kept asking.

I was in Italy. I was in Prague. I was at the North Sea. I was in a café drinking espresso with a man named Ronaldo. I was on a boat, traveling around the Thames with a man named Will.

"Do you have a thyroid problem?" Will asked.

"How did you know that?" I asked. "Are you a psychic?"

"Your hands," he said. "They're really cold. I'm studying to be a doctor."

"Oh," I said, and laughed. "Well, good diagnosis."

Will and I went up on the top level of the boat and put the life vests over our fancy clothes. We wore them for most of the night. We thought this was very funny. We laughed a lot, but I don't remember about what. I just remember laughing. And wasn't that the most important thing? Wasn't that all a person wanted to remember? I was in love by the time we docked. And that's what I was like in Europe—in love with everybody by the time the night was over.

What I like about Ray is that whenever I come home, he immediately announces what I missed.

"Your mom called," Ray says when I return from therapy.

"Of course, she did," I say. "It does not matter that I literally just spoke with her on the phone."

"She wanted to know if we were coming home for the hurricane," he says. "And also, if we were eating well."

"What did you tell her?" I ask.

"I told her we haven't been eating," Ray says. "I said, Oh no. Susan. Were Sally and I supposed to be eating this whole time?"

I swat him on the shoulder. He laughs. He likes it when he's funny. So do I.

"I mean about the hurricane," I say.

"I said we'd consider it," Ray says.

"We can't consider it. You have to work. You have that work boat thing tomorrow."

Ray is a lawyer. He works for a firm that is both rich enough and small enough to take all of the employees and the people the employees regularly sleep with on an annual cruise around the Statue of Liberty.

"I can skip it," he says.

"You can't skip it," I say.

"Please, let me skip it."

"No," I say. "You're going. And so am I. What did you sell your soul for if we don't get to drink free wine on a boat?"

"I knew you'd say that," Ray says, because this is what we say whenever we feel spoiled by Ray's job. "Which is why I told her we would go after the boat thing. You know it'll be good for you."

Ray opens a very expensive bottle of wine, and for some reason, I picture you as you should have been: here, clapping your hands as he pops the cork and pours the wine into your glass. Because you would have loved Ray, the way he always buys overpriced wine, springs concert tickets on me, buys the whole dinner for everybody. Ray grew up without much money, which is why he likes using it so much. It's a toy he never got to play with as a kid. He is not ashamed of how much money he earns or spends, as though being poor from childhood gives him a pass, as though he is not being greedy, but making up for lost time. We always order appetizers, even if we aren't hungry, because he never ordered appetizers as a kid. He never went out to eat.

These are things he tells me in the dark, after sex, which is when Ray talks the most about *who he used to be* and *what made him who he is today*. His mother worked at Tim Hortons, and so that was where they ate, because that was where they always were. But now he's a lawyer who doesn't come home until nine at night sometimes, and on weekends he plays guitar at certain bars. He reads David Foster Wallace and wears hooded cardigans with stripes and plays on a soccer league with Irish people who make him laugh harder than anyone else in the world. I go sometimes, just to see Ray laugh. It's weird watching Ray laugh very hard from a distance with people I don't know. It makes me feel like I don't know him, and this makes me feel less guilty about keeping things from him. Ray is a stranger, too, I think. Unknowable. After sex, he is a little boy from Canada with no appetizers; after work, he is a man with strong soccer legs and a shiny sweat-resistant blue shirt and a lot of hilarious international friends who make jokes I cannot hear. It is only as we get on the subway or enter a party that he feels like my fiancé, when he takes my hand without even looking down, without saying a word.

"You went on a long walk," Ray says, and hands me my glass.

I take a sip of my wine. I am always on the brink of telling Ray about the therapist, because when you live with someone, omitting can at times be just like lying. When I leave, I say, "I'm going on a walk," which is true, because I walk to the therapist. But after a few weeks, it has started to feel like I am cheating on Ray with my own emotions. I leave Ray, once a week, for the Lower East Side, where I sit in a small room with all of my feelings. There is a woman in the room, of course, with ears that are always tipped red. This woman files and organizes my feelings. Then, she looks up, as if she knows something about me. Something I don't know about me. Something I desperately want to know and why won't she just tell me what's wrong with me?

"Okay," she finally said last week. "It has become clear to me that you have no center, Sally."

"No center?" I asked.

"No," she said. She said that this is why I do not know if I want children. This is why I don't know if I want to be married.

"But I'm engaged," I said.

"Yet you are constantly wondering if you want to be," she said.

She looked down at her clipboard, a record of things I've said in past meetings, evidence of me that she keeps to hold against me.

"Quote, I don't know if I want to be engaged to Ray, end quote."

"Did I say that?"

Not having a center is, according to the therapist, the one problem that explains all my problems. It's the thing that connects the dots, the cancer that explains the strange symptoms; for instance, Why don't I want to leave the city and buy a house with my fiancé? People with fiancés love houses. Yet people without centers are afraid of houses. People without centers do not like thinking about mortgages, because people without centers do not value commitment, since they can't even commit to themselves.

"I am engaged," I reminded her again.

"Oh, boy," she said. "Do you want to work on this together?"

"I don't know," I joked. "That sounds like a lot of commitment."

She doesn't appreciate jokes, mostly, it seems, because she's not used to them. But also because the emptiness inside of me is not a joke, she insisted. The emptiness is a black hole, all the more serious because I laughed about it.

"I mean, building a center sounds like a lot of work," I said. It sounded like the project of a politician, like something that might require a lot of funding. I think of all the jokes I could make—jokes I would make to Ray, like perhaps I should turn to the internet, Kickstart some support for my center—but did not make them.

"I mean, isn't it too late?" I asked. "It seems like the one thing you can't go back and add is a center. The center has to be there from the start."

She paused, for dramatic effect.

"You're not a building," she said. "You frequently talk like that, you know."

"Like what?"

"Like you're a structure," she said. "Like you're just a building."

She wrote something down. I imagined it looked something like, *six months and patient still thinks she is a building.*

And how to explain this to Ray? How to come home and say, Well, today I found out I am not a building.

"It was good walk," I say to Ray. "I needed it. And apparently walking is better exercise than running."

"Says who?" Ray asks.

Ray runs a lot. Ray does marathons.

"Valerie posted a study on Facebook."

"Oh, then it must be true," he says.

Facebook: You would have loved it. You would have checked it every day. Called me to marvel at all the great and terrible and inconsequential things that were happening to the people we knew in high school:

Priscilla's unborn child is the size of a lemon.

Valerie's boss made a passive-aggressive comment to her today ("My, don't we look casual").

Shelby Meyers had a really excellent haircut recently.

Then we would have taken the quizzes that Lia McGree always posts, the ones that promise to tell us the hard truth about ourselves, like "What Do Your Bath Towels Say About You?" and "Are You Actually Happy?" And it would have been silly and fun because the internet is sort of like the dark and private space of our bedroom at night, into which we could say and be anything.

But I stopped posting years ago. And I never search for Billy's name anymore. Not since I moved to New York City. At a certain point, I just stopped caring.

"So," Ray says. Ray starts to cook. He drinks his very expensive wine and tells me about his day. "I had to go into the judge's chambers today. He disrobed. It was weird."

"Why was that weird?"

"Because we were only in there for a few minutes and he disrobed. And then we went back into the court and he robed. Pomp and circumstance. Silly."

He tells me how the judge's chambers had tiny model airplanes on the mantle, red velvet couches, a picture of the judge with Ronald Reagan.

"And the whole time I'm thinking, this is right across the street from a store called Ninety-nine Cent Dreams."

"Can dreams still be dreams if they're so affordable?" I asked.

"Apparently," Ray says. "High-end heavily discounted dreams."

During dinner, we drink a glass of wine and watch some documentary. Ray loves documentaries. Something about how mushrooms in the Paleozoic era were as tall as trees. The mushrooms could grow so big and strong like that because there was nothing else in the world that existed.

In the morning, before the boat work thing, Ray and I have sex without kissing. We both act like we don't mind this, the not kissing, but neither of us can get off without the additional sensation, the closeness of mouth. It starts to feel embarrassing, and Ray pulls away. "It's not you," he says. "I don't want you to think it's you. It's my breath."

I laugh, thinking of a hypothetical scenario in which this is the way he chooses to break up with me. *I'm sorry; it's not you, it's my breath. It's really that bad.*

"I couldn't smell it," I say. "Because mine is so bad."

"Then it's official. We're meant for each other," he says.

We brush our teeth, and when we're clean, neither of us feels like starting again. The honesty has sterilized the air between us. Like the Roundup we spray in the garden that kills both the bad things and the good things. Honesty is important to Ray. Ray has been lied to enough in his life. His last girlfriend was a liar. And a cheater. She cheated on him every day, going to the coast of Maine with another guy when he thought she was working at the Dairy Queen.

He told me about the ex who worked at the Dairy Queen on our very first date. He offered up the story like a warning.

"Kill me, punch me, scream at me, but don't ever lie to me," he said. "Don't treat me like a fool. You know what I mean?"

I knew what he meant. I took a sip of wine. I also knew enough about dating by that point to know I was supposed to tell him about my ex now, maybe go into a story about Billy and how he fucked me up—*left me to become a friar! I mean, who does that, right?*—but I didn't want to. I was in New York City, where it felt okay not knowing everything about a person. New York City was a city for people who wanted to be seen without context. I wanted Ray to look at me like a flower, in a vase, cut from its roots. So, instead, I talked a lot about my job at ABC News, which had once been very exciting to me but was starting to lose its luster.

"I basically write pieces about people who get famous for stupid reasons," I told him.

"What do you mean?" Ray asked.

I told him about my most recent stories: A woman from Dover, Maine, who claimed she had never sneezed once in her life. A man who tried to split the atom in his own kitchen. "It's just a hobby," the man told me from prison. "I've been trying to build a nuclear reactor on my stove for years. I don't see what the big deal is. You can read about it in my blog."

"That's pretty cool," Ray said. He sounded genuinely impressed.

"And today, I interviewed this man who claims he can't cry," I told Ray. "Tear ducts damaged since birth, he said. So instead of crying, he punches bags of rice at work."

"Why are there bags of rice at work?" Ray asked.

"He works at a rice factory," I said.

It's not that he was ashamed, the man told me. He had done the research. Men who cried over football games have higher levels of self-esteem. Even medieval warriors sometimes cried. As did Japanese samurai.

"Apparently, he tried everything," I said.

"Has he tried watching *Field of Dreams* though?" Ray asked, and we laughed.

I didn't hear from Ray for three weeks. In the meantime, I went to work. I interviewed a man from Alabama who illegally handled boa constrictors. He brought me to his hotel room, showed me his snake. I took a picture of it.

"You want to handle it?" he asked.

"Okay," I said.

"You sure?" he asked.

Yes.

He liked my gusto.

"Suzanne will like you. She won't hurt you," the man said.

"Her name is Suzanne?"

Suzanne was smooth and slimy up my arm.

"She feels wet," I said.

"It's just coldness," he said.

"Now," he said, "let her tail wrap around your arm. She's a constrictor so that keeps her from squeezing. She needs to feel safe, too, so she needs something to hold on to. But don't hold her head too tight or you'll cut off the windpipe."

I watched the animal's head rise and search. But she was not looking for anything in particular. She was just moving in order to not stay still. "Where her head moves, her body will go," the man says. "Let her. Let her be free and she won't hurt you."

I went on bad first dates with a man who waited for me at a bar while reading a book called *Power*. A man who took me dancing and then talked about how angry he was with Nancy Pelosi. A man who talked about his dead mother and the kitten his father wouldn't let him keep. He kept the kitten in a box outside his house in L.A. "Not inside the house, but still mine," he said.

Then there was the man who mountaineered. Over wine, he explained to me that there were ways to drink your own urine if ever stranded in the desert.

"You piss in a bowl," he said. "And then you put that bowl in another bowl, and the condensation will be drinkable."

"But what if you don't have a bowl?"

The mountaineer looked at me.

"Then I guess you're fucked," he said.

He went to William and Mary. He was also a paramedic. He was always thinking about ways to survive. I was not uninterested by this. He said he had wheeled in a woman the other day who was really obese. She also wrote erotic poetry. The mountaineer thought that was weird. But I didn't understand.

"What's so weird about that?" I asked. "That she's obese or that she's writing erotic poetry? Can obese people not write erotic poetry? I don't understand what you're saying."

"Clearly," he said.

But then Ray left a long message on my phone.

"Sally," he said. "Hello. Two things. One, I am partying at Three World Financial Center tonight. We have vodka and little foam coffee cups. Floral design, for a morale boost. Oh, and paper clips. Lots of those. After, I've been invited to some going-away party for someone I only kind of know at a bar I don't like. I'd much rather see you. Let me know if you feel the same."

I felt the same. I went to Ray's, but we didn't sleep together. We talked. I learned that he was a beautiful and failed musician from Canada who had naturally blond hair and slept very well at night. Now he was a lawyer. He hardly visited his family and didn't think it weird that I rarely did, either.

"Do you know how I know you're not a musician?" Ray said to me on our third date. A concert so good it made me feel high. "Your nails are too beautiful."

I had been getting a lot of manicures with Mom.

"Look at mine. Blown to shit."

His fingers were callused at the tips. Hard yellow skin, years of Ray's life I never knew about. Years he spent growing up in Canada. I liked this about him, how he came from so far away.

"Actually, it's only a two-hour plane ride," he says. "Like getting to Pittsburgh or something."

"Well, what was it like?" I asked. "Growing up in Canada?"

"What was it like?" Ray asked, confused. "I don't know. It was like growing up in a tiny house next to other tiny houses. Did I mention each house was divided by a fence?"

I laughed.

"Sounds like we've had very similar upbringings," I said. "Except I bet your neighbors were nicer."

"Were your neighbors mean?"

"I just meant, the rumor is, all Canadians are very nice," I said.

"Oh, are we? And what are you?"

"Assholes. You haven't heard?"

"Not all Canadians are as nice as you think, you know," he said. He told me about his neighbor, a middle-aged man all the kids in the neighborhood were scared of because he used to pour hot oil down a rabbit hole in his yard.

Ray and I didn't sleep together that night. We didn't sleep together for weeks, something we both felt proud about.

"Anyway, I had a great time, not fucking you again," Ray always said before he left, leaning at my door, and for the first six months we dated, we talked like this about ourselves, joked about all the things we did not share, did not have, and yet I felt we had something. We went to concerts, parties, shows, brunches; we took long walks up and down Manhattan, wearing sneakers and eating trail mix, like we were hiking. We walked and talked and by the time we got to the New York Public Library, my calves felt strong. I was outgrowing my sadness. I was becoming an entirely new person, all muscle and sunlight.

O ne year later, when Ray asked me to move in with him, I didn't hesitate. But Mom was upset.

"Jesus doesn't approve of your cohabitation," she said.

Mom's religion still confused me—it wasn't serious enough to make her go to church every Sunday, but it wasn't exactly a joke, either. She never laughed when I said things like, "Well, the Lord has never lived in New York City, has he?"

She lowered her voice.

"But what will you do if he leaves you?" she asked. "Will you be able to pay for the rent on your own?"

There was a space in my mind, like a small white room, where some of my conversations with Mom existed. A closet where I kept my big winter boots, and only pulled them out when it was snowing.

"Then he leaves me," I said.

*　*　*

Ray didn't leave me. A year later, Ray proposed to me. Then, he started making chicken every night because Ray didn't like to eat red meat more than once a week, and I hated the smell of fish in the trash can. Chicken was the sensible choice, made by two people who are trying to live comfortably, forever.

Ray had many ideas for our future. Ray was always pushing me to do things I didn't believe I could do—why don't you just quit your job if you aren't excited about it anymore?

"Because then I wouldn't have a job," I said.

"Good! You're always complaining about your job," he said.

"Am I?"

"Yes."

I didn't quit my job.

But I did start trying to pitch my own articles. I started to freelance, picked up strange little side gigs writing for websites like eHow and About.com, and I made spreadsheets about how much money I was earning on the side to see what was possible. Because Ray was convincing. Ray was a very good lawyer.

The boat: It is very small. And the wind is a little too windy, something we all feel obliged to address right away. Yes, it is quite windy. Must be the hurricane? Yes, a hurricane is coming, but not for a few days. Someone argues that this wind has nothing to do with the wind of a hurricane.

"This is just like, regular wind," a man named Kurt says, and people nod their heads, because Kurt is a partner at the firm. "Unrelated to anything."

It's difficult to stand, yet we clutch onto side tables and chairs and our slivers of white wine and figure out a way to remain upright.

"Okay, enough about the weather," Kurt says. "For Christ's sake."

"Agreed," Ray says.

Kurt is gruff with thick black hair. Ray hates him yet is always trying to impress him. Not quite a father figure, since he's too young and too much of an asshole. When the husbands are introducing the wives, Ray tells them that I'm not his wife; I'm a writer.

"What do you mean, she's your biographer or something?" Kurt asks. "She follows you around and scribbles notes?"

We all laugh. I feel queasy from the rocking of the boat.

"I'd say it'd be a fairly easy job," another man says.

"A slim book, full of almost no achievement," Ray says.

"Ray was born. Ray makes an argument. Ray sips wine. Shortly thereafter, Ray dies. Something like that."

Ray has been at the company for five years now, and they have just started to make fun of Ray with ease, which Ray says is a good sign. It means they like him. Ray has enough confidence, enough success in life, enough hair, not to get offended very easily. The more they harass him, the more he beams.

"No, no, she's an actual writer," Ray says.

Ray likes to say this. He likes to think of himself as someone who is dating a writer, which I know because I like to think of myself as someone who is dating a lawyer. I like saying, My boyfriend, he's a lawyer. I like watching him get dressed in the morning, the sound of his belt buckle, the way he holds his tie against his stomach as he leans over to kiss me goodbye. I am still in bed, of course, which he pretends to hate but actually likes. It makes him feel like a part of him gets to stay home and write and makes me feel I am headed out into the world to do something notable. And so I stay in bed, make coffee, and turn on my computer as I work. I think of Ray in his office, on the thirty-fourth floor, writing and speaking in a legal language that took him half a decade to master.

"A writer, huh?" Kurt says. "Have you written anything I've read?"

"I don't know," I say. "What do you read?"

In short, Kurt has read everything.

"Does that include eHow?" I asked.

"Excuse me?"

Kurt reads everything, except shit on the internet. He hates the internet. "I don't even know what you mean."

"You know when you don't know how to do something and so you go online and Google, how do I do . . . whatever that thing is . . . and random articles pop up?" I ask.

I give him examples of my recent pieces. "How to Knit a Scarf," "How to Hang Christmas Lights," "How to Keep Your Rugs from Slipping," and "How to Brine a Chicken."

"Do people not know how to do those things?" Kurt asks.

"Yes," I say. "Millions of people."

But apparently, none of those people were Kurt. Kurt is a lawyer, one of those men who lives in one state, works in another, and vacations in a third. These men read the *Wall Street Journal* and fold it into a neat rectangle when they are done. These men wear French collars and read mysteries that always get solved at the very last minute; they hate ambiguity. Their careers are all about pretending to know things they don't really know that well.

Knowledge is power, including knowledge a person pretends to have.

Yet this is what the internet has taught me: No matter how inflated Kurt's chest, he can't store all of the world's information inside of him. He must have wanted to know something over the years. He must have asked Google at least one question—"How to Tie a Windsor Knot," "How to Get Rid of Bad Breath"—two of my articles that have accrued one million hits over time. I know by now that everyone is having an affair with the internet; everyone has shameful moments alone with websites they aren't sure they can trust, yet trust anyway. Everyone wakes up at two in the morning and Googles the name of someone they once loved.

"That's what's wrong with the digital age," Kurt says. "No Picassos. No Prousts. Just . . . all of us. And who are we? We're fucking morons, that's who we are."

I smile at him.

I don't say anything.

You are going too far lately, my editor wrote, taking the reader where he doesn't need to be.

This editor is always crossing out the things I write. The editor is always modifying my thoughts. The editor sees holes, gaps in logic, missed steps, words I cannot think of. It is sort of like being coworkers with the wind, a force that is always pushing against me, though I can't ever see it arrive or leave. After the editor edits my piece, I have no idea what happens to the editor. I close my computer and get on the train that will take me home, and where does the editor go? Does the editor have a home? What kind of table does the editor put keys on? Who calls out the editor's name during the middle of the night? It's hard to picture the editor as a person, but more of a substance, like water evaporating from the hot pavement. Sometimes, it feels like the editor is you, telling me to stop, calm down, cross out my lines:

HOW TO BUILD A PERFECT SANDCASTLE

You wait for perfect weather conditions, so your sandcastle does not get destroyed. ~~Though be aware that your sandcastle will get destroyed. Be mindful of the fact that you are dabbling in an art form that cannot remain. Consider becoming Buddhist.~~

Kurt takes a sip of his wine. I can tell what he's thinking. Fucking writer. Fucking hippie. Fucking feminist. But Kurt is polite. He has made millions off this poker face. It is a lawyer's strength, as well as weakness.

"You sure you're a writer? You sound like a public-school teacher," he says.

"You sound like an asshole," I say.

Kurt and his wife look shocked. Ray stiffens. Then Kurt laughs. Pats me on the back.

"It's what they pay me to be," he says, and his wife looks at me and says, "We really just can't believe the state of things in the public-school systems."

Ray looks up at the sky, which we can't see because it's covered by boat.

"So what are you all doing for the hurricane?" Ray asks.

This is how adult conversations begin and end: with the weather. Like the weather is the only thing that binds us. The weather is the only great battle we have left. Something we are all preparing to fight until death. Everyone on the boat sounds excited about it, even though their language is that of complaint. They're shutting down the subway. They won't let us work. Even though we have that Hughner meeting. And I was supposed to be in court! They sound upset, but I know they are excited, because after years of nothing happening, something is happening. In wind and rain, even the lawyers get to be good guys, for a short while.

"Well, good luck to you and your writing," Kurt says, as if we aren't going to be on the boat together all day, as if I am just at the start of something, though I feel like I have reached the end of something. I am (finally) in a healthy relationship. I (finally) love all vegetables, especially the ones rich in vitamins. I (finally) have an office with a lock on the door and enough free time to go leaf-peeping on week-ends with my fiancé. And last night, when I couldn't sleep, I (finally) took one of those happiness quizzes online. Scored a 9 out of 10, which means that I am very happy.

Ray is quiet on the way home. He is having one of those moments where he wonders if he knows me at all. It makes me want to talk, show him who I am. Or at the very least, what I want to be.

"Well, that was interesting," I say.

"Always is," he says. "That's what happens when you put a bunch of lawyers on a boat."

Ray is on his phone the whole way home on the train. Judging by his body language, you'd think he was negotiating a crucial deal with Samsung or texting with the Russian president, but when I look over at the screen, I see he's playing a game. He keeps throwing red circles at green circles to destroy them. When he's killed all of the green circles, he leans back in his chair, puts his phone away, and smiles.

"You did it," I say. "You won."

"I did it," Ray says. "I'm the fucking green circle champion of the world."

"Congratulations."

Then I check Facebook for three seconds, which is all it takes to feel like shit. Valerie is hiking in the Alps. Priscilla is drinking a virgin margarita in St. Barts with her wife. Peter is at a conference in Silicon Valley. And Will from the Thames River is now in America, living with his girlfriend in Virginia, and is very excited for his first hurricane. He has posted pictures of all the alcohol he's going to consume when it arrives. *Bring it on, bitch!* he writes.

It makes me want to write something angry in response. But I don't. Because suddenly, I see Lisa the Lifeguard post a picture of a beautiful rosebush. She has tagged Bill's Tree and Garden. *Thank you for the beautiful bush!*

I click on her profile to find that Lisa has been tagging Bill's Tree and Garden in almost all of her photos for six months now. Lisa and Bill's Tree and Garden, at a B and B in front of a beautiful mountain. Lisa and Bill's Tree and Garden, at a bakery somewhere in Maine. Lisa and Bill's Tree and Garden, at a jazz concert on the Town Hall lawn. Lisa is featured in every photo, but Billy is not. He must be the photographer, doing his best to capture the beauty of the moment, of Lisa, who often stands on one leg in her photos, like a flamingo.

I click on Bill's Tree and Garden and discover how little I know about Billy now: Billy lives in Aldan, Connecticut. Billy has a beard. Billy likes the Mountain Goats and has recently watched the Lord of the Rings trilogy for the third time and has 344 friends and a lot of photos, which are actually kind of boring, because he only posts photos of things he recently planted: rose of Sharon, a lemon tree, an English ivy.

The train stops and the doors open wide. We stand up.

"I think I am going to be sick," I say.

"What's wrong?" Ray asks.

But before I can explain, a woman behind us loses track of her dog. The dog circles around our legs and then rushes ahead of us out the door.

"Where's my dog!" the woman shouts. "Frankieee!"

The woman is struggling to grab all her luggage. The dog is out the door on the subway platform, not waiting for his owner. The woman shouts louder and louder, and I can hear in her voice that she knows she is losing her dog. Frankieeeee! That is how these things happen. One footstep at a time, one wrong glance left instead of right, and soon it's not her dog. One swerve right, one deer in the road, and soon you are not my sister.

I run out of the train and grab the dog for her.

When the woman sees me, she kneels down with all of her bags, and she laughs as the dog licks her face. I don't know why, but reunions like this always make me want to cry.

Inside the apartment, Ray drops an Alka-Seltzer tablet into the water, and I feel calm as I watch the water foam.

We pack for home. Ray packs all his fancy shirts, which are the only shirts he has. I hate Ray's shirts. They are too formal, too shiny to wear with cargo shorts. Brooks Brothers shirts, the kind that promise never to wrinkle, and under the kitchen lights, I can see the slick coating that makes them wrinkle-free. He wears them everywhere. To the bowling alley with our friends; to brunch in his flip-flops; to his nephew's birthday party and into the moon bounce. It never looks right. But I never tell Ray this. I can't bear the look on his face when he realizes his entire adult life, he has spent all of his weekends wearing the wrong shirt.

"What you need to say is, Ray, just because you're used to the shirts, doesn't mean they are as casual as you think they are," my therapist said.

My therapist believes that being honest is easy. She says that you just open your mouth and that the truth comes out. And perhaps this is so, but this assumes that we all know what is the truth.

"Ray," I say. "Why don't I go home myself?"

"You don't want me to come?"

"I don't need you to come."

"It's not about need," he says. "It's about having company."

"I'll be fine," I say. "I'll be in and out. Back by tomorrow night. Just stay here. It'll be fine. There's never any place for you to sleep anyway."

Ray always has to sleep on the couch, because Dad got rid of your bed. But it isn't just that—our house is musty. The pillows are old. And the white couch—it's not that white anymore. Mom just sits there and watches TV, while the house goes into ruin. Dad stopped fixing things years ago because he thought it might inspire Mom to do something or maybe move to Florida. Dad was still ready to go to Florida. He was cold. He didn't understand how they were going to take care of the house in their old age. "It's too big for us," he always said. "You want to take care of it?"

Mom never answered him, so Dad started leaving Post-it notes on the counter, detailing all the things that needed to be fixed one day, as if Mom might fix them herself. DO SOMETHING ABOUT THE BAT IN THE MORNING, one of them said once.

"Ray, I'll be fine, really," I say. "I'll be back by tomorrow."

And he believed me. He knew about my two-day limit.

"Okay," he said. "If you insist. But be back before the storm."

We get into bed. Ray falls right to sleep, but I can't. So I go out onto the balcony, and I look down at the city, and I understand why our cat always liked to sit atop the bookshelf. From this high up, everything looks more beautiful. The traffic is a long ribbon of white and red.

I sit and I smoke one cigarette—all I will allow myself these days—and search Lisa's profile for more information. Lisa is a vet, apparently. She has a lot of photos of herself, being a vet. There is Lisa, resetting a mouse femur. Lisa, holding the kitten by the scruff of the neck, inserting a long needle, and the kitten doesn't even seem to mind. Somehow, the animal can feel her goodness. Must be something about her smooth skin or the straight edge of her neatly cropped bob. Lisa has grown up to be clean and trustworthy and to the point, like a perfect paragraph. She posts articles about animals and what we can learn about love by looking at animals. I click on all the links—I want to learn from these animals. From Lisa.

When the cigarette turns to ash, I go back inside, where Ray is still asleep. Ray is a good sleeper. So good that he sometimes looks dead. And as soon as I think this, I worry he is dead. I put my phone on the nightstand. I press my ear to his heart. It's so steady, exactly as you would imagine a lawyer's heart to be.

Home is not as bad as I remember it. Mom has a new Brita. There are new chairs in the kitchen, upholstered. And Dad is outside, setting up his ladder.

"Where's Ray?" is the first thing Mom asks.

"Ray didn't come," I say.

"That's too bad," Mom says. "Dad went out and got a mattress for him and everything."

"Oh," I said. "So *now* you guys like Ray."

"What do you mean? I always liked Ray. Ray just never says thank you. Did you notice that?"

I hadn't noticed that.

Dad walks into the kitchen, covered in sweat and bits of tree. He is filling up a glass with orange juice. He takes a big sip.

"Dad," I say. "Do you know how to cut down a tree?"

"Well, hello to you, too," Dad says.

"Do you?"

"No," Dad says. "But I Googled it."

In preparation for the storm, Dad Googled "how to cut down a tree by yourself," and now he thought he was an expert in cutting down a tree by himself. He has been measuring three trees with the naked eye. He has predicted pathways for them to fall.

"Dad," I say. "People like me write those things on the internet!"

"Good," he says. "You're smart. I trust you."

"Call someone," I say.

"It's not rocket science, Sally," he says. "You just pick up a chain saw."

"But why can't you just get some help?"

"I don't need any help," Dad says. "You worry too much about me, Sally."

I drive to Bill's Tree and Garden before it closes. I am nervous, of course. I am unprepared. I haven't thought about what to say, haven't thought about what it will feel like to be in Billy's presence again after all this time. I just know I have to get there before he locks the doors.

Bill's Tree and Garden used to be such a small operation, two small rooms with plants lining the walls. But now the store looks much bigger than it once had, which is usually the opposite of how things work when you return to your childhood town. Everything usually seems smaller, like the town pool, which looks so austere and tiny now, it seems postapocalyptic.

But someone, likely Billy, has put a lot of work in renovating the place. There is a garden out back and out front. Rosebushes everywhere. I start to wander through them, start to trail my fingers over the flowers, when I see him talking to some woman by the counter.

He is still tall. And he still has the neck tattoo. All of this is to be expected, of course. But there is something different about him that I can't quite explain. Maybe it's the beard or the workman's clothing or maybe it's just the fact that he is holding a small pot of geraniums, patiently explaining its features to a woman, which doesn't seem like a thing Billy would ever do.

"Geraniums are actually good for keeping mosquitoes away," Billy says. "Because apparently, mosquitoes don't like the smell of beautiful things. The monsters."

The woman laughs—and I can hear in her laugh that Billy is the kind of guy who does things for people in this town now. People probably depend on him. People probably call him when they need to move something with his truck. When they want to know what kind of tree to plant in the shady part of their yard.

While he talks, I walk around, run my hands on the rosebushes, just as we used to do. We were so little then, spying on Billy. We plucked the rose petals off the bushes and put them in our pockets only to completely forget about them until Mom did the wash and screamed: "Who put rose petals in the laundry machine?" We would hide our fingernails behind our backs, but we confessed. We did, of course. But it was an accident! We swear! And why? Mom wanted to know. Why would we pluck rose petals off of Mrs. Barnes's bush? Well, we couldn't help ourselves, you explained. We just liked them. We liked the way the petals felt against our lips. But I am too old now, too embarrassed to put anything to my lips—so I press one between my fingertips, admire its softness, and hear Billy say, "Sally."

I startle. I pluck the petal off the bush by accident.

"Billy," I say. I hold the petal in the air. "Sorry."

"That's okay," he says. "I always hated that petal anyway."

I laugh. I press the petal between my two fingers. I should have come with something to say, a speech prepared, maybe the one I had been planning in my mind all those years Billy and I have been apart. But all of them seem irrelevant now.

"I have to admit, I'm surprised to see you here," he says.

"I am surprised to see you here, too," I say.

He nods. "I bet."

"You're not a friar."

"No," he says.

"But I thought you were going to become a friar."

"So did I," he says.

"Now you're Bill."

"I am Bill," he says. He made a joke about how Bill made more sense. "It's already on the sign. And wouldn't you rather buy a tree from Bill instead of Billy?"

"Bill sounds like a good guy," I say.

An awkward pause. I rub the petal between my fingers until it shreds, and I scatter the remains on the ground.

"So how may I help you, Sally?" Billy asks. He looks at my hand, at my engagement ring. "Need flowers for a wedding?"

I feel the urge to explain away the ring. I want to say, This is just some ring of some grandmother in Canada I have never met. It means nothing! But then I remember Ray. Our apartment. How he makes Lemon Chicken. I remember why I have come.

"It's my father," I say. "He needs to remove a few trees in our yard."

"Does he know how to do that?"

"No," I say. "He thinks he does."

"That makes it even worse," Billy says.

"I was hoping someone from the store might come by and help him," I say. "I'm sure you must be busy—"

"I'll do it," Billy says.

"You will?"

"Yeah."

"When?"

"When do you need?"

"Tomorrow morning?"

"No sweat," he says. "Really, Holt."

I don't like hearing him use our last name. As if these fifteen years did not even happen. As if I am just a small girl again, in his dad's flower shop, admiring the roses.

"Here's my cell," he says. He writes it down, and it suddenly feels awful, as if we are just two people, enduring a transaction. "In case you need it."

I want to ask him so many more questions. I want to stand there forever. But another woman has come into the store. She is looking for something. Flowers that she can plant in the fall so that they are ready to bloom in the spring.

"Tulips," Billy says, without hesitation. "Let me show you."

Someone from Bill's Tree and Garden is coming to cut down the trees tomorrow morning," I explain to Dad at dinner. I say it quickly, like I am lopping off his head before he can notice. But Dad doesn't flinch. Dad just takes a sip of his beer.

"If it's Billy," Dad says, "tell him thanks but no thanks."

"Richard," Mom says. "He wants to help. We should really let Billy come over."

And it's the same conversation all over again. The same conclusions. The same certainty that it's Billy's fault you are dead. It's Billy who ruined our lives—that's what Dad thinks. And Dad cannot forgive.

"This is your doing, Susan," Dad says. "None of this would be happening if we were living in a condo right now. We would be sitting on some balcony, drinking those little drinks."

"The ones with the tiny umbrellas in them?" I ask.

"Exactly."

Cutting down trees in his yard is exactly the kind of thing Dad didn't want to have to deal with in his old age.

"But every time I bring it up to your mother, she won't respond," Dad says. "Watch this. Susan, do you want to move to Florida?"

Mom eats a piece of bread.

"See?" Dad says.

Mom turns to me.

"Would you be a dear?" Mom says, holding out her wineglass.

Mom is thin now, light and frail, and looks wobbly when she stands. Upon first glance, she looks like something that can easily be blown over. But I am always learning that is not the case; Mom is stronger than she looks, and her love for the house has grown thick and hard over many years. She exists now like a barnacle stuck to the tiled floor, and even though asking her to move is the necessary thing to do, it seems cruel, like we are scraping her off your dead body with a knife.

"You don't need to do it by yourself," I say. "You can have a professional do it. Billy knows—"

"I'm doing it myself," Dad says.

Dad finishes dinner, puts his boots on, and goes out to the yard to stare up at the trees. Dad always loved the trees in our yard. It was why he bought the house, he told us, and why he couldn't bear to chop them down years ago when he noticed they were dying. But now they are dead, he says, dead as dead can be, and it must be hard. It must feel like his responsibility—like shooting your own dog instead of handing him over to the vet.

I follow him out there.

"He's coming," I say. "Are you listening to me, Dad?"

"I'm not deaf yet," he says.

"Yes, but are you *listening*?" I ask.

According to Dad, listening is very different from hearing. Hearing is something birds can do; it is passive and requires no feedback. But listening is active. It's an effort required for actual communication. Communication is feedback. And so on.

"Tell him that if he steps foot on my lawn, I'll shoot him," Dad says.

D on't worry—Dad doesn't have a real gun. Just a BB gun that he bought to scare off the deer. But still. Mom settles down in front of the TV, and I text Billy.

I wouldn't come if I were you, I write. Apparently, you'll get shot.

Shot by what? Billy asks.

A BB gun, I say.

I'll take my chances then, he writes.

"What are you doing on that phone?" Mom says. "Come sit, Sally. Be with your mother."

Mom is sitting on the couch watching the weather. She has gotten so old that she somehow looks like a child, and I find it hard to look directly at her.

"This is hard for your father," Mom says. "We haven't seen Billy in so long. Have you seen him since?"

"A few times," I said.

"Dad is still very angry at him."

"Are you?"

"Sometimes," Mom says.

But a few years ago, she started to notice something. Every year when she went to your grave for your birthday, there were always fresh flowers. Someone was keeping flowers at your grave, and it wasn't her.

"I have a feeling it's been Billy," Mom says. "I mean, who else would it be? Who else has that many flowers?"

Mom is sitting close to the television like we had as children, as if she is in love with the weatherman and maybe she is. Maybe that's what happens to old women who have nowhere to go. They stare at the sea on TV and they lose their vision and inch closer and closer until they fall in love with the weatherman.

"I can't believe this storm," she says. "The weatherman says it will be a bad one."

"The weatherman is paid to be dramatic," I say.

Right now, he is explaining how we will all die in the storm. He claims that if we do not drown in our beds, then our windows will shatter and slit our throats. If we do not die by glass, then we will die by blunt force, high winds, and waves that will take the house. Like someone cleaning a countertop, in one sweep, and everything is gone. If the house stands, then we have to consider other dangers, things like flooding and electrocution. And we should definitely not go downstairs to get that thing we think we need but don't need at all, because downstairs, in the flooded basement, is where people die.

"It happens all the time during hurricanes," the weatherman says.

The weatherman seems excited about all of the death that is to come; he makes it sound like the different ways of dying are like different trails up the mountainside.

"His wife just left him," Mom says. "A terrible thing, to be left like that."

"Whose wife?" I ask.

"The weatherman's!" Mom says.

"How do you know about the weatherman's love life?" I ask.

"He's local! Rick's from our town. His mother and I go walking together. You went to school with him."

Rick. Rick Stevenson? I search Rick's face for signs of familiarity, but Rick has put on weight, the kind that changes the entire shape of his face. It's only when he walks out to the water and stands in direct sunlight that I can see him.

"Wow, that's really Rick Stevenson," I say.

Then it cuts back to a screen, a meteorological graphic of Hurricane Kathy.

"Why don't we watch a movie?" I ask.

And that's what we are doing, watching a movie, when Ray calls. "How are things?" he asks.

"They were better before my mother and I started watching this movie."

"What is it?"

"I don't know what it's called. Ryan Reynolds is in it. Sandra Bullock. And Betty White is in it."

"Well, that sounds promising."

"Betty is doing her best. But it's not enough."

"I think I've seen that one. Is that the one where they're at the lake house?"

"That's the one," I say. "Does it get better?"

"It's a classic boy meets girl, girl hates boy, boy fake-marries girl, girl sees boy in the shower, then boy actually marries girl story."

"Oh. Yes. That classic," I say.

"So that's it? That is my update?"

"I'm trying to think of non-*Proposal* updates to tell you but frankly most of them involve that movie."

I am lying again.

"I understand," Ray says.

I look out the window. I see Dad measuring the trees with his naked eye. Writing things down in a notepad. I see the sun setting through the window. I see Dad with his chain saw. I see the tree, falling in the right direction, as Dad had predicted, but the tree is much larger than Dad predicted and it falls directly on our swing set.

"I got to go," I say. "My dad is probably going to end up killing himself."

In the morning, when Billy shows up, Dad is sheepish. He says nothing when Billy pulls up in a big white truck. He does not get his BB gun. He greets Billy at the door and Billy stands there with his tattoo, the vines still crawling up his neck. Nobody says anything.

"Well," Billy says. "Show me the damage."

And that's when he becomes Bill.

"Follow me," Dad says.

Bill's assessment: All the trees are too big to fell. There is a chance they might fall on the house, or on the neighbor's house. And Bill doesn't want to take that chance. Bill has taken that chance before.

"It hasn't worked out well," Bill says. "It's hard to measure a tree by eyesight. It's always bigger than you think it is."

"So what do you think we should do?" Dad asks.

"I'm going to have to build a ladder," he says. "Nail the ladder onto the tree as I climb up it. Then I can climb and cut off the branches and the trunk, piece by piece."

"Oh, that's ridiculous," Dad says. "You're turning this into a production."

"It *is* a production," Bill says. "I know the process I'm describing sounds tedious. And it is. It'll take the whole day. But it's the only way I would do it."

Dad looks up at the tree.

"That's my professional opinion," Bill says.

"Then do it," Dad says, and goes back inside.

First, Bill needs to get some supplies. He'll need to go to the store to get some wood. He says it to Dad, but Dad doesn't respond. Dad turns on the TV, pours himself a beer like he's retired now.

"Oh, well, if you're going to the store, can you pick up some candles for us?" Mom asks.

"Mom," I say. "He's not the grocer. He's going to get wood."

"Well, I'm worried the power is going to go out during the storm."

"Of course," Bill says. "Anything else you need?"

"Get some batteries," Mom says. "And some grapefruit juice."

"Maybe a few of those hand grenade things," Dad says.

"Hand grenades?" Bill asks.

"He means avocados," Mom says. "Here, I'll make you a list."

Mom starts writing down a list.

"What are you going to ask for next?" I ask. "Lobster?"

"Oh, lobster," Mom says. "That sounds delicious. It's been years since I've had lobster. How about you pick up some lobster, too?"

"No problem," Bill says.

"Let's have a lobster dinner!" Mom says.

"We've got plenty of leftovers, Susan," Dad says.

"I don't want leftovers," Mom says. "I want to celebrate."

"Celebrate?" Dad says. "What exactly are we celebrating?"

"Kathy, of course," Mom says.

"Oh, Christ," Dad says.

But Bill doesn't miss a step.

"A lobster dinner it is," Bill says.

"And some wine," Mom says.

"Mom."

"I don't mind," Billy says. "Really."

Mom gives him the list.

"Thank you," she says.

Then she sits back down to watch the weather.

Rick certainly is very good at his job. He is making it sound like something is really happening. Like he needs something to be happening. I get it. Too many days go by where we just eat chicken and vegetables and forget about it. Too many days feel like nothing. One week without a bill or a phone call and I start to wonder if I'm even really a person. I don't have coworkers anymore to remind me that I'm a person. I have Ray, but even sex with Ray is starting to seem like nothing. Like a tampon or the metal prongs the gynecologist puts inside me. Sometimes it doesn't seem like anything has really happened since your accident, like I have been out at sea for too long, where the weather is too calm and I can't feel the waves.

"I'll go with you," I say to Bill.

It's a relief to step outside and feel the wind, see the birds flying in panicked circles above the house. They seem to know that something is coming. They must already see the storm from so high above, the dark web spun from the equator, coming just for them.

Bill drives the truck.

The truck, I must say, is a little dirty everywhere, except for the cup holder where he keeps a bottle of Perrier.

"What?" he asks, when he sees me looking at it.

"You drink Perrier," I say.

"Of course," he says. "It's the best water there is."

There are always too many things to say to Billy, and it's impossible to say them all at once, and so it's like there is nothing to say, except the basics, of course, what any person might say to any other person while driving in a car, like hello, and how are you? And how strangely formal for a man who once watched me undress in the dark. Hello and how are you, man who once had his cock inside of me. But this is not a thing to say—not to Bill, who drinks Perrier and has a gray streak crawling up his sideburns.

"How are you?" I say.

This is what it's like to be a grown-up. This is what it's like to drive to the grocery store with Bill.

"I'm okay," Bill says.

Bill is always okay. Not good. Not great. As if he has decided that he is never allowed to be good.

"It's okay if you're good," I say. "It's okay if you're dating Lisa. I know."

"I'm dating Lisa," Bill says. "Sort of."

"What do you mean, sort of?"

"I mean, it's not official or anything," Bill says. "She won't admit it, but I think she's a little embarrassed by me."

"Why?"

"Because I grow plants for a living. And Lisa's a neurosurgeon."

"She's a *neurosurgeon*?"

"For animals," he adds. "But still. She's ambitious. She wants more."

"What does she want?"

"Who knows?" he says. "Who knows what Lisa wants?"

We turn onto Main Street. So many years ago, here we were, standing on the side of the road, calling your name. Looking at your dead body. And now we are on our way to get wood. To get lobster. And Lisa is a neurosurgeon for animals? What happened to her swim career? And why isn't Billy a friar?

"Why didn't you tell me you weren't taking your final vows?" I ask.

"I didn't know when I last saw you," he says.

When he saw me in the parking lot of the liquor store, he had planned to return to the seminary. Right after his father's funeral. He had planned to go back and take his vows and spend his life in a quiet silence. But then he saw me at the store. Then I told him I was taking off for London, and he felt this feeling.

"It was a quick feeling," he said. "Just this feeling of, Oh, I want to go with her."

The whole car ride home, he kept thinking, I want to go to London with Sally. But that's ridiculous, so he settled on asking me out for a drink.

"But you never even did that," I said.

"I tried," he says. "I called you. A week after I saw you, I called. But you never picked up."

"I was already in Europe then. I didn't have a phone."

"Right," he says.

"So why didn't you go through with it, though?" I ask. "Why didn't you take your final vows?"

"They say you should question," he says. "But I was always questioning. I was never certain. I thought at some point, the certainty would just come. At some point, I would give myself over to it enough that I would feel some kind of permanent peace. I would feel truly forgiven. But I never did."

That's when Billy realized—he shouldn't join the seminary to be forgiven. He shouldn't be there out of guilt. Others were there because they were believers. Because they wanted to serve God. But Billy realized he wasn't there to serve God. When he was away from the seminary, he did not miss God.

"I missed you," he said. "I kept thinking about those nights we used to spend at the beach."

So he stayed longer and longer in Aldan. He kept visiting the beach. He kept delaying his return.

"I told myself I was just staying longer to get my father's estate settled," he said. "I told myself I was staying so I could sell the store."

It was true, in a way. At first, nobody was buying. And then, suddenly, after the recession, people were buying, but the offers didn't seem high enough to Billy. He rejected them all and kept waiting for something better and passed the time by tending to the plants inside the store. He couldn't bring himself to let the plants die. His own father had sown and raised most of these plants, and suddenly, Billy wanted to understand why. Billy wanted access to his father's brain in a way he never cared about before.

"That's what happens when parents die," he says. "All of a sudden, you want an answer to every question you never thought to ask them."

He read through all of his father's old notebooks. He started researching at night and running experiments with the plants during the day. He started growing seeds indoors during the long winter. He invested in a new lighting system, a new irrigation system.

"I found it much more healing, to be honest, to take care of my father's plants," he says. "Funny, because I always resisted it so much as a kid. I thought it was embarrassing that my father was a florist. Like there was something gay about working with flowers."

"High school boys think everything is gay."

"High school boys are the worst."

"I'll agree with that."

"I remember being proud when he broke his neck at the store," Billy admitted. "I remember telling everyone about it. Like, Look how manly my dad is, everybody! Look how dangerous it is to take care of flowers! But then I started actually working with them."

"High school boys?"

He laughs.

"No. The plants."

When the spring came and the ivy crawled back up his father's walls and the tulips returned from the dead, he knew he was never going back to the seminary. He knew that he had cared for something—truly and deeply—and he saw how those things came alive again. He had been so convinced that the only solution was to run away—to give up his home, his life, his body—to say, God, do what you will.

"But it wasn't," he said.

The solution was always the opposite of what we expected it to be. The solution was to stay here, to plant a rosebush in the middle of Main Street. To wait, to have patience, to watch new life grow up all around him. And now, it's been years. Now, our town depends on Billy. Our town comes to him for help. They ask him to line the walls of the church for their weddings. They ask him to cover the graves of their dead. They have forgiven him.

"So," he says. "What have you been up to?"

It's strange, shopping with Billy. After all this time, here we are, pushing a cart together in the store, putting food in it, as though we are married. At Home Depot, he gets the wood and the brackets. I get the batteries, the candles.

At the grocery store, I say, "I'll get the lobsters. You get the hand grenades."

"Because I'm a man?" he says.

"No," I say. "Because I don't know what to look for in a hand grenade. Never bought one before."

"You never bought an avocado?" Billy asks. He sounds upset on my behalf. "Who are you?"

So we shop together.

"You want it to be soft, but not too soft," he says. "Check for rotten spots."

Then we stand by the lobsters. There is nobody at the counter. We are waiting for the fish boy to come out of the dark hole that leads to the back. He is likely on break, on his phone, wasting his life away. He is probably not expecting anyone to buy lobsters from him on a day like this, hours before a hurricane.

We stand in line. Behind us, there is a man and his little girl. The little girl keeps staring at us. She has the face of a girl who is on her way to a funeral. She reminds me of you. Or maybe me. She starts confessing things with surprising intimacy, a quality I've always liked, but something I like more and more in a person as I get older.

"Did you know I've never had a lobster before?" the girl says.

We did not know this, we say.

The teenage boy finally emerges from the dark hole.

"Oh," the boy says. "I didn't know you guys were here," like he knows us.

The boy asks me how many I'd like, even though it is quite obvious by his tone and facial expression that he doesn't give a shit how many I want. He seems to hate us, simply because I want lobster. Fair enough. I have hated people for less. His hatred is the only power he has.

"Six, please," I say. "Steamed."

"You want them steamed?" the boy asks. "Like, *here*?"

"Yes," I say.

I don't like steaming lobster in the house. I hate the way it smells, as soon as they die. It's instantaneous, and you can smell the death in the house all week.

The boy mumbles something under his breath.

"I'm sorry," I ask. "What did you say?"

"Nothing," the boy says. "I'm *talking* to the lobsters."

The boy puts the lobsters on a baking sheet and says he will be back in a certain number of minutes that nobody can discern, and then turns with the lobsters into the dark hole.

Billy raises his eyebrows, and I know this look well. It means: Some people are just fucked up. A truth learned from spending too much time at the mall in high school. Bill smiles at me. I want to smile back. I want to laugh about how much the boy hates us. I wonder if the boy has a girlfriend, if they watch movies and make out together in their parents' basements, if they drink beers and make up games with their hands and ignore each other's acne and talk about the shit songs on the radio the way I once did with boys. I wonder what it means to be young now and I have no idea. Who is this boy, and what exactly is he saying to the lobsters?

Billy is so close to me and the desire is strong, a giant wave pulling me out to sea always, but I won't. I won't stand there, with your boyfriend, and act like he is mine. As if the joke is ours. A joke is nothing to own;

it is not a house or a family or a small white dog. It's just a wave crashing over my toes, weakest just after it's strongest, gone as soon as I feel it.

"I'm going to get the big one," the little girl says.

She is done scouting. She returns from the lobster tank with enthusiasm, wanting permission. She points to a large red lobster, alone on the right side of the tank. "The Queen," she calls it, but the Queen doesn't look so much like a queen. She looks big, but in a bad way, like her growth is a thing she cannot help. It is a punishment, being too big for your own house. Being two inches taller than your older sister. And it's true—I am.

"You want to eat the Queen?" Bill asks the little girl. "What, are you trying to start a revolution?"

He is talking to the girl like she's an adult. Like she understands what he understands. I can never decide if this is a good thing or a bad thing, to talk to children as if they are not children, but I admire it.

The boy comes back with the lobsters.

"Here you go," he says.

We drive back with the lobsters in silence. We pull up to our yard.

"Why didn't you call me *again*?" I ask.

"I didn't want to bother you," he says.

"Bother me? I loved you."

"I know. And I felt like I had ruined your life enough," he says. "I caused you enough pain."

"Well," I say. "That was certainly true."

Outside, Billy builds the ladder up the tree trunk. I help him. I hold the nails while he hammers the wood into the tree, plank by plank by plank, until it's a ladder all the way up to the top. He climbs up it, and then chainsaws off branch by branch. Each one lands with a loud smack, and I cringe each time, as if the world is ending.

"I don't like this," Mom says. Mom comes out to watch with a cocktail and a floppy hat. "I can't watch. I just can't watch."

But then she watches.

"He'll be fine," I say.

"This is so dangerous," Mom says. "I can't believe your father was going to do this on his own."

Dad is curious. Nervous, too. He can't help himself—he is a safety consultant to the very core, and when a man climbs up a ladder, he can't help but imagine the fall.

"You okay up there?" Dad asks.

"I'm good!" Billy shouts.

"This is too much for me," Mom says, and goes inside and settles herself with another cocktail and the weather. I do some work on my computer. But all I can think about is how weird it is that Billy is outside, cutting down our maple trees, and Dad is standing at the base, worried about him, and you are a storm on TV.

Rick, the weatherman, sounds confident in his predictions of your behavior. He is confident that you are a system like all systems, that can be measured using instruments. He is clearly excited about the storm, about the beginning of hurricane season, I can see it in his posture. Weathermen all over the shore are finally called to action; they are given wind pants and windbreakers and wait along the shoreline, the first front.

It's amazing, how they can track you. They have colored your path red, from the Caribbean to North Carolina to Virginia to Baltimore to New York City and beyond. On-screen, you look like an angry thing. You have something to say. You are a red circle, in Maryland, where you have already killed three people.

"Now I understand that the decision to take a hurricane seriously is a personal one," the weatherman says.

He says he knows how it can divide a town into people who take things seriously and the people who don't. Some residents have been badly burned before; some people have stockpiled flare guns and water and canned beans and the storm passed before they knew it even came. Sometimes the danger turned out not to be danger at all; sometimes the wind chimes barely chimed, and it was embarrassing, all of that silence. Embarrassing to be standing around the kitchen with those jugs of water, the windows boarded. Embarrassing to have drilled holes into your wall, thinking something significant was on the horizon, only to find out that it was just an ordinary day and you spent it drilling holes into your wall.

"But make no mistake. Old and disabled people should do their best to leave the state, to travel to relatives, to make a holiday of it," he says.

"I think you're supposed to say 'elderly,' Rick," I say.

I'm sure someone will yell at Rick for this. He also keeps forgetting to use an "or" instead of an "and" so that being old sounds like being disabled and vice versa.

"Oh, leave him alone," Mom says. "Did I tell you that his wife left him?"

"Yes," I say.

Mom looks at the ocean on TV, which is flooded with surfers on their boards, waiting patiently, like you are something to have faith in. I feel I might scream. All of a sudden, I can't stand it here for one more second, the smallness of our house, the constancy of the waves, the inevitability of disaster. I can't stand how even now, after all these years, I sometimes look down the hall and expect to still see you, coming out of our bedroom, brushing your teeth, toothpaste building like sea foam.

Because you never are. You are dead—I know you are dead. I saw it with my own eyes. I read about it in the autopsy report, over and over again, and now I know too much about your death. Fun facts that are not very fun, things you do not even know about yourself, like that your brain weighed 1,360 grams. Three times what your heart weighed. And your aorta, it was smooth and glistening. Teeth, hemorrhagic. A laceration on your left eyebrow. Cuts on your lower lip and chin area. Rigor mortis present in the upper and lower extremities. A contusion on the chest, and a broken right ankle, which somehow seemed beside the point.

And yet, I used to sit up at night, saying your name, waiting for you to appear before me, waiting for you to turn into Kathy again. Waiting for you to say something. Just one little thing. A simple "hello" would have sufficed.

But it was only silence that followed. And this silence made me feel so stupid. Your silence, it has always been the most perfect punishment.

It gets dark before Billy can finish. He comes into the kitchen, exhausted from his work. Bits of wood sticking to his sweat.

"Why don't you stay for dinner, Billy," Mom says.

"Mom," I say. "He was just here to work."

"Oh," Billy says. "Sure. That'd be really nice. I love lobster."

"Who doesn't?" Mom asks.

"You want a beer?" Dad asks him.

Has Dad forgiven Billy? Or does Dad just like giving beer to hardworking men? It's something I've seen him do with the plumber and the gas guy. And I have no idea what kind of beer Bill likes. Or maybe he likes whiskey? Maybe he's the kind of man who likes a smoky scotch? I dated a lot of those men in my early twenties.

"Don't mind if I do," Bill says.

He sits in our chair. He cracks open the beer. Spreads his legs a bit. The posture is youthful, and he looks like he did a thousand years ago, when he really was your boyfriend, sitting at our kitchen table, madly in love with you. Trying to impress our parents. Talking about basketball with Dad. Complimenting our mother on the potato salad. Telling stories about his dead grandmother.

Does Billy remember any of that? Sometimes, I confess, it is slipping away from me, too. Sometimes, I forget what it was like to be around you, what it was like to have a sister. I am becoming less and less your sister. But it helps when Mom puts out the potato salad. It helps to see Mom acting like this is the most normal dinner in the world.

"Sally," Mom says, "get the place mats. Billy, get us four plates."

He stands. Billy is tall in a way I never expect. When I see him stand up, I think, Who is this big man? This is Bill, and I'm struck by Bill's body. A working man's body. No longer the basketball player who lifted weights in the gym. But more like a tall oak tree. A lean and muscular body, from a different time period, when men grew only the muscles that they needed.

Or maybe it's true what Valerie said once: People start to look like their jobs. Valerie looks more and more like plastic every day. Ray looks like a lawyer, eyebrows furrowed. And Billy, he looks like he could stand entirely alone in a forest and live forever like that. When he carries the plates over to the dinner table, I watch, just to make sure he doesn't drop them, and I have no idea why I expect him to.

Please don't drop them, I think. Mom and Dad are so close to forgiving you. I feel them, softening.

He doesn't drop them. He places them down gently on the table.

"Someone should turn off the TV," Mom says.

On TV, there are boys running into the water in New York. They are greeting you with their chests. They are not afraid.

"Idiots," Dad says.

The weatherman is gesturing wildly on the beach, which at the moment is just a "regular beach." He points to the "regular clouds," which he says will soon become very ominous-looking ones.

"I wonder how much money he gets for standing out there, telling us what a beach looks like," I say.

"This is like the weatherman's Super Bowl," Billy says. "His World Series. Look at him. Look how excited he is."

Dad turns off the TV.

"Well," Mom says over the table of red shells. "This is certainly unexpected. All of us here."

She squeezes Billy's hand in a way that embarrasses me, but not Billy.

"Thank you for having me," Billy says. He smiles at everybody all at once. Somehow, he can do this, speak to an entire group. "I've been looking forward to something like this for a very long time."

Dad lifts up his beer.

"To Hurricane Kathy," he says.

"To Hurricane Kathy," we say.

It's the first time I've heard Dad say your name in years.

We all take a sip of our drinks. And then the doorbell rings.

t's Ray. Ray drove all the way here from New York. "Why?" I ask.

"You weren't answering my calls," he says. "I was worried."

"I was busy," I say.

"I see," he says.

"We're all fine, Ray," Mom says.

"Sit down, Ray," Dad says. "Have a beer. Have a lobster."

Ray gets a beer. He gets a lobster. He sits down. He looks at Billy.

"I'm sorry, but who are you?" Ray asks.

I can hear the panic in his voice.

"This is Kathy's old boyfriend," Mom says.

Mom says it like Ray should know. But, of course, Ray doesn't know. There are too many things I've never told Ray. Billy extends his hand across the table.

"I'm Bill Barnes," Billy says. "I run the Tree and Garden down on Main."

Like that means something to Ray.

"We've known Billy for a very long time," Mom adds.

This is what Ray knows: You are dead. You died too young, in a car accident, and it was all very upsetting. He knows that whenever I say the words "my sister," he has to be serious. Wipe the smile off his face. Become extra polite to our mother. Unload the dishwasher while our mother lights the candles on your birthday cake. Our mother, she still makes you a birthday cake, which I'm allowed to find weird, but my fiancé must think is sweet.

"Let's eat," Mom says.

Mom was the only one who wanted lobster, but she doesn't remember how to eat lobster. I tell everybody I once wrote a piece on this: "How to Eat a Lobster." People are very concerned about this. Apparently, it's a class-based thing.

"I don't see what this has to do with class," Mom says.

I explain to Mom: When you eat lobster, rip the tail off first. The tail, which is not really the tail. It's actually the abdomen. What we call the tail is the thing's entire body. Sever the body from the head, and do this over a plate, because water will come rushing out. Do not be afraid of this water. It's not the lobster's blood. ~~It is not the lobster's life force. It is not the lobster's soul.~~ It's the water you used to ~~kill it~~ cook it.

Some people eat the lobster faster than others. Some have had more practice. Some people will eat the guts and some won't. For example, Grandpa used to eat the guts, and so we all used to eat the guts, but then Grandpa died of a heart attack and now everybody but Dad stopped eating the guts.

When Ray eats lobster, he does not stop for breaks. He does not stop to wipe his hands ever. He keeps moving, working the meat, and it is all so continuous and fluid, like it is a song he can't stop. When he's done, he settles back in his chair before wiping his hands. He looks around at us, and says, "That was amazing."

(He eats the way he fucks, I told Valerie once.)

(No, Valerie said. He fucks the way he eats. He's been eating for thirty years. Fucking, presumably for less than that.)

After, Ray breathes a heavy sigh.

"So," he says. He looks at Billy. He can't stop looking at Billy. "What's with the tattoo?"

"What do you mean, what's with the tattoo?" Billy asks.

"Were you drunk?" Ray asks.

"Actually, I was sober," Billy says. "Very sober. That's the worst part about it. I *wanted* this."

"Why would you want that?" Dad asks.

"It's a reminder," Billy says.

"A reminder to never get a real job?" Ray asks.

"Ray," I say.

"It's just a joke," he says.

"That," Billy says. "But also, a reminder to love. To keep growing."

I can tell Ray is trying very hard not to roll his eyes. This is the exact kind of statement that would make Ray go, Oh, come on. But Ray is a guest. And Mom is struck down by the thought of Billy growing. Of Billy loving. She looks like she is about to cry, but she doesn't.

"Sounds like a cry for help to me," Dad says.

Billy laughs. "Yes, it's certainly that, too."

"I think it's nice," Mom says.

"It's not nice, Susan," Dad says. "It's a neck tattoo."

Billy smiles at me. Billy seems to like it, this teasing. This having an annoying family thing.

"I always wanted to get a tattoo," Mom says.

"You did not want to get a tattoo," Dad says.

"A tattoo of what?" Billy asks.

"Nothing crazy," Mom says. "Just something small. A little heart. On my ankle."

After, Billy offers to do the dishes, because Mom still doesn't trust her own dishwasher (It's from 1981! she says). But Mom says, No. You've done enough. You should go home, before the storm hits. And so we all say goodbye and good luck and please stay off the roads.

Upstairs, in our bathroom, I pull down my pants and it is like something has melted from inside of me. Like those cherry lollipops we used to get for free at the bank, the ones they'd put out in a bowl to thank us for doing chores with our mother. I am not pregnant—not like I expected to be. But still. Every month, it is a relief to me.

I go back to our bedroom, where Ray is sitting.

"That was odd," he says.

"What was odd?"

"Dinner."

"What was odd about it?"

"There was tension."

"Well, it's kind of a tense situation," I say. "Billy was driving when my sister died."

"He was?" Ray asks.

"Yeah," I say.

"Oh," he says. "Maybe that was it then."

There is a huge clap of thunder, so I turn on the TV in our bedroom to see you are a big sprawling thing, headed into Connecticut. When the weatherman speaks of you, he speaks of your strong center, your eye. Yet when I really look at the eye, it doesn't look like a center. You look warm and curled into yourself, like something afraid. You just appear to have a core, a place, a thing that we have always called Kathy. Is that a center?

"A stupid thing to say, but as a kid, I used to feel left out of American storms," Ray says.

He was so close to them but grew up in Toronto and never got to feel the brunt of them.

"I used to be afraid of them, too," I say.

Ray starts flipping through the pages of an outdated *Time* magazine. A terrorist plot, already thwarted. A vegetable that is known to prevent heart disease now gives people liver cancer. And will Donald Trump run for president?

"No," Ray says. "The fucker never runs. Why does everybody always think he will?"

Ray tosses the magazine, like he's done with the news, done with the world, and there is something to be said for people like Ray, who drive forward in conversation when no one else knows where to go.

"But actually, no," Ray says. "That's not it."

"What do you mean?"

"I mean, that man is clearly in love with you," he says.

"He's not, trust me," I say.

"I know tension like that when I feel it," Ray says. "I'm a lawyer."

"What does being a lawyer have to do with anything?"

"I'm trained to know when people are hiding something," Ray says. "I can see it on your face. Right now."

I don't say anything. The rain begins outside.

"I'm going to grab another beer," he says, defeated.

"Don't have a beer," I say. "We should go to bed."

"I have a theory about people who say 'you should,'" Ray says. "'You should do this,' 'you should read this,' are people who don't know how to say, 'This is my favorite book' without saying the word *should*."

I nod. Ray sighs.

"There's something you're not telling me. I can feel it," Ray says.

"There are a lot of things I'm not telling you," I say.

"Try then," he says.

"Billy and I became very close after my sister died," I say. "We were in love, I think."

"Why couldn't you just tell me that?"

"I don't know," I say.

"Because you still love him," he says. "Is that what this is all about? Not wanting kids?"

"I don't know," I say.

Ray goes to get his beer, and the storm picks up. I can hear the house shift, ever so slightly. It's a chorus of weather. The high notes of wind against the bass of thunder. Ray comes back with his beer and pretends to play a bass line to accompany the howling wind. He pretends like everything is fine, and so do I.

I light a lavender candle before the power goes out. Just like Dad. There is a clap of thunder, and Ray shouts, "Yeehaw!" like a cowboy from one of Dad's old movies. We get onto the bed, curl up with excitement like two teenagers doing something they shouldn't.

"I'm sorry," he says. "I'm being jealous."

Ray kisses me, slow and sweet, like he is getting to know me all over again. He makes sure to look me in the eye, so I know that this is a moment; he is getting closer to me, which is all he wants, he keeps saying. He wants to get closer and closer and closer until what?

"You look like you're going to eat me," I say.

"Maybe," he says. "You're kind of cute."

Ray is not the type to be so committed to one woman; he has told me this on a number of occasions. There's something about you, he says, that makes me want nothing but you, and I smile and laugh, like he's crazy to be in love with me, which I know he is. But I realize this night that there is something else. There is something deeply wrong with me. There is a dark hole inside of me, where you used to be; it's the space where I live now. It's soundless and windless and without gravity, and from here, I can see everything. From here, I look back out at the world, at all the regular people, like Ray, living their life so easily. Ray who wants a family with me. Sometimes, when I watch Ray cook dinner or wipe down the counters, I am watching him from afar, and it's like he knows this. He knows there is a distance he needs to travel, a space inside me he is trying to crawl into, and he likes this challenge.

Ray runs marathons.

Ray wants the things he cannot have, like a successful music career. He idolizes the things farthest from him, and right now, the thing farthest from him is me.

But tonight he is getting closer to that space where only you and I live, and it reminds me of old times, not with Ray but with other men. In college, when I got drunk a lot, because that was the only time I felt comfortable crying. Sober, I tried not to let myself do it.

I convinced myself that my grief over you was the ugliest part about me. But Jan was right; grief gets stored in the body. It rots over time. And so I drank, because when I drank I had no control, no sense of myself, and the grief would spill out onto the bed. I would cry, heave, hyperventilate. The boy—whoever he was—would wipe my tears and kiss me, and say, Sorry. So sorry for your loss.

But Ray does not say that. Ray says, "Let's just go to sleep," and then, in a matter of minutes, Ray actually falls asleep.

But I can't sleep. I listen to our house shake in the wind, the windows. Windows and doors, they are the weakest parts of a house. It is through those spaces where you gain and lose the most. It is through those spaces where nothing and everything exist.

Are you awake? Billy texts.

Yes, I write. I am.

I'm coming over, Billy writes. I need to talk with you.

I can still hear the mayor on television. The mayor has said good night and good luck. Right now is the part of the storm where nobody is responding yet. The state has declared a state of emergency, but it is the quietest night I've had in a while. No sirens. No screams from the street. No fireworks. There is no indication of man, or that there ever was man, outside our windows. It is purely weather hitting against more weather. Weather trying to get inside. That seems to be all you want, to get back inside the house, through the cracks. The weather has no place to live because we have sealed the windows shut.

But then I open the door.

And there, outside in the storm, is Billy. If you could have seen him like that, out there in the rain, just standing in our driveway, looking up at the sky, you would have fallen in love with him all over again. I know it.

"What are you doing?" I shout at him.

But he can't hear me. He can't even see me yet. So I run outside to join him.

"You're crazy," I tell Billy when I stand next to him in the driveway, crazy for driving through a hurricane like this, but I don't really mean it. I know that these are the kinds of things you do when you're in love. Love is crazy. Love turns you into something you're not, or something you never knew you could be. It makes a man drive down the highway in the middle of a hurricane. It makes me run outside to feel the dirt in your rain. The strength of your wind.

"I just wanted to see you," he says. "I wanted to tell you that I love you."

"I love you, too," I say.

He takes my hand.

"I know I'm not supposed to," he says. "And if your sister wants to kill me because of it, that seems fair. It seems only fair to give her the chance."

He opens his arms wide, as if to welcome you. I look around the yard. There are a million dangers present; anything can be ripped from the ground and kill us. There are street signs, old trees. In this kind of wind, everything ordinary becomes dangerous.

But then the wind ceases. The rain stops. Your eye is upon us. And I wonder what you see at this hour, with the clarity of your forty-mile-wide eye. I wonder what the top of our roof looks like. What our town looks like. I wonder if you see only the stillness of the trees, and the two of us, standing side by side, holding hands. Can you recognize us? Are you wondering why we are so wet? Maybe you are thinking this is a perfect picture, a perfect day. Maybe you are seeing Billy as I see him. He is wet in the face. He is smiling. His sweater is soaked, and I can see his fine bones through the cotton, and I know that I will love him forever.

In the morning, when the power comes back on, the weatherman cuts through our house and wakes us all up. From my bed, I can hear him announcing what will happen to you: You will go north. You will become a tropical storm. You will make it all the way to

Labrador, and that is where you will come apart. That is where your winds will spread over the ocean until you are no longer Kathy, until you are only air.

But you will return to us, I know. When we are repainting the house or making pancakes for breakfast or digging in the garden or laughing at something funny with our heads back and our mouths wide open—the way you always laughed—we will breathe you in without even knowing it.

ACKNOWLEDGMENTS

Thank you to my agents, Molly Friedrich and Lucy Carson, and the whole team at the Friedrich Agency for reading draft after draft of this novel. I feel so fortunate to have found agents who I trust completely with all aspects of the writing process and business—you are amazing readers, wonderful editors, phenomenal agents, and good friends.

Thank you to my editor, Caroline Zancan. You understood this novel from the very start, and your editorial vision helped me see what it could be (and helped me end my chapters). I'm so grateful for your wit, your humor, and your enthusiasm for the absurd. And thank you to everybody else at Henry Holt who put time and energy into designing, selling, and shaping this book.

Thank you to Eric Bennett, Mary-Kim Arnold, and Katie Hughes, who read so many versions of this novel. I've so valued your feedback and general writerly camaraderie over the years.

Thank you to Diana Spechler and Shelly Oria for reading the earliest of early drafts and helping me figure out what kind of story I wanted to tell.

Thank you to Michael Andreasen, Cristina Rodriguez, and Mark

Polanzak for the seasonal Jeffrey Chester that helped me stay inspired and have fun as I met deadlines.

Thank you to Chris Parrott for your Latin expertise and editorial advice.

Thank you to Abby Rabinowitz and Dan Ryan for reading a late draft of the book, and to Mike Cummings and Mike Bezemek for talking through the plot with me.

Thank you to Providence College for giving me the opportunity to read excerpts of this novel when it was too early to even call it a novel.

Thank you to the Ucross Foundation, the San Miguel Writers in Residence, the Cuttyhunk Island Residency, and the Wassaic Artist Residency for allowing me to work on this book in beautiful places, surrounded by friends.

Thank you to all the friends and family members who put up with me during this ten-year process. I will try to be more tolerable over the next ten years.

Thank you to my brother Gregg for being such a constant supporter of me and my work, and to my sister-in-law Andrea for your creative help on the design.

Thank you to Sarah, who always stayed up very late with me in the fourth bedroom talking about our lives. So much of the sisterly connection in this book was inspired by the connection I felt, and feel, with you.

Thank you to my parents for always encouraging me to write about the hard things and for never shying away from the reality of our grief. You taught me how to see beautiful and funny things in unexpected places, and this is a gift I will cherish all my life.

And finally, thank you to my brother Michael for the time on earth that we spent together, for always being silly with me when we were young, and for teaching me how much fun it is to spend an afternoon talking about nonsense with someone you love.

Alison Espach is the author of the novel *The Adults*, a *New York Times* Editors' Choice and a Barnes & Noble Discover pick. Her short stories and essays have appeared in *Vogue*, *Joyland*, *Glamour*, *Salon*, and *McSweeney's*, among other places. She is currently a professor of creative writing at Providence College in Rhode Island.